CELESTINA'S BURNINGS

By
Annemarie Schiavi Pedersen

Literary Wanderlust | Denver, Colorado

Copyright 2020 by Annemarie Schiavi Pedersen

Published in the United States by Literary Wanderlust LLC, Denver, Colorado. www.LiteraryWanderlust.com

Print ISBN: 978-1-942856-43-6
Digital ISBN: 978-1-942856-49-8

Cover design: Pozu Mitsuma

Printed in the United States

Everything about Florence seems to be colored with a mild violet, like diluted wine."

— Henry James

For my parents, Ennio and Palma

1

Italia, 1491

On a street bedeviled by bonfires, inside a small bakery, Celestina sniffed something burning.

Smoke shaped like the fingers of a ghost spiraled up from her feet. The haziness in Celestina's head cleared in an instant. She looked this way and that but was unable to find the source.

Then the embers in the hearth oven behind Celestina snapped *pop, pop,* and she stiffened at a different scent, the aroma of sweet almond. Her *biscotti*.

Seizing the long handle of the baker's peel, she slid the thin board under the log of almond-laced dough that was baking inside the wall. After inspecting it, she glanced at the timbered ceiling smudged with two centuries of grime and then exhaled her relief.

The dough was not too hard and slightly golden, perfect for the first of its two bakes. She set the board on the marble counter for the dough to cool and stared past it.

Whatever was burning, it wasn't her cookies.

A hollow sound resonated off the cobblestone roads within the city of Florence. She was almost able to smell the stench of blood in the prison courtyard after one bong from the big, black bell called Montanina.

"Montanina?" she asked softly. "Whose head do you call for today?" Celestina crossed herself in a quick prayer for the poor soul who was about to meet his—or her—end. Even those deserving their punishment would be missed by somebody.

And then she forced her attention back to her own work, studying the strip of half-baked dough for portioning. Her grandmother Simona's first commandment of baking was twelve *biscotti* per batch cut in ribbons crosswise. But this loaf was too small. Celestina stroked her throat. Mess up another batch and it would be her neck on a stump.

A devilish smile crossed her lips. She poised the knife tip at the dough's edge. With a deft hand, she cut six strips, picturing the surprised faces of the few lucky customers happening upon extra-fat *biscotti*.

Though she'd have to wait for the second bake to finish before dashing to church and confessing—*Bless me, Father, for I have sinned. I have disobeyed Simona the Crusty*—the idea of losing herself in thirty-three consecutive rosaries, or whatever punishment the priest decided on, always some mind-deadening atonement, was easy enough to swallow after what she'd been through.

She rubbed at the brewing in her stomach. Maybe all that penance would act as a salve for the bitterness that had roiled there.

Bitterness that had started when Papa's life ended.

It ate at her, the belief that Papa's death and the spate of bonfires on the Via Scalia, her street, were tied together. The knife in her hand, flaked with *biscotti* crumbs, glinted in the sunlight streaming from the window. Simona's sharpest knife. Was it as sharp as the sword that had sliced through Papa?

For the thousandth time since that day she wondered: How could his killing not be related to the bonfires that had given the Via Scalia a bad name.

La Via Scalia e un inferno. The Via Scalia is hell.

On both sides of the River Arno, the bonfires were all the people talked about. Everyone except her grandmother, whose idea of a holy day was one in which the bakery made a profit, like a miracle that rarely happened. But it was that sort of backward thinking that put Simona at risk of falling prey to *le streghe.*

Witches.

The word made Celestina's insides bubble like wet yeast. It had been one year to the day that Papa had fallen prey to the witch, as beautiful as she was evil. And in all that time Celestina was barely able to bake without burning, walk without stumbling, or picture her father without his face going blurry.

Everything in Florence was changing so fast. In the olden days, Papa's defense of a sorceress would not end with his soul withering in purgatory. That sort of leniency was in the past.

Still, there was nothing bygone about the show of sadness known as mourning, and Celestina was more than ready for hers to come to an end. The Catholic tradition was like enduring a 365-day funeral Mass. For one year she'd worn only heavy black and lived like a cloistered nun. Her entire world consisted of the bakery, the church of Santa Maria Novella, and the apartment she shared with her grandmother.

In three hours, it would all be behind her.

She glanced down at her nearly threadbare black dress. At noon it was going to the dump. She could only hope that the dark humor hanging over her like a thundercloud might be dispelled as easily.

Celestina let the knife slip. *Clink*. Too bad the blade was unable to cut through the fog inside her head.

"Papa and I are both destined to remain in purgatory," she muttered. "Him caught between hell and heaven and me between Simona and the start of my life."

What a waste. Living in the greatest city on the most interesting street was useless with Simona. Her grandmother wouldn't let her take two steps outside the bakery on her own, unless it was for Mass, though even that caused arguments. In Simona's eyes, a hooded stranger was always lurking, ready to snatch Celestina and sell her to rich people.

And that was *before* Papa died.

Celestina paced before the hot hearth. It hurt her head to bicker with Simona, whose newest fixation was Celestina's modesty. But the past few days, with the mourning period waning, Celestina had experienced stirrings. Florence was full of adventures that she had never tasted. There were young sculptors to meet, flying witches to catch, and foremost and first Papa's soul to avenge.

She fingered the gold charm hanging from her necklace. Papa had cast the tiny *putto* with his own hands. The angel was all she had left of him.

Of course, there were his frescos of cherubs flying across church walls and his stone sculptures of *putti* perched on the city streets. But she was unable to hold a mural or a statue in her hand. If she were to ever mislay her *putto*...she shook her head. Losing it was too terrible to think about.

Terrible. Like Simona's mood should Celestina ruin yet another yield. Celestina rushed the cookies back inside the wall oven for a second bake. Then she lifted the flaming torch from the wall sconce and rekindled the wood in the oven to raise the heat.

Bong.

Celestina startled. "Two rings, Montanina?" she blinked in the direction of the Tower of Boscoli. "So, the black bell tolls for a burning at the stake, not a beheading."

She swiped her perspiring brow, arguing in her head over which would be the worse way to die, one ring or two.

With care, so as not to set her hair on fire and hence answer her own question, she replaced the flaming torch in its holder.

Bong.

Her heart banged in her chest. "No," she breathed incredulously. She was unprepared for three rings. Three rings were rare. Three rings were a cry for the city's youth to rise against tyranny.

"*Madre mia.*" Her hand flew to her chest. "Mother of God, Montanina is talking to *me.*"

She shot a glance out the egg-shaped window. Black horses drawing gold-trimmed carriages began to line the Via Scalia. Her breath caught at handsome young courtiers and their ladies, women with high foreheads in fine brocade collars, sitting with hands in their laps, waiting.

Waiting for what? Not for toasty *biscotti*, she imagined.

She turned her ear to check for her grandmother. The rolling pin seesawed. Simona the Crusty was still in the back room and occupied flattening dough.

Celestina regarded the oven. The *biscotti* needed to bake longer, which allowed her time to step outside for a peek at the street. After stripping the black ribbon of mourning, a ribbon that she hated in all ways, including how it clashed with the mop on her head—an already unremarkable apricot-red shade—she cast it in the corner and started for the door.

Thump. Celestina slid to a stop.

Batting dough against the counter was her grandmother's way of making a point. "Forget Montanina," came Simona's voice from the back of the shop. "Chop almonds for more *biscotti*."

The hairs on Celestina's arms stood like an army of Cypress trees. She hated being yelled at from the back room and was about to say as much when a sudden *snap* outside rattled her.

She dashed to the window, the tip of her nose touching the thin glass. "*Oh, mio Dio*...my goodness...Now I see what's burning."

A gray cloud spiraled from a flaming black dress hanging on a stake in the center of the Via Scalia. She plugged her nose. The bitter stench of burning wool was nauseating.

"You're being too quiet up front." It was Simona, again. Simona. Not *nonna*, like a normal grandmother. Or *Signora* DiCapria, like an ordinary woman. Her grandmother insisted on being called a single word and a single word only: Simona.

"For a person with one name you sure talk a lot," Celestina muttered into her clenched hand.

"A fresh apron will make you feel better," Simona said. "Go ahead and treat yourself."

Celestina batted her forehead lightly against the window. Finding out about the dress burning on the street, that's what would make her feel better.

Outside, a sharp crack pierced the air followed by the shatter of glass. Deep, angry voices chanted, "*Ri-for-ma!*"

Reform? She grabbed hold of the windowsill, catching sight of a band of protesters. *Ragazzi*, street toughs with partially shaved heads in the style of warrior monks, ran past the front window. They bore smoking torches and were dangerous looking. Montanina's call must have wakened them. Light-haired firebrands from the north charged in from the opposite way. She drew her shoulders tight.

The local *ragazzi*, with their faces taut, braced for battle. She quaked at the thud of club against bone. Blood sprayed from noses.

Unable to watch the carnage, she directed her attention at the *biscotti*. For the love of St. Catherine, were they ever going to finish baking? A sound outside like a cannon blast shook an empty basket off the bakery shelf.

Celestina hit the brick floor. Cautiously, she rose to her feet again. She had to see what was happening outside and cast off her apron, ran her fingers through her wavy mop, and brushed flour from her black skirt.

"I'll come back soon to take out the *biscotti*," she called back to Simona.

The long scrape of stool legs against brick floor grated Celestina like fingernails across slate.

"*Basta*, granddaughter. Stop. Stay away from those troublemakers." Simona charged up front.

"I must go out there." Celestina grabbed the door handle.

Simona stamped her foot. "Then no new dress."

Celestina stomped back. "But you promised after Papa's mourning I'd get the orange *gamurra*."

"Not if you go outside."

Her grandmother was so unbelievable in every way. "Fine, go back on your word. The only dress I care about now is the one burning on the street."

"Your papa...my Alessandro...it's been one year to the day," Simona stammered, a sign she'd been drinking. "I can't lose you, too. Stay inside where it's safe."

"I've been in this chicken coop for a year. You can't cage me like one of your canaries, Simona." Celestina flung open the door.

"I'll follow you," said Simona.

Celestina darted onto the Via Scalia, searching for a place to hide from Simona, straight into a cloud of gray smoke. After coughing her way out, she spotted her grandmother in pursuit.

Turning hard to escape Simona, Celestina tripped on a crooked cobblestone. She righted herself before falling and then burrowed deep into the throng.

But the Via Scalia was feet-to-feet with running, shoving, and fighting people who all fell silent at the same moment, their ears tipped toward the rumble in the distance.

Celestina clutched Papa's *putto* at her neck. Beneath her feet cobblestones shook as though an army of demons pounded their way up from of hell.

The people backed up, giving wide berth to the cavalry of horses kicking up clouds of cobblestone dust. There were hundreds of soldiers. Or perhaps they were knights? She ogled their uniforms, crisp and violet blue. The color stirred her. Florence was gold, red, and dark purple. Never blue, until now.

Each soldier bore a white cross stitched on the chest of his tunic. Heavy silver crucifixes hung from blue cords around necks. All donned a black *berretto*, a soft beret with a blue feather at the side. Except for one. The District Marshal, a powerful black-skinned man wore a *barbuta*, a full-headed war helmet with a T-shaped opening for his eyes and mouth. Flapping in the wind was his green cape adorned with blue stripes on the sleeves.

At the sight of his whip, weaved around his waist like a

belt, Celestina stroked the side of her hip, almost able to feel its sting. The top man-at-arms steered his *stallone* around and between the others.

"*Attenzione*," said the Marshal in a distinct Moroccan accent, the word rolling off his tongue with heft. "Montanina rings for the Reform."

Ri-for-ma. The Reform sounded important.

The Marshal then swept his hand to the side, as if presenting a man of great prominence. From the black herd, a *stallone* of pure white emerged. It carried a cloaked figure, face hidden under a black-hooded *cappa*. The mysterious rider straddled a blue-velvet saddle.

The wind kicked up the flap of his cape, which was lined in silk and the color of bright blue gemstones. Celestina's hands tingled. She was almost able to feel its silky blueness slip through her fingers.

But the habit he wore, this religious of some sort, was something else altogether. Stiff and white, it was whiter and stiffer than any she'd ever seen, many degrees whiter than his horse's hide. She swallowed. Only a hard person was able to stand the severity of such a garment against his skin.

As the people closed around him, she rose on her toes to keep him in sight. Squeezing Papa's *putto*, her heart beat fast as an angel's wings. Surely Emperor Marcus Aurelius made no grander an entrance riding through the arched gate of Tripoli.

But the Marshal, clearly irritated by the crush of the crowd, twisted the reins of his ebony horse. It snorted in distress as it was forced to angle its body to push back the people.

The Marshal ordered, "Clear way for the Dominican of North Tyrol, the vice supreme knight of the Reform."

Ehi. Celestina clasped her hands under her chin. Like the Habsburgs, the foreigner was an Austrian. She'd never seen one in person but imagined they were pale as ghosts. She stretched for a better look, wondering if they all bore jutting jaws.

The Marshal brandished his fist. "Move back, Florentines, or I'll lather your hides with my whip. Allow Friar Thane Brucker to advance."

Celestina shuffled back, rubbing her ear. With no pretty vowel to soften the end of his name, Friar Brucker sounded sharp.

When the Marshal ordered, "Bow your heads in respect for Fra Brucker," she snapped her chin to her chest. It was good to hear him called "Fra." That sounded rounder. Nicer.

After proper respect was paid, the Marshal said, "You may raise your heads."

Fra Brucker had tugged back his hood to reveal a jaw that was square and refined. There was a pearly glow to his skin that contrasted with his hair, a mane so black it bore the tint of blue.

Next to her a pair of younger girls, skinny but bearing the hint of womanhood, giggled. It was about Fra's striking looks. Celestina glared at them until they shrank. After they acted sufficiently put in their places, she glanced at the replica of Donatello's bronze statue of David. It stood proud in front of the silk shop across the street.

Now if it were Donatello, the greatest sculptor of all time, sitting on Fra's white horse, she'd lose her morning *biscotti*. She'd even consider losing her modesty.

But for a religious like Fra, no matter how *bello*, she had no loving heart. *Mai*. Never. She could never feel for a man of God that way.

Still, she had the sense his focus was on her. She glanced up and stifled a gasp. He was staring at her. Gray-blue eyes under his lantern brow glowed like the hottest hue in a whisper of fire. It teetered at the edge of indecent.

She looked fast at her feet. His attention made her ears burn. She counted...*uno, due, tre...nove*...surely, he'd be done looking...and *dieci*. At ten she looked up.

His leer pinned her. She squirmed in her slippers. Did he never blink? She tipped her shoulder to create a barrier of coldness between them. A smart smile crossed his lips. Her rebuff was not as subtle as she supposed.

He tapped his horse's neck twice and the *stallone* stepped up and over like a bishop in a game of chess. She stumbled back a step. A pawn in retreat.

He smirked and then faced the Marshal. She dared to breathe.

"The Reform has chosen Florence, the most important city on the earth, to begin its mission to cleanse the world of witchcraft," the Marshal proclaimed. "And Fra Brucker will lead the fight."

Celestina bounced on her toes. Never had she imagined there existed a holy army to save the people from the witches, and to help her save her Papa's soul. It was an answer to her prayers.

Cheering voices bounced off the buildings. Faces beamed. The people were feeling the same way.

The Via Scalia was hell no more.

She dared a peek at Fra. Not with the hope that he'd look back, but to gauge his effect. She wanted to make certain that he understood the people stood with him. But his face was as expressionless as a thousand-year-old stone bust of a Roman stoic.

She scratched her head. An Italian in a similar position would be prancing about on his horse while waving. But

Fra's hand simply cradled the horn of his blue saddle and he dismounted. At full stretch, he was taller than any Italian she knew. His chin was higher than the withers of his horse. He looked to be about 23, or thereabouts, perhaps five years her senior.

He rolled the cuff of his sleeve. Lean muscles on his arms twitched. She flipped a lock of hair over her eye and cast her gaze in the direction of the burning dress. Not a shadow remained. There wasn't a hint of leftover ash, either.

"What are you looking for, Fraulein?"

The harsh sound of his voice was like a bristle brush scrubbing the inside of her ears. His eyes, a set of smoky sapphires, were calculating.

"I'm waiting," he said, tapping his chin.

"I seek the answer to why the dress burned." She prayed no one noticed the tremor in her voice.

The people snickered. Her cheeks reddened. No one was safe from outright derision on the Via Scalia. Fra's silence, however, dangled over her like a nun's threatening paddle.

She stared at the ground, heart beating in her ear.

"Look again," he said.

She regarded where the black dress had been burning. A fresh black dress replaced the old one. She looked from side to side. The people, too, appeared astonished.

"As you can see, there are no lack of witches—or their dresses—in Florence," said Fra.

All nodded obediently.

"So, what do you think, Fraulein?"

Celestina's head snapped around. "Think?"

Thinking often brought trouble when it came to a religious. She preferred if he simply told her what to think. Saved time, and a punishing trip to the confessional.

"Yes, think." Fra hiked up a silky eyebrow. "Do you have the stomach to be a witch hunter?" he asked.

She was dizzy with the idea. "I didn't know such a formal opportunity existed for a woman, a humble baker, such as myself," she said.

"The Reform is a progressive movement of the people. A good woman is part of the people, yes? Do you have the will, Fraulein?"

She clenched her *putto*. For Papa's soul, the answer was absolute. "I am ready," she said.

She detected a bit of mischief in his smile. "Let's see if you can pass a little test."

She wiped her sweating hands against her skirt. "What sort of...test?"

He sized up the hanging dress. "Do you have the fortitude to burn it?"

The Marshal forced the handle of a burning torch into her hand. The powerful flame shook the grip. She needed two hands to hold on. Before anything went wrong, she touched the tip of the blaze to the hem.

Whoosh.

The dress erupted in an orange blaze. The very act of setting the dress aflame emboldened her. "With the power of this flame, I begin my journey to search, find, and destroy the witches of Florence. I swear this, on the soul of my father, Alessandro DiCapria."

Her heart, which only this morning suffocated under a cloak of darkness, lightened with purpose. Before this day she'd yearned for an orange dress to wear and a *ragazzo* with the shoulders of a sculptor to love. But the Reform changed everything.

She now had one mission: to capture five witches and

burn their dresses. She could entertain no distractions. It would take all her guile to succeed.

There'd be a cost, however. Simona's punishments always revolved around the almighty *scudo* and she'd refuse to pay Celestina for work. But for Celestina, the personal sacrifice of not knowing the love of a young sculptor would hurt a *mille* times worse than being poor.

"Very nice, Fraulein," said Fra. "The Reform welcomes you."

Celestina raised the torch higher and shouted, "*Ri-for-ma!*"

The people echoed back, their fevered response a condemnation of all things underworld. They began to riot. A heavy-handed jolt from behind rocked Celestina.

"Quit shoving," she said as someone ripped the torch from her hand. She lost balance in the back and forth of the crowd.

A push sent her sailing through a gap in the people. Her chin hit the cobblestones and she grounded forward, finally stopping with her nose at Fra's brass toecap.

She was staring at the tip of his clog when a rough hand yanked her up by her collar. A foot soldier of about her age, blond strands peeking from under his *berretto*, twisted the neck of her dress until she lost her breath. She slapped at his hand, but it was a vise.

"Release her," barked Fra.

The soldier threw her down. Her knees hit the bricks. A hard sob escaped her throat.

"Don't be an idiot," said Fra, scolding the blond footman.

And then he cuffed the young man. Blood shot from the guard's lip. *Fitting punishment.*

"Stand." With the toe of his clog, Fra prodded beneath her chin.

She tried to rise like an obedient soldier, but to her horror, she was stuck fast. Earlier, when the blond footman discarded her it felt like her kneecaps shattered to a *mille* pieces. She dared not cry less Fra consider her a weakling.

Fra's sigh rippled. "I am running out of grace, Fraulein."

Her bottom lip quivered. Hard pain stabbed her knees. If she stumbled upon standing, it might appear she was wounded, which would give Fra reason to revoke his invitation to join the holy army.

She needed an idea to justify staying down, but being chucked by the young soldier scrambled her thoughts. Inside her head was as messy as a pan of disturbed eggs.

Her lack of explanation as to why she remained splayed on the ground as if she'd been run over by a horse cart was becoming terribly uncomfortable.

At last, she blurted, "As a soldier of the Reform I will service you in any way. And to show my allegiance, I lay prostrate before you."

The people gasped and her jaw dropped. Service the friar? Lay prostrate before him? Her words were dumber than the load of stink that just dropped from the tail end of Fra's horse.

"Your actions are ill-conceived, Fraulein. I'm in no need of being serviced, but then again, you've been rather busy being prostrate, so perhaps you've failed to notice," said Fra.

Face burning, Celestina heard the blond soldier stifle a laugh.

"Now get up," said Fra.

"I can't," she admitted.

He studied her as he might a cobblestone worm: should he step on it or let it live?

"You're fine down there, Fraulein," he said at last.

"*Grazie*, Fra."

"But as long as you're in the position of surrender, practice your Lord's Prayer. And think very hard about its last words, 'deliver us from evil.'"

"Yes, Fra." She feared her voice betrayed her bewilderment. That there was more to the phrase than asking God to keep her safe from the devil, she had no idea. To agonize over such words would torture her brain. But it was an order, and she was a holy soldier, and it must be done.

"And Fraulein?"

She hesitated. "Yes, Fra?"

"While you're down there be careful," he said. "You wouldn't want to ruin your black dress."

2

Rinaldo SanGiorgio hid deep inside the de' Medici Palace, tracing the air, following the lines of the image painted into the plaster wall, risking his life to pretend he was something he wasn't.

Not yet, anyway.

He glanced at his quarry-filthy nails. How his fingers itched to skim Benozzo Gozzoli's masterpiece. Three Wise Men visiting the baby Jesus was a magnificent fresco that cycled across three walls of the Chapel of the Magi. Rinaldo retreated a step, not daring to dirty it with his touch.

It was enough of an adventure just being inside the chapel, which for some reason was where the de' Medicis had moved his favorite girl, the nude beauty created of canvas and tempera. Rinaldo scratched his head. Sandro Botticelli's The Birth of Venus leaning against a wall next to a painting of Mary the mother of Jesus was an odd coupling for the tasteful de' Medicis.

It was almost as if the patricians were hiding Venus.

No matter the reason, Rinaldo was happy he'd found her. He needed inspiration.

That afternoon, Leonardo da Vinci was coming to judge Rinaldo's block of stone. Rinaldo closed his eyes and sighed. Perhaps God was up to tricks and orchestrated that the painting be moved from the dining hall to the chapel to lead Rinaldo there for an extra shot of grace before his important day.

He glanced in the direction of Settignano. Up the mountain in his small *borgo*, the whole town prayed outside at an alfresco chapel shaded by the centuries-old oak, a tree so handsome that Rinaldo would put it up against any from inside Florence's famous Boboli Gardens. There, at Mass, the people of his little suburb were able to listen to the songs of the meadowlarks while taking communion.

Rinaldo scratched his head. City people. How they felt the presence of God while praying inside churches was a mystery. Then again, if everyone prayed outside like him, there'd be no churches or walls. He'd have nowhere to paint the murals he imagined inside his head honoring God and battle.

He stroked the simple marble crucifix hanging from the leather cord at his neck. Usually, after breaking into the palace, he had only moments to visit with Venus before the footsteps of watchmen sent him running, but he figured something important happening in the heart of the city had their attention.

Earlier he'd heard Montanina cry three times, creating an unusual gathering of the people. Some carried clubs.

Rinaldo clenched a fist. He never minded a good fight but was no more interested in the church and politics than he was in living the rest of his life cutting rock at his family's quarry. Discord in Florence did not concern him. He needed to think about only one thing: impressing Leonardo da Vinci this afternoon back up the mountain in his town of Settignano.

His gaze veered back to Venus, eyes following the curve of her tempting hips. Unexpectedly, he winced. An invisible knife stabbed his heart and he clutched his chest. It wasn't the first time a pang of shame stung him when visiting the goddess.

For Holy Ghost's sake, SanGiorgio, you're falling for a painting of a woman standing on a giant clamshell. It's time to find a wife.

A wife.

He *had* tried.

But in Settignano, where his oldest brothers Benedetto and Luca found their girls, he'd had no luck. Not because there was something wrong with the brunettes in Settignano. *No, no, no.* Their lips were luscious as mountain truffles. He knew it to be true because he'd kissed more than a few. The problem was that they giggled in his face when he shared his dream.

It wasn't that the girls were rude, not entirely. In Settignano there was only one kind of dream, and it was set in stone. It was in the blood of Settignano girls to doubt him, just as it was in his blood to run when faced with their doubt.

Forget them all. By this afternoon you will have your answer: fresco painter or family quarryman. Right now, only God knew his fate.

Rinaldo glanced around the chapel for a sense of the time. He couldn't be late for Master da Vinci. But the windowless chapel had no clock machine. Ready or not, he needed to leave, allowing an extra moment of lingering to indulge in the perfection of Venus's uncovered breast.

Rounding the doorway for the hall he spied a guard wearing the red, purple, and yellow stripes of the de' Medici and snoring on a bench covered in maroon velvet. Sneaking past the napping watchman, Rinaldo eyed silk tapestries hanging against a gold-plated wall. He couldn't help but let his gaze linger. Lorenzo de' Medici had good taste in art—as good as Rinaldo's.

Leaping onto the windowsill, Rinaldo studied the grounds below. The colonnade courtyard was open and dangerous. He stroked his neck protectively. If caught, he'd pay the highest price.

He jumped and landed softly on the plush grass. Dashing from column to column, he then scaled the fence. Two stories high, the gate was a piece of art in itself with scrolls threaded through iron bars. And it was deadly with a pointed arrow tip at the top of each shaft. Those, he gingerly avoided.

It was only after blending into the fast-moving crowd on the Via Cavour that his shoulders relaxed. He glanced at the one-armed clock on Arnolfo Tower. *Oh no...che stupido.* He rapped his head. It wasn't quite eleven.

He could've stayed with Venus for an extra one-quarter of an hour. With time to spare, he allowed himself to be swept up in the rush of Florentines answering Montanina's call.

He snaked his way to the center of the crowd, avoiding de' Medici watchmen in their bold uniforms only to cross paths with a different set of guards in good-looking blue liveries.

They protected a tall religious with fancy clothes and a large crest of black hair. He'd overheard that the man was from Salzburg, part of the religious order of St. Dominic. A Dominican. Rinaldo gave the religious the stink eye. The fancy fig from Austria made Rinaldo's chest burn. Friars should look like Jesus, not a Roman god.

Rinaldo glimpsed a young woman lying on the street at the foot of the religious.

His eyes combed her locks. The color made him lick his

lips. Ripe apricots streaked in rays of golden Florentine sun. And then there were the curls: a halo of tresses that danced past her neck and splayed across the small of her back.

The locks of Botticelli's Venus paled in comparison.

The crowd began to fill in the space between them, while at the same time something intense flared within him. Throwing a shoulder this way and a hip that, he rammed into anyone who stood between him and the girl on the ground. With an arm's length between them, his heart froze. And then it pounded with a desire he'd never known.

Her face; he needed to see it. Bending on a knee, he offered his hand. "If I may assist you up, *signorina*."

She kept her eyes locked on the cobblestones. "Go away," she ordered. "I'm praying."

The beauty was pious, it seemed. "It's a funny place to pray, but good for you," he said. "Now please take my hand—"

"I heard you the first time."

His hand fell. The irritation in her voice was unmistakable.

In the distance, the bells of Santa Maria Novella chimed like an impatient taskmaster. It was eleven, and time for him to leave. Master da Vinci was due at the quarry at three, and Rinaldo still had to chip the rough edges off his stone.

"Please, let me see your face," Rinaldo begged, "before I leave."

"That's what I've been trying to tell you," said the young woman. "Leave."

Her tone smarted. He was unused to girls turning him down. For some reason, it made her more alluring. "Where may I find you again?" he asked.

"I'll be fighting," she said.

His chest puffed up. "With whom are you in battle? The blue-and-black Dominican?" he asked.

She answered, "Just *go-o-o*."

The bells insisted he leave as well. Departing turned his heart cold. "Until we meet again." His lips blew a kiss.

Fighting his way back through the crowd Rinaldo glared at the Dominican. He hated how the religious looked at the *signorina* on the ground as if he wanted to bed her.

Seemingly only a few years older than Rinaldo, the Dominican acted like the biggest man in Florence, with his white stallion. Rinaldo clenched his teeth. He wished the lovely *signorina* had not fallen to her face before the religious.

But picturing the *ragazza* in repose, with her sublime curls and waves, outdid his disgust of the friar. Images of her, beautiful as a springtime cloud, floated across his mind. In one, the *signorina* from the street sat sideways, naked on the white horse. Rinaldo saw himself straddled behind her and savored the memory of her scent. Sweet almonds.

Sprinting past the de' Medici Palace he all but forgot Venus. After jumping the city wall, he began his climb up the steep hill for the quarry.

It had never before happened, but halfway up Rinaldo paused to clutch his chest. He struggled to breathe. It was as if a clamshell had slammed shut around his heart.

Never had Celestina heard a voice as savory; it was as delicious as a hunk of Simona's warm *calzone* dipped in twice-pressed olive oil.

And the stranger bore a good heart, she could tell.

After all, not another on the Via Scalia offered his hand to help her up after the blond footman threw her to the ground—they wouldn't dare. Not while she was following Fra's orders to pray.

"Deliver us from evil." Although she'd repeated the phrase, she'd gained no deeper insight of the words. Her hands began to sweat. She feared that she was not holy enough, and that brought worry that her standing in the holy army was at risk.

And the good stranger, while she was sure he meant well, had done nothing to help. The way he kept bothering her to get up when she was following Fra's command proved he was no soldier of the Reform, and therefore served her no good purpose.

Wisely, she'd kept her face hidden from him, the man who possessed vocal cords blessed by the crossed candles of St. Blaise. He'd only seen her hair, which was an unremarkable mix of red and gold, not dyed blond like a fashionable *contessa*. With such a boring mop it was doubtful he'd be able to pick her out of a flock of sheep.

Sheep. The smell of barnyard animals was perfume compared to her neighbor's feet. She stifled the urge to throw up while swiping at their surrounding ankles. "*Basta e basta*," she said. "Enough is enough. Go away, people."

But earlier they'd witnessed her wince, and they weren't going anywhere. Not with the possibility of seeing her trying to stand and fail. Or better yet, puke.

It would help Celestina to save face, and much grief, if Fra Brucker's horse just stomped her flat.

It was a foolish idea, true. So, why then, did she hear a drawn-out whinny over her head? And why were the smelly feet of her neighbors now beating their way down the street, away from her?

Also, the sun cooled. She was now in the shade. There hadn't been a cloud in the sky.

With suspicion, she glanced over her head. The front hooves of Fra's horse were in the air, directly over her. Her knees miraculously stopped throbbing.

"Rolling pin!" It was Simona, shrieking advice from somewhere in the crowd.

Celestina reeled across the cobblestones like a wooden cylinder over *torta* crust. The horse's metal-clad hooves slammed against the cobblestones, shaking the earth and landing within a breadth of flattening her skull.

The people retreated every which way. No place was safe from the *stallone's* stomping legs. Celestina crouched in place. But then the stallion backed up—at her. The great beast bucked. Her arm flew over her face as she awaited the blow.

The moment between life and death was quite long, she discovered. Death by a horse's kick was a slow process. Why she hadn't been pounded into the ground already was a mystery. Surely the end was near. She uncovered one eye to see exactly how long she had to live.

But all she saw was Fra Brucker. He was hanging from the horse's mane, pulling the animal off balance. The behemoth fell down sideways. Its great girth shook like a vat of *gelatina* upon impact with the cobblestones.

A joyous cheer erupted from the people. Celestina jumped up, grateful that her knees worked and flattered that Fra fought his horse to save her.

But then she caught a glimpse of the front of her black dress. *Mio Dio.* My God, she was a mess. White ash was splattered across her black skirt like the stars of Draco in the night sky.

She swiped the old thing clean. Fra mustn't see her black dress dirty. He'd already told her once not to defile it.

He wasn't looking at her, though. He was regarding his *stallone's* heaving belly. Oval-shaped sores, oozing blood, infested the animal's side. It made her stomach lurch. Though it had tried to stomp her to death, she wished it no ill will.

Meanwhile, the friar had drawn a bronze-headed club from the saddlebag. *Thwack, thwack, thwack.* He drummed it against his palm.

Without warning, he cocked the club over the horse's head and before Celestina was able to scream her objection, he thrust it down, stopping short of a killing strike.

It was quiet enough to hear a pigeon swallow. Finally, Fra's lips twisted to a smile. "Lucky for Shadrach the Horse that he is not Shadrach the Witch. Yes?" His gruff voice held the tinge of challenge.

A flock of agreeing heads bobbed up and down.

Fra nudged the cap of his clog under the beast's pink snout. The *stallone* rose mightily. Celestina exhaled. Shadrach was all right.

In one sweeping motion, Fra clutched the stallion's mane and remounted. The Marshal wasted no time in handing Fra a book as thick as an almond cake. She cocked her head to get a good look. Gold letters glistened on its cover. She stepped back in awe. *Malleus Maleficarum.*

Hammer of the Witches.

For months the tome had been whispered about after Sunday Mass, and here she was, a poor Baker Girl, looking directly upon it. It was the world's fourth-most important text, after the Bible, the Koran, and the Torah.

Fra dug his heels into Shadrach's ribs, forcing the already cross animal to circle. Above his head, he raised the *Malleus* and proclaimed, "This manual explains the harm of magic. It tells us how to find and prosecute witches, the carriers of Satan's desires. And I implore the youth of Florence, *ragazzi* and *ragazze*, young men and women alike, to prepare for war."

Celestina sobered at the ominous way the word hung in the air. *War*.

Fra continued, "And though Pope Innocent VIII rightly condemns the use of magic—he has written a papal bull inside these covers explaining as much—the Reform is a movement beyond the Vatican. It is our goal to make Florence a Christian commonwealth, where God and His gospel are the rulers, not a pope. The Reform is the future of the Catholic Church."

Celestina rubbed her hands together. Everyone, it seemed, was ready to start the war. Wild passion sparked the air. Who was the strongest and fastest to stand beside Fra?

All stilled when Fra raised a hand. "At nine hours past midnight, in the piazza of Santa Maria Novella, I will present the Reform's rules against heresy. And as Mass is required on the Sabbath, attendance at tomorrow's sermon is mandatory." His words thundered down the street.

The deep voices of the *ragazzi* rose up. "*Ri-for-ma, Ri-for-ma, Ri-for-ma!*"

The refrain hurt her ears.

"And let me warn you," said Fra, the cords at his neck standing out like tree roots. "Come to my sermon sober, or there will be hell to pay. The devil feasts on those weakened from wine and spirits."

Celestina bit her lip, praying Simona was paying attention. Since Papa's killing, Simona drank raisin wine like it was mineral water. The image of Simona at the bottom of a fiery hole snapped at Celestina's mind like sucking toads.

It was then that a voice from the back of the throng, familiar by its oddness, three parts strong and one part nasal, wrenched her from her daytime nightmare of Simona in hell.

Lorenzo de' Medici's brown *stallone* reared its head. Known as *il Magnifico*, Lorenzo was the secular leader of

Florence and the single de' Medici in the history of de' Medicis to bear the exalted title.

"Do not listen to this zealot from Salzburg. Return to your homes and businesses. Hide every piece of art you own, or you will not have it much longer," shouted the Magnificent.

Il Magnifico was protected by a band of his men, fine-looking soldiers, but anyone could see they numbered far less than Fra's holy army.

Meanwhile, Fra's soldiers in blue raised their clubs and whipped their horses. The people scattered from the street. Celestina clutched her chest. If they were to battle, the carnage between de' Medici soldiers and the Reform would be unspeakable—for the de' Medicis.

"Heed my warning, citizens of Florence," ordered *il Magnifico*. "Go home this instant and shutter your windows before everything you've worked for goes up in smoke."

It had to be much to the dismay of de' Medicis men when a wave of local *ragazzi* awakened from rooftops on both sides of the street.

From the flats atop buildings, fist-sized rocks were flung repeatedly and *en masse* from slingshots. Real-life Davids had caught de' Medicis men off guard. So much for the advantage of the Giant.

For de' Medici's men, a street fight of this magnitude appeared unexpected, and they were nearly knocked from their horses. One rock, the size of a small cannonball, crowned the head of *il Magnifico* himself.

He held one fist to his head to staunch the blood from his wound, while his other beckoned his soldiers to fall back. Celestina was in disbelief that such a powerful man gave up so easily against a holy army and an upstart gang of ruffians. But by not preparing for this level of battle, de' Medici had been outsmarted by Fra.

"We're not through, Brucker. Mark my words, we're not through," cried de' Medici, as he pulled the reins of his *stallone* and led his men in withdrawal back to the sanctuary of the de' Medici Palace.

Fra flashed a haughty smile.

At that moment, she knew Lorenzo de' Medici's retreat was a turning point. If *il Magnifico* remained the heart of Florence, Fra was now in control of the people's souls.

Ragazzi pounded their fists. "Hammer, witches, hammer."

The people answered, "Burn, witches, burn."

Distracted from the uproar, she nearly missed the chunk of marble rock sailing toward her. She ducked in time, but Giovanni LaRossa's window was shattered. *Ragazzi* pulled the artist, a longtime friend of Papa's, from his studio and then tossed his canvases, beautiful portraits of naked women, onto a raging bonfire.

The memory of Lorenzo de' Medici's last words, instructions for the people to hide their art, ripped through her ears like shards of Venetian glass. She turned in every direction, searching for Fra. As a soldier in his holy army, it was her duty to inform him of the destructive rioting so he'd be able to call off the *ragazzi*, who were tearing apart art like snarling street dogs. The Reform was supposed to hunt witches, not hurt artists.

But she was too late. Her heart sunk as Fra and his cavalry departed toward Santa Maria Novella, from where they came. To add insult, a small rock hit the back of her head.

"*Ehi.*" Celestina slapped her hand at the place of the assault.

Across the street was Zola. Her blue eyes mocked as she laughed at Celestina. When Zola flicked her yellow hair,

Celestina had to contain herself from marching across the street to slap the self-satisfied look off of Zola's flat, Florentine face.

They were next-door neighbors and had been best friends once. That was before *Signor* Lombardi, Zola's loathsome father and owner of the *farmacia*, poisoned Simona's canary.

Celestina threw a dirty look Zola's way before seeing Papa's stone *putto* getting smashed. It was the one bearing a halo of fire that stood before the candle shop. One of the finest outdoor stone statues in all of Florence was under attack.

"*Basta*," cried Celestina, starting off to protect the stone statue. "Enough, stop!"

But Zola, stinking of mimosa water so strong it cut through the heavy smoke of the bonfires, spread her arms to block Celestina.

Celestina slapped at Zola. "Move. I must save Papa's sculpture."

In a heartbeat, a pack of *ragazzi* arrived to back up Zola and Celestina dropped her hands, outnumbered.

"Come on, Celestina," said Zola. There was a cool conceit in her tone. "We're going to break that marble *putto* in front of the butcher's shop. It's ugly *and* naked."

"But Papa created that *putto* too." The words tore Celestina's throat.

Behind Zola's shoulder, a *ragazzo* slammed his iron club against the nose of Papa's *putto*. Celestina jerked at the shattering stone.

"Your papa's dead." Zola gave a careless wave of her hand. "He won't care."

"But *I* do. Besides, it's wrong. That's not what Fra said to do."

"Don't be an old *prugna*, Celestina. Everybody's doing it.

It's war."

Celestina regarded one particular *ragazzo* who sidled up next to Zola. He had a perfidious flame in his eye. "And what are you doing with this *ragazzo*?" she asked Zola.

"He's no ordinary *ra-gaz-zo*," Zola drew out the word. "He's a Reform Boy."

So, the boys who took on the great de' Medici from the rooftops had a name. "Your Reform Boy looks nothing like Fra's holy soldiers." Celestina eyeballed the partly shaved skull. "His head looks like the top of the Duomo."

Zola's smile was hard. "*A dopo*. See you later, prune."

Celestina rubbed the spot where the Reform Boy knocked his shoulder against hers as he and Zola departed. Then a whistle pierced her ears. Government watchmen in gold and silver advanced, clubs drawn. Young boys darted furtively, escaping through gaps in the buildings. Merchants scrambled to their shops. Courtiers and their ladies vanished. But the boys of the Reform continued to swing fists as the watchmen swung clubs.

Against the backdrop of smoking bonfires and the orange sun, Celestina spotted a familiar figure swatting her way through the people. Immediately she was reminded that she was in trouble. Still, a slow smile spread across her lips.

"I thought that damn horse was going to pound you into polenta. Barley meal mush on the cobblestones," said Simona, shaking her head.

Celestina allowed Simona to hug her for a heartbeat longer than normal.

"Fra Brucker saved my life," said Celestina. "And I'm in his holy army."

Simona shook her head warningly. "He's a brute, granddaughter. Madness and destruction are what he brings.

Stay away from him."

Celestina didn't have time to argue, not with what was going on behind her grandmother's back. Simona spun to see.

"Simona, no, stay back." Celestina reached and missed her grandmother, who'd already started for the bakery.

At least Celestina *thought* it was their bakery. Draped in gray-blue smoke, the building resembled an enormous *biscotto*, far past its second bake.

3

Rinaldo swung the mallet, cracking the head of the chisel. The toothy edge bit the stone just right. The white block veined in gray-blue was the finest he'd seen. *Pietra serena*. A rock of perfect serenity.

He doffed his brown cap, shaking the stringy wetness from his hair, admiring his final swipe at the stone. From the sunbaked perch high on the marble cliff, he blinked past the valley to the rust-colored, tiled rooftops of Florence.

Twisting the white crucifix dangling at his neck, he thought of the girl with the golden-red locks, wondering if she had arisen from the terra-cotta cobblestones.

The only thing he knew for certain was that the clip of ox hooves was nearing.

The cartman navigated the red wagon up the tight lane, followed by a stream of Rinaldo's cousins, uncles, brothers, and father—all *scalpellini*, stone men, like Rinaldo.

Master da Vinci sat alone in the cart, straight-backed, holding his floppy white hat and looking like a painting against the ice-white wall of stone behind him. A gold rope of rubies glinted at his neck.

Rinaldo regarded the marble block before him. "My future is in your hands, my friend." He glanced at his thumb. Which way would Master point his: up or down?

The cartman pulled the ox by its nose ring straight up to Rinaldo's block. Master da Vinci leaped from the cart.

He lifted Rinaldo in a bear hug. "What's your name, *scalpellino*?" asked the Master.

Rinaldo's feet dangled like that of a boy. He could only grunt. "*Um...um...*"

"This is the first time my youngest son has needed to search for his words," said Jacopo SanGiorgio. Rinaldo's father was sticks and bones compared to Master da Vinci. "Perhaps, Master, my boy needs to look you in the eye to speak."

Master unhanded Rinaldo.

"My name is *R-iii-nal-do*." It came out as windy as the backend of a horse.

"Good to meet you." Leonardo tapped Rinaldo's cheek three times. "You can call me *L-eee-o-nardo*."

Benedetto, the eldest of Rinaldo's three brothers, also the tallest and broadest, snorted a laugh. "There's no need to introduce yourself to our youngest brother. He speaks of you so often that your name burns our ears."

Rinaldo's shoulders curled. Benedetto's mouth was always too honest.

His second eldest brother Luca, forever angry that he'd grown only as short as their mamma, made sucking noises. With Leonardo present, Rinaldo was unable to punch his brother in the teeth.

Instead, he stared daggers at Giacobbe in attempt to ward off further embarrassment. Cobbe, not even a whole year older than Rinaldo, was his best friend. And though Cobbe wasn't a donkey's ass like Luca, too many quarry rocks had clunked him in the head, which made his thinking a bit thick.

And there was Cobbe now, hand raised for Master to call on him.

Rinaldo's neck burned.

"Master," Cobbe started, "perhaps you can give Rinaldo fresco lessons here in Settignano. You can paint the quarry walls. That way he doesn't have to leave me."

Rinaldo wanted to run.

"What's this talk of frescos?" Master faced Rinaldo. "Jacopo tells me that of the SanGiorgio stone masons, yours are the hands blessed by God."

"My brothers are good at it, too," Rinaldo added, to temper Benedetto and Luca, who were sure to take insult and cause him untold trouble before the Master.

"You must be better," said Leonardo, seeming to enjoy stirring the pot. "Jacopo said that you alone cut my block. Listen to me, jumping ahead, calling it *my* block. We won't know if it's fitting for a horse sculpture of the most exquisite detail until I inspect its worthiness."

"I hope it pleases you." Rinaldo's insides shook like a cocoon ready to break open.

Leonardo pointed. "This is it? Twelve foot by ten?"

"Exactly."

"Now it's time for you to pray that it's worth the fifty gold florins your father quoted." Leonardo's gaze stroked the stone.

"I have spoken to God about it many times," said Rinaldo.

He watched speechlessly as Leonardo kicked the stone, stroked it like a pet, and whispered sweet words to it.

"What's he going to do next?" whispered Luca. "Nibble its ear?"

When Leonardo spit on his thumb and rubbed saliva into the marble, Rinaldo held his breath. A crystal-like flash sparkled under Leonardo's fingerprint. Rinaldo clutched his chest to catch his leaping heart.

"The goodness inside the marble has been ignited," declared Leonardo.

A hopeful flutter tickled Rinaldo's rib. Leonardo sucked marble dust from his thumb. But when Master's lips puckered, Rinaldo cringed.

"*Vieni qui*. Come here, Rinaldo."

The urge to flee was overwhelming. He must have failed to cut the rock right, otherwise Leonardo would have approved it by now.

His father nudged him. There was no way out. Rinaldo's deerskin slippers clutched the cliff with each tense step forward.

"Does my stone displease you, Master?" Rinaldo bowed his head.

"Look up," said Leonardo.

Rinaldo slowly lifted his gaze.

"Now smile," said Leonardo. "This rock has been quarried to perfection. If I took a chisel to you in the way you've done to this stone, I'd uncover a talented sculptor inside."

The other SanGiorgio men roared in victory but Rinaldo's shoulders dropped. Rinaldo dreamed of tempera, not marble. And even though a gray blanket of gloom covered him, he shivered feverishly.

"*Silenzio tutti*. Everyone be quiet," said Jacopo. The men hushed. "And our commission, Master? Is it as we discussed?"

Leonardo pecked a kiss on either side of Jacopo's wiry mustache. "You have earned full payment, Jacopo. Fifty gold florins."

"*Grazie*, Master," said Jacopo, turning to Rinaldo. "Now, do you have something to ask Leonardo?"

Rinaldo's tongue grew thick as a brick.

"The skunk has my boy's tongue," said Jacopo. He faced Leonardo. "So, it's up to me to say it. Is there any way you can take Rinaldo as a student?"

Rinaldo held his breath.

"I don't teach sculptors," said Leonardo.

Rinaldo's heart jumped in hope. "That's all right because I want to paint frescos."

"I see you had no trouble saying that," said Leonardo.

"Please give me a chance to learn from you," begged Rinaldo.

Leonardo studied Rinaldo's shoulder span. "The way God built you and the way you cut my rock, you look like a sculptor to me, boy."

"But I want to leave stone."

"There's no escaping it, boy. Stone runs in the blood of the Settignese."

"But it's my dream to paint...*per favore*," Rinaldo said, searching Leonardo's face for a change of heart. "Please."

"I no longer take apprentices of any discipline," Leonardo's tone was gentle.

Rinaldo kicked the quarry dust. "Of course, you don't."

"I see you are upset," said Leonardo. "And you are angry."

Rinaldo stared at the back of his hands.

"Look at me," said Leonardo. Rinaldo peered up in slow defiance. Leonardo stroked his beard. "What is your age and how much formal education have you acquired?"

"I'm aged twenty...and two years of general school," answered Rinaldo.

"That's two more years than most quarrymen." Leonardo's tone was contemplative. "But you're too long in the bones for a formal apprenticeship."

"Then please, Master, advise us," Jacopo said. "Every spare moment the boy draws. His work is on parchment, on cliffs, on his poor mamma's walls. He never stops drawing. Tell us if he has a future in fresco or put these dreams out of his head. Tell him whether the life of a painter is possible, or impossible, for him."

Leonardo sighed. "A boy as gifted as you believe Rinaldo is doesn't need me for success, Jacopo."

"Without someone like you to teach me, I don't know how to succeed," said Rinaldo.

Leonardo crossed his arms over his generous belly. "A boy who speaks with such frankness has earned a bit of my wisdom."

Rinaldo's heart quickened.

"A man must meet three conditions to be a fruitful artist," said Leonardo. "First, he has to have the right look."

Rinaldo's heart hardened. He'd already failed. Quarrymen were considered artisans, but in reality, they were laborers. Rinaldo was all ropy muscle and sun-browned skin. Leonardo, by contrast, was beefy pink and soap-polished.

"What's this look of which you speak?" Jacopo asked. "Rinaldo has a handsome face, square and even."

"It's not what's on the outside," Leonardo explained. "It's a look of hunger. And it's in the eyes."

Jacopo flapped his arms. "Well, it's over then. Our life is hard, but Rinaldo's never gone hungry. His eyes have always had enough to eat."

Leonardo howled. Rinaldo checked the top of the mountain, fearing a rockslide from Master's echoing laugh.

"It's not a physical hunger, Jacopo," said Master, sobering a bit. "It's a desire that comes from the inside. You can see it in a boy's eyes."

Jacopo beckoned Rinaldo closer.

"Do you see it, Papa?" Rinaldo presented one side of his face, and then the other. "Do you see the look of desire on me?"

Jacopo studied him from every angle. Finally, his father shrugged.

Rinaldo looked to Leonardo for an answer. "Rinaldo has the right look," Leonardo assured.

Rinaldo beamed.

"The artist smiles," said Leonardo. "Now the second requirement is money. Rinaldo will need five gold florins to even be considered to have the chance to work beside a skilled artist."

"With today's commission, Rinaldo has earned his florins," said Jacopo.

It was going so well Rinaldo dared to hope. "What is the third requirement, Master?"

"It's the most important," said Leonardo.

Even his stupid brothers leaned forward to hear. "Tell me," said Rinaldo.

"It's a muse."

"Muse?"

"Yes. And you need to find one," said Leonardo.

His brothers glanced around. Jacopo scratched his chin. There was no way around it. Rinaldo had to ask. "What's a muse?"

"A pretty woman who is your inspiration," said Leonardo.

"Girls?" Pretty ones grew like sunflowers all over Settignano but not one helped him become better as a painter.

"Not plural," said Leonardo. "Singular. One. *Uno.*"

"Only one girl!" cried Luca in fake distress. Leonardo shook with laughter. Even Jacopo cracked a smile but Rinaldo turned red as the rubies in Master's necklace.

"Yes, only one." Leonardo wiped an amused tear. "But she has to inspire you in the best possible way."

"What's the best way?" Rinaldo asked.

"She should possess hair as sublime as a goddess," said Leonardo.

Rinaldo's heart quickened at the memory of the *signorina* on the cobblestones. "Should it be the color of strawberries and apricots, a color more sublime than even that of Botticelli's Venus?" he asked.

"Well, that was specific," said Leonard. "Does this girl you have in mind make the *cazzo* under your tights hard as the marble you stand on?"

Rinaldo scowled at his brother's and cousins, braying like donkeys. He wished they'd laugh themselves off the cliff.

When the stupidity died down, Rinaldo said, "I saw a girl like that once, on the Via Scalia in Florence. But she ignored me."

Leonardo winked. "You have to return to Florence and win her over, then."

"Do you think I can?"

"If you can mine a stone of such beauty, as you did for me and my future horse, you can figure out anything."

Rinaldo threw back his shoulders. "Papa, may I have my share of money?" He presented his palm.

Jacopo frowned, "You'll get paid with the others."

"*Per favore*, Papa." He extended his hand farther. For the first time, he did not back down under his father's stern glare. Jacopo dug through his money purse. Rinaldo slipped the five golden coins in his pocket.

My fortune is changing.

"Papa's favorite." Luca's nostrils flared.

Rinaldo yanked Luca's ear. "So long, stupid brother."

Rinaldo leaped from the cliff where they stood, landing on the one hanging underneath. He then vaulted from cliff to quarry cliff, taking a dangerous shortcut down the mountain.

"Rinaldo, you're going to kill yourself," Jacopo shouted. "Where are you going?"

Rinaldo paused and waved. "To satisfy my hungry eyes. *Addio*, Papa. I'm off to grab a clean shirt, fetch my sketches, and give Mamma a kiss goodbye."

He saw his father point at Cobbe. "Rinaldo, stay with Giacobbe. He'll keep you safe," Jacopo shouted.

Though Cobbe possessed the fastest legs in the family, he always managed to slow Rinaldo down in ways that had nothing to do with running.

Expectedly, Cobbe caught up to Rinaldo in no time.

"Where are we going?" Cobbe asked.

"*I'm* going to Florence," said Rinaldo.

Giacobbe sized up the great city in the distance. "Why can't you practice painting here? Why do you have to go there?"

Rinaldo leaped up and swatted the leafy branch of a pear tree. "To find my muse, of course."

Cobbe passed him going down. "Brother?" he asked. "This muse of yours, does she have a friend?"

4

Rolling smoke tumbled through the bakery. Simona tried to clear the air by flapping her apron.

Celestina thought her grandmother resembled an ill-tempered angel, with good reason. *Biscotti*, now the color, size, and shape of bat *cacca*, lay scorched on the oven floor.

"You should be ashamed of yourself, granddaughter." Simona threw a blanket over the ruined yield, suffocating the smoke.

"*Mi dispiace.* Sorry for leaving." Celestina's throat hurt like a *biscotto* turd had lodged there.

Simona waved her hand through the fog. "I'm talking about the *angelo del buio*, that priest from the north. He's an angel of darkness and you fell before him like a *puttana*," said Simona.

A *mille* little knives stabbed the inside of her ears whenever Simona talked of modesty. "Don't call me a whore, not when I'm still a virgin," said Celestina.

Simona wagged her finger. "And you must always be good. But sometimes you're a little *stupida*."

Celestina slumped. "What do you mean, stupid?"

"Why didn't you let that handsome stranger help you up from the street? What a *Herculino*." Simona whistled. "And Little Hercules looked respectful, too. I can tell these things about people. He's nothing like that damned friar who took vows to freeze his *cazzo*."

Celestina slapped her hands over her ears.

She was still able to hear the ranting. "That friar's vow of chastity has not been tested and he's going to destroy all our lives because of it. Mark my words," said Simona.

"I'll be careful." Celestina hoped that ended it.

"Also," Simona continued, and Celestina winced like she'd been pinched. "For punishment, you will not be getting the orange dress. The fabric shop can put it on a scarecrow, for all I care. And another thing, you are not joining the Reform. That devil priest is just using you," said her grandmother.

"Using me?" The heat inside Celestina spiked. "If you mean to defeat the heretics, then I agree. Think anything else and you're the one with the dirty mind."

Simona snorted. "Fra is *merda* beneath my feet."

Celestina spun for the water bucket, which was always filled in case of fire. "Stink under your feet, you say? I know how to clean up a mess like that," she said and hurled a splash of water across the floor, pushing Simona to the back.

Celestina fled before the litany of Simona's obscenities following her out of the door burned holes through her ears. She glimpsed Papa's stone *putto* lying in pieces on the street. The sight of it was unbearable and she turned away, which was when she spotted a lively fire burning in front of the *farmacia*.

Strangely, the flame was not anchored to the street. It floated at Celestina's eye level, and the flame glowed brilliant, even in the day.

She blinked for a respite from its brightness, glimpsing

the ghostly image of a book. It floated inside the flame.

She glanced around. For the first time in her life she was alone on the Via Scalia. The watchmen had cleared the street. There were no witnesses to confirm what she was seeing, which was a book hovering inside a fire, with the book not burning.

Her gaze returned to the book. Its pages began to flip open, each bearing a whispery picture of Papa. Chestnut whiskers. Paint-splattered artist's smock. Blue-green eyes the color of the outdoor fresco he'd once painted of the Adriatic.

She savored the sight. Papa appeared so vivid. She hadn't realized how much of his color she'd already lost inside her head. She blinked, in hopes of capturing the image in her memory, like a painting. When she looked again, Papa had been replaced. The new image left her aghast.

It was a witch. Not any witch. *The* witch. Papa's witch: the enchantress with the long, black hair.

She was kneeling at the communion rail during Mass at Santa Maria Novella, exactly as she'd been that fateful day. And still, even in the flames, her head was uncovered.

That was a sin. Everyone knew that a veil, scarf, or hat was required inside church of girls over the age of seven.

A murderous rage spiked inside Celestina. By foregoing the veil, Papa's witch had committed an act of rebellion so heinous that it set in motion the wheels of his death.

The page flipped, and Celestina's breath hitched. Next to the witch was Monsignor. Miserable Monsignor. Celestina's body shook as if she were back in time, one year ago to the day, when he refused to serve the witch the Eucharist.

"I would sacrifice my life before I would allow a witch with an uncovered head to corrupt the holy host," boomed Monsignor from inside the fire. The familiar words and force of his voice thrust Celestina back a step.

The pages flipped faster. Monsignor drew back his hand. *Slap.* It cracked the witch's cheek.

Celestina quaked like she was there all over again. Next, the pages reenacted Monsignor dragging the witch out of church by her hair.

"*Je me attens a mon juge, c'est le roy du ciel et de la terre.*" The sound of the witch's mysterious words, perhaps French, wavered through the flames.

By now Papa was back in the fire. Celestina swallowed a bitter lump, watching as his hand stroked the witch's uncovered head. Though her face did not look evil, Celestina remembered that demons were successful only through trickery.

Watching Papa as he kissed the witch's lips produced tears of hatred in Celestina. She was already bracing for what came next—the church's white-uniformed watchman impaling Papa with his curved sword.

Celestina squeezed shut her eyes. After calming down a bit she dared survey the fire again. The witch was gone, but Papa remained. Dead on the ground, his blood seeped between cracks in the cobblestones.

A hard snap in the fire startled Celestina. Papa vanished, the book was gone, and the fire had extinguished.

She shook her head. Inside she was numb. If she didn't know better, she might think a witch had cast a spell over her. Or perhaps she'd simply fallen asleep on her feet and it was all a dream. Whatever it had been, it was going to remain her secret because if she told the wrong person it could very well be her dress burning on the stake in the middle of the Via Scalia.

In a fog, she paced before the bakery. Eventually, she'd

have to go inside and face Simona.

Trying to postpone that misery for as long as she was able, she glanced down the street. She slammed her back against the façade. The real Monsignor was storming up the Via Scalia.

She hadn't seen him since the Tribunal of Faith shipped him to Siena's Cathedral after he slapped Papa's witch. Sent away to rest was the official pronouncement of the Tribunal. And now Monsignor was back, and with a formidable strut. The year of sleep had worked, apparently.

Celestina edged her way toward the door, hoping she could enter the bakery before Monsignor saw her. She'd made no progress on the task he'd assigned her, an order given while she stood over Papa's dead body.

His words chewed at her ears by night and day.

"For the sins of his mother and father, and for sacrificing his God-given life for that of a heretic, may the soul of Alessandro DiCapria be doomed to remain forever in purgatory until which time his earthly people repent and deliver proper penance for their sins and God sees fit to release him."

And what he'd demanded next was impossible for her to accomplish while she was in mourning:

"The daughter of Alessandro DiCapria must capture the dress of the witch who tempted her father, plus four more for extra penance, to burn in the piazza. Only then will Alessandro's soul be released from purgatory to see the face of God."

And here was Monsignor, nearing. She dashed inside, but he'd legged it over fast and he was nearly on Celestina's heels.

The hem of his blue *magna cappa*, a spectacular cape of a type she'd never seen—certainly never on him—flapped around his quick-moving feet.

She hadn't expected an old man to be part of the Reform, but Monsignor certainly looked the part with his silver-and-black hair cut in short snippets and brushed forward like Julius Caesar's. The new style framed his deep-set, black eyes. He still smelled of Bergamot orange.

He glanced around the bakery like it had been a long time since he'd been there but during his years at Santa Maria Novella he'd never been in Simona's shop, not once that Celestina recalled.

"*Buon pomeriggio*," he said, but it was not a good afternoon the last time she saw him when she pleaded for him to administer extreme unction to Papa as he lay bleeding in the piazza.

She curtsied in grudging respect. "If you are here to judge my progress in catching five witches, I've been unsuccessful."

Monsignor looked bewildered. "What?"

Her head flinched back. Had he forgotten what he'd ordered? She wished she never had to talk to him again, but with Papa's eternal life at risk, she dared not ease up.

"I have just recently been welcomed into the Reform, and I swear upon my dying breath that I will capture the dresses of five heretics," she said.

"That's fine," he said, but his mind seemed elsewhere.

"*Ri-for-ma!*" she raised her fist. But the word just hung in the air. She reddened. It didn't sound the same with just her saying it.

"You really do favor my old friend," he said.

She glanced over her shoulder. That was his answer? And whom was he talking to? There wasn't a single customer in the bakery.

He stroked the crucifix of white silk stitched on the chest of his cape. "But you do not, however, resemble your grandmother. Not even when she was your age."

Celestina stared at him blankly. He was talking to her like a roll of salami had hit him in the face. Simona never attended Mass, even on Sunday, so it was always puzzling how they were even acquainted and why Simona despised him.

"Exactly how do you know her, Monsignor?" asked Celestina. "My grandmother."

"She's one of my oldest friends."

Celestina blinked obviously. "Friends? Are...are you talking about my Simona?"

"There's another? Now, where is *Signora* DiCapria?"

Celestina rubbed her neck. If they were such good friends, how was it that Monsignor didn't know that Simona refused to take the surname of any man, even her own father?

"*Scusa*, Monsignor," said Celestina. "Call her only Simona—no last name. Otherwise—"

He chuckled deeply. "I know your grandmother well. I will not provoke her."

From the back of the shop, Simona sauntered in sans apron, fanning her face, looking like no grandmother ever in a linen dress the yellowish color of citrine that clung to her womanly curves. Wisps of her honey-gray tresses, which she wore loose and wavy to her shoulders, never in a braid or bun like other women her age, waved in the air with each back and forth of her hand.

Monsignor was correct that Celestina looked nothing like her grandmother. Simona was a remarkable beauty in body and face, with eyes the color of shimmering basil.

"Well, if it isn't Guilio Baldasare," Simona said. "What brings you to my bakery for the first time in thirty years?"

Monsignor gave a sly smile. "I come in peace."

Simona sniffed the air. "Even in this stench of burning I

still smell your stink of orange."

His eyes narrowed. "You used to like the scent."

"I *liked* my son," said Simona.

The words rocked Celestina. *Naturalmente* a mother liked her son. Simona loved Papa, of course. Where was her grandmother going with this?

"Alessandro chose evil over God and brought on his own death." Monsignor saying Papa's name brought fever to Celestina's forehead.

Simona poked her tongue in her cheek. "You're like Dante, telling stories, but you tell them only to yourself," she said. "That sword that killed my son, you didn't touch it but your hands were all over it. You wanted Alessandro dead from the moment of his birth. You couldn't bear the thought of who he came from—"

Monsignor cut in before Celestina was able to ask, who did Papa come from?

"If that's what you believe," said Monsignor, "you're the one telling the stories."

Celestina's attention seesawed between Simona and Monsignor. "I can't tell. Are you talking about Papa's father? Who is he?" Celestina asked.

"*Nessuno.*" Their joined response, a hard "no one," left her slouching and with no room to pester.

Monsignor planted his feet. "I'm famished from my travels and in need of refreshment. Fetch me something to eat, Simona-with-No-Surname."

"What's your pleasure, Baldasare?" Simona's voice was tight as a string on Nero's fiddle.

"I no longer eat soft, white bread," he said.

"And you never cheat?" asked Simona.

Monsignor glanced at the back of his hands. "Only once."

Simona eyed him derisively. "You look bad in blue, Baldasare."

"That's a shame," he said, dusting flakes of ash off his shoulder, "because that's what I now wear. This is my new habit. Perhaps you haven't heard. I'm back permanently from Siena and am now the Supreme Master of the Reform."

Celestina was stunned to hear Monsignor had risen so high. She was only a soldier; he was all the way above her, like God.

Simona brushed her fingertips beneath her chin in scorn. "I should have known you were the brains behind that Austrian skunk. Yes, I've heard your virtuoso from Tyrol. Well, Baldasare, your mission is working. Did you know that you and the young friar have me praying again?"

"And what is your prayer, my child?" There was nothing pious in the way Monsignor asked.

"For God to damn you and the Reform," said Simona.

Celestina gasped and made the sign of the cross. Damning was a mortal sin. *Simona doesn't mean it, St. Catherine.*

"Support the Reform, Simona," said Monsignor.

"Not on my son's dead body. Or my granddaughter's living one."

Celestina raised a tentative finger. "*Scusa*, Monsignor. I support the Reform—"

"*Stai zitta*," Simona snapped. "Shut up, granddaughter, and do not say another word to this devil."

"Let the girl speak," Monsignor growled.

"Fra admitted me into his holy army and I'll hunt witches for the souls of both Simona and Papa," said Celestina.

"*Basta*, granddaughter. Enough." Simona pointed at the back room. "Stay there until this monster leaves."

Celestina skulked to the back. She hated being away from

the action but at least she was still able to listen.

"Cibo doesn't know about your Reform, does he?" Celestina cupped her ear. It was Simona, saying a new name, "Cibo."

"I have the youth on my side. Cibo's supporters are old. His days in the Catholic Church are numbered." It was Monsignor, sounding like he was in a fight with Cibo.

"Our friend in red has never lost a single battle to you. What makes you so sure you can beat him now?" Sounded like her grandmother was on Cibo's side.

"The Reform is blue and red is dead." Monsignor again.

"Politics, pope, and Holy Roman Empire. No wonder I've always hated the color red." That was for sure Simona. "And now I detest blue, as well."

"If I don't see you at the young friar's sermon tomorrow in the piazza, there will be trouble." Celestina grimaced at the ruthlessness of Monsignor's tone. "I'll call for a boycott of your bakery." There was a tense pause. "Wait," Monsignor's voice rattled. "What are you doing?"

Feet shuffled and the door opened and slammed shut. From the back, Celestina peeked. Monsignor didn't bother to say goodbye, and who could blame him with her grandmother ready to impale him with the iron poker in her hand.

Celestina marched up front. "How does Monsignor know you? And who's Cibo?"

"Forget Baldasare and Cibo," said Simona.

"What other secrets are you keeping from me, besides the identity of my grandfather?" asked Celestina.

"Grandfather?" asked Simona. "Why did you bring him up?"

"Does Monsignor know my grandfather?" Celestina pressed. "Is Papa's papa still alive? Are there living relatives besides you and me?"

Simona jabbed the kindling in the hearth with the poker. "You're casting for fish in the air."

Celestina grabbed her grandmother's arm. "Answer me."

Simona yanked free. "It's the friar from Tyrol who I want to talk about. Stay away from that black-haired demon. He's worse than any poor soul he demonizes."

Celestina slapped her hands on the counter. "Stop talking bad about Fra, and start talking about our family secrets."

"I will take my family secrets to my grave and whisper them to the devil," said Simona. She turned for the back room. "And no going to that sermon tomorrow."

Celestina rubbed her closed lids until she saw black spots but nothing erased the vision of Satan gnawing on her grandmother's thigh and sucking the marrow.

Once again she felt the urge to escape Simona. But this time she had a real place to go—to Fra's sermon.

5

"The bakery next to the *farmacia* smelled good," said Cobbe, rubbing his stomach and staring down the Via Scalia.

It took most men just short of two hours to make their way down the mountain path from Settignano, but Rinaldo was on a mission and he and his brother made it to the heart of Florence in half that time. The fast pace burned strength, however, and now Cobbe was acting like he'd starve if he didn't shove fresh *pane* in his mouth every two heartbeats.

"My muse is not at some bread shop," Rinaldo said, quickening his step toward Santa Maria Novella. "If you're so hungry, go back there without me."

"Can't. Promised Papa I'd look after his baby boy," said Cobbe.

Rinaldo rolled his eyes. When they reached the piazza, he sliced through the crow purposely, to loose Cobbe. Rinaldo was looking for the young woman from the cobblestones, while the throng waited for the Dominican's sermon.

Coming upon a sign stating "Keep Out" in big black and square letters, Rinaldo saw it pointed to the back of the church.

His pulse quickened. The sign stirred him to thinking. At yesterday's rally, his muse had refused to view his face. Possibly, she was shy. If so, it would be smart of her to seek a private area from which to listen to the Dominican's lecture.

In the meantime, Cobbe found Rinaldo, who eyed him flatly. His brother wasn't easily sidetracked.

"We're taking a shortcut," said Rinaldo.

Cobbe spied the sign. "You're not rotting in prison for some girl whose name you don't even know."

Rinaldo pushed him. "Get out of here, then."

Cobbe squeezed Rinaldo's ear. "And live to tell Papa that his favorite was hanged in the piazza for trespassing? Forget about it," said Giacobbe.

Rinaldo pretended to baby his sore ear, and then in a trick move cut away from his brother. "*Ciao ciao, stupido.*"

"*Ehi*, who are you calling a stupid?" Cobbe shouted.

Rinaldo bounded over a rough-cut sawhorse that acted as a gate and then edged past a pair of alert watchmen in blue guarding the restricted area.

The guards waved him through. Biting back a surprised smile, he sauntered in like he belonged. If only his muse could see him now, she'd surely be impressed; the guards seemed to be.

There was a good chance they deemed him a great artist who made serious frescos inside Santa Maria Novella. Otherwise, why would they have allowed him to pass?

Rinaldo nosed around, searching for the *signorina* and the Dominican. The friar's conceit made Rinaldo's skin crawl. Rinaldo had no doubt that the religious warred against his vow of chastity and he desired the girl from the Via Scalia.

It was after that hideous thought that a claw cinched Rinaldo's tunic and pulled him back.

The devil Dominican. He's going for my soul.

The grip securing him was strong as a rock-clenching *gradina*. How did a priest get so damn strong? Then the hand fell away, replaced by a familiar voice. "Is baby Rinaldo going to cry?"

He swung on his brother, to put him in his place, but Cobbe was always faster and ducked in time.

"How did you sneak past the blue guards?" asked Rinaldo, glaring at his useless fist.

"They waved me in," said Cobbe, matching Rinaldo's stride.

"But you don't look like an artist." Rinaldo slowed his step.

Cobbe eyed the expanse of Rinaldo's shoulders. "Neither do you, in honesty."

Glancing first at his chipped fingernails, and then at the pack of grunting laborers pushing against the *culo* end of a colossal white horse that refused to enter past the door of the church, Rinaldo slumped in understanding.

Squinting into the sun, he saw that the *stallone* belonged to the Dominican. The guards had thought that Rinaldo and Cobbe were there to shove a horse that refused to go inside, perhaps because it hated the friar.

That gave Rinaldo an idea. Since the Dominican was sticky for the *signorina*, he may have invited her inside the church, so they could be alone together.

Rinaldo elbowed his brother. "What do you say we help those Florentine weaklings move the horse?"

Cobbe covered his *cazzo*. "If that thing bucks, it'll kick off our balls."

"Help me, for once," said Rinaldo.

"And all I wanted was some bread before home."

"Giacobbe, *per favore*...please."

Cobbe scratched his chin, his elbow, and the back of his neck. Rinaldo's skin itched. He could have chiseled a small pony during the time it took Cobbe to decide. Finally, his brother blinked. "How can I say no to helping men when they're working outside a house of God."

Rinaldo clapped his brother on the back and together they approached a fat-necked man, clearly the boss. "Give me and my brother a chance," said Rinaldo.

The boss surveyed Rinaldo from foot to head. "You're not one of us. Get out." The boss glanced over at the blue watchman.

Rinaldo waved his hands. "No, no, no. You don't have to pay us, Boss."

The boss cocked an eyebrow. "Move aside, boys. Let's see what these big mouths can do." The sweaty laborers retreated, giving no argument.

Rinaldo rammed his shoulder into the horse's flank. Cobbe pushed against Rinaldo, doubling the force. The horse whined a "leave-me-alone" warning. Rinaldo dug deep until his lungs hurt.

Push, SanGiorgio.

A moment later the horse's stance broke. The laborers cheered and the boss sucked the inside of his flabby cheeks.

Rinaldo stroked the long nuzzle of the *stallone*. "I owe you a favor one day," he whispered in its twitching ear, leading it through the church doorway. Its heavy hooves clipped against the beige-and-gray church tile. Cobbe and the men followed in silence, reverent of their surroundings.

Seeing the full interior, Rinaldo's stomach fluttered like he'd swallowed a choir of tiny angels. God was present from the candlelight to the architecture. For the first time in his life, he understood why city folks chose to pray inside.

The vast interior was shaped like a Latin cross. The nave was long and slender. There was a center aisle, and two side aisles running along the walls decorated in winged *putti* and stained-glass windows.

Rinaldo gazed at the ceiling. The vault consisted of pointed arches with diagonal buttresses in black and white. At the altar, a formidable winding staircase led to the marble pulpit.

He brought the horse with him to the Tornabuoni Chapel, where Rinaldo studied the frieze of musical *putti* in bas-relief and the fresco of the newborn Christ and Virgin Mary. He marveled at the hands of the master who created such a masterpiece. A gold plate sunk in the wall was emblazoned with the name Domenico Ghirlandaio.

Rinaldo whacked his chest in order to breathe. The magnificence before him was nearly too much to bear. Ghirlandaio didn't simply paint. He shaped life.

Rinaldo weaved his fingers through his hair, staring at Ghirlandaio's modern vision of ancient peoples. Art belonged to those who succeeded in finding their life's muse. Men like Leonardo and Ghirlandaio.

How about you, SanGiorgio? Will you ever be this good?

Born a *scalpellino*, he'd surely die one if the Tornabuoni Chapel indicated the measure of skill he'd need to paint frescos inside city churches.

He stared at his fist. He needed a punch in the face— punishment for being wrong about everything. There was no friar with a blue-lined cape or girl with golden-red locks hiding inside the church. He was never going to paint frescos. It was time to collect his brother and leave behind all memories of Florence.

It was back to the quarry for him.

In his search for Giacobbe, he glimpsed a *putto* in fresco on the back wall and mindlessly dropped the horse's reins. The clomping of hooves faded as the horse meandered off.

Rinaldo neared the painting. Though the image was fading—the *putto* hadn't been cured correctly in the wall, even Rinaldo knew that—it enticed him nonetheless, particularly its hair.

It was the same color—flaming gold—like that of his muse. He narrowed his stare in stricter study. *Mio e Dio.* My God. It *was* his muse.

He grabbed the back of the pew, horrified that another already claimed her for his muse. Though it shouldn't have mattered anymore, now that he'd given up his dream of painting, it did. Why else was his soul so rattled?

His mind raced for answers. Would a man paint his muse, the woman who stirred his dreams at night, as a chubby winged cherub with flowing sashes covering the interesting parts?

No, SanGiorgio, he would not.

A muse needed to be painted like a woman, sensual and arousing. The *putto* on the wall was beautiful, but not created to stroke a man's desire. Rinaldo broke into a wide smile. Whoever had painted this *putto* had loved the subject as a child.

He fell to his knees before it. The artist had created letters within the fold of the sash. C-e-l-e-s-t-i-n-a. It was most definitely the girl from the Via Scalia. She was called Celestina. A plaque named the artist: Alessandro DiCapria.

Her papa?

Rinaldo dropped his face in his hands. The fresco was a sign from God. His path was now set. He was going to remain in Florence and find Celestina even if he had to wear out his feet hunting for her.

He ran through the pews to tell Cobbe the news but slowed at the strange sight of his brother, among the laborers, near the door leading out to the piazza. They were still as statues staring at the Dominican.

He *was* there, after all, and he'd found his horse, but the animal's demeanor was far different from when Rinaldo walked it around the church. It seemed afraid of the Dominican, who was now circling the agitated animal.

With hands so fast they flashed, the religious bolted the animal's bridle against its chest plate, bending its neck forward at a near lethal angle. The horse's pink eyes flashed wild. No wonder the poor thing did not want to be near its damned master.

Rinaldo scowled, but the Dominican, with the shock of black on his head, brushed erect as a cock's comb, appeared not to notice. His eyes, like blue slate, a color seen nowhere in Ghirlandaio's godly frescos, were solely on his horse.

More warrior than priest, the Dominican's back was rigid, stance wide, and chest high. Pale feet were bare on the cold church tile.

Rinaldo sidled up to Cobbe. A sun-shriveled laborer, standing next to his brother, leaned over to Rinaldo.

"*Inquisitore,*" the man's voice was low. Rinaldo glanced in the direction of the Dominican.

"Inquisitor?"

The old man gave a sharp nod.

The unseemly word sounded about right for a *stronzo* religious. Rinaldo snuck behind a column to gather more information on the little shit pretending to be a man of God. Cobbe was at his back.

In one swift poke, the Dominican jabbed the tip of his rosary crucifix into a festering blister on the side of the horse's stomach.

Rinaldo muffled his gasp. Though his heart was in a twist for the frightened animal, Rinaldo stayed hidden to uncover the reason for the Dominican's cruelty.

The Dominican proceeded to poke expertly at the wound for it to bleed. Clearly, he'd experimented with this torture earlier. The horse snorted into its chest while the friar spread its blood on the top of his own bare foot, and then the other.

Rinaldo steamed. How he'd like to dig the end of that rosary between the friar's ribs. Giacobbe, too, wore a look of hurt and confusion. Together they advanced to the closer pillar.

The friar dragged his hands over the animal's muscular flank. "Be still, Shadrach," he said in a calming tone. "All must sacrifice."

Rinaldo prayed the Dominican's words meant Shadrach's torture was over, but when the friar stabbed the horse again, on the new side, Rinaldo staggered back into Giacobbe.

Shadrach's long whine made Rinaldo's stomach churn.

The friar streaked Shadrach's blood across the left panel of his white habit.

After the Dominican's third stick, and after he rubbed the horse's blood around his hands as if it were soap, a murderous rage ignited within Rinaldo.

"Enough, *frate*!" Rinaldo stepped from behind his cover.

The Dominican spun around.

Rinaldo yanked free of his brother's grip.

He cast a dirty look at the religious and then nodded toward Shadrach. "Why must you torment this beautiful creature?"

The Dominican raised a cool eyebrow. "Your name, Italian?"

"Rinaldo. Family name SanGiorgio."

"Are you proud of yourself for standing up to a man of God, SanGiorgio?"

Rinaldo upped his chin. "Pride is a sin. So is hurting a defenseless animal."

"I can see you're well-versed in Catholicism."

"Of course." Rinaldo tried to sound confident so as not to wither under the Dominican's cool stare.

But the Dominican continued to glare icily. "Bet I know something that you don't."

Rinaldo crossed his arms over his chest. "What?"

"I'm going to guess that you cannot speak Austrian."

Rinaldo's mind raced to find a Germanic word he knew, but his life had been too simple to hear anyone other than his countrymen. "I know only Italian, that is true."

"I'll teach you a phrase, then," the Dominican offered.

Rinaldo swallowed. "All right."

The Dominican leaned in. "*Leck mich im arsch.*"

"What does that mean?" asked Rinaldo. It sounded like gargling.

The Dominican's face lit with amusement and then he stepped forward and, unexpectedly, pecked Rinaldo on the lips.

"*Puah,*" Rinaldo retched, slapping at his mouth in an effort to rid his face of the kiss. Before he could make a fist to crack the Dominican's jaw, the friar had him by the hair.

"Ready for part two?" asked the Dominican.

But Rinaldo was unable to speak. His face had already been slammed into Shadrach's rump.

The religious twisted Rinaldo's arm behind his back, near

the breaking point. The searing pain in his arm immobilized the rest of his body, which made it difficult to ward off the Dominican's continued push of Rinaldo's face toward the horse's dark crack.

To create a sliver of breathing space, Rinaldo dug the heel of his free hand into Shadrach to thrust the horse forward. But without Cobbe to back him up—the battle was *mano a mano*, hand to hand—Shadrach was unyielding as a wall of stone.

His only chance of breathing was to move the friar. Rinaldo spiked back his elbow. It struck the soft spot under the friar's chest. Perfect aim. The Dominican keeled over.

Freed, Rinaldo indulged in a long breath, but the Dominican was on him again. His arm was a noose around Rinaldo's neck.

Thrusting back his hips, Rinaldo raised the friar off his feet, and then Rinaldo fell back so that the Dominican slammed back first onto the tile, with Rinaldo on top.

But then the Dominican, with the skill of a Grecian wrestler, flipped and switched places so that he was now on top of Rinaldo.

Pressing his fist against the apple in Rinaldo's throat, the Dominican asked, "Now, Italian, tell me, what does '*Leck mich im arsch*' mean?"

"Kiss...my ass...Dominican," choked out Rinaldo.

The friar sprang to his feet and Rinaldo gasped for air.

"Let's see the sharpness of your wit after a decade in chains." In a guttural roar, the friar shouted, "Watchmen, arrest this Italian—"

From the back, a hand grabbed Rinaldo's collar. His heart leaped to his throat. Wrenched to standing, he was hauled away at frightening speed.

With each backward step, Ghirlandaio's frescos grew

more distant, as did his chances of ever again seeing the real Celestina.

※

"*Crocifiggilo!*"

Not only was Rinaldo unable to see the miserable pig who was dragging him by the back of the collar through the fevered crowd in the piazza at Santa Maria Novella, he could not believe what he was hearing. The people had worked themselves into a fever waiting for the damned Dominican to present himself.

"Crucify him," they shouted at Rinaldo, as they kicked at him and tried to punch him in the face. He landed a few back, despite being dragged backward.

But what Rinaldo really wanted was a second chance to attack the Dominican. How he wished he could avenge Shadrach, tied up and wounded by the friar. It was the Dominican's dirty secret that the blood on his hands and feet belonged to the poor horse—a trick to fool the people into believing he bore the wounds of the crucified Jesus.

While Rinaldo panted for each breath, he cursed the piece-of-*merda* dragging him. The guard who had him could possibly give Shadrach a fair race.

"Show me your face," growled Rinaldo.

Finally, his captor spoke. "A pain in the cock, that's what you are."

Rinaldo broke out in a grin. A heartbeat later he was released. "For the love of God, Cobbe, I thought you were a guard for that damn Dominican."

Cobbe shook his head warningly. "You picked a fight with the wrong person this time, brother. That Dominican is a bastard. Now let's get out of here before the real guards find us."

"You go home and tell Papa and Mamma I'm staying until I find my muse," said Rinaldo, planting his feet.

Cobbe's mouth dropped. Rinaldo left him standing there. Stupid squash, Cobbe. A few long steps later he glanced back to see if Cobbe had left.

It was then a soft gasp escaped Rinaldo's lips. He'd found the person he was looking for, and it wasn't his brother.

His breathing turned ragged. There was no mistake. It was his muse, reddish-gold hair shining under the bright Florentine sun.

With Celestina less than a hundred heads away, Rinaldo thrust his fist and shouted with enough force to crack the sky. "Thank...you...God."

There was a slap on his shoulder. His stomach tightened. Was it a guard? He spun around with his fists up—and had never been so happy to see his brother.

"What now?" asked Cobbe. "I heard you shouting from back there."

"She's here," Rinaldo's voice cracked.

Giacobbe checked. "Where?"

Rinaldo pointed in a high arc in Celestina's direction. "The girl with peaches for skin."

Cobbe glanced heavenward. "Here we go again."

"Celestina," bellowed Rinaldo, but she appeared not to hear. The people made great noise. Her attention remained on the phony Dominican.

"Celestina?" asked Cobbe. "Since when does she have a name?"

"Tell you later. Come." Rinaldo pulled Cobbe by the wrist.

Cobbe snatched back his hand. "There are too many

watchmen near her. You saw what that damn religious did to his horse. If we get caught, that will be us."

"Don't you see, Cobbe?" Rinaldo bounced from foot to foot. "Nothing will happen. God is with us. It's a miracle that I found her."

The strength of one hundred men filled Rinaldo as he lowered his shoulder and plowed through the crowd. He was going for her, Cobbe or no Cobbe.

But when the press from Cobbe's shoulder boosted him from behind, Rinaldo was heartened all the more. Only ten people, or thereabouts, now separated him from Celestina.

He was close enough to see her eyes flicker green-blue. Her lips were even and the color of pink roses. He imagined her round and firm breasts perfect under her pretty green dress. One more shove and he'd be there.

Then the glint of metal flashed. He lurched back. The blade of the watchman's sword just missed his nose.

The people screamed, pushing every way to flee from Rinaldo. He stilled, eagerly examining faces. Where was Celestina?

He met the glare of a watchman in blue. The guard was heavy with fat and muscle and bore a formidable sword. With an even thrust, the soldier swung his weapon. Rinaldo leaped back. It missed slicing his stomach by a slip; at the same time the swing threw off the watchman's own balance. The guard stumbled to the ground.

With the angry look of a man not used to missing, the watchman stuck a finger inside his cheek and whistled. At the shriek, the people parted. Two guards barreled through the crowd. Keeping one eye on them, Rinaldo searched desperately for Celestina.

He heard Cobbe's shout above the fracas, "If we don't

leave now, you will never meet Celestina."

Rinaldo froze at his brother's wise words. Celestina had no idea he loved her even before he knew her name. And she'd be no worse for it if he hung from the gallows for simply trying to meet her.

Cobbe was right. Rinaldo would not allow himself to die before he reunited with her. "*Andiamo*, let's go," he swung his arm at Cobbe.

But the watchman, whose hand was coming for his throat, had other ideas.

)(

The bells of Santa Maria Novella chimed nine times. Celestina smoothed Simona's hand-me-down dress, a sage-colored smock that fit Celestina quite well, and then watched with anticipation as the church's tall door swung open to the piazza. She anchored her feet. No one was shoving her from her good spot. She'd been waiting since sunrise for Fra's sermon.

Finally, the tips of Shadrach's ears flickered like a set of white flames inside the dark doorway. Fra, in a bright white habit with a blue stripe cuffing each sleeve, ducked his head to pass beneath the arched doorframe. He was standing on Shadrach's back, and when they advanced into the piazza, Fra appeared to be moving on white water.

Celestina bounced on her toes. It was the most exciting moment of her life until the stink of mimosa water filled her nose. Once she loved the flowery smell but now it made her stomach roil, like the person wearing it. Zola and her father had pushed up all the way to where Celestina was standing. A faint purple bruise clouded Zola's eye. Celestina glared at *Signor* Lombardi.

But he was unshamable. When he should have been cowering under Celestina's slow burn he was piping up as loud as a horn. "*Fra, Fra, Fra,*" he shouted, pumping his fist. Even looking at that hand of his soured Celestina's tongue.

Celestina turned her back to the Lombardis. The angle gave her a better view of Shadrach anyway. Fra had raised his arms, exposing his palms.

The people fell silent. Like a crucified saint who'd fallen from the clouds, Fra was streaked in blood, bearing punctures in his palms and feet. A slash bloodied his robe beneath his heart.

"Fra wears the five wounds of Christ."

Naturalmente, Signor Lombardi was the first to shout.

As then, as one, the people cried, "Stigmata, bloody Stigmata."

A trumpet blared and the crier rang his bell. "*Silenzio,*" he bellowed. The people again hushed.

A flash of light caught her eye, followed by an immediate explosion, causing Celestina to jump. A fire roared under the feet of a woman tied to a stake in the center of the piazza. She was wearing a black dress.

"Help," screamed Celestina. She must save the woman and searched this way and that for a bucket of water to douse the fire.

"The witch burns in effigy."

It was again *Signor* Lombardi.

She flinched from his voice, feeling impossibly embarrassed from her overreaction. She was now able to see it was a life-sized, straw doll. Though she was relieved *Signor* Lombardi was right, it annoyed her more than anything.

Her eyes riveted back to Fra, arms straight out at his sides, like Jesus on the cross.

But she was unable to give him her whole attention. There was a ruckus that was taking place. Fra's guards were chasing a troublemaker.

She turned to throw the culprit a dirty look, but the image of Papa being stabbed ripped through her like a burning javelin. His killing had happened in the exact spot where the young *ragazzo* was now causing a problem.

She brought a shaky hand to her forehead, tunneling in on the face of the young man fighting. He was as handsome as Papa, if not more.

And like Papa, he was in an unfair fight. It was many against one, and the one had no weapon. The fighting *ragazzo* was in unfathomable danger, but he moved like a wasp, all grace and strength, swiping at attackers and ducking from danger.

It's how she'd always pictured Donatello. Broad shoulders, tapered waist, and legs that looked like they'd been cut from rock.

She tugged at her *putto*. What was wrong with her? Her heart cheered for the *ragazzo*, though he was clearly an enemy of the Reform; otherwise, Fra's guards would not be on the attack.

"*Fra, Fra, Fra.*" This time when the people cried, their squeals did not ignite her so much as give her a headache.

But this was no time to wane in her commitment to the Reform. Turning her attention to Fra, which was the reason she was there in the first place, Celestina discovered the religious was no longer standing on Shadrach's back. She was barely able to see him over the taller heads, and so, there was really no more use in trying.

Instead, she looked back at the *ragazzo* and sighed. What a waste for a tanned face such as his to pale in prison.

"*Malleus Maleficarum!*" Fra's voice jerked her from her reveries.

She set her jaw. Fra was the man of the moment.

Forget young Donatello.

But the *ragazzo* was growling like a tiger fighting his hunters.

She needed to sneeze. Covering her mouth, she looked off in time to witness the *ragazzo* leaping in the air and dodging a watchman's swinging knife.

"The *Malleus* proves witches exist." Fra's words cut through the noise of the piazza. The people hushed. She faced Fra determinedly.

Ignore the ragazzo.

"But you may wonder, exactly what is a witch?"

She tipped her ear toward Fra, a move that allowed her to check for the *ragazzo*. But she could no longer find him. The people had filled in the space where he'd been fighting. Her teeth began to chatter. His odds of beating capture were bad.

St. Catherine, protect him.

"What...is...a...witch?" The command in Fra's voice shattered her mind's picture of the *ragazzo*.

She forced herself to behold Fra and no one else.

"First," the friar proclaimed, "a witch is practically always a woman. She's a weak-minded purveyor of infanticide, cannibalism, and casting evil spells to harm her enemies, as well as the power to steal a man's privates."

Celestina began to settle down. Fra was an excellent orator, on the level of Cicero, she suspected.

With his booming voice, he further explained, "And this is why you must not drink spirits. Witches pray on the weak-minded."

Celestina clutched her heart; Simona was at risk. Her mind

wandered to the *ragazzo*. She bit nervously at her fingernail. Perhaps he'd been drinking, which was causing him to fight, putting him in the same bad spot as Simona.

"Second." She looked over the people's heads, catching sight of Fra's two fingertips. "A witch has the power to change the weather. She makes it cold when it suits her purposes or hot like hell," he said.

Celestina fanned her face. Was a witch in her midst? It was hard to know. Perhaps the heat inside her was ignited by the fighting *ragazzo*.

"Third," Fra raised a triumvirate of fingers, "a witch fornicates with the demon in exchange for magical powers. These are told to her through voices only she hears in her head. She then uses the magic in potions or curses to turn the head of a lover in her direction or away from another."

Celestina covered her ears.

She prayed Satan would never speak to her—though, she wouldn't mind hearing what the *ragazzo* sounded like.

"Fourth," the friar waved his hand, "a witch has the ability to raise a bird from the dead."

Celestina shook from limb to limb, thinking again about Simona. And as she might have suspected, *Signor* Lombardi took the opportunity to cast a deadly glare at Celestina. Her blood boiled.

After snorting her disgust, she pivoted away from *Signor* Lombardi to find Fra flapping his arms like they were wings.

"A witch has the ability to fly, whether on a broomstick or by turning into a flying animal," said Fra with a caw. His croaking sent shivers up her back. "Flying is how she quickly gets to her faraway sabbats. But make no mistake, not all witches participate in sabbats. In some cases, she remains at home on her rooftop in the dark of the night, performing her acts of heresy."

Did the handsome stranger, fighting for his life, realize any of this?

"And fifth and last..." The air stilled. "When a woman, particularly one not far past girlhood, hears voices inside her head from the heavens above, or hell below, it's one sign she's a witch. Remember, we can speak to God. But the heavens speak to us through miracles, not with voices in our ear."

Zola swung around to find Celestina. The bruise under Zola's eye grew redder as she scowled accusingly. Celestina shrunk in her slippers. Of course, Zola had remembered.

Celestina heard voices. She was always uncertain if they belonged to Mamma in heaven or St. Catherine. This was because she'd been born on St. Catherine's Feast Day and grew up hearing distressing stories on how Mamma bled to death immediately after her birth. All the stories mixed her up. At one time she even thought St. Catherine was her mamma.

Revealing all that to Zola a long time ago was one of the stupidest things she'd ever done. Zola mocked her and never let her forget it.

By now Fra had remounted Shadrach and Celestina was more than happy for a respite from Zola's judging eyes.

"There will be a one-day grace period in which a witch can turn in herself and her accomplices," said Fra. "If she comes to us first, she won't be condemned but simply given penance to reconcile with the church and God."

Celestina was heartened. The Reform was merciful.

"After that, we need your help, good Florentines. If you find a witch, catch her. If she bears a black dress, all the better. Then, bring her to us. The Reform will take care of the rest. This will please God, and that good act will absolve you and your loved ones of sins."

"Burn the witches," the people chanted.

But not *Signor* Lombardi. His dirt-pitted nose appeared like an unwelcomed pox before Celestina's face.

"I'm reporting Simona for not being at the sermon," he said.

Celestina threw back her hand to slap him, but he slipped away like a poisonous snake, serpentining through the people toward Fra.

Celestina turned for Zola, to threaten her with hell if her father reported Simona. But Zola's stare was fixed on the spot where the handsome *ragazzo* had been fighting the sword-wielding soldiers. He was now gone. The blood drained from Celestina's face. There was something special about the *ragazzo* and she felt the need to protect him from Zola—if he were still alive.

As worried as she was about the *ragazzo*, she was just as concerned for her grandmother. Celestina ran for the bakery to warn Simona not of witches, but of something just as evil.

The man next door, with a nose as dirty as a garden of poppy seeds.

){

Giacobbe tripped the soldier going for Rinaldo. With the Dominican's voice trilling in his ear, Rinaldo and Cobbe ran away and dove for cover into a mound of hay in a farm cart outside the piazza.

"What the hell's he talking about, witches?" asked Cobbe, still panting from their fight in the piazza.

"That son of a bitch has everyone fooled." Rinaldo spit out dried grass.

"There's nothing for us here, brother." They crawled out

from the hay. "Let's go home."

Rinaldo brushed dirt from his tunic. "I'm staying."

Cobbe slapped his cap against his knee. "If the friar's guards catch you—"

"My life is worthless without my muse." Rinaldo peered to where he last saw her.

"I *did* see a blonde next to her." Giacobbe gave a low whistle.

Rinaldo rubbed his hands together. "Watch out girls, here come the SanGiorgio men."

"You look for the girls. I'll keep an eye out for the guards," said Cobbe.

The Dominican had finished jabbering and the crowd had thinned. Rinaldo and his brother pulled their caps low on their brows and approached the blonde who'd been standing next to Celestina.

Rinaldo tapped her shoulder. "*Scusa, signorina*? May I ask you something?"

Her face brightened, "Aren't you the *ragazzo* who escaped the guards?"

"*Shhh.*" Giacobbe's finger tapped his lip.

"You shut up," she snapped. Then, sweet as fig *torta*, she faced Rinaldo. "*You* can ask me anything."

The blush of an injured eye made Rinaldo hurt for her, but beyond that, he found her unlikable. She was pretty, no doubt, but he was put off by the way she sneered at Cobbe.

"A girl your age with pretty terra-cotta hair was here and now she's gone. I believe she's called Celestina. Can you tell me what direction she might be headed?" asked Rinaldo.

The blonde tapped her fingers on her cheek. "I need your name first. "

His brother stuck his thumb into his chest. "I am Giacobbe

SanGiorgio."

"Not you," she snarled. Cobbe flinched. She pointed at Rinaldo. "You."

Cobbe jumped in without hesitation. "This is my younger brother Rinaldo."

"Rinaldo," she repeated.

Cobbe pushed aside Rinaldo. "Now that you know who we are, please tell me who made your eye like that and I will find him and make him sorry to be alive."

She spoke through clenched teeth. "My eye is fine, Giacobbe SanGiorgio." Her shawl slipped from her shoulders into the crook of her elbows. "I fell down the stairs, that's all."

Cobbe cried, "But you appear as graceful as a swan—"

Rinaldo could stand it no more. He grabbed Cobbe's sleeve, pulled him aside, and growled in his ear. "Quit courting her, she's not interested. We need to find my muse before she gets away altogether."

Cobbe shoved back. "Do not call my muse not interested."

Rinaldo's hands flew to his cheeks. "She is not your muse. Let's go, because I'm not leaving you here with her—"

Unexpectedly, the cold lips of the *ragazza* touched Rinaldo's ear. What she did next made the world blur. Then she walked off, winking over her shoulder.

"What did my muse say to you?" Cobbe demanded.

Rinaldo stammered, "Told me...where...Celestina lives."

"I know that's not all. Tell me or I'll break your jaw." Cobbe made a fist.

"She's called Zola Lombardi and she lives upstairs from her family's *farmacia* on the Via Scalia, next to Celestina," said Rinaldo. What Rinaldo did not tell Cobbe was that she stuck her hard tongue in his ear hole.

"That must mean Zola wants me to walk her home," said

Cobbe. He caught up to her easily.

Rinaldo threw up his hands. Only Giacobbe could fall in love with a woman, who in her own way, was as fast as him.

6

Celestina dug her finger under her coif and scratched her scalp to no relief. She ripped off the white linen cap altogether, throwing it past the hot oven, and shook her messy mop of curls and waves.

The shift she wore under her dress clung to her body. Her insides had been on fire since Fra's sermon.

She was worried about the fighting *ragazzo*, but there had not been a moment since to consider what became of him. Fra's flock was starving after his lecture, and she worked like a demon to satisfy them all, which left the bakery's shelves bare.

In fact, business had been so good that Simona hadn't the chance to announce that Celestina had earned a cut in pay for disobeying by attending Fra's lecture.

And now she had to start baking all over again, but her apron was making her swelter. She tore it off and flung it to the corner alongside her black mourning ribbon that was still there from yesterday. It seemed so long ago.

Santa Maria Novella's bell chimed once. It was a polite ring to tell the time. Normally, she loved the sound, which was her signal to yawn and head upstairs to the apartment for afternoon *riposa*.

But today she was too worked up to consider sleep. *Signor* Lombardi's words about Simona were like worms under her skin.

Before anything else, she must warn Simona of their old enemy.

Celestina peeked around the corner. Her grandmother sliced fig *torta* on the worktable in the small back room. "Simona? *Scusa*—"

Simona glanced up, wrist poised to cut. "The bread for our neighbors will need to leave the oven soon," she said.

"Simona, listen—"

"I admit that damned friar's visit had one benefit." Simona shimmied her shoulders. "The hatred he grows in his followers makes them hungry. We earned a small fortune this morning."

Celestina bit her lip, holding back a chuckle. If fire rained from the sky, Simona would plant dough seeds so they'd spark into bread rolls. "You should have been a banker instead of a baker," said Celestina.

If only women ran the world," Simona said and stared off for a moment. "But no matter, Baldasare was wrong about the boycott. Nobody stayed away. I'll rub his nose in it next time I see him, which I hope is never."

Celestina plucked at the neck of her dress. "*Ummm*, Simona, we need to talk about that boycott. *Signor* Lombardi tattled to Fra—"

Simona shrugged. "Lombardi brings depravity wherever he goes."

Sweat trickled down Celestina's temples, fanned down her cheeks, and made her hot with loathing for *Signor* Lombardi. Simona was the only woman who'd ever stood up to him.

And, it had cost her a thriving basil plant, which was mysteriously dosed in salt after Simona called the watchman to make *signore* quit hitting Zola. Also, her oven had paid the price. It was filled with sand and out of commission for three days after Simona wrestled away the belt he had used to strike Zola.

The front door squeaked open and Celestina's heart dropped. God willing it was a customer and not *Signor* Lombardi. Either way, she wasn't done warning Simona.

"Attend to our patron," said Simona. "And don't forget to remove the bread from the oven."

Celestina cringed at the memory of the burned *biscotti*. "But I'm afraid to leave you. *Signor* Lombardi—"

"Don't give our customer a chance to leave for Carino's down the street."

Out of habit, Celestina ran her hand over her waves, but they never straightened. She stepped out front and then froze at the sight of the young fighter from the piazza.

He gazed dreamily at the countertop. His sun-bronzed finger followed a streak in the marble and he seemed not to notice her, which gave her the opportunity to stare openly at him.

He was lean as a strip of veal, while at the same time strapping as a bronze statue of a Roman god. He was wily and, without question, dangerous. Though he appeared nonthreatening at the moment, bad men had a way of luring money from their prey.

She readied her lips. One short whistle would bring Simona up front yielding her Umbrian dagger. But his sun-reddened cliffs of cheekbones, and the way she yearned to keep looking at them silenced any intention to call for help.

Instead, she took in his brown wisps, the color of balsamic

from Modena, circling the edge of his cap. A sweet tartness filled her mouth. He was too good-looking, to be honest.

Call a watchman.

But before she could yell, he spoke. "High in the hills and close to heaven, do you know my small town, Settignano?"

"I haven't been there." Though his deep voice was somehow familiar, she barely recognized her own, resonant and velvety in her ear.

The side of his fist polished the countertop. Faded scars scored his knuckles. "Settignano is nothing like Florence," he said. "All we know is marble. Take your countertop. From the vein in the stone, I can see it started as a block from our quarry. Perhaps my grandfather cut it, or his father before him."

The stranger lifted his eyes, brown and flecked with gray, warm and lively; nothing in them said he was bad. Her heart hurt to think of what accident befell him, leaving the pink scar that sliced through his square chin.

Otherwise, his skin was unblemished, with light stubble shading his jaw. His nose was slightly broad but in harmony with his features. And his lips were the color of pink marble, shaped like a faraway mountain.

A drop of sweat rolled between her breasts.

Stop thinking immodest thoughts.

He slid off his cap, and she shuffled back, unsure of his intent, fearing a hidden weapon. But when his fingers simply circled the brim, she saw the weathered cord around the muscular neck that beheld a holy crucifix, carved from white stone, perhaps mined from his quarry. It rested beneath the notch on his collarbone. A boy who was fully bad would not bear such a cross.

She glimpsed at his tunic, a long-sleeved *farsetti* that

pulled across the span of his broad shoulders. The coat's tight fit brought chills to her skin. Beneath it was an indigo vest tied up front with a leather lace. His camel-colored hose held together in front by a cloth codpiece.

She refused to look, but that didn't stop her from imagining what was closeted beneath the triangular barrier. But just like when he was fighting in the piazza, she was unable to look away from him for long.

He was chiseled beautifully in every way and it was only a matter of time until a great master sought him for his subject for a canvas or sculpture. Masculine, yet boyish, it was the face she wanted her children to bear.

Stop making marriage plans.

She blinked back to the present.

You have witches to catch.

But that didn't mean she had to look unkempt. She tried tamping her hair before he noticed it was a bee's hive of messiness. But instead of wrinkling his nose, he grinned. He seemed to like her mop.

And what was that spark in his eyes? His expression hinted that he'd solved his own little secret, which appeared to embolden him.

He reached across the counter, pausing before touching the tip of her curl. "It's nice to see you again, Celestina."

She scurried back, almost into the hot hearth. "How do you know my name?"

The look of alarm on his face passed, suggesting relief that she hadn't fallen into the oven. "I saw your name on the pretty *putto* in church. You are called Celestina, yes?"

"My Papa," she said and nodded, "it was the last *putto* he painted before he died. He never really finished it."

The stranger bowed his head. "I am sorry about your

father. He was a great artist, I can tell from the heavenly way he captured you in his fresco. And he was smart, naming you for the heavens."

Ma che. She fanned herself. His words were honey. Perhaps he was a charlatan, tricking her with sweetness. She must discover his intentions before both she and Simona ended up robbed. Or worse.

She narrowed her gaze. "I saw you fighting the Reform watchmen in the piazza. I will give you bread, but no money."

"I am not a thief or guilty of anything except fighting for the honor of a good horse," he said and chuckled.

She had no time to inquire about his silly answer because he was reaching inside his satchel. She clutched her chest. So that's where he stored his weapon.

She opened her mouth to scream for Simona, but when he drew out a charcoal pencil, she let out a huge breath.

A teasing smile spread across his lips as he rolled his charcoal stick between in his fingers. "Now that you know I'm a defender of horses, can I ask you another question?"

She stroked her neck. Never had she wanted to hear a question more, but it was immodest for a young woman to act eager. In her plainest tone, she asked, "What is it you desire to know?"

He aimed the sharp tip of his charcoal stick inches from her lips. "Can I make you my muse?"

She lunged back. Was her desire for him so obvious that he felt he could proposition her on the spot? Did he not know to whom he was talking, a modest young woman set to fight witches as a soldier in Fra's holy army?

"What kind of *signorina* do you assume I am?" she said.

He eyeballed her up and down. "The sort who will become my muse."

"Celestina DiCapria is no notch on anyone's charcoal stick."

"Why are you angry, *signorina*?" He blinked hard. "What I seek is good."

Celestina slapped her hands to her head. Did he not know the level of which she was insulted? Was he stupid? Celestina thought one of his precious quarry rocks must have fallen on his head.

"This is the first time we've met, and you ask to...to...to... what did you call it, make me a *muse*?" She drew out the word.

He shook his head with vigor. "Yes, but this is not the first time we met."

And then a memory bubbled up. That spicy voice. He was the *ragazzo* from the Via Scalia. She'd been right about him. It was a damned good thing she didn't allow him to help her up. God only knew what idea that would have given him.

She stomped her heel. His brashness was beyond anything she'd encountered. "Stop asking me to be your *puttana*."

"Celestina...*may-may-may* I be familiar and call you that?" He was the one shaken now. "I fear you misunderstand. I'm not asking to make you my whore, only to draw you. Becoming a muse means you're the best."

Her eyebrows jumped. "*Gia*...go on, I'm listening."

"Master Leonardo da Vinci told me to find one, and God brought me to you. I want to draw you and make you famous, like all the great muses."

"Famous?" She ground her fist into her hip. People knew the names of the women who sold their bodies at the bordello down the street. "There are different kinds of famous, *scalpellino*, what do you mean? And it better be nice or I'll call for my grandmother to charge at you with her hot poker."

Jamming the charcoal back in his satchel, he waved

his hand. "No, no, no...I am not asking for you to disgrace yourself. Or to mate."

Celestina's hand flew to her chest. "*Caspita*. Good heavens."

He recoiled. "What a mess I'm making."

She was unable to hide her exasperation. "Then what are you asking?"

"I want to capture your image, like your papa did, only not as a baby cherub." The sincerity in his tone was palpable. "I want to draw you the way you appear right now, with the sun streaming over your hair. I swear it's the color of golden grapes flaming on vines under the burning Settignano sun."

She stroked her waves, the veil of misunderstanding now lifted. Being a muse sounded divine. "Go on," she said.

"Well, just look at your face." He framed her with his hands. "Both sides are perfect, like a butterfly's wings."

She ran her fingers across the curve of her cheek, over her jaw, to the rounded point of her chin.

"And your eyes. They are clear as the stream that comes through the quarry, where each day I take long draws of cool water."

She was unused to seeing herself from the perspective of a young artist, who really looked like a young sculptor, which was all the better. His words were overwhelming and wonderful, and, she was concerned, bordering on sinful.

"Well, my nose is not so good," she admitted humbly, to placate God. "I do have this bump." She rubbed beneath the bridge.

"Oh, but Celestina, *Celissima*, it is those small imperfections that make a woman all the more beautiful."

"Thank you for your compliments." Celestina turned her face so he could view her profile. "But you really must stop now."

The young *scalpellino* bent on one knee and placed his hand over his heart. "The only way I will cease is if you agree to accompany me to the Vines. There's a spot by the pretty stream where I can draw—"

Her heart dropped. "My grandmother would never allow it."

His gaze drifted over her shoulder. "Is that your grandmother?"

Celestina twisted to find Simona listening. "Yes. That is she."

"I see the source of your beauty," he whispered. He stepped up and bowed before Simona. "*Signora*? May I respectfully draw the image of your granddaughter this afternoon?"

Celestina cringed, waiting for Simona's wooden spoon to crack against the set of boulders that made up his behind.

When there was no breaking of baking tools, Celestina let down.

Simona winked at her. "You have earned an afternoon off, granddaughter."

Celestina's mouth dropped. What angel had Simona swallowed? It wasn't even Twelfth Night and Celestina was being given a gift. But her heart sank like fallen dough when she realized that Simona, in her probable drunken state, forgot the rules.

"But, Simona, mustn't you stay here to serve our customers?" she asked.

"*Si, certo*. Of course," Simona answered.

"But," Celestina stammered, "then there is no one...to accompany us."

Simona faced the stranger. "Are you worthy of my trust?"

His hand covered his chest, in pledge. "*Si, si, si*."

Simona wagged her finger in his face. "If you dare to even think about taking my Celestina's modesty, you know what will happen, correct?"

The stonecutter gulped, then nodded.

Simona turned to Celestina. "Do not make me regret my indulgence."

Celestina sprang up and down in her slippers. "I promise on Papa's soul to keep my modesty."

"*Allora*," said Simona. "Go now, and be home before the sun sleeps."

"*Grazie mille, signora.*" The young stranger straightened to full height, even seeming to grow taller.

The scorch of burning bread, however, snuffed Celestina's joy.

"Again?" cried Simona.

Her grandmother jabbed the peel inside the oven, pulling out smoking rounds of blackened bread. The ruined loaves thudded when she chucked them in the scrap basket. Simona then stormed to the back, using swear words Celestina had only heard flying from the mouth of the incinerator sweep.

Celestina blinked away tears, not because of the smoke, but because she'd messed up again after Simona had been so kind. Not only had they lost profit, now she'd never be allowed to go with the *scalpellino* and be his muse—fitting punishment for once again neglecting the dough.

It was only a matter of time before she made a fool of herself in front of the quarryman anyway. She was unable to look at him, for she knew he'd be laughing at her—or worse, pitying her. Her opportunity to be a muse was finished before it even started.

But when there was no laughing, only the scrape of busy feet, she dared glimpse up. He was flinging the bread from the scrap basket out the door and into the gutter. A pack of street dogs fought over it.

He returned with the empty bucket. "Burned bread smells good." He sniffed. "Like toast."

When he picked up the broom to gather up the ash her heart warmed in awe. She dared check with Simona in the back to see if it was still all right to go.

"We're already back in the hole," said her grandmother, working in a puff of flour. "Go ahead with Herculino, but just to let you know I'm knocking down your pay."

She beamed at Simona and then turned to join the *ragazzo*.

It occurred to her that he knew more about her than she did him. "What are you called?" she asked.

"Rinaldo." He swiped ash from his brow. "From the family SanGiorgio."

"Rinaldo SanGiorgio." The words danced on her tongue. "SanGiorgio," she repeated. "Saint George."

With charcoal-smudged hands, Rinaldo made horns on either side of his head. "*Ahaha, Celissima—*"

An excited shiver ran up her back.

"You will soon see I am no saint," he said and grinned.

Rinaldo rubbed his chest. The thought of being separated from his muse for even one heartbeat was like a chisel stab to his heart.

"You don't have to change dresses," he begged.

"But I want to be a *simpatico* muse." Celestina slipped by him. "And I only have to go up there," she pointed to the ceiling.

"But the only way to get there is to run all the way around

the block and up the stairs." He pretended to try and catch her as she dashed off.

He dropped his forehead to the cold counter. He desired everything about her: the hint of breast curving under her blouse, the pearly patina of her skin, and the hips that made him burn with fever.

But he'd promised her grandmother he'd be respectful, and he intended to act honorably. He glanced at the hourglass. She was taking forever.

The bakery's front door creaked open and Rinaldo's heart leaped. When he saw it was Giacobbe, his reaction went the other way.

He gave his brother the once over. "My God, why do you look like the runt in a litter of goats?"

Cobbe mumbled, "I can't talk about it."

Rinaldo searched Cobbe's downcast face. Melancholy was not his brother's natural way. "Are you...crying?" Rinaldo asked.

Cobbe slapped his hands over his face.

Scanning his brother for wounds, Rinaldo found no blood, bruises, or breaks. He whacked his brother's shoulder. "You're feeling sorry for yourself. Now speak or I'll give you something to cry about."

"Zola hates me." Cobbe said it like his mouth was stuffed with mealworms.

Rinaldo rolled his eyes. "Girls in Settignano love you. You have your pick. Forget Zola."

"My *muuuse*," Cobbe cried.

Rinaldo threw up his hands. The door creaked again. This time it was Rinaldo's gift from God. She was even more sumptuous in a red skirt than she was in the green dress.

He fought an overwhelming desire to bury his face in the

bust of her velvet blouse trimmed in white rabbit fur. The color of her tufts peeked through a black lace veil. His stomach, and other parts, hardened.

But she barely looked at him. Her horrified stare was on Cobbe. "Rinaldo, what have you done to this poor fellow?"

Before Rinaldo was able to explain, Cobbe stepped forward to sob on Celestina's shoulder. "I'm Giacobbe. Rinaldo's older and uglier brother."

God help him if he ruins her blouse with his slobber.

Celestina cradled Cobbe's wet face. "Before me, I see the very handsome replica of Rinaldo. You two could be twins."

Rinaldo could not help but smile. Not only was Celestina an angel on the outside, on the inside her heart was perfect.

Rinaldo edged his elbow between them, dislodging Cobbe.

"Congratulations, brother. I see you have found your muse. I wish you much happiness." Cobbe backed up like a scolded puppy. "And now I must sink into the Arno."

Rinaldo groaned and caught his brother's shirttail. "You're not doing that," he said. "Go ahead and tell us. What happened with the girl next door?"

Celestina's head snapped. "Zola?"

Cobbe moaned the name.

"God help us," said Rinaldo.

"I tried to make her my muse, but she has no interest in me. She is in love with only one man," Cobbe said.

Celestina scowled. "Tell me, Giacobbe, who is Zola suddenly so in love with that she has left you in this pathetic state?"

Cobbe wiped his nose. "It's best not to say."

Rinaldo tried to control his impatience. "There are no secrets here. Talk."

Cobbe nodded at Celestina. "She'll get mad."

"Giacobbe," said Celestina. "I've only known you a few moments, but already I feel brotherly love for you. And Zola was once like a sister to me. I will not get angry."

Cobbe rubbed the back of his neck. "Zola loves...Rinaldo."

Celestina's hand flapped over her heart. "When did all this happen?"

Rinaldo could tell she was hurt. "Don't listen to him," Rinaldo said. "It's all in Zola's mind. Nothing happened—"

"Well something happened because Zola said Rinaldo is her muse," said Cobbe.

Rinaldo kicked his brother in the back of the pants, "*Chiudi la bocca*. Shut your mouth. Zola doesn't know what the word means and either do you." Rinaldo pointed at the door. "Get out of here."

Rubbing his bottom, Cobbe slogged out of the bakery.

Celestina turned away from Rinaldo. "If you and Zola are together, I cannot be your muse."

He edged around to face her. "Never Zola, only you, and always you." He inhaled her sweet scent. "The girl who smells like sweet almonds."

"Are you saying I'm nutty?" A shy smile spread across her lips.

"I'm saying I want to eat you up."

Just when he thought they were all right, she again sobered. "Perhaps I should stay. I have other responsibilities. Important work to do," she said.

"But your grandmother gave us permission," he said.

Celestina stared off. "It's not the bakery..."

"Whatever vexes you, there must be a way to work it out."

Her expression turned sharp as a hawk's. It was clear she was thinking hard. He felt like heaving. What could be more important to her than being his muse? He shook away the thought. Her barely knew her and had no idea what was going on in her heart.

"I've made a decision," she said.

He held his breath.

"I'm going to attempt to do both."

His relief was thwarted by the presence of a shadow through the back doorway. "Herculino, come with me to the back room," said Simona.

The blood drained from his face as he followed Simona into the back. She changed her mind, he feared.

Simona dug her finger into his shoulder. "Listen to me, Herculino."

He gulped. "*Si, signora.*"

"Do nothing to dishonor my granddaughter."

"You have my word."

"But just as importantly, do what you must to take her mind off witches. And, for all our sakes, make her forget that goddamned inquisitor."

7

It wasn't the aroma of Sangiovese grapes sweating on vines in the mid-afternoon sun that made Rinaldo swoon like a drunken fool. It was staring at Celestina's coral lips, picturing her sipping cool wine sitting on a bench, her hair dancing in the breeze coming off the Arno River.

"I've never been past the city gate," she said, glancing over her shoulder at the city of Florence on the other side of the wall.

He blinked back to the present, face reddening. He never considered that she might be uneasy outside the city. He'd been so excited to show her *Le Vigne*, an ancient vineyard that had grown into a forest, that he hadn't realized the dense flora might be too much *alfresco* for a true Florentine.

"Small forests grow everywhere on the Tuscan hillsides. They're soft heeled and green shaded. Perfect for sketching a muse." He hoped the reassurance might settle her worries. "But if you're afraid, we can—"

"No, no, no," she said. "The Vines will be a good place for me to start becoming used to the woods. As a soldier of the Reform, I will have to venture to where the witches live—

forests and the like. So being a muse is also an opportunity to learn the whereabouts of my enemies."

Damned Reform. Whenever she mentioned it his stomach clenched. The Dominican was weighing her down like a jack-snipe on the wings of a butterfly.

"Can we forget about witches for the afternoon?" He hadn't succeeded in keeping the contempt out of his voice.

"Witches make people die and leave others orphans, Rinaldo. A Reformer never forgets," she said, her tone fat with indignation.

He wished to take her in his arms and squeeze out the burden her heart carried, from whatever it stemmed.

She plucked a purple grape and nibbled delicately. It stained her lips violet, like diluted wine. He drank in the picture of her, and then, feigning blindness from the sun, pulled his cap low in order to cloak his own worries. It remained to be seen whether his artistic skills were worthy of her beauty.

Taking her hand, he led her toward the makeshift entrance into the woods. He jerked back when she balked.

"What's wrong?" he asked, fiddling with the crucifix at his neck, hoping she was not doubting his level of skill, too.

She peered into the thicket. "It's so dark in there."

He let out a big breath. That was all? "There's pretty light, too. Don't fear."

Somewhere nearby a bull bellowed. They both startled, but the animal's deep moan gave Rinaldo an idea. Of course, he grinned. It made sense now. She'd been afraid of meeting up with some big animal.

He patted Celestina's hand. "I will protect you from bears and bulls."

She stared glassily into the woods. "There are things scarier than bears," she said.

His shoulders fell. It hurt that she didn't fully trust him. "But I can protect you from anything." He flexed the ball of his upper arm. "Pinch it."

She poked at his muscle. "You must eat bulls for supper," she said. He detected that her humor was lightening. He pretended to nibble her wrist.

"Bulls are my snack. I feast on pretty girls for strength," he said.

"Yes, I see your horns," she said with a quick glance at his head.

"And I'm a good fighter." He showed off his fists.

"I remember you in the piazza during the sermon," she said, the spark in her eyes returning, "I would expect nothing less from a boy who eats bulls."

Rinaldo raised the crucifix from his chest. "I swear on Jesus, if you become frightened, we will leave."

She yanked a sprig of parsley from a wild plant and nibbled. "There *is* plenty of light left. All right, *Torino*, my little bull. Make me your muse."

Rinaldo liked his new nickname. Torino sounded brave.

Inside the Vines, they made camp near the modest waterfall feeding the stream. The sky-blue water dropped in drapes, but Celestina was far more beautiful.

In a spot where the sunlight streamed through the crooked branches of the gnarled olive tree, Rinaldo helped her onto the cap of a giant rock curved like a toadstool.

With the *gurgle, gurgle* of water in the background, she adjusted her skirt so it settled in a wave, matching the ripple of the stream at her back.

"The way you position the fabric shows you possess an artist's touch." He studied the effect with admiration.

"When I was little Papa sometimes sketched me. He

would have let you study under him, you know, as he learned under Master Botticelli."

Botticelli? Rinaldo needed a swig of Chianti. She was farther above him that he'd imagined. "The same Botticelli who painted Birth of Venus?" he asked, to be sure.

"*Si*, Sandro," she replied.

"You call him by his Christian name?"

"He and Papa were great friends, though Papa admitted his paintings didn't measure up to Sandro's. But whose do?"

Rinaldo's tongue dried to paint pigment. Celestina was worldly. She'd been exposed to great art. She would know if he drew worse than Botticelli and her father.

"Maybe this wasn't a good idea. I should take you home," he said.

"Did I say something wrong?"

He wiped his forehead, praying Celestina didn't witness that his hand trembled. "Your words are perfect. It's me. I...I...I don't know a lot about—"

She tapped her finger to his lips. "Show me how to be a muse, and I'll teach you what I know about art. We'll learn together."

Thank you, Jesus, for Celestina.

He caught her wiping a tear from her face. He sidled next to her on the stone.

"Why do you cry?"

"I miss Papa. He would have liked you."

Rinaldo leaped off the rock, facing her. "I pray that your father blesses my drawings so I can earn a position as an artist and create frescos inside churches to make a perfect life for his daughter."

She straightened the folds of her dress. "That's what I want, too," she said with an air of reflection.

Pleased he'd planted the seed about their future, he knelt upon the mossy earth, removing the sketchbook and charcoal from his satchel. He turned to his sketchbook, "Let's start—"

"But I have one question," she said.

His heart skipped a beat. Already he'd told her everything he knew.

"Why do you bring me to the woods," she asked, "when you can just as easily paint me inside a room?"

He considered his answer. "I like to pray outside, attend Mass outside, and so I guess I like to draw outside, too. Is there something wrong with that?"

"*Aha*, so you prefer to create outdoors, with nature as your canvas," she said.

His dry mouth returned. "What are you saying, Celestina? Do you not believe that I can work inside, like a true artist?" His voice was as tight as canvas stretched and nailed to a frame.

"Of course, I know you are able, but there are many ways to be an artist, Torino."

He dropped his chin and stared at his blank page. He didn't know where to begin.

"Torino?"

He looked up. "Yes, *Celissima*?"

She raised her finger to her lips. "How should my face look, when I pose?"

He straightened. This he was able to answer. He held his thumb between his eyes to gauge dimension. "Like the face of a muse, how else?"

"Should I be a happy muse?" She grinned widely. "Or a down-hearted one?" She pouted. "Perhaps I should pose as one who is all-knowing." Her curly eyelashes fluttered.

A flush crept over his cheeks. That she had to be feeling

something while he sketched her was something he never considered. What a fool he was. His muse, with Botticelli's wisdom running through her blood, knew more about art than he ever would.

But a thought did come to him. "Be sad. That's one feeling I understand."

She attempted to dull her expression, screwing her mouth this way and that, trying to be gloomy. Her bad acting caused her to giggle.

The lilt it her voice was so alluring it forced him to bury his anger. "Your smile's perfect," he said, pointing his charcoal against the paper. "Stay just like that."

Celestina's majesty surpassed that of a goddess, so it wasn't her fault when he struggled to draw the simple line of her face.

He confused the lacy scallops of her black veil with her golden-red hair. Her face was heavy on the page, shaped nothing like a rose petal, the way he intended. And her slender neck could have been mistaken for a casing of salami.

He pressed the charcoal harder. The sharp tip tore the sheet. The pad toppled from his lap, and in angry frustration, he chucked his charcoal into a pine tree.

She craned her neck, watching the pencil fly, and then slid from the rock to retrieve his pad from the ground. After brushing off the dirt she placed it back in his lap. "What's wrong?" she asked.

Rinaldo raised his hand. He glared at it. "My fingers are stone."

"Let me see." She took the sketchbook and paged through. "The trouble," she cocked her head, "is that your drawings lack movement."

Rinaldo stared at her until his eyes crossed. His *Celissima* wasn't as smart as he'd imagined. "I cannot give life like God. Not even the Divine One, Leonardo da Vinci, can create a figure to run off the page."

He saw her bite back a smile. "You misunderstand," she said.

His back became rigid. She'd delivered her words with patience as if he were a child. "So then why doesn't the daughter of the friend of the great Botticelli tell me?" He tasted the acid in his words.

She pursed her lips, admonishment for his smart tongue. "You draw well. But you must relax so that your pencil can copy your feelings," she said.

Her soothing tone turned his blood to lava. "That's easy for you to say," he sniped.

And then she began to knead Rinaldo's drawing hand as if it were dough from her grandmother's bakery. Warm blood flowed into his quarry-hardened calluses. Her fingers climbed his arm, rubbing his stony muscles. His entire body, once heavy with expectation, lightened under Celestina's loving touch.

He pulled her delicately to her feet. The scent of almond clung to her graceful neck. The veil she wore—the same one that troubled his hand with its intricate lace—slinked off her head and past her shoulders to the ground. He watched a pair of intertwined strands of hair that stood up from the rest and danced atop her head in the light of the sun.

With his fingertip, he drew invisible circles on her back.

"Why do you use my body as your canvas?" Her voice teased.

"Just giving my drawing 'movement.'"

She tapped the tip of his nose in teasing rebuke. He snared her finger in his mouth. She giggled, tickling the underside of his tongue.

She withdrew her finger, and he caught it with a kiss. It tasted of the purple grape and curly parsley she'd nibbled earlier, sweet with a pinch of savory.

He saw her body tremble, as though his simple touch was new to her.

He drew her close. The stroke of her heart tapped his chest.

"Rinaldo." She cooed his name. Her voice was light, a beautiful pairing with the sweet song of lovebirds calling for one another in the trees.

"*Celissima.*" She was the single torch that lit all his longings: love, marriage, and the burning desire to make great art.

He nuzzled the curve of her ear, fingers twisting a tender tendril at the nape of her neck. Her back arched, and she nuzzled her nose into the notch at the base of his neck.

He fought to contain a coarse struggle that reared inside him. He promised to protect her modesty but yearned to take it. To keep her safe he let her go, leaving his entire body craving.

She nodded softly. "We must slow our desire."

He grabbed his hands to keep them from touching the top of her soft, white breasts, swelling in the confines of her bodice. No saint, Rinaldo had chiseled his way inside other girls, who never told him to slow anything.

"I want to kiss you, *Celissima.*" His voice was thick. "Does that count against keeping you modest?"

"I want it all, but we promised. Simona is very protective."

"I would never hurt you." His voice broke with huskiness.

"If you take my modesty, or if I give it, it doesn't matter. She will cut your throat." The way she said it dispelled any notion that she was exaggerating. Her fingers combed a stray lock around his ear. "One step at a time, Torino."

While his only desire was to be chained to her body, he must prove he could be a good provider before she would ever marry him. These pictures he planned to draw meant everything, and he needed to get on with it, with the beginning of his life, their life. He ground out each word. "Time...to... draw."

She whispered and her breath steamed the inside of his ear. "Attack the paper with your desire." He helped her sit back on the mushroom-shaped rock.

Then she shook out her hair. Her curls danced in the ray of sun peeking through the leaves, and the craving inside him doubled. She sat and fixed her skirt to drape over the stone while with trembling fingers he dug through his satchel for a new stick of charcoal. Energy surged through his hand and upon the paper. This time, drawing was effortless.

Circling her like a wolf, his look stalked every curve and line of her body. His charcoal dashed around the page outlining her figure as if his hand possessed a soul of its own.

Her full and sensual lips were completed in the time it took him to draw a breath. He flipped the page and drew another sketch of her tapered brow.

They never spoke, but she didn't require instruction. Slanting her head toward the stream for one drawing, she turned her shoulders the opposite way for the next. Reading his mind, she knew exactly what pose he wished her to strike at each angle.

Every phase of her head was complete, and still, he was unready to stop.

"Please, *Celissima*." He bowed his head quickly, to remain respectful. "I'm not asking to touch, just to see. Show more."

Celestina twisted her lips, seeming to consider his request with agonizing thought. She wiggled her blouse down her shoulder but only a hair's breadth. She did the same with the other. A sliver of cleavage appeared.

"That's what I want," he said.

"I feel naughty." She bit her lip. He captured the hint of guilt on her face in a quick sketch. "Go fast," she said.

Putting charcoal point against the paper, he said, "Count to thirty and then I'll be done." She gave a quick nod.

His hand was lively. Her shoulders and chest breathed on the page. Never in his life was he so satisfied after being denied a kiss. He was ready to draw again, from another angle, and he returned to the source of his greatest artistic success, Celestina's bare shoulders.

"*Ventinove...*" Celestina drew the word out. "And thirty." She covered herself, and said, "Time's up."

He looked at his hand in marvel. Celestina and her heaven-blessed body had magically transformed it into an artist's hand. "I have enough sketches to satisfy any Master and they are my best, by far." He blew charcoal dust from the page. "But I plead to draw one extra, with a hint more skin, for my eyes only."

But her attention was trained on the treetops. "Do you hear that?"

He set his sketchbook on the ground, turning his ear. "Sounds like a village crone. Or maybe a crazed bat."

"We must catch it. *Now.*" She flew off the rock, grabbing hold of his hand. "*Vai*, Rinaldo. Run."

He fumbled to retrieve her black veil and his drawings. What was she talking about, catching a bat? But Celestina yanked like she was the horse and he the chariot.

He could have easily bridled her, but he'd pledged to Jesus

he'd guard her, and so he didn't pull back for his drawings and her veil. He would recover them after she settled down. But she led him on a mad dash. To gain some control, Rinaldo overtook her stride, being the first to duck hanging limbs and vault treacherous roots.

"A bat is impossible to find in the day," said Rinaldo.

"It's getting to be dusk, which is a good time. We must catch it and still not break our promise to Simona...to return... by sundown." She was panting.

Dark came and still, they'd seen no bat. With Simona's promise on his mind, he led her outside the woods. She looked up as they ran back through the city gate.

He waited until they crossed the Via Strozzi, safely into the heart of Florence, before they slowed. The moon hung boldly in the sky.

"Are you all right, *Celissima*? Why did you want to catch a bat? *Che schifo*. They're disgusting."

Her chest heaved. "The sound of that particular bird was strange...which led me to believe that was no ordinary bat."

"A bat can be unordinary?" he asked.

"Promise you'll believe me." She grabbed hold of his hand. Her skin was ice.

He slapped his free hand across his chest. "I trust every word you say, even if I don't understand."

"*Allora*." She raised her brow. "Would you still believe everything I say if I told you that just this morning that *pipistrell*o was a person?"

He jerked back his head. "The bat was human?"

"A witch," she said with conviction.

They passed a burned-out artist's studio on the Via Scalia. "You're starting to sound like that lying Dominican," he said, in a not-kind tone.

"Witches are real, Rinaldo."

He tried to reason with her. "But the Vines is small and dense. We would have seen them walking around."

"You have to look up," she said and bent backward, face to the starry sky. "They turn into *pipistrelli* and gather in remote places. The Vines is a perfect place for their sabbats."

Her grandmother had warned him about her and witches, but her belief in them was worse than he imagined. "We abandoned my sketches to rot...on the ground...because of some witches?" His tongue was heavy with irritation.

She stomped her foot. "You're either with the Reform or against it. If you're against it, I can no longer be your muse."

He was unable to hide his bewilderment. "But that damned religious has you so worked up—"

"Decide, Rinaldo Saint George."

)(

Rinaldo's mouth hung open, round as the moon behind him. His astonishment was honest and genuine. She could see he was struggling for an answer. Her ultimatum, Reform or no Reform, had caught him off guard.

But her commitment was clear. She would not walk away from the holy army. At the same time, she prayed her vow wouldn't cause him to walk away from her.

Please, Torino, don't make me choose.

His head rocked back and forth as though his mind was in turmoil.

If you say no, we cannot remain together.

He exhaled and crossed his arms.

I will never meet anyone I love more and will end up a nun.

He cleared his throat.

She stiffened her shoulders.

"Your battle..." he said.

She held her breath.

"...Is my battle, *Celissima*. I stand before you with my heart."

She celebrated with a cheer and fell into his chest, a tile of rock-hard granite.

"I'm overjoyed," she said, "but also now worried about your drawings that we left in the dirt. Also, the black veil I left there was Mamma's. It's the only thing I have of hers. We must return for them at sun break."

He scratched his neck. "By then buzzards will have ripped my drawings to shreds. Pictures of your hair will be woven into their nests," he said.

"Not if we return before the birds rise," she said.

"But your grandmother?"

"I'll start the dough before she wakes. If I get up extra early, we'll be back before she notices I'm gone."

Rinaldo gave her a doubtful look. "I'll go alone."

"Absolutely not," said Celestina. "When she sees the dough, she'll know I returned safely. Besides, I cannot let you go alone. An artist and his muse must work as one..."

Celestina clamped shut her lips. A rustling in the shadows between the bakery and Zola's *farmacia* caused Rinaldo to look at her quizzically. She motioned for him to remain silent while leading him inside the bakery.

She closed the door behind them and turned up the oil lamp, but they barely needed it. The moonbeam shining through the window was glorious. Rinaldo swept her in his arms, and the noise outside, most likely Zola spying on them, soon was a distant memory.

The touch of Rinaldo's soft lips behind her ear took away

her breath.

"Why do you hate witches so?" he whispered.

She stiffened. He was right to ask. An explanation was called for after the way she'd acted at the Vines.

"A witch had a hand in killing my father. It's causing his soul to languish in purgatory, where he will stay until I catch her and four other heretics in return," she explained.

He appeared startled. "Who has told you of such rules?"

"Monsignor."

He looked at her incredulously. "God's words tell us of heaven and hell, *Celissima*. But did Jesus worry about witches in the shape of bats? *Mai*. Never. I have not heard that."

Her back arched. What did he know of it?

"It must be wonderful to have a big family to protect you from the troubles in the world," she said. "My grandmother won't even tell me who my grandfather is, and she drinks. Her soul is in danger, Rinaldo. I must catch witches for the sake of what's left of my family."

He was silent. Every heartbeat was an eternity in this time of truth. He was either with her or against her. There was no in between when it came to Papa and Simona and witches.

"Forgive me, Celestina. I cannot imagine what you have endured," he said.

She sagged against him, her heart assured. "You understand?"

He stroked her wet cheek. "For the sake of you and your family, I will fight in the battle against the witches while you stay here and keep your grandmother safe."

Her heart clouded with uneasiness. "Together we will fight. *Si*?"

He straightened his shoulders. "I will proudly fight for both of us."

She reeled from him. Did he not speak Italian? "I am not staying home and baking bread for the real soldiers in this war. I am fighting," she said.

He had the gall to throw down his hand. "I don't like you being near the Dominican."

"You're not my papa, and it's not your decision," she said.

"He's a liar, *Celissima*." Rinaldo flashed his wrists. "Five wounds of Christ, my ass. The stigmata were fake. He injured his horse to reap its blood for his brutal act."

The words "injure his horse" were like three stabs in her ears. On the one hand, it was true that Fra was part madman. On the other hand, Florentines wouldn't follow a pleasant, round friar into a holy war. Only a true *guerriero* was able to take on the task of ridding the city of witches.

"It's true he's hard as stale bread, but he's a warrior who the people believe in," she said.

Rinaldo swung his arm in the direction of the church. "The same people who are burning their city to pieces? What will they set aflame next? Beautiful Santa Maria Novella, where your image graces the wall?"

She would do anything to save Papa's work, and she pounded the counter to make it clear to Rinaldo. "I will defy anyone who seeks for Santa Maria Novella to burn, but I must fight the demons that threaten what's left of my family and city."

Rinaldo stepped forward to embrace her. She slapped away his hands.

"I hate that *stronzo* Dominican," said Rinaldo.

"But we need Fra for his knowledge of witches."

"I can't rest knowing you are anywhere near him."

"Can't you see, on the big canvas, that doesn't matter?"

"So, you don't care what I think?"

She was able to tell Rinaldo was wounded.

"It doesn't matter," she said, trying to sketch it in a way more familiar to him, "because you will be there with me. Can't you see us fighting side-by-side, slaying demons?"

He gave her the once over. "Sorry, but I cannot."

She clasped her heart. Now it was she who was wounded.

"But I can see you fighting behind me. That's the only way I'll agree. I must always take the first strike," he said.

"That I can do," she said. It felt like her insides were gleaming. "So, I can keep my eye on *you*."

"That's funny," he said flatly, before catching her by the waist and lifting her over his head.

"In Settignano, we never make big plans. This is the most excitement I've had in my life," he said.

Celestina flapped her arms like she was flying. "You must leave now, Rinaldo. Sleep well so we can depart at first light."

He set her down as if she were fragile as blown glass.

"Giacobbe and I have taken a room across from Ghiberti's doors." He bore a disoriented look. "But Florence is all a maze to me in the night."

She pulled him outside, back onto the street. Sweeping her arm across the city, she explained, "Florence is laid out in squares, similar to a chess board."

He shrugged. "Chess?"

"It's is a hard game, but here's what I remember. Our little bakery is a pawn." She grabbed his hand and pointed their fists due north at Santa Maria Novella.

"The church stands as a great queen for us to protect. When you get to the church piazza," she positioned their hands westward, "the Baptistery stands in this direction. Walk in a straight line and you will be able to knock on Ghiberti's bronze doors."

Rinaldo's voice was tender. "I like the way you say things."

"I like your muscles."

"But tell me something?" he asked. "How does a bakery girl know so much about chess?" He kissed her entwined hand.

"My favorite customer is a great ocean explorer." She gently stroked his scarred knuckles. "He finds out where other people in the world live and gives them the word of Christ. Sometimes he comes back to Florence, and when he does, he brings his black and white board to the bakery. He taught me the game."

"Why are you always playing these chess games with him?" Rinaldo's back stiffened.

"He's a friend of our family, somehow," she said. "Well, a friend of mine, but not of Simona's, even though he swears she makes the best pear *torta* in all of *Italia*. He tasted it long ago when he brought over a chessboard as a boy and played with Papa. But for some reason, she's just always hated Cri's guts. That's his name, the explorer."

Rinaldo poked her teasingly in the ribs. "But your grandmother loves my guts, right."

She pulled a wisp of brown hair that snuck out from under his cap. "Simona doesn't love anybody, except me. But I think she secretly likes you too."

"I've nothing to worry about with this 'great' ocean explorer?" He stroked her shoulder.

She crossed her heart. "He's old. I've never had an uncle that I know of, so he would be like that."

She yearned to keep staring at Rinaldo's face in the full moonlight. But she also wanted him home safely. "Meet me here at daybreak," she said.

He offered her his elbow. "First I walk you to your

apartment."

She crossed her wrists behind her back. "Absolutely not. You'll get all mixed up and never find your way home."

His brow furrowed. "But what if—"

"I insist you go," she said. "I know this block like you know the Vines. I will be fine."

He leaned forward as though he was going to kiss her, and then wrenched back. She understood his struggle.

"See you first thing in the morning, my *Celissima*, my star."

"Follow the full moon," said Celestina, "and don't step out of the light. I don't want the witches to snatch you in the dark."

"Just let those witches try and get me." His broad shoulders blended into the dark. "They'll be sorry they ever met *Ser* Torino."

St. Catherine, turn the faces of witches from Sir Rinaldo.

Looking around at her own predicament, she tagged on an extra request.

And don't forget me. I have to make it home alive, too.

)(

A screech pierced the dark. Celestina startled. Was it an owl, or a witch beckoning Satan?

She stole a quick glance at her apartment above the bakery and then anticipated her walk home down the Via Scalia. Reform Boys, their shadows long in the moonlight, dashed furtively back and forth across the street.

She hadn't been outside at nighttime since Papa's killing, and with the presence of the Reform Boys, the Via Scalia had turned threatening in the dark.

It was stupid to have refused Rinaldo's offer to walk her home. But his sculpted face in the moonlight had made it difficult for her to think straight. She knocked the side of her head to make the fear spill out of her ear.

A holy warrior is not afraid of the dark.

She threw back her shoulders and rushed past Zola's *farmacia*. Celestina had assumed the earlier rustling outside the bakery was Zola spying on her and Rinaldo.

She braced for Zola to jump from the shadows, and worse, to have with her that Duomo-headed Reform Boy.

Celestina buried her head in her shoulders and pressed on. Zola hadn't attacked, which Celestina considered a small miracle.

As she approached the *lupanare*, Celestina pulled her blouse close into her chest. Some nights the bordello sat empty, but tonight there was light inside the house that Florentines called "the wolf's den," with its fitting bull-hide flap that served as a door.

It was said that simply walking near the place brought the "burning" disease to a woman's *patata*. Striding long and quickly, Celestina crossed the street to stay clear of the floating disease.

Clouds sailed fast across the moon now, and the good light from the sky faded. The Via Scalia turned black and foreign, and suddenly she felt like an uninvited guest on her own street.

"Fraulein?"

She stopped so hard she nearly fell out of her slippers. "Fra?"

"What is a girl like you doing out at night?" he called out from across the street.

She could ask him the same thing about being in front of the *lupanare*. "Going home," she said, hearing the strain in her voice.

A street torch illuminated half his white habit. His other half was cast in silhouette. If she were an artist, she'd draw him as he appeared to her at that moment in that exact light, as a sort of mysterious creature of the night.

"Come across, Fraulein." His voice was broody.

Her mind raced. Had he discovered she bared her shoulders for Rinaldo and was now disappointed in her? Would he allow her into the Reform after such a violation of modesty?

In the dark she picked her way across the cobblestones, careful not to fall prostrate before him again, stopping a little distance away from him so he couldn't hear her insides tremble.

She sweated in her dress. It was torture waiting for him to speak. Unable to bear the silence any longer, she blurted out, "What a surprise to see you—in front of the *lupanare*." She slapped her hand over her mouth. She needed to think before she spoke to him.

"Is that so?" he asked.

"I meant no disrespect," she said.

"Of course not."

"I'm sorry for any confusion."

"I'm not confused."

"Of course, you're not confused, you know everything," she said.

A rush of air slapped her face as he whipped off his *cappa*. "Not...everything," he replied.

She scrubbed her face with her hands. Why had she led him to say something bad about himself when all she wanted was to get on his good side? She must mention his virtues to convince him that she believed in him and his cause.

"But for one so young to be in such a grand position, you

must be very smart," she said.

"I've had a head start. The Dominicans raised me in the abbey since age seven." For the first time, he sounded slightly like a normal person.

"Where were your papa and mamma?" she asked.

"That's none of your business."

She was thankful for the dark so he was unable to witness her face redden. "Of course not."

"Tell me, Fraulein, what are you called?"

She said her name.

"Celestina." He repeated thoughtfully, almost like a caress, then said, "Now, Fraulein..."

Her shoulders dropped. She hoped he might stop calling her that harsh word, now that he knew her name.

"Tell me a story," he said.

His twisted way of talking was making her squirm, and now he wanted a story? There were a *mille* of different kinds of stories. Perhaps he wanted something religious.

"Do you mean...one of the parables of Jesus?" she asked.

"*Nein*," he chuckled, shaking his head back and forth slowly. "Tell me about witches."

She smiled. Denying her a position in his holy army would be impossible after what she was about to tell him. "Witches fly in the Vines."

"How would you know such a thing?"

The question sounded like a trick. "I...heard a bat there that sounded different, almost human in its cry."

"So, you were there?"

Her heart beat faster. "Yes."

"With who?"

The image of Rinaldo fighting Reform guards in the piazza ripped through her mind like a runaway bonfire. She had to be careful. Fra's questions could lead the Reform to Rinaldo.

"I was there with a friend." She tried to keep her voice even.

"Male or female?"

As if his thumb pressed the apple in her neck, she choked out. "*Ragazzo*. A man."

He snapped, "With an escort?"

"My grandmother works." She stroked her neck, but it did nothing to take away the ache in her throat.

"I see. And why were you and this man at the Vines?"

If she happened upon a horse and carriage clomping down the street, she swore she'd throw herself under the wheels. Anything to get away from his incessant questioning.

"He wanted to draw my picture," she said.

"This artist, what is his name?"

She swallowed hard. Betraying Rinaldo was unthinkable. "I call him Torino."

Fra sighed. "His real name."

"Unsure, Fra," she lied.

Telling a falsehood to a religious was a dirty sin, of which she'd most certainly confess, but not to Fra. Confessing to such a man was unimaginable.

"Is Torino a sorcerer?" he asked.

She exhaled in relief. If that was all he was fishing for, she'd been worried for nothing. "*Mio Dio, no*. His dream is to paint frescos."

"Does he paint Satan or angels?"

"He loves the *putto* in Santa Maria Novella." It was a good answer, and better because it was true.

He stepped closer. "By chance, was he inside Santa Maria Novella today, before my sermon?"

A pain stabbed the back of her throat. Replying either yes

or no was bad for Torino. She needed an answer as smart as King Solomon's.

"He did not bring it up in our discussions," she said and held her breath, hoping it appeased his questioning tongue.

Fra nodded at the ground, "I see," he said like he had the answer to all of his own questions anyway. "Your grandmother was absent, however, according to *Signor* Lombardi—"

Celestina cut him off. "*Signor* Lombardi is a *miserabili pezza di merda.*"

Fra stepped back. "Your temper gets in your way, I see."

"You have no idea how horrible it is to live next door to him."

Fra held up his hands to ease her fury. "He is a miserable piece of shit, I agree with you, but a useful one."

Under normal circumstances, she'd clasp her hands over her ears so as not to hear a religious swear, but talk of *Signor* Lombardi coarsened her instincts. Exhausted from the day and this infuriating conversation, she retreated a step, yearning to get home so she could think about Torino in peace.

"Oh, Fraulein..."

"Yes, Fra?" Did he never quiet?

"I already knew about witches and the Vines, so you are no further ahead as you've brought me no news. But you will have the chance to prove whether you will make a worthy warrior of the Reform tomorrow at midnight. There's been word of a sabbat."

She clapped silently. Before her was the opportunity to capture five witches in one fell swoop. By the following morning, Papa would be singing with the angels.

"*Grazie*, thank you, Fra. A *domani*, Fra. See you tomorrow."

She dashed off. Only when half the block was at her back

did she risked glancing behind her shoulder. Someone had already joined Fra in front of the *lupanare*. Bald-as-a-worm Magnaccio, *papi* of the bordello.

Austrian friar and whoremaster, together—they were the strangest pair she'd ever seen. She wondered what they were up to. With Magnaccio, it had to be no good.

Gypsy men huddled under torchlight casting lots in the alley. Hand at her throat, Celestina rushed past. Their stares bore into her back and she sped her step. At the end of the narrow passageway, the low-hanging moon greeted her. She was able to see well as she headed home.

Thud.

The sound was high up and made her heart lurch. Pulse quickening, she scowled this way and that. Bats? She thought about a net they had at the apartment. They used it as a sieve to lift dead vermin hiding in sacks of grain. It was perfect for her to practice with before the sabbat. She doubled her pace to fetch it, passing Zola's apartment. Then she raced up her own stairs.

She reached for the door handle, but quickly withdrew her hand, worrying at the prospect of a witch in the form of a bat had followed her home. Such a monster could fly through the open door and steal Simona.

Thud.

There it was again. But this time she was able to pinpoint the sound to the Lombardi's side of the flat roof, a roof their apartments shared.

She snuck up the second flight of stairs leading to the roof and gasped. So many small fires were lit up there.

Celestina started for them to stomp them out before they

flared and put the Lombardi's in danger. But as she closed in, she saw the fires were set in concentric circles around the roof. It looked like a setup.

She stopped in her tracks. Zola was in the center of the fires and on all fours, kicking like a possessed horse. Also, Zola was naked.

Celestina buried her face in her hands. Zola was acting like a demon. It was hard to bear, but Celestina's curiosity soon got the better of her. She allowed her fingers to slide down her cheeks.

Zola had fetched her dress from the floor of the roof and was proceeding to seesaw the innocent garment back and forth between her legs.

Searching blindly for a step on which to sit, Celestina needed a break to keep her head from floating off and drifting to the moon. When she caught her breath, she began to count the candles on the roof. Thirty-three.

It was the age of Jesus Christ when he died upon the cross. Celestina turned away. Thirty-three was never chance. Whatever Zola was doing, it was with the intention of spiting Jesus.

Zola was clearly out of her mind and needed help from above.

St. Catherine, save Zola from her rebellion.

The sound of a horse whinny drew Celestina's attention back to the rooftop circus. Zola had swiped up a horseshoe and held it over a flame.

"Dear Horseshoe, I do not strike you to make you fit an ass, or hammer you to the foot of a mule. Oh, no, lovely horseshoe. Instead, I think of a hammer to pound the heart of Celestina."

Celestina jerked back. How dare her name be invoked in

sacrilege.

Zola continued. *"As I feel the heel of my father's hand against my cheek, the Great Satan will make Celestina feel the pain of my hammer. Great Satan, I implore you to hurt Celestina for running away with Rinaldo today, for using her magic upon him when he loves only me."*

And then Zola flung the horseshoe off the roof. Somewhere a window shattered.

She kept chanting, *"And in that way, may my horseshoe unhinge the foot of Rinaldo if he doesn't turn away from Celestina and toward me."*

Poor Rinaldo. If Zola loved him, why did she wish him injury?

And then Zola raised a fist and spoke to it. *"One bean represents me. One is for my beloved Rinaldo. And the third is for my greatest enemy, Celestina."*

Celestina choked the railing while Zola jiggled the beans in her fist.

"The girl whose bean lays closest to Rinaldo's is meant to be his lover. Be with me, my stars."

Zola cast the beans. After examining one, she crawled to another, and after staring at that one for several heartbeats she thrashed as if she were fighting her way out of invisible puppet strings. *"Nooo,"* she screeched, pounding her fist against the roof.

"Bravo, little bean," Celestina whispered, eyes narrowed in contempt for her neighbor.

Finally, Zola lurched upright. *"I stand as close as I can to the heavens and pray to Auriga, the chariot in the stars. Send a love arrow through the heart of Rinaldo and make him mine. And then, throw a death arrow through the heart of Celestina."*

Celestina slapped her hand against the roof. She'd heard enough. "*Basta*," Celestina yelled. "*Sta zitto*, Zola. Shut up."

Zola's back arched. "Cele-*s-s-s*-tina?"

"Quit hissing," Celestina upped her chin. "You're neither witch nor snake. You're a fake."

"*Ahahaha*. Look at you, acting like you're the one who Rinaldo loves," said Zola.

"Go find your own artist." Celestina stomped her foot.

"I have," Zola taunted.

"You have in your pitiful nightmares," said Celestina. "And you better pray I don't tell Fra that you're playing witch."

Zola wagged her finger three times. "Remember what happened the other times, when your stupid grandmother ran and lied to the guards that my Papa hit me."

Celestina glared defensively. "The basil dried up from salt, the oven turned useless from sand, and Valentina, Simona's pretty canary, exploded from poison, a type known to be made by your father at your *farmacia*."

"And then your witch grandmother put a spell on it and it came hopping back to life," Zola said.

"It was a trick," Celestina shouted. "Your father was too stupid to know that."

Zola's fingers curved into claws. "Good story, Celestina. But like my Papa, I'm not playing games. You'll understand that when my unspoken hex comes true—it's against someone you love."

Celestina glowered. "Leave Simona alone, faker."

"I'm not talking about your stupid grandmother," said Zola.

Celestina's mind raced. "Rinaldo?"

"Giacobbe," said Zola.

Celestina flinched. Had Zola no heart left? "But Rinaldo's

brother is the only one who likes you," she said.

"His heart will break like a sick bat," said Zola.

"You have no power," Celestina cried.

"You want to save Giacobbe's life?"

"Of course."

"Then denounce your love for Rinaldo."

Celestina crossed her fingers behind her back. Two could play at this game. "Fine, it's over between Rinaldo and me."

"And with that, whenever Rinaldo thinks about you, he will face great pain," said Zola.

"You've gone mad," said Celestina. She stormed down the few steps toward her apartment. As she was about to open the door a flying object tangled itself in her hair.

Zola laughed maniacally while Celestina slapped like crazy at her head. It ended with a plop and a bat lying at her feet.

Celestina kicked the dead thing away. She then threw open the door and slammed it shut. Breathing raggedly, she barricaded the door with her back, considering the possibility that Zola wasn't a fake witch after all.

Celestina lowered the flame burning in the oil lamp to a flicker. Flopping in the cane chair, she covered her mouth to mute her sobs so Simona was unable to hear them as she slept in the other room.

Gelosa, gelosa, gelosa. Gnawing jealously had made Zola turn her back on God, which left her soul unguarded, giving the devil the perfect opportunity to take over.

Celestina swiped her tears as her stomach moaned, aroused by the aroma of pork hocks in chicken broth and parsley wafting about. Celestina ladled a bowlful of Simona's *minestrone.* In her home, beans were for eating, not silly love games.

She sipped a spoonful of soup, but her stomach revolted. She was still too worked up over Zola to eat. Celestina set down her spoon and checked the empty space against the wall, the place where her *forziere* should have stood all these years.

Mamma hadn't lived even one day after Celestina had been born and had no time to put together a dowry chest. Without a dowry, would Rinaldo want her?

Her body tingled, remembering the fevered way he gazed upon her. She couldn't wait to see him in the morning. Still, she was tired to the bone and in need of rest. She tiptoed into the narrow bedroom she shared with her grandmother.

As Simona breathed lightly in her sleep, Celestina hung her dress on a wall peg. She changed into her soft nightdress, spun from silkworms. How fortunate she was to have a grandmother who spoiled her. Zola never wore anything nice.

Celestina slipped into bed next to Simona. The blanket they shared was frigid against her skin. Images of the day ripped through her mind like slivers of glass: Fra's stigmata; Zola's body writhing in the moonlight; and the bump that swelled between Rinaldo's thighs.

Unable to endure the heat swelling between her own legs, she flung off the goose-down blanket. She flipped onto her stomach and rocked, softly at first.

Stop panting or Simona will wake.

Balling her fist, she rubbed her *patata* and panted into the mattress.

I am sinning.

Was Rinaldo suffering the same way in his bed, across from Ghiberti's doors?

The harder she rubbed, the more she filled with the

desire to smell the heady musk that clung to Rinaldo's chest. Purposely, she stiffened. Her lower part was swollen and she feared it might burst. She stayed still, which made the pressure build. Every pant caught in her throat.

Simona is going to awaken.

She rolled from the bed to the floor, pounding her *patata*, but that only caused more ripening.

She pulled at the flaps on either side of her woman parts until her yearning peaked and she gasped. Finally, she was able to let down. But the wanting for Rinaldo's hard body rubbing against her own had only been stalled, not satisfied.

Climbing back into bed with Simona, she honed in on her grandmother's light snoring and settled down.

In Celestina's dream, Rinaldo smiled, nicely at first. And then he laughed wickedly at her while she boiled like *minestrone* in a black cauldron in the forest. Jerking alert, she leaped from the blanket in a wild sweat.

The floor planks were cold against her knees. A sliver of wood dug into her skin, but she didn't move. The pain helped her focus.

Keep Rinaldo good and both of us safe.

She kept praying that way until it was time to get up.

8

Across from Ghiberti's doors, Rinaldo's room was only a fraction wider than a coffin. He and Giacobbe shared a ropy mattress, lying in opposite directions.

Awakening with his brother's dusty feet in his nose sent Rinaldo out of bed fast, rubbing the strain of sleep from his back. At one *scudo* for the week, the room cost more than he'd spent in Settignano in a half a year. But it was worth it. Smelling like a wild boar from sleeping outside was no way to court his muse.

He left Cobbe and started out for Celestina's, down the Via della Avelli. The cool air blowing in his face awakened him. The moon still hung low, but the sun was on the rise. Rinaldo's stride was long. Pigeons, pecking scraps of breakfast between the cobblestones, scattered from his path.

Slipping onto the Via Scalia, he scratched his head. One building appeared nothing like the refined brick, stone, and wood-slat buildings that gave the Via Scalia its rich feel. He stopped to study its strange façade. It had the look of a stucco cave. Out of curiosity, he flipped open the bull-hide flap styled as a door.

Once inside he edged along the wall, pinching his nose at the stench of salty musk, the aftermath of people mating, and the extra scent of lavender trying to perfume the stink from the air. The itch that stirred under his tights left him longing to bury his nose in Celestina's almond-scented shoulder.

He gazed about the large room, fixed into separate sections not by plaster, but by heavy Oriental carpets hanging from the ceiling. In one corner, two flabby rumps humped. It left him gasping into his fist.

But that was nothing compared to the naked man in the other corner, face toward the ceiling, pressing a wild-haired head into his crotch.

He burned with embarrassment, being present in this Florentine version of a Roman orgy. As he started to leave, a gnarled hand clawed his shoulder.

Rinaldo spun about. Kohl-smudged eyes stared at him. The woman bore a long face and sunken cheeks cracked in the design of spider webs.

Sweat rained down Rinaldo's forehead. Was this creature one of Celestina's dreaded witches? The crone bid him into the empty stall. He followed as though in a trance.

"Why you're a healthy one," she said in some sort of liquidy accent. "Welcome to *lupanare*. I'm Daciana from Transylvania."

Tran-syl-where-ia? He swallowed. "*I...I...I* shouldn't be here—"

"*Why...why...why* not?" She gave a wet chuckle.

"Because I'm...going to Celestina's."

From behind Daciana appeared a man in a brown cassock, his bones jutting like arrows and daggers beneath the cloth. His face looked like a *rospo*.

Run, SanGiorgio.

But the man who looked like a toad blocked Rinaldo's getaway. "I'm Whoremaster here. I know Celestina."

Rinaldo lowered his brow. Now it was impossible for him to leave. To allow the whoremaster to say aloud the beautiful name of his muse, to insult her in this grave way, was a breach of all that Rinaldo considered decent. "What do you know about her?" Rinaldo narrowed his eyes.

"That she's prettier than Botticelli's Venus," said the whoremaster.

Rinaldo's face burned. He'd been stupid to think he was the only man who saw the resemblance; still, this toad wasn't fit to look at his muse.

"What's that to you?" Rinaldo snapped.

Whoremaster rubbed his veiny hands. "Pay Daciana thirty *baiocchi*, and talk of Venus DiCapria goes away."

"Why should I pay?" Rinaldo looked between them.

"Confess, confess, confess." Whoremaster taunted. "You know you were looking at Daciana."

"I seek nothing from her," said Rinaldo.

The whoremaster shoved Daciana at Rinaldo, who caught her safely before she fell face first into the stone floor.

"Inside *lupanare* it costs to look, but more if you touch," said Whoremaster. "Fifty *baiocchi*, now."

Rinaldo threw his hands in the air. "I didn't look at her, and I didn't touch her until you pushed her at me."

Daciana rubbed her fingertips before his face. "Money, money, money."

Rinaldo slapped at her greedy hand. "I'm not giving you *merda*."

She wagged her finger. "Anything with shit is ninety *baiocchi*."

Rinaldo's mouth filled with spit. "*Bleah! Che schifo.*

You're all disgusting."

For no reason, at least none that Rinaldo saw, the whoremaster swatted Daciana's behind, good and hard. She covered her *culo* and yelped like a hurt puppy.

Rinaldo's hand balled into a fist. Someone had to teach this cassock-wearing, bed-pissing whoremaster a lesson. "No one hits a woman, not even a greedy whore with a horse's face," said Rinaldo, reaching back to strike the toad.

The whoremaster flicked his wrist. There was a flash of metal, and then a slice across Rinaldo's chest, leaving a thin wound. Blood seeped through his shirt.

"You don't want to pay my lady, so I take it from your hide," said the whoremaster, slipping his knife back into a fold of his cassock.

Rinaldo backed away, protecting his wound with his trembling hand. With his other hand, he fiddled for the opening of the bull-hide door and then stumbled into the middle of the Via Scalia. The crest of the morning sun over the mountain was bright. The change of light bit at his eyes.

But that was nothing compared to the sting of the whoremaster's knife. All at once he yearned for the high cliffs and narrow ledges of the quarry. They were safe compared to the flat streets of Florence.

If Rinaldo wanted to be with Celestina, in the end, it could cost him much more than the *scudo* for his sparse room across from Ghiberti's doors. He glanced longingly at the mountain. Was that the echo of his name being called?

He glanced down the street at the bakery. Deafening silence.

He turned again for the hills. Was that small spark of light, far up in the peak, the candle that Mamma always kept lit?

He looked back at the bakery. Cold darkness.

Jesus, give me a sign in which direction to turn. I promise to follow.

He pivoted for the bakery. A hot pain shot through his ankle. He was unable to take a step without enduring blistering agony. "*Mannaggia*," he cried. "Dammit."

Rinaldo growled in agony. Jesus had delivered the sign, and it rested at Rinaldo's feet.

Celestina kneaded the last of the dough, double the amount she usually made, the extra to ease her guilt for leaving Simona with the bulk of the morning baking.

She glanced out the window for Rinaldo, wishing she was able to welcome him with light from the lamp, but last evening she'd mistakenly left it burning and there was no oil left. A smile crossed her lips. The empty lamp was Rinaldo's fault for having a face that glowed handsome in the moonlight that had streamed through the window.

The sky was brightening by the heartbeat. Her pulse quickened. What if witches nabbed him or Zola's curse killed him? She dashed from the bakery, ready to raid the city in search of him, and then padded to a stop. She was overcome with giddiness.

Rinaldo was at the end of the block. But he was going the wrong way. She whistled. *His inside compass really did get mixed up in the city*, she thought. "*Ehi*, Torino," she called cheerily. "The bakery is over here."

He spun and stumbled.

She clutched her chest. Zola's curse. She ran for Rinaldo as if flames nipped at her heels. "You've been hobbled by an evil horseshoe," she cried.

He spread his arms. "I've become a clumsy ox overnight,"

he said.

Her hand flew to her mouth at the slash of blood seeping onto his white tunic. "Two of Zola's curses have come true," she whimpered. "The horseshoe, and Auriga's arrow, which has pierced your chest."

"I wasn't with Zola." He looked at her like she was talking gibberish.

"You do not need to be in the presence of the curser to suffer the curse," she said, and then plied her fist at the stars. "Why, Auriga, did you spare me and not Rinaldo?"

"The man who looks like a reptile is called Auriga?"

Celestina cocked an eyebrow. Perhaps in his small town, there was scarce knowledge on the stars. "Auriga is not a real man, Rinaldo."

"The hell he's not," said Rinaldo. "And what do you mean he spared you? If he's ever touched one strand on your beautiful head, I will string him up by his—"

She pointed upward. "Auriga is the charioteer in the sky. Zola asked him to hunt you, and he listened."

"This cut to my chest didn't come from a charioteer or Zola," said Rinaldo. "I was knifed inside the *lupanare*."

Celestina lunged back, mouth agape. Perhaps he wasn't so perfect. "Rinaldo...how could you?"

He flashed his palms. "I was nosy."

Nosy? While she lay tormented next to her grandmother, yearning to be with him, he was satisfying his needs with a *puttana* at the *lupanare*.

She yanked his ear. "You dog, Rinaldo SanGiorgio." He yipped, and she was glad it hurt. "A prostitute. Truly?" she accused.

"It wasn't like that." Rinaldo waved his hands.

"Then what did you do inside?"

"A wild woman talked to me. She was from Transylvania."

Transylvania sounded silly and made up. "So, this... Transylvania snake...cut you?"

"No. It was a *rospo*," he said.

She folded her arms. Now he was creating stories with abandon. "A toad, with a knife?"

He rubbed his bad ankle, saying, "Perhaps you know him because he knows you. You have to believe me, *Celissima*, or I will have no choice but to go back in there and trap the toad and bring him to you so he can tell you himself."

She snapped, "Why do you keep calling him a toad? Whom are you talking about?"

And then the answer to her own question hit her like a brick falling from the sky. "Bald Magnaccio cut you," she said with a shiver. "We should alert a watchman and show him your wound so that miserable whoremaster will be sent to wither in Bargello."

"Forget him. I've got a hundred scars. This will heal fine."

"But Magnaccio must be punished."

"He has done me a service in a way, and so I will let his attack slide, this time," said Rinaldo, bearing a faraway look.

"What good comes of getting sliced like a piece of prosciutto?" Her tone was uneasy.

"It's a sign from God," he said coolly.

Not only had his limbs been injured, his soul sounded broken as well. "A sign that you're no more important than a hunk of spiced ham?" she asked softly.

"That I should leave Florence forever," he said.

She grabbed his arm. "But why?"

"I am not good enough for Florence or you. My wounds are signs."

She slapped her forehead. She must change his mind.

"You are everything," she said. "Without you, I will become a nun, because there is no other man, now or ever."

"Don't say that," he said grimly. "Any *ragazzo* from Rome to Verona would cut off his hand to spend one day with you."

She combed through her hair with ice-cold fingers. "Listen to me before you decide," she said. "Then, I will not stand in your way."

He nodded wearily.

"I believe it's the curse making you think this way. You were slashed not by Auriga, but by the evil Magnaccio, who did the constellation's dirty work. Then when I called you, it wasn't a horseshoe that hobbled you, but your own shoe. Zola's curses have come true in roundabout ways. And they are working to take you away from me."

He was silent and she hoped he was taking good measure of her explanation.

"My decision has nothing to do with your neighbor," he said finally. "I can give you nothing. God has confirmed it."

Her spirits drained into a swirl inside her stomach. "When you walked in the door of my bakery, I believe that was *my* sign from God, that *my* love had finally arrived."

"It's no use," he said with a sad inevitability. And then he turned for Settignano.

Her breath caught in her throat. She hadn't expected this ending. To lose him because of Zola's curse was unthinkable.

She must do something to get him to stay. Without time to make sense of it, she kicked him in his one good ankle.

She could almost see his scream waving through the air. He tottered sideways until he finally toppled.

"You, too, Celestina?" he asked, tone burning in betrayal.

She dropped her head, not blaming him for being angry. He'd endured many wounds in a short time. "I'm sorry I hobbled you, but it was for a reason. I don't want you to walk away from—"

He cut her off. "From what? Love?" He batted off cobblestone dust that clung to his tights. "Feels more like hate."

She licked her lips. Worried lips. Sad lips. Celestina-loves-Rinaldo lips. Why had God given her lips if she was unable to use them when they were needed? She hoped St. Catherine viewed her next act as noble and not immodest.

Leaning in, she asked Rinaldo, "Does this look like hate?"

His chest muscle stirred at the touch of her lips against his slash. "But your modesty..." His protest was weak.

"*Shhh*," she pressed her finger against his flushed lips. "Immodest? No." The scent of his manly musk made her mouth steam. "I'm simply tending the wounds of an injured artist."

She swiped her lips gently over his raw wound, the taste of his blood and sweat salty on her tongue. She exhaled as though her warm breath had healing magic. His nipple hardened.

Rinaldo nuzzled the top of her head. "But if I fail to learn the art of fresco," he whispered into her ear, the rumble of his voice making her own nipple blossom, "how could someone like you ever love a simple *scalpellino*?"

"I would love you if you were a galley slave," she replied.

"I think I can do better than that," he said flatly.

"Come back to the bakery. I'll bind your wounds," she said, pulling him to his feet.

"I'm all right," he said, grasping her hand and rising to his feet. "We must get to the Vines before my drawings become squirrel litter."

She was overcome with relief, enough that she saw their future bright and clear. She started to tell him about the upcoming sabbat, pausing only when she saw him looking over her shoulder with a terrified expression. "What's wrong?" she asked.

"It's the toad," his voice broke. "Coming straight at us like we're a couple of flies from Transylvania."

9

Magnaccio was fast, but Rinaldo had more to live for, or it seemed to Celestina, who marveled at his ability to run away with two hampered ankles and her in tow.

They hopped over a pack of runaway pigs, twisted to avoid beggars, and shimmied over the city gate, running all the way to the Vines.

With the sweet song of the wood warbler caressing her ears, she let out a huge breath. They could be at peace, at least until the sabbat that night.

Pretty birds did not appear to soothe Rinaldo, however. He searched anxiously for his sketchbook.

Perhaps peace was not so much on her horizon, either. She hadn't yet told Rinaldo about the sabbat, and since she sensed it was not his favorite topic—especially since Fra was going to be there—she hesitated to do so while he was presently vexed.

He threw up his hands and sniped at her. "*Celissima*, please turn your back."

Acting on orders from a *ragazzo*, without knowing why, was not in her makeup, though she owed Rinaldo a favor after she'd left him partially hobbled. She gave him her back but his splashing in the brook threw water on her resolve and she peeked.

Rinaldo's shoes and stockings were strewn along the bank. He was wading through the fast water, arms tensed above the blue stream, and spying the bottom of the clear creek.

She hoped the coolness of the brook at least healed his swollen ankle and shin because it would serve no good purpose for his sketchbook. With a flutter in her stomach, her gaze perused the hem of his tunic. It clung wetly to the cuts and muscles of his torso and it crossed her mind that it wouldn't be the worst thing if a gush of water swept up his shirt to unmask his man parts.

Control your impure thoughts.

A moment later Rinaldo's shadow was busy behind an old olive tree. His clothes were gone from the bank of the water.

"I'm going up to swing around for a better look," he said, walking out from behind the tree.

"*Uh*...excuse me?"

He used his fingers as a comb. "Going swinging," he said.

She cocked an eyebrow and glanced at his legs. "Two injured pegs aren't enough? You want to break your neck, too?" She punched her fists to her hips. "You certainly are not 'going swinging.'"

He fingered a hanging vine, testing its strength "Excuse me,'" he teased. "But, yes, I am."

Mio Dio. He charmed her even when he mocked her. Still, she hated how he took chances with his life.

"A good Roman soldier doesn't travel by air or sea." She thought it was something St. Catherine might say. "He keeps his feet securely on the ground."

"*Ahhh*, but *Celissima*, the Settignese have more grace, looks, and honor than Romans. Didn't I ever tell you that?"

"But your ankles—"

He rotated one foot, then the other. "Healed," he proclaimed, much to her doubt. "Stay here and look for your mamma's veil. I'll be back before you find it," he said.

She reached for the closest vine, straining to pull up. "Then I'm going with you. You need my help."

His hand masked his smirk. "Somehow I'll manage without you."

"Are...you...teasing me again?"

"Never," he managed to slip out before indulging in a belly laugh.

She unhanded the vine and dropped to her feet. "But if you fall, you'll die." She grabbed her chest. The thought of losing him stabbed her with grief.

"I work in a quarry, remember?" He climbed up a vine before she could blink. "Feet of a mountain goat."

She stomped her foot. "Come down."

He called down from high in the branches. "Now that I found you, *Celissima*, do you think I'm going to let anything happen to myself?"

Celestina leaned back to look up. He'd started to swing. "Have you forgotten that you've been cursed by Zola?" she shouted, her voice echoing behind him.

"And by the way," she said into her shoulder, which he could not possibly hear, "Fra said there's a sabbat tonight."

)(

Rinaldo moved to and fro through billows of smoke wafting up the branches. Fearing the Vines was on fire, he stopped to land on a high branch. If necessary, he'd turn back for Celestina, to sweep her away before one flame touched her glorious head.

Then from the side of his eye, he spotted an old woman below, at the edge of the clearing, stirring a stick in a bubbling cauldron. Satisfied that's where the smoke stemmed, he leaned over the branch for a better look. A black veil covered her head. Celestina's veil.

Sliding down the long vine, he landed on a pile of dry pine needles. His ankle held, and he got on with his mission. With silent feet, he advanced. Pieces of his sketchbook cover, unmistakable swaths of chestnut leather, lay torn next to the pot.

Rinaldo approached with caution. "*Scusa, signora,*" he said evenly.

Perhaps her hearing was bad. He repeated, with a bit more force, "Excuse me."

Her attention remained on the pot.

"*Signora!*"

Slyly, she reached under the veil, confirming to him that she had indeed heard him but was going about things her own way. When she withdrew a hidden ax, it was clear that he was right.

Rinaldo raised his hands, a sign he meant no harm. Though the ax was no more than a blade tied to tree lumber, it was a formidable weapon.

She raised it threateningly over her head. That she'd be more scared of him than he was of her was a thought that hadn't occurred to him until that moment.

Heart pounding, he stepped back. "*Signora,* I come in peace and with a simple question."

Her phlegmy eyes were set wide and deep under her broad forehead. "If you come closer, Druda will chop you bit by bit." Her voice was a rolling rumble.

He swiped up a scrap of his notebook cover. "What have

you done with my drawings? Point me to them and I will be gone, along with my muse's black veil." He waited for her to hand it over.

Druda pulled the veil close around her throat. "Pictures?" she asked.

"*Si, signora,*" he said, unsure if she didn't understand or was playing games. "Of a girl, a beautiful *signorina* with long waves..." He moved his hands like he was caressing Celestina's waist. "Perfect curves."

She winked a slit of an eyelid. "Naked?"

He sputtered, "My Celestina is a woman of modesty."

"Poor you," she said.

Rinaldo regarded the ax. "Did you burn my pictures to make your fire?" His shoulders tensed.

She spit in the cauldron. "I inherited this fire."

"From who?" Rinaldo glanced around.

"The Gathering. Lucedio told me to keep the fire alive until tonight. When they return, they promised to make me young again," she said.

Rinaldo snorted, "No one is able to turn back time."

She wagged a craggy finger. "Never misjudge Lucedio."

Rinaldo's skin crawled. "Lucifer?"

She nodded. "King of the Bottomless Pit."

Devil talk scared the *minestrone* out of him. "Can we discuss my book of pictures?" Somewhere in her crazy mind, she had the answer, he was sure of it. "Have you seen them anywhere?"

Her eyes danced. "You're good-looking." She leaped forward like a sprite, and he stumbled back. His ankles had begun to once again torment him. "Are you Lucedio, come early to make me a girl again?" she asked.

"My God, no."

She shrugged. "If you want your pictures, come back tonight—the gathering will witness Lucedio rise and make me young again. Come see. I'll be pretty tonight."

Rinaldo swallowed hard. "There's a sabbat tonight?"

She opened her toothless mouth in a smile.

His stomach flipped. "And witches and Satan will be here, inside the Vines?"

"Yes," she said. "They can watch me and you fuck."

He ordered his feet not to run. "First, I need my sketchbook and Celestina's veil covering your head." He reached out, trying his best to be commanding.

"Fuck first," she said, shutting one eye and glaring at him with the other.

Rinaldo raised his end fingers like bullhorns to fight off the *malocchio*. If she cast the evil eye against him, he'd be under her spell. "You think you're going to fuck me?" He aimed the horns at her. "*Vaffanculo!*"

"Fuck you, too!" She threw her hands in the air triumphantly.

Rinaldo scrambled backward. His ankles slowed him like he'd turned into a turtle. She was coming at him, ax in hand.

He clutched a ropy climber and shimmied up the vine. At a safe distance, he glanced down. Druda was extracting a sheet of paper from her bosom, which she then waved over her head like a victory flag.

"Come and get your picture of the modest Celestina," she shouted from below.

She had what he needed, so he shoved down his loathing and descended the vine. But Druda had run away and disappeared into the brush.

Hand over fist, he climbed back up. He kicked off from the trunk of the tree and winced at the sharp pain that ripped through his ankle as he swung over her wobbling figure.

She taunted him with the picture, finally shoving it inside her dress top. "Come and get it," she called.

Rinaldo didn't notice the fat tree trunk, smack ahead of him, in time to change course.

Celestina shoved aside hanging vines. "Torino," she called.

Rinaldo hadn't returned from his swinging adventure. She shook from her head the worry that she was going to lose him before they could start their life together.

Trampling creeping groundcover, she came upon a black pot boiling over a steady fire. She froze at the sight. Witches? A distant grunt made her jump and she scurried to hide behind a stump. On the other side of the clearing, an old woman dragged a man bound in vines lying on his side.

Leaping from behind the stump, Celestina shouted, "Let go of my Rinaldo."

The old woman turned—she moved faster than Celestina thought possible—and poised the blade of an ax at Rinaldo's neck.

Smoke rolled off the top of the kettle, creating an opaque wall between them, making it hard for Celestina to determine the expression on Rinaldo's face; however, he was lying still as a log. But she held back her urge to cry out for him, so as not to startle the old crow into dropping the sharp blade on him.

The old woman's button eyes stared into hers. "If honorable Celestina takes one more step, Druda cuts off Rinaldo's head. But head or no head, Druda turns young tonight and fucks Rinaldo," she said.

Rinaldo's feet shifted slightly. At least he was alive.

Help us, St. Catherine.

Ahi. Celestina doubled over in seething pain. She hadn't expected a kick from the saint at that moment, thinking she had enough to contend with, but St. Catherine always had a good reason for what she did.

And then in the throes of her pained breathing, she saw there was a scheme to St. Catherine's aggression. The blow was St. Catherine's way of telling Celestina to make Druda angry, too.

"But after tonight," Celestina said wickedly, "won't you be even older?"

As St. Catherine must have suspected, the old woman's nostrils flared. "I will be *younger*. Tonight, the gathering takes me back in time."

Celestina spotted a heavy stick, sturdy and weapon-like, on the ground. She hadn't seen it earlier. St. Catherine must have dropped it there.

Celestina glanced up at Druda, "Tell me, how is the gathering going to make you fertile again?"

"First, Lucedio will plant his seed in me, followed by me fucking Rinaldo, who will be my son's father on earth," said Druda.

Celestina crept toward the stick. "I see. So, it's you, Rinaldo, and Satan—"

"*Lucedio*," she corrected sharply.

"My apologies," Celestina added quickly. "The three of you will create one beautiful baby, I'm certain."

Druda petted Rinaldo's hair. The ax slipped from her other hand.

Seizing her opportunity, Celestina clutched the stick. The old woman burst into action, swiping up the ax and flinging it at Celestina, who used the stick like a baton to bat away the ax.

It was then, in a gust, that Rinaldo swiped his bound feet

across Druda's ankles, toppling the old shrew and rolling on top of her to keep her down. Celestina dashed over, sliding on her knees to help untangle Rinaldo from the vines roping his wrists and ankles. Their gazes met unexpectedly and his eyes gleamed. Her chest swelled with pride in saving him.

Free from bondage, Rinaldo flung Druda over his shoulders like an old sack of flour and then dangled her over the cauldron. "If you ever look at Celestina again, I'll throw you in this pot to boil."

Druda kicked and screamed and Rinaldo finally allowed her to roll out of his arms. She scampered into the cover of overgrown vines like a nighttime forest creature escaping the light.

At the same time, Celestina fetched the ax and heaved it deep into the brush to hide it, temporarily at least, from Druda, while Rinaldo swept up her mamma's black veil.

They came together and Celestina dug her face into his rising and falling chest. Softly, she stroked his wrist, red from the tight wrapping of vines.

But his gaze was far into woodlands. "My business with Druda is not finished," he said.

Celestina moaned. "Tell me you are making a joke."

His jaw twitched. "I wish."

Did he never tire of danger? "In the name of St. Catherine, why?"

"Druda has a drawing of you inside her dress. I have to go in there," he stifled a gag, "and get it out."

She had no intention of helping him dig around Druda's stinky bosom. "What good is one sweaty sketch?"

He sighed in anguish. "It's all I've got, and I have to find work, today if possible. It's the key to our marriage."

She perked up. "Marriage?"

He blushed. "I loved you the moment I saw you lying on the street before that damned Dominican."

She clasped her hands to her chest so her heart would not break through and float away. Good had come of her making a fool of herself on the Via Scalia.

"For me, it was at the sermon in the piazza when you ducked the swinging sword of the Reform guard and he fell on his fat *culo*," she said.

He pulled in a deep breath. He seemed in agony with the weight of his many injuries hanging heavy on him. "Since we both want to get married, that leaves only one answer," he said.

"And what is that, Torino?"

"I must draw you all over again."

She stepped back, a wave of apprehension coursing through her. "I must say no."

He threw down his hands. "What do you mean?"

She cast her gaze to the side. "My muse days...have finished," her voice broke.

He bent on one knee. "But you are my muse, now and forever. I must draw you or I will die," he said.

She stroked his jutting cheekbone. "Since you met me your life has changed. You've been hobbled and cut, and bound in vines. *Ahi*. I am beginning to believe Zola truly is a witch, and her curse has power. For your own good, you must find another muse."

"*Mai, mai, mai.*" He rose from his knee. "Never."

"But your terrible luck is not going to cease until you stop drawing me."

He pounded his fist in his hand. "I am unafraid, *Celissima*."

"But the way it's going you won't survive our courtship," she said.

He shot up and kicked at groundcover. And after stomping and snorting like a bull, he turned about with a new and purposeful glow.

"If we return to Settignano today, I can return to work in the quarry. My uncle is a religious and he can marry us by nightfall," said Rinaldo. "In the eyes of God, will that kill Zola's curse?"

She clasped her chest. That he would sacrifice his happiness made her lightheaded. "But you hate the quarry," she said.

"I don't care. I just want to be your husband. You can be my muse at night."

She stepped back. "It's not all about you, Rinaldo." She surveyed the sky, now blue but tonight it would be black. "I have a mission. Tonight's the sabbat. I know I haven't told you until now, but I'm going and I hope that you choose to join me."

"I heard from Druda," he said. "And like her, your thinking is not sound."

She looked hard at the *scalpellino*, not having realized he'd turned into such an opponent. "Saving Papa's soul from purgatory—to you, this is considered the talk of a mad woman?" The tension in her voice could have snapped a branch from a *mille*-year-old olive tree.

"Not the part about saving your papa. I want that as much as you do, but must you be so single-minded?"

"I'm sorry, SanGiorgio. Everything comes after Papa," she said.

He turned from her and brushed both hands through his hair. She reached out to stroke his back but pulled back. They were at a stalemate and she hadn't felt so alone since Papa died.

She massaged the lump in her throat. After meeting who she thought was the quarryman of her dreams, it now seemed that aloneness was to be her way of life, her God-given destiny.

She started to leave, to go her own way home to prepare to fight solo at the sabbat, when Rinaldo said, "I have an idea."

She stopped cold.

"Tonight, we hunt the witches and end their reign of terror so that tomorrow we may marry and live with your grandmother until I find a master to teach me the art of fresco," he said.

Joy bubbled inside her. She wanted to kick herself she'd been so wrong to worry. "*Si*, Rinaldo." If they were able to catch the witch who caused Papa to die and four others it would make for a perfect future.

He grabbed her hand. "I will go round up weapons." He turned, and his ankle buckled, resulting in his tumble to the ground.

"The witches are punishing you for ignoring Zola's spell," she said nervously.

"We're not going back around with that, *Celissima*. No more talk of Zola," he said and rose to his feet.

She let him pull her close. "I swear, no more Zola," Celestina said.

He looked deep into her eyes. "Make love to me, in case we die in battle tonight."

She was too startled to do anything but laugh. "Nice try, Torino," she said.

His mouth pouted, and then the corners turned up.

"But what I will do is this," she said, unclasping the chain around her neck. Her golden *putto* glistened in the sunlight. She reclasped the chain around his neck. "This is my most cherished possession, made by Papa's hand. I bestow it to you to show the strength of my commitment."

Slipping off the thin leather strap that bore his white marble crucifix, he slipped it over her head. "Take this as a pledge of my love from today until eternity," he said.

Their lips hovered. The sweet warmth of his breath on her skin made her *patata* throb. Fearing her modesty was crumbling, she stepped back and so did he. Only he pretended to clutch his chest as if he were dying.

"And now you must leave me before we go too far. Remember our promise to Simona," she said.

He shook his head. "I will honor my pledge."

"Meet me right here at nightfall," she said, and once again he was up the vines and swinging.

She watched, heart in throat, once again all alone.

10

The crash of pottery striking plaster was more than familiar, but the mystery was what had happened to upset Simona in the short time it took Celestina to fetch water from the well.

Her grandmother had been quite generous earlier, even thanking Celestina for making a double batch of dough. Simona had said she thought they missed passing each other, Celestina going back to the apartment to rest after the harder work, while Simona went the other way to the bakery to start the fire in the oven.

And Celestina didn't explain otherwise, which was that she had made extra dough out of guilt for sneaking back to the Vines with Rinaldo. It was a sin of omission that she'd have to confess.

Celestina tucked Rinaldo's cross inside her blouse. Simona hadn't seen it yet. Sneaking out for the night's sabbat was going to be tricky enough without adding more spice to the soup.

"Why are you throwing dishes?" Celestina peered around the corner into the back of the bakery, arm poised to protect her face.

Her heart jumped at the unexpected flash of lively blue eyes.

"*Ciao, bella.*"

"Cristoforo Colombo," Celestina said and they both ducked. Simona's flying cup missed their heads.

"*Passerota*, my little sparrow. You've grown into a beautiful swan."

The cord of St. Francis cinched his red robe at the waist, giving the garment a regal air as it hung from his tall frame.

"And the high seas agree with you," Celestina said.

Simona drew a swig from a green bottle. "If only you two knew the truth," she slurred.

Celestina gritted her teeth. Simona never missed a chance to abuse Cri. He, however, navigated her as easily as a choppy wave.

"*Signora*, either tell *passerota* and I your big secret, the one you always tease us with or stop speaking in riddles," he said. Celestina nodded in full agreement.

Simona swiped her lips. "Never mind."

Celestina sighed and Cri gave an oversized nod. "That's what I thought," he said.

Simona eyed the poker. Celestina quickly beckoned Cri to the front of the shop.

"What brings you back to Florence?" she asked, donning her apron so it would appear to Simona she was working.

He bowed his head. She caught a glimpse of his grays and nervously brushed her hand over her own untamed locks. They did share the same hair color, and looking at the top of his head was like peering into her own future.

"I've come to pay my respects. I'm sorry about Alessandro's passing," Cri said. "I heard he died bravely. Though I met him only once as a boy I liked him as readily as I might a long-lost brother."

She was much comforted by his words. "And you remind me of him," she said, overcome with newfound grief.

Cri tossed a roll at her. She fumbled, and then caught it, thinking that's exactly what Papa would have done to lighten the moment. When she flung it back at Cri, he bit off a chunk.

"I also have a taste for a big slice of Simona's famous *torta* before I set sail," he said.

"We're out of *torta*," said Simona from the back.

Celestina waved off her grandmother's lie. She produced a whole pear *torta* from under the counter and wrapped it in linen.

He handed her a fistful of coins.

She stared at the mound in her hand. "Cri, this is much too much."

"I heard rumors around town that the bakery is in trouble. Boycott coming. Your grandmother will take them, believe me."

Celestina couldn't argue.

"Now fetch your girlfriend next door, the alchemist's daughter," he said, removing the chessboard from his well-traveled leather satchel. "I'll judge your competition."

She didn't want to spoil his visit by talking about Zola so she simply mumbled, "Zola cannot play today."

His eyebrow kicked up. "Why not?"

Her grandmother staggered forward, saving Celestina from answering. Simona pushed aside Cri and faced Celestina. "Does it have to do with Herculino?"

"*Aspetta*, wait..." Cri bit back a smile. "*Passerota* has a boyfriend?"

"Rinaldo's a *scalpellino* who wants to paint frescos like Papa," she said, feeling her cheeks flush.

"Would your papa like this *scalpellino*?"

"*Si, si, si*. Rinaldo is brave, handsome, and—"

Cri cut her off. "I should stand in for your papa and meet this Rinaldo. After all, only yesterday you were a baby."

She wished he'd stop teasing. "You were already sailing across the world at my age."

The corner of Cri's lip twisted in a devilish smirk. "Your *ragazzo* might want to join me on the seas, that way he can stay far from Simona."

Hatred harpooned from Simona's eyes.

"Actually," Celestina cupped her hand so Simona couldn't hear, "she thinks he's special."

"I've met people from all over the world but to me, *Passerota*, you're the special one. Take care of yourself."

"It's the same for me," Celestina said, basking in the glow of his attention. "Where are you off to now?"

"Last voyage I sought Christians, but this time I'm looking for the Lost Tribe of Israel in the New World."

She was dying to tell him of her own upcoming adventure, the sabbat, but didn't dare with Simona near. "When you return, perhaps I'll have stories to tell you," she said.

He narrowed his gaze. "A beautiful young woman such as yourself may find trouble if she goes looking for stories that are too good."

"I will be careful, I promise."

He gave a worried sigh before turning for Simona. "*Addio, signora*," he said and saluted.

Simona brandished her fist. "May your boat fall off the end of the earth."

"I love you, too, Simona," he called over his shoulder and was out the door.

Celestina tore a hunk of soft bread from a warm loaf and

spread it with butter. She glanced at Simona, now with her head over short towers of coins, counting them.

With feigned casualness, Celestina said, "Another one of your secrets, I know, but why does Cri's very existence make you crazy?"

Simona pursed her lips and continued to stack money. "Don't worry about it."

Celestina licked her butter-smeared lips. "But you have to admit, Cri *is* getting more handsome with age."

Unexpectedly, Simona's hand flew up, aimed to strike. "Never say that again!"

Celestina lunged back, the bread sailing from her hand. Simona had never before raised a hand to her. It was almost like Celestina had committed a horrible, unspeakable sin. "What...what...what did I say wrong?" asked Celestina.

"Just don't speak about him like that. Or think about him like that, either."

"*Gia.* All right." Celestina dropped Cri's coins on the counter.

Simona scraped them into her leather purse, cinching the cord tight so nothing would spill out, as nothing ever did. Then she took a long drink from the green bottle.

Celestina just shook her head. The sabbat could not come fast enough, and neither could the capturing of five witches.

To save Papa's soul. And Simona's.

)(

Standing with her back to the counter Celestina smelled oranges.

"Monsignor?" She spun around.

"Is your grandmother about?" His tone was sharp.

Before Celestina could come up with an excuse to keep

them apart, her grandmother was already sauntering up to the front, hot poker at the ready.

"One defiant baker woman is hardly worthy of a second visit from the leader of the new religion. So, what do you want, Baldasare?" asked Simona.

Monsignor glowered at the poker. "I will not allow you, or anyone, to mock my dream of melding the spiritual wisdom of Christians, Jews, and Muslims into one great Catholicism. The New Templars of the Reform surrender to no one, or no thing, not even the Vatican."

"What you describe is an abomination, not a religion," said Simona. "What religion despises half the people in the world?"

"Again, with complaints on how the church treats women." Monsignor struck his fist to his chest. "I am the leader of men."

"So as a woman that means I don't have to follow your rules." Simona threw the poker into the corner with a clank, which Celestina thought may have been premature. Monsignor had a threatening look in his eye.

"In the end, all will subordinate to me. Even Holy Cibo," said Monsignor.

Celestina's ears perked up. That name again: Cibo.

"His ordination was *your* dream," countered Simona. "Cibo struggled with that idea, let alone forging a new religion."

Monsignor leaned in. "You distracted him, with your womanly *carisma*."

Simona bent forward so they were nearly nose-to-nose. "You stole him from me like you tried with Alessandro."

Monsignor flicked his hand. "You weren't so special. There were at least three who birthed him sons. Anna Colonna was the most beautiful, but the least formidable."

Simona's eyes glistened. "I'm aware of the son Anna bore

him." The hurt in her grandmother's voice was like a knife in Celestina's chest. Monsignor had found Simona's scab and he knew the most painful way to pick at it.

"I heard he's in town," Monsignor fished.

Simona upped her chin. "Though I despise Anna's son, and make no mistake, he will always be Anna's son, I'd never tell you his whereabouts, not even under torture. You've already ruined his life once by ripping him from the arms of Anna and then farming him out to the Genovese wool trader and his wife, so all of you could appear as good little priests. I refuse to take any part in hurting him further," said Simona.

Monsignor shrugged. "His life didn't turn out so bad."

"The lies the religious tell," said Simona. "That time Anna stole her son back—poor Anna had only hours with him until your rats sniffed them out—she brought him here to hide, but I couldn't have that.

"So, I threw her out for fear it would lead you to Alessandro as well, but not before feeding mother and son, and allowing him and Alessandro to play for a while," said Simona. "After that, as an adult, Anna's son came here often looking for Alessandro but they never crossed paths again. I saw to it."

Simona slowly reached under the counter.

Monsignor fixed his stare on her grandmother. "Listen, Simona, I didn't come here to argue."

"Then why did you come, Baldasare?"

"To inform you that the Reform has called for a boycott of your bakery."

Simona withdrew her dagger. Its blade was as long and pointed as a Venetian's nose. By the way Monsignor bolted for the door, the hem of his blue cape flapping at his feet, it was clear he read the look on her face: one of murderous rage.

Celestina waited for Monsignor to pass by the window

before she dared to ask a question that she imagined unfathomable only a few moments earlier, but Simona's extra-thorny conversation with Monsignor led her to it.

"Did you lay with Monsignor?" Celestina held her breath.

Simona steadied herself against the counter. "Don't start, Celestina."

"That's not an answer." Celestina's voice strained. "Tell me, because it sounds like he may be Papa's father."

Simona tightened her lips.

"Why aren't you denying it?" Celestina 's insides quivered. "Saying nothing means you rolled with Monsignor."

Simona's gaze was steady as she stared into the oven fire. "He wasn't exactly a *monsignore* when I slept with him," she said.

Celestina stumbled back. Did her grandmother not understand the magnitude of her sin? "How could you?" gasped Celestina.

Simona threw the knife against the wall.

Celestina cringed at the clatter. "That's your answer?" she asked. "And what about the other man? This Cibo character? You rolled with him, too?"

Simona reached blindly under the counter, producing a bottle of raisin wine, which Celestina promptly swiped from her grandmother's hand.

"Give me." Simona lunged for it.

"Not until I get answers." Celestina held the bottle high. "What is this about a new religion, and a man named Cibo?"

Simona reached through the pile of rags beneath the counter, producing a new bottle hidden there. She guzzled it down.

Celestina choked the bottle she was holding. "Is Cibo my grandfather?"

"I've done many horrible things in my life, but I don't regret lying with Cibo once or twice, a long time ago," said Simona.

Celestina slammed the green bottle against the counter in an explosion of glass and red wine. The walls looked like there'd been a stabbing. She just glared at her grandmother, who was nothing more than a charlatan.

"All you do is talk about my modesty, but when you were young, you'd given yours away twice, at least."

Simona slipped down the wall. "It's in your lineage to be better than me," she said.

"Is that so," said Celestina, wiping her wine-stained hands and marking her apron. She'd had heard enough of Simona's betrayals to last her a lifetime.

"Well hear this, Nonna/Grandma/Old Lady *Signora* DiCapria." Celestina untied her apron and chucked it in the corner. "I quit," she said.

But Simona, now asleep in the cloud of drunkenness, heard none of it. Celestina ran out the door and didn't look back.

The Reform's boycott would break Simona's business in three days' time, but that was no longer Celestina's concern. Her new plan was bigger than anything her grandmother was able to imagine.

After the night's sabbat, she was running away with Rinaldo. Perhaps they'd board Cri's ship and dock in a foreign land and catch witches there. But wherever they ended up, one thing was certain.

Celestina's modesty was staying in Florence.

11

Rinaldo paced like a bull under the full moon outside the Vines, grinding his teeth as he watched the purplish billows of smoke stain the Florence sky. Art burners. If the Reform Boys hurt Celestina in any way, he'd unchain hell against the lot of them—especially the Dominican.

Red ants nipped at his ankle. He slapped at them, and then inspected his sack of weaponry: rope, netting, rocks, unlit torch, and flint, all there.

Fighting witches was new to him. He had no desire to fight women, and in truth the only one he'd ever looked crossways at was Zola.

Flexing his hands, he considered the proper amount of force needed to catch a witch. To hurt a living thing possessing feminine qualities was impossible for him. But an underworld necromancer disguised as a bat...for that he should not hold back.

The whole idea of a sabbat left him with so many other questions, too. After they were caught and caged, did the bats transfigure into women? And what about stripping their dresses? He scrunched his nose. That would be Celestina's job. Even a witch needed privacy.

He shook out his tingling hands, searching this way and that for Celestina. Perhaps, wisely, she'd changed her mind and stayed home to allow him to fight for the two of them.

He slapped at something nibbling his arm, knowing in his heart there was no chance of her retreat. Celestina thought she was a warrior, and though she possessed far more brains than brawn, he had to respect her wishes.

A disharmony of chirping gave him skin bumps. His instinct was right. A tornado of bats twisted in silhouette before the full moon. He dug his nose into the crook of his arm. Flying feces soured the midnight air.

They circled low, and one dove at him. He punched and the bat exploded, its cold blood splatting over his knuckles.

He swiped the back of his hand against his coat and then, realizing what he might have done, turned cold as a dead man. Perhaps he had just killed a witch. A woman.

Pulling his cap over his ears to protect his hair, he repeated, "It was a bat...a stinking flying rat. You did not kill someone's wife, daughter, or mother."

Ahi. Next a bat as big as a barn cat swooped at his head. He stooped in time and it missed him. His mouth gaped as he watched it zigzag away, picturing Celestina hanging from its claws, dangling in the moonlight.

He gave his head a hard shake. He must get his imaginings under control.

He crouched and rested his arms across his knees, dropping his head. A new picture flamed across his mind. Magnaccio had Celestina by the back of her skirt and was dragging her inside the *lupanare*. The filthy whoremaster had roped her golden-red hair around her throat.

An unexpected tap on his shoulder jolted him to standing.

Fists drawn, he swung into the blackness.

"*Attenzione.* Be careful, Torino. It's me."

Celestina pegged her arm to her face. When she dared to lower her shield, she found Rinaldo, glowering at his clenched hands.

"I would chop these off to keep from hurting you," he said with a voice so pained it hurt her.

"Why are you acting crazy?" Her fingertips examined his neck for punctures. "Did a bat bite you?"

He knocked his head. "It's not bird fever. I thought you were Magnaccio."

"Now I look like a toad?"

"You look nothing like him, and beautiful in all black." She saw him giving her dress a second look.

"Mostly all black," she corrected, stroking her cuffs of white ermine fur against his cheek.

"Simona made it for me before Papa died," she said. The very mention of her grandmother's name angered her. "It was too fancy to wear when I was mourning, and so I've saved it for a special occasion."

Free of her promise of modesty, she purposely nuzzled her nose into his chest. Shooting stars flared inside her head. Touching him made her mind circle the moon in ecstasy. She came roaring back to earth when he clutched her shoulders.

He squeezed too hard. "What are you doing?" she demanded.

He flung her to the ground as if she weighed no more than a rag doll, and then he jumped on top of her.

"Get off *immediatamente.*" She kicked beneath him, but his body was a blanket.

A heartbeat later, when the rush of low-flying bats aimed for them had passed, she stopped protesting, understanding why he used his body to cover her.

He helped her to her feet. "*Mi dispiace*, I'm sorry," he said, "but when you didn't move..."

She brushed debris from her dress, grateful for his quick action. "Simona probably sent them to chaperone."

"*Gia*," spat Rinaldo. "The little bloodsuckers are flying chastity belts." He gave one straggler the back of his hand. She cringed when it smacked against the tree.

After shooing away a pair fighting over Rinaldo's head, she asked, "How's Giacobbe?" Thinking of Zola and her curse against Rinaldo's brother made her want to vomit.

"Probably throwing stones at Zola's bedroom window, begging for her love." Rinaldo created a helmet with his hands to protect her hair from more bats.

"So, Zola's curse didn't work." She dared to feel relief.

They dodged a band of bats flying at them sideways. "His only sickness is love sickness," said Rinaldo. "I'm tired of talking about Cobbe. Are you ready to battle some witches?"

"First, we must pray." Celestina laced her fingers between Rinaldo's. Closing her eyes, she began: "*St. Catherine, please let Rinaldo and me capture five witches in order to free Papa from the island of purgatory. Guide Rinaldo and me in every step of our fight against God's enemies.*"

Rinaldo bowed his head. "Amen."

And keep Simona safe from evil.

It was as good as she was able to muster, considering she hated Simona and never wanted to see her grandmother again.

"*Celissima*." Rinaldo poked her shoulder.

She was unready to break prayer, attempting to ask St.

Catherine to remind God to free Papa's soul from purgatory at the moment his witch was taken, but Rinaldo kept jostling her shoulders.

Mai, but Rinaldo required a lot of attention. She looked at him. "Can't a girl have a moment alone with St. Catherine before battle?"

He jabbed his finger at the Vines. She swung around to find bats, thousands of them, forming a solid curtain blocking their entrance.

"They're trying to keep us out," Rinaldo shouted above the near-deafening flap of wings. "We should heed their warning."

Celestina set her jaw. "I'm going in."

"Not now." Rinaldo grabbed her sleeve.

She tore away her arm. "Don't try to stop me."

"I forbid it." Rinaldo caught her around her waist.

"Stop trying to be my papa, SanGiorgio."

She jerked from his hold and rushed the wall of birds, slapping at sharp beaks and claws, only stopping when she was left alone and swatting bare air.

A ball of light appeared, followed by a monumental *swoosh*. The bats fled toward the moon. Spitting feathers from her mouth, she glimpsed Rinaldo and his torch.

"Seems they're afraid of fire." He sounded quite proud and offered her a skin of water.

Her throat drank like a thirsty tree. "Now let's find some heretics to catch," she said, wiping her lips.

Rinaldo blocked her path. "Please go back to the bakery where it's safe. Let me fight the witches alone," he said.

Her skin prickled. "Don't fuss," she said, and tried to push past, but he was a wall.

"That gate of vermin was a sign," he said. "When you asked God to protect you, He sent bats to keep you from the sabbat."

She edged past him, blood boiling. "Perhaps they were angels in black, meant to keep you away from the sabbat. I will fight alone if I must."

She stomped forward, the night dew soaking her slippers. But when a spot of light approached from behind, a slow smile crossed her lips. Rinaldo overtook her stride, and she let him lead into the darkness, the torch throwing suitable light.

Ahead lay the clearing. She tugged his tunic to stop him.

"What is it, *Celissima*?"

"After our victory, we can celebrate in our own special way," she said.

"But Simona?"

"Do not worry about her any longer."

He replied, "I see—"

"I see what?" It's what she wanted to ask. She'd expected him to start swinging from the vines in excitement, but he remained quiet as a dead tree. Her insides turned icy as bat blood. She was totally bewildered by his silence.

Say something. Please, Rinaldo.

Rinaldo pounded his fist against his thigh. It did nothing to resolve the rising between his legs. He'd been ready to create love with Celestina since the moment he witnessed her lying before the Dominican on the Via Scalia. He said nothing because he wanted to say exactly the right thing.

"With your words in my ear," he started, "I will fight like a warrior tonight and in the end, we will come together as one." He thumped his fist to his chest.

She let out a huge breath, though he could not imagine that she doubted his absolute love for her.

"I pledge to lose my modesty to you, tonight," she said.

He could not wipe the smile off his face as he followed at her heels into the clearing. Ahead of them, wild flames danced from torches. He snuffed his own so no one could see them, and then they paused to listen to the ringing mix of voices in a chant spiraling through the Vines:

Flying on broomstick women of the night

Pray, pray, De-mon-e

Sick of hollow hearts under stark moonlight

Pray, pray De-mon-e

Take us Lu-ce-Dio, yes the undead

Pray, pray De-mo-ne

Lay beside us upon hell's fertile bed

Pray, pray De-mon-e

"They're calling up Satan." Celestina's voice shook. "The sabbat has begun."

"Climb aboard your mule." He pointed at his back. He wanted her as near as possible. God forbid they became separated in the Vines.

She wrapped her arms around his neck and slipped her legs around his waist. Her soft breasts pummeled his back. The heat between his legs became unbearable and all he could think about was finishing up the sabbat and lying with Celestina.

He groped the rough bark of a tree. It didn't feel hollowed out, although he could never be sure about termites. He secured his weapon-filled sack against the base of the tree for safekeeping.

"Hang on," he said, "we're going up." She clung tight.

High in the tree, he tested a springy branch. It was young and thin, but suitable. Also, the moonlight was *stupendo* up high and he was able to see far.

He secured Celestina closest to the trunk. "I will guard you with my life."

"Are you scared?" she asked. The tremor in her voice told him that she was.

He counted at least six necromancers, all nude, dancing wildly down in the clearing. "I fear nothing," he lied.

What an evil sight the witches were. One woman straddled a goat. His heart ached for the poor creature, to be humiliated in such a foul way. Another hoisted a wooden cross over her head as though she were Jesus, and then threw it on the ground and stomped it.

He sneered at the blasphemy. Other women passed a bottle of brew and swigged. Glass crashed against a rock below. Celestina jerked and the branch beneath them cracked. He wrapped his arms around her and the tree trunk so she was secure.

"Soulless creatures," said Celestina, looking away.

"Do you see the witch who led your papa to his death?" he asked, eyes on the hunt.

She scanned below. "No one favors her. And even if she were here, I couldn't steal her dress..."

"Because no one down there is wearing any clothes," he finished her words.

"Look at the hunched lady, it's Druda without clothes." Celestina pointed straight at the crone.

His stomach lurched. "Stirring her brew of children's bones."

"Don't give me any worse thoughts. I can't let go to cover

my ears."

A trio of new women, clothed in flowing garments, danced into the clearing and started a circle. Rinaldo stiffened, ready to pounce. "Is your papa's witch among them?"

She bit at her lip. "It doesn't appear so."

It was then that Rinaldo spotted a new threat. A man, naked as a snake, walked from the bush into the clearing. The women flocked to him as if he was their king. Two knelt at his backside, and one in front.

Rinaldo swallowed revulsion. "They're kissing his ass..."

Celestina gasped. "And eating his front."

"It's a living fresco," said Rinaldo, "of hell." He clutched Celestina's shoulder. "I'm getting you out of here. You're going back to your grandmother's. I'll return to fight these demons alone."

She slapped his hand. "I'm not letting you out of my sight. And I'm not leaving without catching at least five witches."

He tried to block her view of them. "I don't want you to see this."

"It's not your decision."

He winced at the sharpness of her tone. "Are you sure you want to do this?"

She gave a hard nod. "I must free Papa's soul so that he may look upon the face of God."

He could not deny the conviction in her voice, but he had beliefs too, ideas that mattered as much as hers.

He planted his feet and then hugged her. "God gave you a fiery heart, *Celissima*, but you can do better things with it than to capture some witches and hope God accepts that as payment for your father's death."

She tensed. "Like what?"

"Fight the Reform and the Dominican," said Rinaldo. "His

movement is not as big as he claims. Where is his holy army, the men dressed in blue? They were a formidable lot, that is true, but all who remain are the Reform Boys, and they're nothing more than Huns."

Celestina shot back," His holy army has fanned out. They're bringing word of the Reform to all of *Italia*. That's what we'll do if you're still with me."

"Of course, I'm with you. I'll always be with you, but he's destroying the city and his thugs are destroying the very art you profess to love. They are actually killing your papa's memory."

She chopped at his arm. He refused to release his hold in fear she might fall. "You sound as old as Simona," she spat with contempt.

He scowled at her peevishness. "Then you should listen to your grandmother."

He was immediately sorry. She was under much duress and he didn't want to be angry about what he did not understand. "Tell me the story of this witch who your papa saved, so that I may grasp what vexes you so."

"She was beautiful and perhaps French and she kissed him."

Rinaldo looked at her incredulously. A kiss? "Did he kiss her back?"

"Yes."

Rinaldo blew the air out of his cheeks. "Exactly who said that this woman who your papa kissed was a witch?"

"Monsignor," she said. "The witch was inside Santa Maria Novella and she wore no veil, which is one telltale sign of a heretic."

She'd spoken of him before; the one named Monsignor reeked of the Reform. "Do you trust this religious?" he asked.

"*Gia...*"

"Perhaps? That's your answer? Think about what you are saying, *Celissima*. You are doubtful whether this Monsignor is even a good man."

She shrugged, seemingly bewildered. It tore his heart.

"He and Simona have a secret between them," she said. "Then, when Papa was dying, I begged Monsignor to give him extreme unction, but all I saw was red. And then Monsignor said words that turned to chicken stew inside my head."

He fought the urge to throw Celestina over his shoulder and flee the festival of hell beneath them. "In the middle of Last Rites, this is when Monsignor told you to capture the five dresses?" he asked.

A stream of bats swirled at their heads. "*Si*," she cried, hugging the tree trunk. "But he hasn't asked me about it since. It seems like he's forgotten it, but it's *all* I can think about."

Rinaldo ducked out of the way of a flying rat. "And your grandmother and Monsignor know each other from long ago?"

"Again, yes."

"Are they friends or enemies?"

"Enemies."

"And it is Monsignor who claims to know how to save a loved one's soul from eternal purgatory?"

"*Si*, Rinaldo."

He gently lifted her chin. "This all sounds like a pile of bat *merda*. Nothing about it makes sense."

He glanced at the bacchanalia below. "Those people down there are lewd, but I haven't seen one turn into a bat, or a bat turn into one of them. As for Monsignor and five witches, to me, it sounds like people are making up lies to hurt other people. It's all foolishness."

"But Papa's witch, she didn't wear a veil. That has to mean

something," she said.

"I know sometimes you feel rebellious, *Celissima,* because I do too. But what if this woman had her own good reason not to wear a veil? What if your papa fell in love with this supposed witch and that's why he kissed her? Love at first sight? The way I first started to love you."

She was quiet and he could tell she was listening.

"Listen, *Celissima*, my love. I'm nothing more than a simple *scalpellino* who works in the quarry from sunup to sundown, sometimes never hearing another voice in all that time. Gives me room to think. And now I think this whole witch hunt is little more than a way to bring vast power to that skunk friar and Monsignor."

She stared into the distance as if her thoughts danced outside her heart.

"Celestina, what are you thinking?" he asked softly.

She nibbled her bottom lip. "You've made me go back over what happened." Her voice was tiny as a baby mouse. "I've been so angry that all I see is red and blue, and nothing in between."

White smoke from below swirled up the tree. Rinaldo clasped his hand securely around her shoulders. "We're leaving. Now."

She eased her hold on the tree trunk. He took that as a good sign. But then she surprised him and clutched hold of the tree even harder.

"But Simona has done bad things," she said. "I have to prove to God that we're a good family. If there's any way possible, I must save Simona's soul from the devil, even though I'm angry with her right now and never want to see her again."

Rinaldo breathed deep. He was frustrated and had the

feeling he might lash out if he didn't calm down.

"It's that damned Reform that has put these ideas in your head. The Reform is about power on earth, not God in heaven." He worked to keep his tone even. "It's the Reform we should be fighting," he cocked his head toward the orgy beneath them, "not those maniacs."

Celestina bit back a sob. "What do you know of it? You have a papa, a mamma, and brothers who love you, who will always be there for you."

His heart ached that she felt so alone, but it was a feeling that he was familiar with too. "What is also true is that sometimes a *ragazzo* gets lost in a big family. I love them, but if I stay in Settignano I will become as petrified as the marble in the quarry. You, and you alone understand my dream for a different life."

He hadn't expected her to throw her arms around him, and he had to shuffle his feet to keep stable.

"There is no one else under the stars like you," said Celestina.

He tapped his lips to hers, salty from her tears and sweet from her words. "Let's climb down, get out of here, forever away from these demons," he said.

Celestina pressed her finger to his lips. "Hush. Look down."

A flash of baldness danced at the base of the tree.

"*Mannaggia*," Rinaldo cursed, catching himself before he toppled off the limb. The naked bedlamite from the orgy was Magnaccio. The last fight Rinaldo needed was with a dirty whoremaster.

Rinaldo clung to an overhanging limb, stretching to get a good look at a nearby tree so as to make their escape. He needed a vine strong enough to carry them away.

The branch lurched. Celestina swayed dangerously. He caught her before she fell. And then reptile-like hands slung a vine around Rinaldo's neck. With expert quickness the knot was yanked tight.

A set of bony fists jabbed his back and Rinaldo's feet slipped from the branch. He swung from his neck.

Celestina's terrified scream cracked the night air like a hammer shattering a mountain of rock.

Rinaldo gasped for breath while his hands tore at the knot.

Celestina extended her arm dangerously. "Grab my hand," she cried.

Choking, he was unable to tell her to get back. He swung his legs to gather momentum to reach out and push her back against the trunk. But then she stretched out farther for him to take hold of her hand. It was too far.

"*Rin-al-do!*" she screamed. She fell past him, while he hung uselessly.

)(

Rinaldo clutched the vine over his head and pulled up. It allowed a sliver of air to stall the black creep of death while he picked at the knot around his neck.

Jesus, let me live to help my muse.

He tore at the vine until it surrendered, and then caught hold of the tree trunk. Climbing down was taking too long so he let go and dropped, landing square on his feet.

Magnaccio stood a couple of arm's lengths away.

"Snuff the torches," the whoremaster ordered. Fire and light vanished. A blanket of black fell inside the Vines. Even the clouds listened and covered the moon.

Rinaldo was unable to see Celestina, but he'd know her anywhere by her sweet fragrance of almonds.

"Grab my hand, *Celissima*, wherever you are." His voice was weak from the hanging.

A smaller hand locked with his. He sniffed almond. He squeezed her palm reassuringly and led her through the Vines, away from Magnaccio and the monsters of the sabbat.

The reek of sulfur followed them—or perhaps it was the devil chasing them, carrying with him the stench of hell.

Jesus, save us.

A moonbeam cut through the trees. Rinaldo ran toward the light. It disappeared, cloaked by a cloud, but it served its purpose. He was able to guide her outside the Vines.

She kept up with his pace better than he expected after her long fall, but she was silent, which was all right with him. He'd rather not talk and further hurt his throat.

But he was having trouble breathing and slowed his pace. Though it was still too dark to see it, he knew of a stone farmhouse guarded by an army of Cypress trees.

"I know where we can hide until it's safe." The words scratched his throat.

She squeezed his hand sharply. A sign she was ready to forge onward.

He blocked tree limbs for her, taking the brunt of their scaly leaves to save her tender skin. In no time they arrived at the farmhouse. He groped the wall for a spot free of spidery vines and guided her there.

He wished for a shard of light to see her beautiful face, but at least he was able to smell her skin. It was Celestina's almonds, though the scent was not as sweet as he remembered. Most likely the smoke dulled its usual aroma. He kissed the crest of her brow, damp with her sweat.

Voyaging downward, he sought the treasure of her mouth. But he took a detour, wishing to pause at the small bump on her nose. He must give her singular flaw its proper due.

He enlisted the help of his tongue, its sensitive tip trolling for the tiny pebble along her bone, but he found nothing. Her nose had turned flat. Perhaps it had squashed from her fall.

"Where is it?" he whispered hoarsely. "The lovely bump on your nose?"

With the heels of her palms, she struck his chest. Air gushed from his lungs. The blow left him dazed and flat on the ground. "I meant no insult. I...I...I love your nose," he stammered.

She leaped atop him. As she reached under his doublet, groping like a blind woman, he told her to slow down. "We have all night," he said. After the hanging, the words burned his throat.

But she did the opposite. Her busy hands yanked the top of his hose without bothering to undo the lace that tied together the two columns at his waist. He rocked one way, then the other. He had no choice but to assist her as she stripped him. His bare behind scraped the cold ground.

She hurled away his leggings, which brushed against his face before flying past his head. She wiggled about and it seemed like she was tearing off her dress. Her elbow stabbed his eye.

"*Aye*," he cried, embarrassed at how the pain in his face made his pole grow hard. "Slow down." He needed to catch his breath and find her face. "Let's start with a thousand kisses—"

She shoved him flat on his back. He grunted and looked around, for the first time relieved it was pitch dark with little chance of anyone witnessing her domination of him.

His mouth slacked when she sat on him backward, her legs bent at the knee to straddle his thighs Her backside was bony, not round like he remembered seeing underneath her skirt when she posed for his sketches in the Vines.

"Turn around," he begged. "Let me taste your honey-sweet lips."

Instead, she turned and slapped his face. His head snapped to the side. The blow weakened his spirit more than it stung his cheek.

He stared openly into the dark sitting up as best as he could. She wiggled her behind in this newly formed seat, bracing herself by grabbing the back of his thighs.

"Tell...me...what you're doing." His heart beat so hard in his ears he doubted he'd be able to hear her, even if she bothered to answer.

She bounced. A squawk burst from his lips. Between humps, he stroked the back of her hair. It was less silky than he remembered. Shorter. Coarser. Perhaps dirty from her fall from the tree.

He inhaled her scent and was newly heartened. At least she still smelled like his *Celissima*.

He cried out when she spanked his thighs as if he were a horse and she its backward-riding master. His rod was on the verge of breaking under her thumping buttocks.

She moaned, "*Unca, unca, unca,*" and kept bouncing. The ugly sound from deep inside her throat made his toes twist.

Digging his fingers into her shoulders, he attempted to sedate her wild riding. She only sprang harder. He feared the pounding against him would crack the ground, sending them crashing through the gates of hell.

Their coupling was miserable. This was nothing like he dreamed their first lay would be. "I know it's black as coal out here...Celestina...but I want to see your face," he stammered.

She paused a moment, lifting her thigh. A rush of cool air slipped under her leg, giving him chills. But she coupled again, her slit tight around his *cazzo*, jerking up and down.

"Turn...around. I want...our faces...to touch," he moaned.

She only thrust harder. His stone sac nearly exploded.

"Celestina," his throat caught, "Please turn around."

She smacked his thighs. "*Unca, unca, unca.*"

"Use words...talk to me."

"*Unca, unca, unca.*"

The pressure between his legs mounted. "Stop...hit...ting."

Her hand only swatted harder. The sound snapped the night air like a bullwhip. And then he peaked. A shower of burning rain sprayed into her. She slipped off him. Panting, he lay on the bare ground like a bird with a broken wing.

But in no time her gusto was back. With cold hands she clawed at his neck, yanking the gold chain bearing the winged cherub over his head.

He rose on his elbows. "Why take it back?" Then to add insult to rudeness her arm hit him in the head as she tossed it toward the farmer's garden.

"But your Papa's *putto*," he said in disbelief. "How can you throw away your proudest treasure?"

Her answer was to shove him back on the ground, but he was fed up with Celestina and her "*unca, unca, unca.*"

With the side of his fist, he pounded the earth. A girl who claimed modesty had turned out to be anything but chaste. He'd never considered that their first time would be backward...and angry. And now she was quiet as a ghost.

"Celestina, please say something," he said.

A deep and familiar voice answered, "Brother?"

Rinaldo twisted. "Cobbe?"

His brother nodded with the torch in his hands.

"What are you doing by the Vines?" asked Rinaldo.

"I broke into Zola's bedroom," said Cobbe.

Rinaldo rolled his eyes. "So why aren't you there?"

"Her sister said she was around here. Have you seen her?"

Rinaldo's lip curled. "Zola's a witch?"

"Do not say that about my muse," Cobbe flicked the torch and the flame veered dangerously close to Rinaldo.

Rinaldo scrambled back, but after Celestina, he was not going to be pushed around by Cobbe. "Stay away from that demon." Rinaldo glanced around. "Am I right, Celestina?"

Where was his muse? Rinaldo rose to find her. "Celestina?" He threw up his hands. Celestina was not acting like herself at all.

A spike of heat at his bare bottom made Rinaldo jump. "What the—"

Cobbe smirked. He had positioned the torch to illuminate Rinaldo's naked ass. "Cold, brother?"

Rinaldo covered his *cazzo* with his hand while his foot swept the ground in search of his tights. He winced at the tenderness remaining in his lower half. "Shut up and help me find Celestina."

But Cobbe didn't answer. Why was no one talking to Rinaldo? And where were his damn tights? He threw an irritated glance at his brother, whose arm was sticking out straight, his torch burning wildly, mouth agape.

Rinaldo snapped, "I said help me—"

And then he saw her in the torchlight. Rinaldo stumbled back. She was nude, blonde, and not Celestina.

His breath hitched in his throat, stabbing him like a beak in the neck.

She smoothed her limp locks. "*Ciao*, Giacobbe. Did you just arrive?" Her voice burned Rinaldo's ears like boiling sap.

"*Si, si, si.*" To hear his brother grovel, like a slave before his queen, made Rinaldo's back stiffen.

She teased, resting her finger to her lips. "*Aspetta*. Wait. If Giacobbe just got here…that means…heavens…Rinaldo, did you trick me into laying with you?"

Rinaldo shot a look at his brother. Cobbe's face was murderous in the light of the torch.

Rinaldo faced the naked Zola. "*Unca, unca, unca*…So that was you, not Celestina?" He thought his throat might be bleeding. "I should have known."

Zola stroked her throat. "I thought I was laying with Giacobbe. I had no idea it was you, Rinaldo." Her voice was sickly sweet.

Rinaldo grasped his hands to keep from choking her. "But…but I remember you smelling of mimosa the day we met. Why today do you smell of almonds, like Celestina?"

"I splashed on almond water. Is that a crime?" she asked with feigned innocence.

Rinaldo glowered. "You tricked me."

"I never said I was Celestina."

"You never said anything!"

Cobbe's flaming torch began to shake. Rinaldo faced him. "Brother, I know you're upset, but can't you see she's no good, with the desire to ruin everything good around her?"

Zola dashed to Cobbe, falling to her knees before him. Another trick. Rinaldo boiled. Cobbe cast the torchlight so it glowed on her face as she looked up at him.

"Me and you…you and your brother…you boys look and sound the same. I could not tell who was who in the dark," she said.

Her whimpering made Rinaldo's teeth twist. "If she wasn't a woman…"

And then Zola doubled over as though she'd been impaled.

Cobbe stabbed the end of the torch into the earth and fell next to her, but with her history, Rinaldo suspected she was faking. Watching his love-stricken brother rubbing her shoulders made Rinaldo's stomach turn bitter.

"Where do you hurt?" Cobbe asked.

Zola grabbed her belly. "Rinaldo's seed has just taken root in my stomach."

"A baby?" Giacobbe gasped.

Rinaldo threw up his hands. "It's impossible to know so soon."

"But you squirted your vinegar inside me," she said.

Rinaldo was unable to scramble back from his brother's fist, coming fast and hard. "That's from her father," said Cobbe.

Pain rocked up Rinaldo's jaw.

The horned beast stood on its hind legs, pointing its green *cazzo* at Celestina's *patata*. She gasped awake, her horrific dream shattering like a mirror before her eyes.

A loud snort over her head made her jump. Shadrach's drool dribbled on her forehead. Fra Brucker, sitting high in the saddle, loomed over her.

She straightened her dress, which was tangled around her waist, hoping the religious hadn't seen anything that he had no use to see. A heartbeat later she remembered what last happened.

"Where's Rinaldo?" She sat up clumsily.

When she looked high at the tree where she'd last seen him hanging, the ground flipped. She thought she was going to throw up. She tried to stand but fell back down.

"The *scalpellino*? I hear he's taken a witch." It was Fra.

She exhaled. "So, he is safe and no longer hanging?"

"Yes, Fraulein. Now let's see if you can do your part for the Reform."

Fra dismounted and then proceeded to circle her. She was dizzy watching him.

"Remember the little test I asked you to perform on the Via Scalia?" he asked.

"Burning the witch's dress?"

"Very good, Fraulein. I have another test for you."

"Yes, Fra?"

"Stand up." Then, Fra whistled. "Magnaccio," he called.

She stumbled to her feet. "But Fra, he's a whoremaster."

"Every army needs one," said Fra. She caught a tinge of amusement in his voice.

Magnaccio dragged over a dark sack. Celestina glared at the whoremaster; he was always making trouble and she was sure it was he who tried to hang her Torino.

The sack wiggled. Celestina didn't know if it was her wobbly eyes playing tricks or whether the bag was alive. It was then that a spindly old woman unfolded from her hunched position.

Although the poor thing tried to pull away from Magnaccio, she had no luck. The woman's raspy rattle led Celestina to believe she was diseased.

"I caught a witch," Fra said it in a singsong way, much too teasingly for the scared way the old woman looked. She was clearly more frightened than evil.

Magnaccio thrust a wild-flamed torch in Celestina's hand. It burned so hotly it seemed to melt the air. She slowly turned to Fra. "Do you want me to burn her dress?"

"No," said Fra. He nodded at Magnaccio, who began to tie the witch to the tree.

The torch was heavy and much too alive in Celestina's hand. It was difficult to hold and control. One wrong move and the Vines would be set aflame. "What do you want me to do with this, then?" she asked.

"Burn her," said Fra.

Celestina's insides chilled to ice. She was almost embarrassed to ask him to clarify because what she thought he said was too outrageous to be true. "You want me to...burn the old woman?"

"Yes."

Celestina squeezed the handle of the torch. "Why don't I just ask her for her dress, and then I can burn that?"

"That won't do," he said. "This is the test to see if you are worthy to be called a witch hunter. And heed my words, Fraulein. If you cannot burn a witch, then it is my duty to accuse you of being one."

"What?" She laughed nervously. This had to be a joke, like the presence of a whoremaster in a holy army. "I thought witch-hunting meant I captured the witch and stripped her of her dress. When the dress burned, she had the chance for reform."

"My patience is at its end, Fraulein. Burn the witch," said Fra.

Celestina looked from the old woman, trembling against the tree, to Fra, who glowered at Celestina. Rinaldo was right. Fra was a maniac.

She looked about anxiously. "Where's Rinaldo?"

"I assure you, Fraulein, he has done more than capture a witch's dress."

She held out the torch for Fra to take. "I will not burn the old woman."

"Are you disobeying a direct order?" There was a scalding

fury in his tone.

She nearly dropped the torch, shocked at his wretchedness. She knew enough not to give him a direct answer, which only led to more warped questions.

The torch swayed and for a heartbeat, it illuminated Shadrach's bloody belly wound. It gave her an idea. "Give me another job. Put me in charge of taking care of the horses," she said, hoping it placated him enough so that she may finally be through with this insanity and free to find Rinaldo.

Fra swiped the torch from her hand. His air of disgust told her he'd had enough. "Take her to the Passage of Witches," he ordered Magnaccio. "And no witch should bear a crucifix at her neck. Remove it."

With a flick of his knife, Magnaccio cut the cord and flung Rinaldo's precious cross into the brush. Then he grabbed the back of her collar.

"I'm no witch." She struggled to break free from Magnaccio. "Let me go. I need to find Rinaldo."

Magnaccio dragged her through the Vines. In the distance, a great flame burst through the trees. It was the spot where the old witch was tied.

Celestina screamed for the poor old woman, and in doing so seemed to beckon another. Druda emerged from the brush.

She followed at their heels. "Stupid girl, stupid modesty."

"Where's Rinaldo?" Celestina begged. "Please, Druda, tell me if you know."

"Stupid question," said Druda. "Rinaldo fucked Zola. Cobbe didn't fuck Zola. The brothers had a fight."

"What?" Celestina slapped at Magnaccio's hand, but he held her fast. *Rinaldo fucked Zola?*

Sick, sick, sick," said Druda. "Rinaldo-Zola-Cobbe."

"*Mio Dio*, Druda, did you see them?"

"Over by the farmhouse. *Unca, unca.* Fuck, fuck."

She must have seen it played out when she was spying on them.

Celestina tried to grab the gold necklace that Druda spun around her finger, but Magnaccio was moving too fast. How did Druda have Papa's *putto* when she'd given it to Rinaldo?

Overcome with vicious jealousy as she'd never known, Celestina roared and then bared her teeth.

Rinaldo once thought she was afraid of bears and bulls. But Druda's news had just turned Celestina into the most bloodthirsty animal in the Vines.

12

Rinaldo's jaw throbbed. The lark's throaty whistle stabbed his ears. His fingers swept his neck. Celestina's *putto* was still missing.

He opened his one working eyelid—Cobbe's fist made sure the other was swollen shut—and searched the outside ground. Celestina's precious gift was nowhere. Damn Zola for ripping it off his neck.

A chill up his legs reminded Rinaldo that he was also missing his stockings. Lucky the husband of the farmhouse wasn't standing over him with a pitchfork.

Like falling apples, memories from the night before thumped him in the head: the sabbat, hanging from the tree, and Zola's trick.

Ahi. He slapped his hand over his chest to control his panting. He must find Celestina.

He located his clothes, dressed, and ran fast to the Vines, scaling the first tree he came across. Despite smoke that lingered from the bonfires and torches, he had good sight of the clearing.

A hooded figure scampered among the trash. His lip

curled at the sight of her. Druda had to know something.

He latched on a vine and swung toward her. Cool air hit his face and made his mind strong again. Landing on a solid limb, he was feeling almost back to normal as he slid down the trunk. The grass beneath his feet was stomped flat. He gagged from the lingering stench of leftover screwing.

Reaching past a thorny bush that pricked his hand, he caught Druda by her bony shoulders and shook her. "Where's Celestina?"

Druda plopped a shiny object inside of her mouth, and then spun for the brush.

He clutched the back of her dress. "That's Celestina's *putto*. Give it back."

Druda opened her mouth. It was perched on her tongue with the chain nestled around and looked like a baby in a snake's lair.

"Kiss. Kiss for it." She smacked her lips.

He'd rather hang from the noose again. "First tell me where Celestina is. I know you know. You're everywhere in these woods."

"Kiss first." She opened her hollow mouth.

He caught a whiff of her breath and gagged. It stunk worse than Cobbe's work slippers.

Get it over with, SanGiorgio.

He poked his tongue around the slimy heat of her toothless cavern, finding the *putto* sunk between her gum and lip. He swept the chain from the crone's mouth and spit it onto the palm of his hand. Despite being covered in sticky saliva bubbles, it was in fine shape.

"There's your kiss," he said. "Now where's Celestina?"

"Bad kisser, bad kisser." She pointed at her *patata*. "Kiss me better. I want a *festa* in my *figa*, or I no tell you about

Signorina Modesty."

His gaze traveled down to where she pointed. *Merda.* He'd give her a party she'd never forget.

Holding his breath, he thrust his tongue inside her mouth. He thought about Celestina, and his tongue came alive remembering the sweet taste of parsley on her fingertips.

Druda pushed back against his tongue, shoving his dream out of his head. It was all work now. Sweat poured from his upper lip. He rooted his feet so he wouldn't run.

For good measure, he cupped her crotch and gave it a good boost. Holding his hand there, outside her dress, he squeezed until her tongue slipped from his mouth and her back arched. He cringed as she screamed like a feral cat. He hoped he'd done enough to tickle Druda's dried-up cherry.

"I know you felt that." He pushed her away. "Now where's Celestina?"

Druda hiked up her dress, pointing her thumb at the bald bird between her legs. "She's hiding. Come inside and find her."

"You...you..." His hands shook as he reached for Druda's neck.

Don't kill her Rinaldo. She's not worth your soul.

It was Celestina's voice in his ear.

He tripped backward to get away, swiping up a good-sized rock. He shimmied up a tree, stopping near the top to eye Druda.

He aimed for her. Then he shook his head softly and let the rock fall from his hand.

It would have been a good throw.

From his spot on the street, Rinaldo stared through the bakery window. The shelves were empty. Neither a loaf of bread nor a single *biscotto* graced the shelves.

With a lump of sorrow hurting his already bruised throat, he softly opened the door, fearing that confessing he'd lost Celestina was going to result in his death. Simona was surely going to try to kill him, but whatever the cost it had to be done.

Simona was wailing at the ceiling:

"St. Catherine, our Celestina loves you. You brought Herculino to us to free my granddaughter from the pain in her heart. I beg of you, bring her back so she may find peace."

Fixated on the ceiling, Simona appeared to be waiting for a response.

Rinaldo shifted about. He wouldn't blame Simona if she skinned and tacked his sorry hide to the doorframe of the bakery. Glancing in the direction of the *lupanare*, with its bull-hide door, he gulped and it hurt.

The aroma of almond jolted his heart. It wafted from the back room. He clasped his hands, praying he was going to see Celestina again.

Moments passed and he slumped. Of course, it was the air of unused nuts giving off the scent. Simona was still waiting for an answer from the ceiling.

"Signora?" he said humbly.

She dried her wet cheeks with her palm. A shaky gasp escaped her lips as she shuffled over. He stiffened, bracing for her wrath.

Instead, she wrapped her arms around his chest. He held his breath, still unsure whether she was going to sink a dagger in his back.

He patted her shoulder. "It's my fault she's missing. I should have kept her from the sabbat."

"There was nothing you could do to stop her, Herculino.

She was taken to hurt me."

"To hurt *you*?" It was an incredulous thing for her to say. "You are certain that she wasn't taken by witches?"

She stomped her foot. "I thought you were smarter than that."

Rinaldo stammered, "I...I...I...don't know what I believe anymore."

She shook her finger in his face. "There are men inside the church, those yielding great power, who are evil. Who they call 'witches' are powerless women, poor souls driven crazy by some man, no doubt."

Rinaldo winced. It was the first time he felt guilty for being a man. "If only I had been smart enough to make her stay back, this would never have happened," he said.

Simona shook her head in absolution. "She has a mania—it's all witches, witches, witches with her. Stems from Alessandro's death. We can talk to her until our blood runs blue, but in the end, it's up to her to understand the error of her ways."

Simona had said "we." She had included him. That one simple word made him part of the family.

Before that moment he hadn't realized just how much he wanted to belong to Celestina and Simona. His resolve, to bring Simona's granddaughter home, strengthened even more.

"Do you know where they are keeping our Celestina?" he asked.

"Whoever is the *piece-of-merda* who snatched her doesn't hold the strings. He was just a pawn," said Simona. "I'm sure of it."

"Then who has the power?" asked Rinaldo.

He caught Simona before she slumped to the floor. "We're

never getting her back."

Rinaldo flushed. Her claim was unfair. "Don't think so little of me, or of my love for your granddaughter. Tell me whatever you know."

She squeezed his hand. "That she was captured last night at a supposed sabbat is unimportant. It could have occurred anywhere—at the next sermon, at the next bonfire, at the arrival of the next handsome friar riding on a great horse. At the sabbat, he simply had the benefit of using the witch hunt against her."

Rinaldo's nostrils flared. "It was that damn Dominican. He arranged the sabbat to draw Celestina. He took her, didn't he?"

"He's part of it, I'm certain, but he has a superior named Monsignor Baldasare." Simona flicked her nose. "Smells like an orange."

"Celestina spoke of him."

"I knew something like this would happen, Herculino. I just didn't know when."

Rinaldo helped her to a stool. "But why does a *monsignore* want to hurt you and Celestina?" he asked.

"I have a terrible secret that only Monsignor knows," said Simona.

"Tell me." He hoped she knew she could trust him.

Simona wrung her hands. "He's punishing me because a long time ago I chose someone else and not Monsignor."

"But who? Perhaps the other can help us."

Her expression glazed and she seemed to travel to a far-off land.

Rinaldo pressed on, "*Signora*, please. Stay with me. Who did you choose?"

Faint lines around her mouth deepened. "Who he is

doesn't matter for now," she said. With the touch of a mother, she stroked his cheek. "Find Monsignor Baldasare and you will find my granddaughter," she said.

He wanted to hurt Monsignor and to make the Dominican bleed. "Yes, *signora*," he nodded.

"And Herculino?"

"*Signora*?"

"Celestina is in trouble. I feel it in my bones. Find her, and be quick as a priest inside a whore house about it."

13

The earthy musk of patchouli worsened Rinaldo's headache. Doubling his pain was the vision of Zola with her back to him and shaking her hips while dusting green medicine bottles inside the *farmacia*. She was acting like she didn't know he was there, even though bells jingled when he opened the door.

But he wasn't leaving until she confessed what happened to his muse. "Where's Celestina?"

"No greeting?" Zola turned, dangling his marble crucifix between her fingers.

"I gave that to Celestina," he growled, easily swiping it from Zola, securing it safely in his fist. "How did you get it?"

"It didn't take much to buy it off Druda, a few *baiocchi*. All that it's worth."

Druda. He rubbed the cross to clean it, sick with fear. What tragedy had struck Celestina that she'd lost it? He stared at the small crucifix as though it might answer.

"Look," Zola said.

Caught off guard, he glanced up.

A handful of pink dust flew in his face. He reeled and

knocked into a table. Glass bottles crashed to the floor, unleashing the foul stink of more patchouli.

He spit out pink-laced phlegm tasting of medicinal clove. The burning mist also snuck up his nose and settled over his tunic. He rubbed pink granules from his eyes.

"Loathe the girl named Celestina, and follow Zola everywhere." Zola's chant was aimed straight at him.

His eyes clearing, he witnessed her slip an object into her mouth. Then, with no warning, she kissed him.

Snorting like an enraged bull, he shoved her off. He had to hold himself back from pushing her all the way into the River Arno. Never again would he allow her to make him her fool.

They both retreated, catching their breath when a new scent sweetened the air. Orange.

"What is that in your mouth, *signorina*?" Looming behind them was a religious carrying the air of the Reform. He was clothed in a spectacular *cappa magna* of the richest blue and his voice rumbled like the tail end of a lion's roar. It had to be the man called Monsignor.

Accompanying Monsignor were three broad-shouldered watchmen in blue. Rinaldo edged up against the wall at the sight of them. None of the guards were familiar from his brawl in the piazza, but he needed to stay as invisible as possible in case they recognized him and to listen for word of Celestina's whereabouts.

"Daughter, answer Monsignor," said another, who bore all the charm of a black-and-white garter snake. He slithered between the watchmen and faced Zola.

Signor Lombardi.

At the sight of her father, Zola withered. A watchman, as big as Benedetto but without a hint of his brother's goodness, shook her by the shoulders. Her head bobbed to and fro and finally, the guard let her go. "Answer Monsignor," he shouted at her.

"*Niente*, Monsignor. Nothing." Whatever was inside her mouth had her speaking with a lisp.

"Then why do you drool like a she-monkey with coconuts in her mouth?" asked Monsignor.

Zola wiped her mouth and stared at her feet.

Signor Lombardi raised his fist threateningly. "Remove it now, daughter, or I will beat it out."

Just as Rinaldo was starting to feel sorry for Zola, he spotted Cobbe sneaking into the *farmacia*.

"*Va*, go," Rinaldo mouthed at Cobbe. "Stay out of trouble."

His brother shook his head in defiance.

Hot air shot out of Rinaldo's nostrils. Cobbe was hopeless.

By now *Signor* Lombardi was starting to count to three, baiting Zola to show what she'd hidden behind her teeth. "*Uno...*"

She slurred "no" through tight lips.

"*Due*," said *Signor* Lombardi. He raised his fist higher.

Cobbe's own raised fists signaled he was willing to sacrifice everything, even his life, to defend Zola from them all.

Zola remained disobedient.

"And..." said *Signor* Lombardi, "*numero tre...*"

"Spit it out."

It was Cobbe speaking.

Rinaldo slapped his hands to his cheeks but froze when Zola spit into her father's waiting palm. Perhaps Cobbe *was* good for her.

Signor Lombardi studied the object. "Why do you suck on a magnet?"

Rinaldo wondered, too.

"I don't know, Papa." Zola spoke at the floor.

Monsignor crossed his arms. "I know what you've done, *signorina*, now explain it to your father."

Zola squirmed. "The pull of the magnet is to attract Rinaldo to me," she said.

Cobbe's head dropped like a dead sunflower and, in a fury, *Signor* Lombardi chucked the magnet to the floor. Rinaldo remained still. Celestina had warned him of Zola's hexes. This one hadn't worked, and in fact, it had the opposite effect. He despised Zola more than ever.

Hands clasped behind his back, Monsignor orbited Zola with a methodical pace. It was torturous to watch.

"What did you throw in the face of the young man behind me?" Monsignor glanced over his shoulder.

Rinaldo braced himself. Until that moment he was unsure if Monsignor realized that he was present. But it was clear now that the mighty religious missed nothing.

Zola began to thrash about, which Rinaldo hoped took Monsignor's attention away from him. She was looking for an escape, but the watchmen fanned out in defense and there was nowhere for her to run.

"It was Love Dust," she finally admitted, "made from minerals mined from the east."

Ahi. Rinaldo swiped at the pink sand still clinging to the front of his vest. Love Dust hadn't worked on him. Not even close.

Monsignor kept circling her. "And from where did you get these minerals?"

She looked over Monsignor's shoulder. "From Papa's back room."

Monsignor cast an accusatory glance at *Signor* Lombardi.

"Allow me to explain, Monsignor," said *Signor* Lombardi, in the manner of a groveling servant. "These minerals, they are not meant for Love Magic—"

"*Basta*, Lombardi," Monsignor interrupted. "Enough."

Signor Lombardi backed up a step and nervously pinched his fingers against his thighs.

Monsignor returned to Zola. "You know that Love Magic goes against our beliefs, do you not?"

Before Zola could answer, her father replied, "She knows nothing but she'll learn now. My eldest daughter is none of your concern, Monsignor. I will beat her for her sins until the skin curls off her bony ass."

"Of course, as her father, you are more merciful than I." The coolness of Monsignor's words belied the flare in his eyes. He signaled for the watchmen. "Strip her of her clothes so I may examine where the devil has laid his mark upon her body."

Rinaldo pulled his cap low on her forehead. Not even Zola deserved to have to bare herself in a room full of men. He averted his gaze and saw Cobbe take a quick step forward.

"My name is Giacobbe Massimo SanGiorgio. There is no need to make her strip. She is no consort of Satan. In truth, I plan to make this woman, Zola Lombardi, my wife. I planned to ask her father this very afternoon."

Rinaldo's mouth dropped and even Zola gasped, but *Signor* Lombardi's face brightened.

"Yes, of course," said the *signore*. It was clear he was grasping hold of the opportunity to save his daughter or, Rinaldo thought, his own hide. "This fine young man has been courting my daughter."

Zola's expression grew sunny as well. It was unbelievable. She looked happy. But it was short lived. Monsignor had the floor again.

"So now what my informants tell me has been confirmed,"

he said like he'd caught them all in a net. "*Signorina* is courting two men. Brothers, I'm told. Who is to say she is not under the devil's spell?"

A ball of sweat rolled down Rinaldo's forehead. Both he and his brother were now in danger. Monsignor was too smart for all of them.

Signor Lombardi fell to his knees before Monsignor. "But my daughter has provided valuable information on the bakery girl. That should count as loyalty."

Rinaldo squeezed his crucifix. Blood dripped from the side of his fist.

"My words came from a jealous heart," Zola cried out. "A heart that Giacobbe has healed."

Rinaldo stared at his bleeding hand.

"She told the truth on that little witch next door," said *Signor* Lombardi. Rinaldo had no idea what lie Zola had told about Celestina, but *Signor* Lombardi was selling it like a snake oil *montambanco*.

Rinaldo shoved his fists under his arms. He needed to find Celestina more than he needed vengeance against the *signore*. Vengeance would come later.

Monsignor addressed the oldest of the watchmen bearing a gray mustache that curled down at the tips. "Take her away," said Monsignor.

The other watchmen restrained Cobbe as the mustachioed guard flung Zola over his shoulder.

"Where are you taking my Zola?" cried *Signor* Lombardi.

"Where we keep all the evil ones until their judgment day," answered Monsignor.

Rinaldo could hold his silence no longer. "And where is that?"

Monsignor turned slowly. His cold-hearted eyes found

Rinaldo.

Rinaldo straightened his shoulders and looked back at Monsignor with all the bravado he was able to muster.

"Bargello," said Monsignor. The word hung in the air like the sword of Damocles, the way Monsignor surely intended.

Rinaldo's one knee buckled. "Isn't that...a man's prison?"

"Women who consort with the devil can hardly be given special accommodations," said Monsignor.

Rinaldo licked his cold lips. "Is that where...*Signorina* DiCapria stays?"

"The bakery girl's being charged on several counts of heresy as we speak. And don't bother trying to see her. There are no visiting privileges for witches," said Monsignor.

"I understand," Rinaldo said evenly, edging his way toward the door.

"Good boy. Smart boy," said Monsignor.

Rinaldo nodded falsely. If he had to hitch a ride on a broomstick, he was busting into Bargello and breaking out Celestina.

Monsignor snapped his fingers at the watchmen. "Restrain poor, lovesick Giacobbe Massimo SanGiorgio until this evening."

Cobbe glanced at the door, and Rinaldo took it as his brother's way of telling him that he was all right and that it was safe for Rinaldo to leave. But Rinaldo paused a heartbeat to view his brother in this new way. Although Rinaldo would never understand, his brother truly loved Zola.

Slipping outside the *farmacia*, Rinaldo bolted down the Via Scalia for Bargello to free his own love, who'd captivated him without any need of Love Magic.

He paused a heartbeat, spitting a wad of phlegm that had built up in his throat. On the cobblestones, his saliva was laced with pink.

    The last of Zola's Love Dust?

    He could only hope.

14

"*Ciao*, Baker Girl. I'm Capo."

The young prison guard greeting her was no gargoyle, Celestina had to admit. Velvet brown skin, golden ringlets falling to his shoulders, and eyes that shimmered green like Simona's; Capo's smart features were angelic compared to the whoremaster.

The man who'd dumped Celestina without ceremony at Bargello's gate.

If she were able to be happy about anything, it was seeing the back of Magnaccio's hairless head as he left her behind.

"*Benevenuti al Bargello*," Capo said. She shrieked at the clang of the prison gate behind her. "Welcome to hell."

Capo tugged at her and she stumbled and then tripped face first into a dry patch of grass. More sand than foliage, it was spoiled with dark red splatters that led to the bloodstained blade of an ax stuck in a tree stump. Beside the stump was a pole. Her gaze drifted to the top, her mouth dropping open at the grisly sight. She could have been looking in a mirror because the severed head was frozen in a silent scream, too.

She was hurtled up the outdoor staircase to deep inside

the prison, where Capo led her through a corridor of wild-haired, ill-kemp, and sickly women. At the start of the hall, there was a sloppily painted sign hanging from the ceiling. Apparently, she was heading into the Passage of Witches.

At the end of the passage, Celestina faced a half-circle of attached cells separated by iron bars. There was an open space, a miniature piazza of sorts, with an ambit of perhaps five feet.

Three of the four cells were occupied. Capo pointed at the first, to a woman with patchy hair, Celestina's elder by about a decade. The woman rolled a sheep hock between the bars with her neighbor, together they were playing a spirited game of knucklebones.

"That's Anastasia. Evil Anastasia, I'm talking to you. Tell this one why you stay in Bargello," said Capo.

"A monk fucked me but I killed him before he went to hell," said Anastasia, without remorse.

Celestina was taken aback at the graveness of the mortal sin, and of the indifference with which the woman talked about it.

Capo faced the second cell, pointing at Anastasia's knucklebones partner. "Giovanna, tell Baker Girl why you're here."

Giovanna shuffled over. There was a spinning madness in her eyes. "I killed my baby and offered him to the demon to eat for dinner."

Celestina tried to reel away from the woman, but Capo had her.

The girl in the fourth cell had golden brown tresses, which fell like an open fan across her slender shoulders. She was younger than Celestina by two or three years. Her lips were bright as poppies. A smudge of dirt stained her cheek.

"I'm Juliana," she offered. "I refuse to eat pig meat."

Celestina raised her eyebrow. "All right. But why are you in prison?"

"Only heretics refrain from pork," Juliana said without a hint of guile.

"Are you a Jew or a Muslim?" asked Celestina.

"Catholic. I simply do not like pork," Juliana said.

Celestina stared at her, openly perplexed until Capo diverted her inside the empty third cell. He followed her, flashing his dagger and sawing the twine binding her hands.

Beneath the ermine cuffs, she rubbed her raw wrists. Then she glanced up and was hit in the eye with a stinking drop of water that dripped from the flat ceiling.

"Nello," hollered Capo, "bring our newest witch prison clothes."

Nello's stomach jutted like he was pregnant with a calf. The guard even smelled like a cow. He was nearly as tall as the ceiling, with features squashed in the middle of his face. Greasy hair parted on the side fell in wavy clumps.

Her eye twitched as she watched Capo leave. Alone with Nello, her heart sank. She tried to put off his lecherous smile with a deliberate glare, but it wasn't working.

He threw a prison dress at her to put on, and at the same time unclothed her with his ogling eyes.

The frock smelled sour and unwashed from the last women to wear it. It was no more than a converted gunnysack with a faint stain of blood on the backside.

"Change clothes," said Nello. "Then give me your dress."

"Don't look." She held up the gunnysack to hide her front.

"I don't take orders from witches. Get moving before I strap you."

She pulled the prison dress over her black dress, and then

maneuvered out. The hem of the prison dress was to her knee, half-a-leg shorter than her own dress had been. A chill from the open window blew up her legs.

She gave one last, gentle stoke to her handmade black dress and then chucked it at Nello. He rubbed the ermine fur cuffs across unshaved whiskers, which galled her further, and then he ambled down the corridor.

Sick with exhaustion, she looked for some place to settle but there was neither a chair nor a bed in the cell, although there was a mound of straw.

She eyed the three witches surrounding her. Once all she thought about was catching them. If she added in herself, she'd be close, but in need of one more to free Papa from purgatory.

She slid down the wall, considering Papa's witch, and who that might be.

)(

Celestina awakened with a fuzzy feeling in her hand, having dreamed she'd slapped Rinaldo across the face for rolling with Zola.

She attempted to shake her hand awake, but it was caught on something. Quickly she realized what happened. While she'd been sleeping her wrists had been shackled to the wall.

She clamped shut her knees. God only knew what else occurred while she slept.

"What am I doing in here?" she whispered to herself. The real prisoners, Anastasia and Giovanna, were snoring. She didn't know about Juliana yet—she was still confused about the trouble with pork—but the younger girl was also asleep on the bare floor.

A torch flickered in the dark. She squinted at the hooded figure outside her cell.

"*Bon giorno*, Fraulein—"

She cut him off. "You've reconsidered, I see." She raised her shackled hands as far as she was able. "You know I'm not a witch. Now unleash me and allow me to leave."

Fra grasped hold of the iron bars. "I want you inside here, Fraulein, where I can keep you safe." His words were as smooth as butter, but his heart rancid.

"Safe?" She was so angry her voice quivered. It was a ridiculous excuse. "Safe from what?"

His gaze skimmed her breasts. "The correct question is safe from whom?"

"I...I...don't understand," she said, now scared. It appeared he'd contrived some new reason to keep her detained.

"I'm speaking of someone very close, Fraulein."

She made a show of glancing around and down the corridor to prove him wrong. He had no good reason to keep her locked up. And the sorry part was, it appeared not to bother him in the least. She was reminded of how coldly he ordered the burning of the old woman at the sabbat. Celestina had been unable to stop thinking about the poor thing's fate.

The heat inside her turned to chills. "I must know so I can pray for her soul. What happened to the old woman?"

"To whom are you referring?"

He knew very well who she was talking about. "The one you ordered me to burn."

"Don't worry about the crone, Fraulein. She wisely repented."

Celestina looked down and away.

"What? You don't trust I can be merciful?"

As usual, his question left her unsure. Perhaps he'd been telling the truth, and she *was* in grave danger.

A familiar voice, deep as hell ran hot, cut off their

exchange. "Who speaks to the witch?"

Celestina pressed her back to the wall. What was *he* doing here in his fancy blue *magna cappa*, while she shivered in a gunnysack?

"Isn't it late for you to be out, Monsignor?" asked Fra. She was unable to tell if Fra wanted Monsignor to stay or go away. Celestina was clear on what she wanted—the latter.

"I could ask the same question of you, Thane," Monsignor replied.

Fra glanced at her and brushed his finger past his mouth, seeming to say that he had a secret.

She was too busy steaming under Monsignor's stare to care.

"Even in this dim light, I see the resemblance to your grandfather," Monsignor said to her.

Her head fell back. She was past sick of his game. "Why do you torment me this way, with talk of my grandfather?"

"*Torment*? You will soon find out what that truly means," said Monsignor.

"Wicked old man thinks he's God."

"Wicked?" Monsignor's eyes bulged.

If her hands weren't shackled, she'd have slapped them to her mouth. What had possessed her to say that out loud? The bottom of her feet began to sweat. It was the devil. She could feel his unholy presence.

"How dare you call God wicked." The ferocity in Monsignor's voice made even Fra step back.

Streaks of red and black swirled before her eyes. "I was just angry with you for teasing me about my grandfather. And you've twisted my words. I never meant to insult God," she said.

"So, you meant to insult me?" Monsignor drew out the

last word.

She felt on trial. "Why must you alter everything I say?"

"Wailer," he snorted in disgust. "I expect nothing less from the spawn of a bastard."

Celestina yanked at her chain. "Call my Papa that again and you'll be sorry!"

"Your disrespect has earned you a visit with the *strappado*."

"*Strappado*?" she rasped. The hanging strap left arms twisted the wrong way forevermore.

"May I speak?" asked Fra, raising a finger. Surely, he was preparing to intercede on her behalf, to tell Monsignor he'd gone too far in his threats.

"Be careful, Thane. We've already discussed your lack of humility and thirst for ambition," said Monsignor.

"Of course, Monsignor." Fra bowed his head.

"Sometimes I think you forget that it is I who wears the *magna cappa*."

"Never, Monsignor."

"All right then, go on."

I'm experienced in the art of torture. I'd like to offer my skills."

Her breath burned in her throat. Fra was a wolf in a holy habit.

"Torture is a messy business, Thane," said Monsignor.

"Please allow me the task of breaking this little witch," said Fra.

"You may supervise," said Monsignor, "but I'd like Raphael to lead."

She shuddered. The only Raphael she knew was an astonishing young painter. The walls of her cell were closing in. Heaven forbid if Bargello's Raphael was equally adept in the art of torture.

"Let me prove myself," said Fra.

Monsignor scratched his chin. "All right, but bring Capo."

"Yes, Monsignor."

Monsignor cupped Fra's shoulder. "You are growing into a fine leader, Thane. But do not disappoint me or I'll bust you down to a parish priest."

"That won't be necessary...Monsignor."

She detected a change, a hint of trepidation, in the friar's response. Fra, it appeared, only wanted to serve God in a dramatic way on a big stage.

Her mind was filled with bitter thoughts. Rinaldo, Fra, and Monsignor—they all talked and acted big while her life hung in the balance.

)(

"Glory Be Only to God."

The words written across the back wall of the torture room were in blood.

Capo steadied Celestina, but he couldn't help her breathe. Metal face masks hung from the walls, along with iron bridles bearing spiked mouth depressions. She studied a contraption with four, bear-styled claws.

"Breast Ripper." Capo glanced at her chest and then winced. "They heat it, clamp it on a *tetta*, and rip."

She shuddered at the heinous images building in her mind.

Fra Brucker stepped between her and Capo. "I will take it from here, guard," he said.

"But I usually stop the torturer when he goes too far," said Capo, giving Fra a skeptical once over.

"I said that will be all, watchman," said Fra.

Capo stepped back. "As you say. But I will assume my post outside in case I'm needed."

The heavy door banged shut. Her stomach knotted. Like a rodent, she scurried about for a nook in which to disappear, but there was nowhere to hide.

Fra, meanwhile, had locked a metal weight around his own ankles, and then took hold of the rope hanging from above.

"Tie this around my wrists," he whispered.

"I don't understand," she said, guarded.

"You know how to secure a good, strong knot, don't you?"

"*Si.*"

"Quickly now." He crossed his fists behind his back.

The hanging rope was thick and difficult to bend, but she managed to tie it around his wrists. Her gaze followed it upward, where the rope passed over a beam and around the circumference of a large spinning wheel secured to the floor.

"Now turn the wheel so I hang from my arms until the weight chained to my ankles clears the floor."

She stepped back. "I cannot...though you've wronged me, I will not torture you this way."

He glanced toward the door. They heard Capo talking, perhaps to another guard.

"In the name of God, turn the wheel, or...or...or I will grab that grandmother of yours by her collar and drag her here to take my place."

Celestina's nostrils flared. How dare he invoke Simona. Without hesitation, she gripped the handle attached to the wheel and pushed. The angry squeak pierced her ears. She dug her feet into the floor and shoved until it stuck in place halfway around.

It was only then that she was able to look at the young

friar hanging by his arms behind his back. The heavy ball at his ankles swung just above the floor. The extra weight had to make hanging unbearable.

"Think about a person you hate," he grunted. "And scream."

That was easy. It was Rinaldo. Though she was beginning to understand what Fra was up to, the idea of shouting about Rinaldo was too private a matter. Refusing to cooperate, she picked out a rusty mask from the wall and hid behind it.

"Scream...or we're both dead," Fra said.

She was beginning to feel guilty. The cords in his neck protruded like sticks. Thinking that could be her up there, she yowled through the mask, which sounded like the mating cry of a feral cat.

"That's not good enough. Fraulein, scream...scream like you're watching me strip the hide off your grandmother's wrinkled ass."

That did it. The mask clanged to the floor. Celestina howled like she was at the Coliseum being gored by a gladiator.

And then she thought of Rinaldo lying with Zola, and anger rippled through her soul. She screamed until she was out of breath and then doubled over and sucked in more air to start again.

Fra cut her off. "That's quite enough, Fraulein. Let me down now."

She yanked the wheel backward. The ball of weight banged. Surely Capo heard it loud and clear. Fra collapsed in a heap on the floor.

His head hung and he didn't move.

She held her breath.

"Fra?"

He didn't answer. She feared he was dead.

"Fra!"

He raised his head.

His eyes were a bloodshot blur of grayish blue. She undid the rope that bound his wrists. When she reached to unshackle the weight from his feet, he swatted her hand and did it himself.

He stumbled to standing and without warning reached out and messed up her hair. "Needs to look like...you've been thrashing in pain." By the weakness in his voice she knew he was hurt.

"Are you all right?" she whispered.

"I haven't felt this good...in a very...long...time."

His tortured state aroused within her a burning heat. His sacrifice was sinking in. "But why did you take my place?"

"Why do you think?" He stroked the back of his arm.

"Because you know I'm not a witch, as you accused?"

"*Ahhh*, Fraulein, you are anything but innocent," he said. "But, then again, neither am I."

15

Celestina rolled her tongue around the clay cup, searching for a missed drop of broth—anything to stave off the hunger. Three days in Bargello tasted like Rinaldo's betrayal.

"Rinaldo fucked Zola."

Druda's words circled inside her head. The crone was a maniac, but her possession of Papa's *putto* and description of the unholy alliance between Rinaldo, Zola, and Cobbe rang true. Despair gnawed at Celestina's stomach.

Rinaldo and Zola were together in bliss, and she was in prison. Even Papa's witch was free, Celestina believed, and at liberty to put good men in purgatory. Of the many heads of long hair inside Bargello, none possessed the glossy blackness of Papa's witch. Celestina feared she'd never find her now that she was the one in prison.

A commotion down the corridor distracted her from her gloom. The prisoners were whistling at a new arrival. Her curiosity spiked. Witches came and vanished regularly with little notice. Why this one caused mayhem was a mystery. Also, two other guards assisted Capo and Nello, which was unusual.

As the newcomer neared, Celestina noticed hair that was chopped short like a man's, but also there was the presence of a black dress. Visible at the ankles were black hose, the sort worn by soldiers. Male soldiers.

Celestina rubbed her stomach. Hunger was playing tricks on her. Florentines did not see a half-and-half every day. A half-and-half was a rarity, said to have sprung to life on the moon.

The guards stopped at the threshold of Celestina's cell. Nello jiggled the skeleton key in her lock.

"No, no, no," Celestina begged.

The guards did not heed her plea.

St. Catherine, save me.

Nello shoved in the prisoner.

Celestina huddled in the corner, rubbing her pounding forehead. Some horrible ill might befall her simply by being in the vicinity of such a curiosity.

"Strip," said Nello to the moon person.

Celestina held her breath. The unholy body parts hiding beneath the clothes of the half-and-half were unimaginable.

Doffing the dress, the moon person exposed another layer of clothing: a man's doublet as well as the tights. Celestina breathed, relieved that no skin was exposed.

She watched the moon prisoner fold the dress with care.

And then, with extended arms, the dress was offered to Celestina.

She'd been looking for the dress of a witch, not a moon person. But since the moon person offered it without menace, Celestina felt it would be rude not to take it. After all, they had to live together.

Oddly, the dress was quite warm in Celestina's hands.

Then the temperature of the garment surged. Celestina

shrieked as though she was handed hot coals. She flung away the dress.

Nello caught it like a hot potato, tossing it back and forth from hand to hand. Soon he slowed and then stopped altogether.

"Not hot," he said.

Celestina displayed her palms to show the burns.

Nello scowled. Capo, Juliana, Anastasia, and Giovanna stared at her curiously, as if she were the moon person.

Celestina checked her hands, now cooled. Not a blister. It was her cheeks that burned now.

Capo grabbed the dress from Nello and then glanced disappointedly at Celestina. He said to the moon person, "No more tricks."

"Angels don't need tricks," said the moon person.

Celestina was taken aback. The foreign accent was familiar, as was the feminine voice, though she could not place it. The short hair, however, was completely strange to her.

"No angel." Nello manhandled the moon person, shackling it to the wall. "You are *sodomita*."

He and Capo started to leave. "Stay," Celestina begged Capo. "Don't leave me with him. Her?"

"You'll be fine, Baker Girl," said Capo. And that fast she was left unattended with the sodomite.

Next Celestina sought Juliana, but she was crouched in the corner of her own cell. Anastasia and Giovanna clutched hands between the bars.

Celestina's gaze probed the alien, finally gathering the courage to converse with it.

"How...did...you...get...here? Did you...jump off...the moon?" She spoke deliberately so it could understand.

The exotic creature gave a high-pitched laugh. "The

moon? France? What's the difference?"

So not from the moon, and French; however, the bigger question remained unanswered.

"So, then what are you...*uomo o donna*?" asked Celestina.

"What does it matter, man or woman? We are all made in the image of God."

"*Mah*, but if we are to share—"

"Do not worry, I am a woman."

Celestina remained unsure. "But your hair is short, and is black its real color?"

"The color is all mine," said the woman. "And I am no witch."

Celestina flushed, not realizing she'd been so obvious. But she needed to press to determine why the woman was so familiar. "But it's said only a witch can change the temperature. Your dress burned my hands."

"My dress did no such thing," the Frenchwoman replied.

Celestina stuck her thumb in her chest. "Are you saying *I* made the dress burn my hands?"

The Frenchwoman shrugged. "Your heart needed a dress to burn, and so it did. You should be pleased."

"I did no such thing." Celestina crossed her arms.

"Then why did it not burn the big guard?" asked *la francese*.

"Because you have witch magic," Celestina cried, heart filling with hatred.

"Witches are not your problem, *Ma Mie*. No, my dear. The need to blame others for what is angering you, that is your problem."

Celestina's back arched. "You don't know what you're talking about."

"I did not mean to upset you," said *la francese*.

"You didn't." Celestina upped her chin.

"Please accept my heartfelt apology, anyway."

Though her head remained painfully hot, the rest of Celestina cooled. She had no idea what it was about the Frenchwoman, but Celestina was unable to stay angry with her.

"*Va bene*," Celestina said. "We're all right now."

La francese smiled halfway, raising a swollen ankle. "May I give you two words of advice?"

The woman's foot was bruised deep purple and likely broken. Celestina didn't know how she bore the pain.

"Go ahead, if you must," said Celestina.

The Frenchwoman stroked her puffy foot. "The first bit of advice is this: never jump from the second story of a church-prison."

"You escaped?" Celestina's pulse quickened.

"Had to get away from crabby nuns," the Frenchwoman said with a slight smile.

Juliana giggled. Anastasia and Giovanna cackled. But the pain in Celestina's head spiked. "So, what's your second lesson?" she asked, now cranky.

"Dear Celestina—"

Celestina's head jerked. "How do you know my name?"

"Your dear papa, Alessandro, said it aloud that day, of course."

Celestina's heart skipped. "You know Papa?"

The Frenchwoman gave a prolonged nod. She appeared to be waiting for Celestina to recognize her, but Celestina's memory remained blocked.

La francese finally broke the painful silence. "I met him for the briefest moment, but his goodness touched me forever. Alessandro was brave. It was not easy to stand up to

Monsignor on behalf of a stranger."

The image of Papa kissing the dark-haired Frenchwoman outside Santa Maria Novella broke through the wall in Celestina's head.

"Are you...*are you*?" Celestina clutched her skull to keep it from shattering.

"*Oui*." said the Frenchwoman. "Yes. I am she, Geneve Romee. The woman your papa saved."

)(

Rinaldo hunkered behind a crumbling patch of stone fence across the street from the iron-gated fortress called Bargello. He'd sacrifice both his hands and his feet to trade places with Celestina.

His mission, however, was not to take her place but to free her in order to start their life together in the best way he knew how—though his drawings.

He sketched fast, nearly burning up the page in his sketchbook. His plan needed to be complete by dark, or he'd have to wait a whole other day to rescue his *Celissima*, and only God knew what troubles might befall her in the middle of the night.

The tip of his charcoal snapped, and he rummaged in his satchel for another, rubbing his watering eye against his shoulder. With smoke from the bonfires, nothing was easy.

Though he hated the Reform Boys with every rope of muscle in his body, he was almost thankful that today it was the Via del Proconsolo where they picked to protest. On a more peaceful evening, he would not so easily get away with hiding across the street from the prison.

The guards were stretched to the limits trying to douse the fires set by the radicals, who had tossed arts, books, and women's face paint on a bonfire raging in the center of the street.

Rinaldo felt the heat but barely looked up; he was on a mission and too busy drawing. He wasn't even so much bothered by thoughts of the damned Dominican, whom he saw nowhere. Perhaps the fig was too fancy to soil his bloody feet on the streets near Bargello. For Celestina's sake, Rinaldo prayed it was true.

With the side of his hand, he smeared the charcoal waves surrounding Celestina's sublime face. That one small technique gave her hair "movement." He prayed Celestina would be pleased when she saw his progress.

He added a cascade of stars falling from the sky in homage to his muse's celestial name. A whisper of her breast showed, for his enjoyment.

Finally, he added himself to the drawing. Though he was nearly a head taller than Celestina, he created her as the stronger presence. Good art told the truth.

Finished, he ripped his sketch from his notebook, folding it into a three-sided packet. He tied it with the leather cord of his necklace. The attached marble crucifix, the one he bestowed in promise of their love, gave the package needed heft. He slipped it in his tunic pocket and tucked his sketchbook under his arm.

A whistle shrieked. Rinaldo crouched for cover. A dark-skinned prison guard with wild yellow curls led a contingent of watchmen. The guards followed him like a line of feral cats. Rinaldo waited for the smart-looking capo to pass before enacting his plan.

Earlier he'd seen a giant prison watchman, one who reminded him of Silenus, the statue outside the winemaker's shop on Celestina's street. Rinaldo sought him out. He was now guarding the prison gate.

Bearing a pale face, thick lips, and a squat nose, the big guard wore a coarse cape and brown leggings at their limit over his elephantine calves. Despite the riot around the corner, he looked sleepy on the job.

Rinaldo doffed his cap. "*Ciao*, boss."

The watchman looked skeptical. "I'm Nello, not Capo. I guard only the women."

Rinaldo's eyebrow jumped. He was getting closer to Celestina. "*Scusi.* I'm new around here. I thought *you* were boss."

Nello beamed. "You did?"

"Why wouldn't I? You look important," said Rinaldo.

Nello thrust out his chest. "What do you want, *ragazzino*?"

Ragazzino. Little buddy. It was going better than Rinaldo imagined. "I'm an art student," said Rinaldo, tipping his cap. "May I draw your image to show my Master?"

The watchman's whole face jumped. He checked the courtyard over his shoulder and then steered Rinaldo through the gate and inside. The hard click of the gate reminded Rinaldo where he was. If he had any doubts, there was bloodstained grass and a head on a stick.

Rinaldo fought the urge to run. *Jesus, keep Celestina safe.*

Nello waved Rinaldo on to a shadowy area.

"Why do you want to draw me?" the big man asked.

"You look strong as a moose. Take off your cape and make a muscle," said Rinaldo.

The guard flung back his cape and flexed a mountain.

Rinaldo flipped open his sketchbook. It wasn't Nello he was drawing, exactly. It was Atlas, an image he drew a thousand times as a boy. With a crisp rip, he tore the page from the sketchbook.

Rinaldo's heart beat in his throat as Nello studied the image. "*Allora*...Well?" asked Rinaldo. "What do you think?"

"It looks just like me. I'm holding the whole prison on my shoulder." Nello beamed.

But when Nello's face started to fall, Rinaldo felt that cursed urge to run away. His plan depended on Nello being flattered, and suddenly the big man appeared disappointed. Rinaldo tried to keep the worry out of his voice. "What's wrong, Nello?"

"You said this drawing was for your Master. Now you have to take it back."

Rinaldo exhaled in relief. "No. No. No. Don't worry. I have your image set like stone inside my head. I can easily make another for my teacher. Keep that one."

Nello bounced. "I'm giving it to Mamma."

"She will love it." Rinaldo smiled teasingly and shook his finger. "But not as much as she loves you."

Nello stared pleasantly into the distance.

"Say, Nello," Rinaldo elbowed the guard somewhere in his rib region. "Where do they keep the new girl, the one they caught at the sabbat?"

Nello cupped his mouth conspiratorially. "The saucy, sunshiny redhead that we all want to fuck? *Si*. I know where she is inside."

Rinaldo's fists balled. A murderous rage spiked in him. But he needed to stay calm; he had a bigger mission than landing a killing blow to Nello's face. He must get to Celestina before Nello—or anyone else—did.

Rinaldo unclenched his fists. "Point to where she is inside."

Rinaldo followed Nello around the corner onto the Via del Proconsolo and past a band of Reform Boys tossing kindling at the base of a wooden cross.

Nello pointed to the second story at a barred window. "She's in that cell."

A staccato of whistles sounded, and like rats flushed from a building, Reform Boys piled onto the street. Prison guards swung clubs. Rinaldo quickly counted eleven windows, which put Celestina in the center, before dodging a swinging baton.

That's when, from the side of his eye, he glimpsed the white *stallone* and the damned Dominican.

"You are not Geneve Romee," said Celestina, pointing at her cellmate, finger burning in accusation. "That witch's hair was long."

The Frenchwoman looked surprised. "But you have never heard of shears in *Italia*?" she asked.

Celestina flushed. This woman had an answer for everything. "Burn in hell," said Celestina.

But when it was Celestina's hands that burst into invisible flames, it was clear that she was the one who'd been cursed by the devil's fire. She screeched from the searing pain.

"*Ma mie*," Geneve Romee snapped. "Be at peace."

Celestina's hands cooled as if she'd plunged them in a bucket of ice water. But now her tongue needed to taste blood. She flung her head this way and that, searching for any makeshift tool to plunge into Geneve Romee's heart.

With no suitable weapon, she raised her hand to slap the witch across her face. But her arm refused to move. It hung petrified.

Why, oh why, was she unable to strike the heretic?

She told herself that she did not care that Papa liked Geneve Romee, or that the arms of the woman dangled helplessly in chains, or that Monsignor had already slapped her once inside the walls of Santa Maria Novella.

Celestina glared at her useless hand. First, it had been unable to burn a witch, and now it was unable to even strike one. Perhaps she was a witch herself, as Fra accused.

Exhausted, Celestina hung her head. Her arm, no longer willful, followed suit and dropped. She stayed that way until Geneve Romee spoke.

"*Ma Mie*, may I tell you something?"

Celestina wiped her wet nose against her shoulder. "What?"

"You are not one of the Reform, and you never will be."

Celestina swatted at a fly in the air. "How do you know?"

"Because *they* would have struck me."

The words registered as a challenge, stoking Celestina's hatred of Geneve Romee above that of all witches. She drew back her hand in defiance. She must prove the witch wrong. But an invisible rope sprouted from the wall and wrapped around her wrist. Her arm shook in the air.

Strike the witch, coward.

Fra had proven that enforcing God's word required brutality and ruthlessness. She must hit the witch.

"*C'est assez.* That's enough, *Ma Mie.*"

Celestina's arm dropped like an anchor. She swallowed hard and boldly met the gaze of the Frenchwoman.

"Give me one reason why I shouldn't kill you for what you did to Papa?"

A pained expression pulled at Geneve Romee's face. "But what did I do?"

The gall of the question nearly made Celestina's head explode. "You have kept Papa from God," Celestina cried.

The Frenchwoman looked horror-struck. "Is that what

Monsignor told you? *Ma Mie*, that is not true—"

"He said I must deliver penance for my family's sins. And men of God do not lie," Celestina screamed, "Witches lie."

"I am no more a witch than Monsignor is a man of God," she said, looking pointedly at Celestina.

Celestina threw up her hands. "What do you know of Monsignor, other than he told you to cover your head at Mass?"

"Tell me if I am right about this, then."

"Speak," snapped Celestina.

"Monsignor promised that God would free your dear papa from eternal purgatory if you performed some penitent act, such as herding up a passel of witches and burning their dresses, only that was not enough for the Reformers. Am I close?"

"Five witches." Celestina looked around. Juliana, Anastasia, Giovanna, Geneve Romee, and herself; there they all were. "How do you know such things?" Celestina demanded.

The Frenchwoman's face softened. "I am not so smart, *Ma Mie*. It's what men like Monsignor tell orphans to lure them into the Reform to do their dirty work for them. As much as Monsignor is run by his dogmata, he also acts out of spite. Make no mistake—Monsignor hates me above all for challenging him and the paternalistic ways of the Roman Catholic Church."

Celestina searched for the meaning behind the woman's words. "But what does that have to do with me?"

Though burdened by shackles, Geneve Romee leaned closer. "By allowing myself to be captured, I'd hoped to save you. I am here to bear the brunt of the evil men who have put you here, to the best of my ability."

Celestina's heart sparked back to life. An uncontrollable sob escaped from her lips, accompanied by a new lightness in her chest. "You allowed yourself to be captured to help me?"

"You are the young woman they talk about, aren't you?" Geneve smiled softly. "The one with the 'sunny red hair' who fell on her face before the Austrian inquisitor?"

Celestina felt the flush in her cheeks, "*Si*, that was I."

"It is the least I could do to help the daughter of the man who saved me. *Non*?"

Celestina gave a serious nod. "But I must learn the whole truth if there is to be peace between us."

"Ask what you must," Geneve said.

"If you are not a witch, then why did your dress burn me when I held it?"

"*Ma Mie*, the answer lives inside of you."

Celestina set her jaw. She must think harder and better. Shutting her eyes, she prayed. *St. Catherine, give me wisdom.* It was then that her soul and heart joined as one, and there was a great spark of warmth that filled her chest. It was in the heavenly afterglow where Celestina found her answer.

"I now know," Celestina said purposefully.

"Tell me, my lamb," said Geneve.

"I needed to feel punished because I did not fulfill my false mission to free Papa. But, by participating in the Reform, with its hatred of art and all that is beautiful, I have hurt Papa's artistic legacy. And this is why I am so angry. I am angry at them, not at you."

"*Exactament*," said Geneve. "Exactly. Good for you, *Ma Mie*."

Celestina let out a miserable cry. "My life is a lie."

"No, it is not, not anymore," said Geneve. "But I see you require more information. I thought perhaps you might be satisfied when I asked St. Catherine to send you the book of pictures in the fire, on the day the black dress burned on your street."

Celestina's mouth dropped. "That was you?"

"That was St. Catherine working through the Holy Ghost, but I gave them the idea." Geneve smiled humbly. "I wanted you to see that your papa saved my life and died a hero. I believe Alessandro was saved at the moment of his death. What more could God ask of a man?"

The pain in Celestina's head was fading. "So, God does not condemn Papa?"

"If God is as I believe, He celebrates your papa's life."

Celestina stood taller. Briny tears drained down her throat, warming her insides. How stubborn she'd been. Simona had tried to tell her the same thing. But it was Geneve who said what she needed to hear in just the right way.

"I have felt no peace since Papa died, but I now see that there are angels inside Bargello," said Celestina.

But that peace was short lived. The scent of orange filled her nose, and a shiver so cold it burned up her spine.

Celestina could hardly hide her disgust when Monsignor, draped in the *magna cappa*, stood squarely before her cell. Capo and Nello were behind him, and Fra, protectively holding his shoulder, was to the side.

Though Fra had sacrificed by taking her place on the *strappado*, Celestina felt little sympathy for his pain. Geneve's arrival severed all loyalty to the young religious.

"*Signorina* DiCapria, you let the Frenchwoman's dress slip through your careless hands, I hear," said Monsignor. "Poor Papa Alessandro is doomed to purgatory. But all is not lost. Let's put our heads together and think up a different penance for you to perform to save your papa's soul."

Celestina crossed her arms over her chest. No longer did she believe that every pronouncement uttered by Monsignor was the word of God. To trust that Papa was with Mamma in heaven felt true now, thanks to Geneve.

Geneve rattled her chains. It stole Monsignor's attention from Celestina.

"God alone is judge, not you, Monsignor," Geneve said. "And if Alessandro is not in heaven, what hope is there for any of us?"

Monsignor's face was stone. "What the French Witch says is ignorant."

"But if what I say and believe is meaningless, then why do you charge me with heresy seventy times over?"

Celestina slapped her hand over her mouth. *Madre mia.* Seventy.

"And guilty of each, I am sure." Monsignor's lip curled.

"I expect such condemnation from one who orders women mortally wounded and masterpieces burned," said Geneve.

"My mission from God is to make Florence pure," said Monsignor.

"So, you destroy culture in the name of Jesus Christ?"

"You are getting dangerously close to seventy-one accusations, *signora.*"

A drop of sweat rolled down Celestina's back. She wished Geneve would back off. Monsignor was acting defensive, which always brought dire consequences.

But Geneve persisted. "Your Florence is a place of inequity, where women are slapped as slaves for disobedience, but where men are hailed as pious when they strike."

Monsignor smiled with malice. "You understand my

vision of the New Jerusalem all too well."

"Understand, never. But I do see through your delusion," Geneve said.

"That's seventy-two charges." Monsignor's jaw twitched.

Celestina scowled at Fra. It seemed he purposely did not look at her. Was he seeing the evil his superior wrought?

"I demand to see Lorenzo de' Medici," said Geneve.

Celestina cocked her head. It was an odd turn that Geneve took. Monsignor pounded his chest, swallowing a newfound cough.

"And why is that?" Monsignor swiped his eye.

"So that *il Magnifico* can view the deplorable condition of this prison and remedy it," said Geneve. "And before you say anything else, I know, Monsignor, that's indiscretion number seventy-three."

Monsignor stared narrowly at Geneve. "You've been inside Bargello for half of one day, and you're already complaining." He looked her up and down. "Missing the nuns at your cozy church-prison, *signora*?"

"This is not about me." Geneve swung one shackled hand in Juliana's direction. "Why is this child in prison?"

Juliana's chest swelled at the attention. "They say I am a heretic because I do not eat pork, but I simply retch at the taste of pig meat."

There was a new defiance in Juliana's manner and tone. Geneve was rubbing off; however, in Juliana's case, perhaps it was not a good thing. Monsignor would make the girl pay.

Not even a heartbeat later, Monsignor gestured for Nello. The guard charged Juliana's cell. Celestina was never so sorry to be correct. He dragged out the girl. When Nello banged shut the cell door, it was so calamitous that Celestina had to clutch her heart to keep it from jumping through the wall of her chest.

Geneve jangled her chains furiously. The strain bloodied her wrists. "Take me for torture instead. The girl is barely old enough to bear a child," said Geneve.

"Perhaps next time you will think before you stir up the others," he said.

Geneve stomped her swollen foot. Celestina recoiled at the thought of the pain, but her friend did not flinch. "Lorenzo de' Medici will set free the innocent. Now bring him to me," said Geneve.

"Seems you are behind in the news, *signora*. De' Medici is no more," said Monsignor.

Geneve's mouth twisted. Celestina simply froze. *Morto.* Dead. Now she knew why *il Magnifico* didn't stay true to his promise to take on the Reform.

Although Celestina had met him only once, years ago while holding Papa's hand, it was as though she'd personally lost a dear friend. Lorenzo de' Medici helped Papa like he did many artists. And Papa always admired the way *il Magnifico* patterned Florence after civic-minded Rome. Without his steady hand, the fire-brandishers of the Reform would turn Florence into hell.

"And no doubt you damned him on his deathbed," accused Geneve.

"How dare you?" Monsignor began to breathe fitfully. Geneve had apparently slung a rock that bruised Monsignor squarely in his soul.

"I am close to the truth, am I not, Monsignor?"

Monsignor threw back his shoulders. "Bearing false witness against your neighbor is a mortal sin, *signora*, or don't they believe in the Ten Commandments *en France*?"

"France believes," Geneve snipped. "But do you,

Monsignor?"

Monsignor began to pace before the cell. "Everyone here knows who the heretic is, *signora*. You are the one claiming that Archangel Michael, St. Margaret, and St. Catherine of Siena all talk to you. Proof you're a heretic, through and through," he said.

"No, no, no, Monsignor." Celestina barely recognized her own voice. It was strong and sure. It was her turn to save Geneve from Monsignor. "Geneve is no heretic. She is practically a saint herself." She caught Fra's expression, a proud smile, which she hadn't expected.

"*Zitto*, woman," snapped Monsignor.

"Shut up? No, Monsignor. Not when I have now found my voice," said Celestina.

The seething in Monsignor's face was palpable. Celestina was about to tell Monsignor to go to hell when Geneve cut her off.

"I see it threatens you that I receive words from the heavens," said Geneve.

Monsignor turned hard for the Frenchwoman. "It is my duty to judge you."

"*Je me attens a mon juge, c'est le roy du ciel et de la terre,*" said Geneve, repeating the same mysterious words she recited outside Santa Maria Novella on the day of Papa's execution.

Geneve answered Celestina's question before she was able to ask. "It means, I trust in my judge, who is the King of Heaven and Earth," said Geneve. "Not my words, *Ma Mie*, but those of my countrywoman Jeanne d'Arc."

Celestina gave a quick nod. Joan of Arc faced seventy accusations of heresy, too. She understood now, completely.

Monsignor fisted his hands. It looked like he wanted to throttle Geneve. "*You* have the *vaine glorie* to say that to *me*?"

His jaw pulsed.

He didn't bother to wait for her answer and spun for Capo. "When that little witch who abstains from pork gets back from torture, take the vainglorious *Signora* Romee," he said.

Celestina detected a slight hesitancy in Capo's nod, and then the image of the breast ripper grabbed her mind. She now knew how Papa felt and of how deserving Geneve was of defending.

"You are the leader of the true reform, and your words must be known," Celestina spoke directly to Geneve, with no regard to Monsignor's fussing behind the cell door.

Geneve's pale face glowed like a pearl. "Now that you understand that Monsignor and the Reform are bad and that God is good, I have done my job well. Wounds of the flesh come and go. Do not worry about me," she said.

Monsignor paused, finding Celestina. "I'm not finished with you. As your grandmother knows, I never forget." And then he turned for Fra. "Thane, *andiamo*. Let's go."

Fra tapped his fist against his lips, hesitating for a heartbeat before following Monsignor in obedience the rest of the way down the Passage of Witches.

※

Celestina hugged her knees and looking fixedly at Geneve, who was in a trance.

Geneve finally blinked awake. Celestina smiled; it worked.

"What is it, *Ma Mie*?"

"Why soldier clothes and man's hair?"

"*Mais, oui*, but yes, of course, you are curious. Always I am on the run and in need of disguise."

"Constantly?"

Geneve nodded. "I have made enemies of many men in

many churches in many countries."

"Aren't you afraid they are going to kill you?"

"These men can easily take my life, that is true, and sometimes I am afraid," said Geneve. "But God has the final word regarding our souls, theirs and mine. In the end, I am less worried about mine."

"Why do these men hate you so?" Celestina loathed them with all her heart. Geneve was too good for all of them, one *mille* times over.

Geneve's dark brown eyes glistened with an inner light. "My mission on this earth is to teach women that we are equal to men before the face of God. *My* Reform movement is far different than Monsignor's."

Celestina nibbled her lip. "You sound like my grandmother Simona."

"Your papa got his bravery from Simona then."

"Perhaps," said Celestina. "He never knew his own papa."

"One day you will meet your grandfather," Geneve said.

Celestina shrugged. That seemed impossible.

"May I share a dream that came to me on the night your father so valiantly sacrificed his life for me?" asked Geneve.

Celestina raised an eyebrow. "You dreamed about Papa?"

"Yes and no," said Geneve. "First, I must explain that my dreams are more than dreams...they are what I call 'my imaginings.' Both the living and the dead speak to me, like your papa and our saints."

Imaginings? Celestina perked up at the very word. "How?"

"That I do not know. Oftentimes, I have never met those who come to me. Still, they introduce themselves and ask me to deliver a message to someone they love."

"Are you saying someone in your imaginings cares about me?" Celestina cozied up to Geneve. "Tell me."

"Yes, this young man who I dreamed of, he loves you," said Geneve.

Celestina stiffened. She couldn't bear another disappointment like Rinaldo. "Please don't play with my heart," said Celestina.

"I would never consider it. Now, let me tell you about him. He has the perfectly masculine face of Michael the Archangel. And while his body is strong as an ox, his soul is gentle as a baby rabbit. His name is, how do I say it in Italian, Ronaldi?"

"Rinaldo?" Celestina breathed the word. "Rinaldo," she repeated. "But I hate him."

"*Oui*," said Geneve. "I know that's what you think. But your heart tells a different story than your mouth, *non*. Either way, he has a message for you."

By now Celestina's composure was no more than a fragile shell. "I must know," she said.

"Geneve Romee." It was Nello calling, his voice resonating down the corridor. "Torture time." His unexpected interruption made Celestina seethe.

Geneve, however, simply drew in a slow, unflappable breath. "I am sorry, *Ma Mie*, but you will have to wait to hear the rest of my imaginings."

Nello tossed Juliana into her cell. The girl rolled into the position of a newborn baby.

Next, Nello found Geneve. He keyed their lock and stepped past Celestina. It was only then that Celestina discovered Fra Brucker was there as well, hidden behind Nello.

Celestina gave him a hard sneer before facing Geneve, who'd been flung over Nello's shoulder as if she were a chicken about to boil in a pot.

"Don't hurt her." Celestina beat on Nello's back. Each strike unleashed a plume of odor, stinging Celestina's throat, but she fought on, stopping only when he flung back his hand and swatted her as if she were no more trouble to him than a fly.

Her bones cracked against the wall. Sliding down, her eyes implored Fra to do something.

But the religious did nothing but watch.

Nello, meanwhile, kicked the door shut. It was a punch to Celestina's heart. She watched helplessly as Nello chugged down the corridor with Geneve flopping on his shoulder.

Only after they were gone did Fra step to the bars. He pulled the cuffs of his white habit, crisp and clean underneath his black and blue *cappa*. "What exactly do you think I can do?" he asked.

She stumbled to her feet. "Help Geneve, like you helped me."

"She is not my concern, Fraulein."

Celestina jumped to her feet, clutching the bars that separated them. "So, what are you going to tell me next, that I'm your concern?"

"You are."

"Funny, because why have you never told me exactly why I'm here. I demand to know," she said.

"It's the only place I can keep you safe," he said, as though no further explanation was needed.

"Safe?" There it was again, that word. She squeezed the iron bars. "From who? Nello? Is he safe? Starvation? Is that safe? And I know you endured the *strappado* for me once, but do you think being anywhere near that torture room is truly safe for me?"

"Yes," he said like it was an indisputable truth. "Otherwise you'd be outside, with the Reform hunting you down and most certainly killing you for your bewitching ways."

Her head flinched back. "What is this word 'bewitching?' Some horrible Habsburg nonsense?"

"It means you've switched on my internal heat, and if that isn't witchcraft, then what is?"

Her hands slipped from the bars. "*Non capisco.* I don't understand."

"It's all in the book," he said. "Hammer of Witches."

At once she hated that book and its ugly name. Simply thinking the words *Malleus Maleficarum* made her empty stomach twist. She was now at a terrible disadvantage. He had all the knowledge since she'd never read even a word on witchcraft. She narrowed her gaze. "Go on."

"Since taking my vow of holy orders, I have been impotent, which for a religious can be both blessing and curse."

He said it like she should care about his *cazzo*. She fought the urge to slap her hands over her ears but refrained in order to keep listening and make sense of what was happening.

"Go on," she said again, this time guardedly.

"The first time I saw you I became stirred. Now, even if you're not present, simply when I think of you, I become... roused. And there's no relief. I am driven to madness by your witchcraft," he said.

She gave him her most hostile glare. Only God knew what was going on underneath that habit. Simona had been correct about him. His vow of chastity had been untested, and now he'd developed this strange sort of delusion.

She stared at him straight on. "It is not my fault you chose the life of a cleric and now cannot control your desires."

"I cannot argue with the first half of your statement, Fraulein." His tone was ice.

Conversely, her own internal temperature was rising. It was as if her body decided to spite her on purpose. She dared not wipe the sweat beading on her brow. He mustn't know that he rocked her composure.

"Release me from this hellhole, *if* you are any sort of *man* at all," she said.

"That is quite impossible, Fraulein. It's not just this Love Magic you use against me," he said. "You've been accused of hearing voices."

"Who is my accuser?" she demanded.

"I'm sure you know."

"I have such great neighbors," she said with bitterness. Would she never be free of Zola's and *Signor* Lombardi's hatred?

"And Fraulein here's a word of advice. I know the Frenchwoman is your new hero and an escape artist."

Celestina glared back. "*Si*, so what is that to you?"

"Remember this. If you ever try to escape from this cell, for any reason, the Frenchwoman will suffer unspeakable torture. You saw the breast ripper the other day, I know you did."

Celestina clutched her chest. Poor Geneve. She would never do anything to harm her friend.

And then Celestina had a most selfish thought. What if Geneve never came back to finish telling Celestina about Rinaldo and her dream? It was a reprehensible thing to be worried about, a dream when Geneve faced such grave danger.

Though Geneve would surely understand the ramblings of Celestina's lonely mind, Celestina hated herself for it, which was exactly what Fra and Monsignor would want. They truly were experts in torture.

And somehow, she swore to St. Catherine, she'd strip them of all their evil might.

))((

Juliana stroked her shoulder and moaned. "You hide the hurt of the *strappado* well, Celestina. I am not as brave as you."

Her comment caught Celestina unaware. "What? I'm not in any pain."

But then her mind cleared and she figured out what Juliana was saying, which led Celestina to clamp shut her mouth. She knew better than to breathe that Fra had taken her torture. If word got loose, Geneve would suffer the cost.

Juliana coughed weakly. "But I heard you scream from inside the torture room."

"*Ahi.*" Celestina faked a wince. "So, tell me again," she said in an attempt to change the subject, "why are you here?"

"I told you—I hate pork," Juliana said with exasperation. Celestina didn't blame her for being tired of repeating it.

"But how is that equal to..." Celestina gave a quick nod toward Giovanna and Anastasia. "Monk Killer and Baby Killer," she whispered.

Juliana dropped her head. "The father of my friend saw me spit out a bite of dried pork on my way to work at Papa's shop. He always was jealous of my Papa, who is a successful *candelaio*." She glanced at the candle burning outside her cell. "And, so, he wanted to hurt Papa and our business."

Celestina nodded empathetically, thinking of Zola. Juliana's tale was all too familiar. "Everything bad starts with a jealous person," said Celestina.

"Speaking of bad things," whispered Juliana, glancing at Giovanna, who was staring at the ceiling. "Do you want to know the true story of Giovanna? She told me it in one of her... clearer periods."

That there was more to Giovanna's story, Celestina didn't doubt. "*Naturalmente.* Of course," she said.

"Giovanna fainted in childbirth," said Juliana. "When

she awakened the midwife told Giovanna that her baby was stolen. That it had been given to a sterile husband and wife with enough money to pay for him."

"I've heard this sort of story before." Celestina grabbed hold of the wall, remembering Simona's account of Anna Colonna's baby and how Monsignor stole him and delivered him to a Genovese couple.

"Then the healer lied to Giovanna, telling her she did this awful thing of killing her baby and feeding him to the devil," said Juliana. "Their secret—their lie—would be safe because no one would believe Giovanna if she was inside the prison, accused of witchery."

Celestina glanced over at poor Giovanna. How Celestina's cheeks burned. She'd been unfair to blindly believe the worst.

A deep roar from the street outside the prison gave her a welcomed distraction. She dashed to the long, skinny window with a view of the Via del Proconsolo.

"*Ma quanto fumo.*" Celestina waved her hand before her face.

So much smoke wafted in through the window from a bonfire on the street. If Bargello caught fire, with her and Juliana and Anastasia and Giovanna trapped at the end of the corridor, and Geneve in the torture room, they'd never all make it out alive.

Celestina sized up the riot. Monsignor stood on a platform next to the big fire. Across the street was a smaller one, where a crucifix was burning.

He raised his arms like a prophet. "Pope Innocent VIII is bastardizing our great religion before God. But the Reform will once again make the church and Florence wealthier, stronger, and more magnificent than ever," he proclaimed.

Monsignor remained in the center of the circle. "*Mon-sig-*

nor, Mon-sig-nor," shouted Reform Boys, shoulders clasped and swinging back and forth.

Celestina choked the bar supporting the window, the bar that kept prisoners from wiggling through in case of fire.

Monsignor's words about Pope Innocent VIII were no less than blasphemy. Why were she and her friends behind bars, and he was free to sprout bombast?

Monsignor continued, voice whirling like an orator. "In the name of God, I denounce clerical corruption, despotic rule, and the exploitation of the poor that is the reign of Pope Innocent VIII."

"*Ri-for-ma! Ri-for-ma,*" chanted Reform Boys.

Monsignor growled savagely. "But by far Innocent's greatest sin is bestowing favors to family members, lovers, and illegitimate children. The scourge of nepotism is everywhere, even inside the halls of that giant prison." He pointed straight at her window. Reform Boys followed his finger with lewd expressions on their faces.

She leaned back out of their sight. It had to be a coincidence, she assumed, that he pointed at her window.

Furtively, she peeked again. She spotted one head, alone in its blackness and luster. With a straw broom, Fra batted down flames sprouting from the burning cross.

When the smoke from the small fire cleared, Celestina was able to make out what Fra was trying to save. "It cannot be so." She squinted to make certain.

"What do you see that vexes you?" asked Juliana.

"The Reform Boys are burning...*my* dress." She was insulted, enraged, and wholly sure it was her dress. The white ermine cuffs gave it away.

Fra Brucker, at least, had tried to salvage it but now she'd lost sight of him in the chaos. But the reason for his action stumped her. He had called her a witch, after all. What was it to him if her dress burned?

She searched the crowd for him, but finding Fra in the upheaval was like looking for a slug in a sack of coarsely ground wheat. Impossible.

It was then that she saw another. Her breath hitched. She leaned forward so her forehead pressed against the window bars. The young bull from Settignano lunged forward, reached past the fire, and ripped the ermine cuff off her burning dress.

She retracted her own hand as if she could save him, but after Rinaldo rubbed the scrap of fur against his cheek, she let out a huge breath. He remained unburned.

Celestina no longer bothered to look for Fra among the others on the street. She was starved for Rinaldo and couldn't keep her gaze from his finely chiseled features.

Even the sharp whistle from the street didn't distract her from Rinaldo. Not even the onslaught of rocks, thrown by *ragazzi*, hammering the outside wall of the prison like a hailstorm, made her turn from him. It was only in the next barrage that she lost sight of him. Because, instead of watching him, her eye was on the small package he threw her way. It whirled through her barred window and onto the floor of her cell.

She had to duck or it would have smacked her in the lips.

Celestina stared at the small bundle that sailed through the window like a shooting star, though it looked to be a page folded to the size of a barley cake rather than anything celestial.

She stepped away from it, and then toward it. Rinaldo had tied his leather necklace and marble crucifix around the packet, which was why it was able to fly so far. Seeing her betrothal gift again made her jumpy. Somehow Rinaldo found it after Magnaccio cut the cord from her neck.

Cautiously she reached for the packet, wondering what it meant. Was Rinaldo trying to make up for his betrayal with Zola? It seemed impossible that he'd know she'd found out. She snapped back her hand. Perhaps the paper contained something bad that would make her upset.

She pinned her fists to her hips. What audacity Rinaldo SanGiorgio possessed. A great heat flushed through her. Did he foolishly believe her betrothal promise stood after he coupled with Zola?

She glared at the packet. What did Rinaldo expect her to do with that thing, intriguing as it might be? Was she supposed to slide across the filthy floor on her knees, rip it open, and then faint in joyous gratitude?

Never again would she fall for his tricks. She wasn't opening his packet.

The only way she'd change her mind was if an angel appeared in her cell and convinced her it was a good idea. And she needn't worry about that. With Geneve in the torture room, there wasn't a good spirit within throwing distance of Bargello.

Outside on the Via del Proconsolo, a man screamed. It was so pained a cry that she tried to escape it by sinking her head between her shoulders.

She was not wrong about the absence of good spirits.

She left the packet where it was and peered out of the window. On the street, watchmen swung spiked balls on chains. She looked for Rinaldo, but there was no sign of him.

The bonfire now raged like a scene in Dante's Inferno. Prison watchmen had taken command of the riot, shouting and corralling Reform Boys.

City guards barreled down the Via del Proconsolo, flat clubs striking at knees and hobbling protesters. Off to the side, a young man with brown, wavy hair had his back to a watchman with a long spear.

"Rinaldo, watch out," she cried. His name ripped her throat, but her voice was no louder than a calf's in a stampede.

The spear pierced the young man's back and he crumbled onto the street. It was only then she saw that the victim was of slight build and no more than fourteen years old or thereabouts. She slapped her hand over her mouth, *Thank you, St. Catherine, for sparing Rinaldo.*

She tore away from the window. Why had St. Catherine spared Rinaldo and not the younger boy? And why was Celestina still praying for Rinaldo? She hated him.

It was then that a cinder drifted through her window. She dodged before it hit her face. It landed a thumb's width from Rinaldo's packet. Loyalty for the vexatious packet spiked inside her, and she dashed over and stamped the ember dead. Then she stomped her foot again for good measure.

She loomed over the packet. What an *idiota* she was. She should have let it burn.

Down the corridor, Nello ordered prisoners to back away from their cell doors. If he discovered the packet, she'd face a whipping for concealed contraband. She kicked Rinaldo's little gift to a dark corner. Then, she heard a rustling on the other side of her cell door.

She pinned her hands against her stomach and spun around.

In the doorway stood something else she'd like to kick.

16

The Via del Proconsolo smoked from bonfires. The Reform Boys had either escaped or were captured. Prison watchmen were inside proceeding with the new hoard, and Rinaldo was feeling blessed with opportunity.

The waxing moon threw good light, making it easy for him to hammer at the outside prison wall. Within moments he'd cleaned the flaking mortar surrounding a four-foot-wide by two-foot-tall brick. Never had he expected it to give way so easily. To keep up his strength he mined his pocket for a strip of dried pork, tore off a celebratory bite with his teeth, and saved the rest for later.

Everything was going his way. With the wall almost breached, he was that much closer to Celestina. And with the guards occupied, what could go wrong?

But, then, his back stiffened. There was a shuffle on the street. He started to hide when a mangy dog appeared in the moonlight.

"*Shhh*. Go now, eat," said Rinaldo, fetching the remaining pork strip from his pocket and throwing it across the street. The dog scampered off and Rinaldo resumed prying and pushing until the brick toppled inside the prison wall.

He considered how to angle his body through the open rectangle but was interrupted by more footsteps. He turned to run off the dog, but when a wide-shouldered figure ran through the shadow cast by the building, Rinaldo's tongue dried to dust.

Mannaggia la miseria. Rinaldo rose quickly, standing flush to the wall, trying his best to hide the hole. It was then, from the new angle, that he recognized the *ragazzo*. He slapped his thigh in irritation. It was Giacobbe.

Heart banging inside his chest, Rinaldo threw tools through the hole and shimmied inside. He must find Celestina before Cobbe became involved and Rinaldo's near perfect break-in broke down into a mess.

It was pitch black inside the prison. He floundered in setting the large brick back inside the wall as the dark was making matters harder. He finished securing the brick only to discover another barrier. The damned fortress Bargello had a second inner wall.

He punched it, but his fist was no wrecking ball. Doubling over, he cradled his bruised knuckles to his chest. If he was going to make it all the way to Celestina, he needed to keep his head.

He groped the bulwark with his good hand, found a damp area, and dug out sludge-like mortar. The bricks were simple to push, and he slipped easily through the passageway.

Going forward he stumbled into the bottom step of a hidden staircase. At the top, he was thwarted by another barrier.

His hand examined a door, thinning with dry rot and sticky in the frame. A hard shove broke the seal and he was inside. Light from wall torches was suitable enough for him to see.

Before him were three corridors. Celestina could be ten steps away in one direction or a *mille* in the other.

He picked the left corridor and ventured around the corner. He ran smack into another wall, this one with beady eyes.

"Where do you think you're going?" asked Nello.

Rinaldo's gaze darted around the corridor, searching for an excuse. *Ahi.* Above Nello's head, there was a long row of notorious-looking portraits.

Rinaldo pointed at them. "I'm studying the paintings."

"What business do you have with the *Pitture Infamanti*?" asked Nello.

"I'm not only your little buddy, but I'm an art student, remember? *A proposito*, by the way, by the way, when you left to eat, did you have a chance to show mamma the picture I drew of you, Signor Adonis?"

Nello lit up. "Mamma said your drawing looked just like me, her baby ox."

"It's a good pet name. Suits you."

Steady yourself, SanGiorgio.

He lowered his shoulder in an attempt to squeeze past Nello. "*Allora* then, I'll be on my way. I have to draw now."

Nello caught the back of Rinaldo's neck. "Draw what?"

"The witch, of course." Rinaldo squirmed.

"The sunshiny redhead? I just saw her. Think she likes me."

Rinaldo's stomach flipped. He hated when Nello talked about Celestina and he forced himself to take a deep breath to remain calm so as not to throw a punch. The only consolation was at least he knew she was still alive.

"*Si*. I've received a commission to paint her for the *Pitture*

Infamanti." Rinaldo pointed at a bare spot. "It's going there."

Nello's hand slipped from Rinaldo's neck, and a considerable weight lifted. The big man began to grope his underbelly. Rinaldo rubbed his eyelid while Nello serviced his huge groin.

"We need a lady on the wall so draw her good," Nello grunted. "Then every time I pass, I can shoot her with *madre d'acido*."

Rinaldo had to hold himself back from lunging at the *pezzo di merda*. For now, he'd play like they were true countrymen, but he swore he'd get even with the piece of shit in his own way after Celestina was safe and far from Bargello.

Swallowing his disgust, Rinaldo asked, "So where do I find the little witch?"

Nello's face jiggled like a plate of congealed gristle. "Straight past the men's corridor...then keep walking...she's at the end of the Passage of Witches," he panted.

A sharp whistle from behind sobered Nello cold. Rinaldo's blood turned to ice, too. With Nello blocking the narrow corridor, there was nowhere for Rinaldo to run.

"Nello, fetch that French witch from the torture room," shouted a nervous-voiced watchman who'd appeared at the end of the corridor.

"*Sodomita?*" The big man turned to question. Rinaldo, heart pounding, slipped behind him for cover.

"*Si, si, si,*" the other guard responded with urgency. "We need every convict in their cell and accounted for. Some son of a bitch breached the wall and he's going to help some other *bastardo* escape."

The anxious guard's footsteps faded. Nello turned to Rinaldo, who clenched his jaw, preparing for the back of Nello's hand, which could break Rinaldo's chin in one blow.

Surely Nello realized it was Rinaldo who the other guards hunted.

Instead, Nello clamped Rinaldo by the shoulders. The end was near. Nello was simply going to break Rinaldo in half.

Goodbye, Celestina, I'll see you in heaven.

Nello swung him around like he weighed no more than a stick of charcoal.

We can have our first dance with the angels, Celestina.

And then Nello set him down and let go.

Fighting the urge to run away, Rinaldo hung back in order to fake the air of innocence. Nello, meanwhile, pounded down the corridor and shouted, "*Sodomita*, here I come."

Before Nello had second thoughts and returned for him, Rinaldo fled the *Pitture Infamanti*. He paused a heartbeat to consider who might be around the corner before proceeding, and he thanked God he did. A pair of men who he was unable to see, but could hear, talked nearby.

Rinaldo slid into a shadow and crouched, safe from torchlight. The men talking were a dozen footsteps from him, perhaps less.

"Check on the status of the break-in," said one.

Rinaldo's eyes widened.

It was Monsignor. The man he was talking to remained a mystery.

"Then come fetch me. We need to talk about that little witch, Simona's granddaughter," Monsignor continued.

Rinaldo checked his gasp. *Mio Dio*. If *Celissima* didn't need him to escape, he would have risked everything for one crack at Monsignor's nose.

"But what disobedience has she committed, Monsignor?"

Rinaldo seethed at the sound of the other voice.

It was the Dominican.

So now the *stronzo* religious cared about Celestina? Rinaldo tried to tamp down his wild breathing to hear what trick the lying Dominican was up to.

"If I didn't know better, I would say you were reconsidering your vows, Thane." Monsignor's jab was clearly intended for the Dominican, but it stabbed Rinaldo like a double-bladed dagger. He could not allow a single one of these *luridi branco di cani bastardi*, these filthy bunch of sons-of-bitches, near Celestina.

"Or you're plotting against me to take over as Supreme Master. Which is it?" asked Monsignor.

"I seek only to create in Florence a Christian state, free of demons," said the Dominican. Rinaldo shook his head. He wasn't believing a word of it.

"Not the world?" asked Monsignor.

"I will leave the rest of the earth to you, Monsignor."

"All right, then, Thane. But watch yourself with that girl—the women in that family have beguiling ways."

"Always, Monsignor. Chastity and obedience are everything to me." There was a hard edge to his words, but Rinaldo knew better. The religious spoke false.

"Then do not make me question you again, Thane."

"Yes, Monsignor."

Rinaldo's clenched fists swelled. The perfectly calibrated way in which the Dominican spoke to the *monsignore* betrayed his lust for Celestina. The Dominican was up to something bad.

In his flight from Monsignor, the Dominican's stiff habit grazed Rinaldo's knee. Rinaldo bit hard on his lip to prevent even a wisp of sound. Gauging footsteps, it seemed Monsignor went the other way.

Rescuing Celestina was not going to be as easy as Rinaldo

had once imagined, not with the unchaste Dominican going for her, too.

))(

Celestina rushed the iron-barred door, shouting after Capo. "You take away Geneve...and bring this...this...two-timing wet rag in her place?"

Capo shielded the new prisoner. "Don't make me mad, Baker Girl. I've no time for lady games, not with Monsignor's damn witch burning coming up later."

Bong.

Montanina. Celestina's stomach rolled.

Bong.

"Is it Geneve?" Her voice caught in her throat. "Is she going to burn, Capo?"

"You think I'm in their inner circle?" asked Capo. "Now don't make trouble, Baker Girl," he said and was off.

"Backstabber," shouted Celestina after him.

The leftover echo of Montanina rang in Celestina's ear as she clutched the front of her prison-issued sack, sizing up Zola's dark-gold *gonnella*. Her Via Scalia neighbor and new cellmate had never owned a garment anywhere near that nice, until now.

"So, did you couple with Capo in order to earn such a pretty garment?" It was mean, but Celestina thought the question fair.

Zola swiped the wrinkles from the flowing sleeves. "The one I seduced is higher than an everyday capo. And I did it for us, Celestina. Your cute Capo now has orders to take care of both of us."

"Capo has always been all right to me. I don't need you for that," Celestina snorted. "And since when are you worried about me?"

Zola's expression turned pained. "If I could, I would put back time, make it all like before."

The scent of savory Pecorino wafted into Celestina's nose. Her mouth watered so bad it hurt. Zola drew the chunk from her pocket. "Eat some. You're skinny as a rabbit," said Zola.

Celestina's mouth puckered. "No." There was glory through suffering and she'd rather die starving than owe Zola.

"Perhaps later." Zola slipped the cheese into her pocket.

The strong odor lingered, flaming Celestina's bad humor. "Why are you here?"

Zola dropped to her knees and stretched her arms. Celestina hadn't expected the antic and leaned out of reach. "You must help me," said Zola, face twisting pitifully.

Celestina raised an eyebrow. "First confess the charge against you."

"Monsignor saw me blow Love Dust," said Zola.

Beans, horseshoes, and the constellation Auriga rolled like rocks inside Celestina's head, but Love Dust was new.

"And who's the victim?" Celestina sighed as if she needed to ask.

"Rinaldo," said Zola. "I threw it at him after I tricked him into coupling."

Celestina crossed her arms, lamenting that Druda had indeed told the truth, perhaps one of the few times ever. She scowled at Rinaldo's packet on the floor.

"So, it was a trick? But how could he not know it was you, with your constant stink of mimosa water?"

"I purposely doused myself in almond water to smell like you, from your *biscotti*," said Zola. "And at times during that night, the sky was black as Monsignor's heart. Rinaldo couldn't see that it was me."

Celestina pursed her lips, "Mmm...You're telling me that for once you couldn't get a man to believe you."

"Monsignor distrusts all woman," said Zola. "And here is another truth. I no longer love Rinaldo. Giacobbe has asked for my hand in marriage, and I have accepted. He is loving, gentle, and his mouth tastes like overripe, bursting-with-sweetness cherries."

Celestina considered Cobbe's taste. She loathed giving Zola the satisfaction of knowing the answer, but had to ask, "Is that what Rinaldo tastes like?"

Zola shook her head. "Oh, no."

Celestina's head jerked back. "Does Rinaldo taste bad?"

Zola made a calming gesture with her hands. "Rinaldo tastes of berries and lime. Different than Giacobbe, but as nice."

Celestina licked her lips and looked away. "Who cares about berries and limes and kisses? At least I'm chaste."

Her lie burned even her own ears. Zola was no fool. While Celestina starved on sanctimony, Zola feasted on the special taste of Rinaldo.

"And you alone own Rinaldo's heart," said Zola. "He cried your name, you know, not mine, back at the Vines."

Celestina clasped her chest, unprepared for Zola's kind words.

"If he'd known it was me, he'd have run away," Zola continued.

Celestina stared openly at Zola. Giacobbe's love was rubbing off. She *was* acting less horrible. Perhaps, Celestina reconsidered, they could be halfway friends.

Down the corridor, Nello's footsteps thudded against the floor.

"Boss said all witches back in their cells," huffed Nello.

Geneve, slung over his shoulder, bounced with each of his steps.

At that instant, Celestina forgot Zola, Montanina, and the poor soul who actually did burn on the stake.

Thank you, St. Catherine, for sparing Geneve.

What she was ungrateful for was Nello's body odor. He stunk like cow *merda*. She slapped her hand over her nostrils and mouth, aching to tend to Geneve but instead having to hug the corner to make room for Nello.

He chained the fragile Frenchwoman to the wall. Her eyes were marred blue and black; dried blood crusted the corners of her mouth and her already injured ankle was now swollen twice as fat. And that was the carnage Celestina was able to see.

As Nello stirred to leave, his stink filled the cell with a nearly unbearable ripeness. Celestina held her breath until she no longer heard his footsteps down the corridor. She then bent over and exhaled with a force that almost made her pass out.

Celestina started for Geneve, but she was already too late. If only it were so easy to wipe out the stink of Zola, who'd snuck over to minister to Geneve.

Celestina drew in slow, steady, fiery breaths. First Rinaldo, and now Geneve. Would Zola allow Celestina any one special to love? Mostly she hated herself for ever trusting Zola.

And now Juliana was acting up. She was being silly and girlish. Anastasia and Giovanna had begun to pant like a pair of she-wolves in heat. Celestina felt her cheeks burn. What was going on? Was all this because of Zola?

Celestina looked back and forth between Zola and Geneve, both perfectly still now, their attention trained outside the cell door.

Celestina crossed her arms and cocked her hip, asking everyone at once, "Who are you all looking at?"

Without bothering to wait for an answer, she spun to see and nearly wet her gunnysack dress.

){

He looked at her the way he did at the Vines as if he was sketching her with his eyes.

And all at once she trusted him without reserve, like she had that day, back at that mushroom-shaped rock.

She glimpsed the pulse at his throat, throbbing in the face of such danger. Papa's *putto* hung from his neck. Somehow, he'd recovered it from Druda. Could nothing, or no one, thwart his determination to be with her?

Rinaldo tapped his lips for her to stay silent and she covered her mouth so as not to allow even a whisper of breath to escape, thus alerting Nello or the other watchmen.

From behind his ear, he extracted a metal toothpick. With the expertise of a Carthaginian pillaging a Roman villa, Rinaldo picked the lock. In less time than it took for her to blink, the lock clicked.

She scooted back. His face saddened, as though it hurt him to think that she was frightened of him, but that wasn't why she needed space. The excitement in his hazelnut-gray eyes was simply too alluring, and it was her way of fighting the urge to run into his arms, so leery was she to show her true feelings in front of Zola.

"Celestina." His deep voice shook around the edges. "My *Celissima*. In the madness of the past days, I nearly forgot your beauty. Botticelli's Venus pales."

Her fingers examined her hollow cheeks while her gaze sank to her ankles, stained with dirt. Next to Zola, Celestina was about as appealing as a peach that fell off the horse cart and rolled under the wheels.

But, still, he seemed entranced by her, and her alone.

A shudder passed through her. "Why have you come?"

"I've come to break you free," he said as if that had been a funny thing to ask.

She saw he glimpsed the packet he'd thrown earlier, still wrapped with the strap of his crucifix. Though a cloud of hurt passed his eyes, he asked, "Shall I take it with us?"

She fetched Rinaldo's packet from the floor and dusted it with the hem of her gunnysack, taking care to be extra gentle with the white marble crucifix dangling like a charm from the leather strap. She held it to her heart.

"I cannot go," she said.

She heard his breath catch. "But, why, *Celissima*—"

"Take me, then." It was Zola.

Celestina dropped Rinaldo's packet.

He flinched when the crucifix jangled against the floor.

"No," he said, looking at Zola in disbelief. Celestina, who closed her hanging mouth, was heartened by his quick denial.

But Zola was tenacious. "Do it for your brother. For the sake of Giacobbe, who loves me, take me."

Rinaldo stared at Celestina across the sudden ringing silence.

"I...I...I have to hear from Celestina first," he stammered.

She could not believe it had come to this, but Celestina knew it was only right that Zola take her chance. "Take her," said Celestina to Rinaldo. Fra hadn't threatened Zola with Geneve's life, after all.

"That cannot be what you truly want, *Celissima*," said Rinaldo.

She crossed her arms in front of her chest. "Leave me."

"But, *Celissima*, I love only you," he said, half-whisper and half-cry.

"I know that but I have my reasons, and I will not speak them aloud."

She forced herself not to look at Geneve. She mustn't reveal Fra's threat that if Celestina escaped Geneve would pay the price. The Frenchwoman would force Celestina to run, without regard to her own life.

Geneve seemed to have picked up Celestina's unspoken thought. She rattled her chains, exactly as Celestina was learning to expect from so selfless a woman. "*Ma Mie*." Geneve's voice was weak. "You must escape with this dear man."

Celestina tightened her lips.

"You heard her, Celestina. Quit playing modest and let's get out of this hell hole," said Zola.

Celestina's lip quivered. The image of Zola and Rinaldo coupling at the Vines rolled around her mind. And then came a picture of Geneve, the bloody breast ripper hanging from her chest.

"*Ma Mie*, it is your duty. Run for your life," said Geneve.

"Please come, Celestina," said Rinaldo. "You refused me when you lay on the street before that damned Dominican. Don't make that mistake again."

Rinaldo's words slew her like an arrow. The last person she needed to be thrown in her face was Fra Brucker. If only Rinaldo knew what Fra had holding over her head.

Juliana broke the stalemate. "I hear voices. They're coming," she whispered.

Rinaldo glimpsed down the corridor. He extended his hand for her. "Come with me, Celestina. Now, or we're all finished."

"Celestina, make a decision," Zola snapped. "Escape with *us*."

Us? Celestina turned from hot to cold. That not-so-innocent word—us—had just made her task easier. She recalled Druda's trill—*Rinaldo fucked Zola*—and forced herself to once again feel the hurt of that night at the sabbat.

"Go before I call Nello myself," she said in a proud way, hoping it appeared she was reducing herself to some stubborn and primitive emotion that prevented her from leaving with Zola and Rinaldo.

Her denial visibly rocked him. "I cannot make you return my love, Celestina. But I ask you do one thing." He eyed the unopened packet dropped at her feet. "Unwrap the strap and open it."

She stared at Papa's golden cherub dangling from the chain around his neck as he softly clicked shut the cell door, disappearing with Zola into the shadows.

And it was just in time. Watchmen swarmed the corridor. Nello and Capo kicked open cell doors and shouted questions. No one asked about Zola, not that Celestina would say anything. It was Rinaldo they were after anyway.

After the guards moved on, and the Passage of Witches settled down, Geneve's head rolled to meet eyes with Celestina.

"Oh, *Ma Mie*," she sighed. "Why are you such a fool?"

Savage grief overcame Rinaldo. Everything had turned out wrong.

He was nearing the end of his escape at the bottom of the hidden staircase inside Bargello with Zola, not Celestina. To add salt to his bleeding heart, Zola was panting. *Unca, unca, unca.* He swore he'd rip off his ears if he had to hear any more of her grunts.

Stay disciplined, SanGiorgio.

Once again, there was no light. For a frantic moment he was unable to find the spot on the inner wall where he'd dug out the brick, but then his hand went through the hole. He dove through first and then steered Zola.

He fingered the golden cherub at his neck. If only Celestina were here with him instead of Zola. He'd fight a thousand gladiators with his bare hands to get her to safety.

As it was, he was more than happy to get out of such cramped quarters with Zola and her infernal *unca, unca, unca.*

After handily hauling out the loose brick from the outer wall, he poked out his head to scan the Via del Proconsolo, looking this way and that. Fortunately, the street was as bare as St. Jerome's head. It seemed that while the watchmen knew of the escape, they were clueless as to where he'd breached the wall.

He swiped his sleeve against his sweating forehead. "I'll go first and then help you through. When your feet hit the cobblestones, run like a rabbit with a wolf on its heels," said Rinaldo.

Zola tugged him back.

He glared over his shoulder. "I've no time to talk to you."

"I need to tell you something before we go out there."

He rolled his eyes. "What?"

"Celestina still loves you. You should have picked her up and made her come with us."

"So now you tell me?" He was shaking. "You're probably not telling the truth."

"As Celestina always says, 'I swear to St. Catherine.'"

"*Grazie.*" His breath quivered. "It's good of you to say so."

"*Prego*," Zola affirmed. "You are welcome."

"Now, let's get you to Giacobbe so I can figure out how to free Celestina," he said.

Rinaldo slipped from the hole as easily as a mouse through a tight crack in the marble. He then secured Zola beneath her arms and drew her forward, allowing her a moment to squint past his shoulder. Rinaldo whistled for Cobbe, the way they alerted one another in the quarry, hopeful his brother was still skulking around Bargello.

A figure jumped over the crumbling wall across the street. A breath later Cobbe had Zola by the hand.

"Take Zola home and hide her in the quarry," said Rinaldo. Cobbe stared at her with a simpering look on his face. "Get going, you idiot." Rinaldo could not hide his impatience.

"Brother?"

Rinaldo glanced over his shoulder. "Run, Giacobbe!"

"I owe you for saving my muse," said his brother.

Rinaldo's head fell back. "Just go and we'll call it even, you stupid squash-head."

He watched Cobbe for a few heartbeats to be sure he and Zola were safely on their way, but he wasn't too worried. Even if Giacobbe carried Zola on his back he'd be faster than any watchman in Florence.

Finally, it was Rinaldo's chance to slip away. He looked to the south, knowing exactly where he was going: Rome. And he was starting straight at the top to help him in his quest to free Celestina.

But first, he had to make one important stop.

17

When Rinaldo found Simona, she was crouched in a cane-backed chair staring at the bakery floor. The place was quiet as a coffin. There was still no bread on the shelves. She hadn't seen her granddaughter in more than half a week.

"*Signora*?" Rinaldo kept his tone soft as if speaking any louder would break her into shards of glass. Her gaze was slow to find him. "I've seen Celestina inside Bargello."

"Take me to her," she said, snapping to life.

"Witches are denied visitors. And that's why I'm going to a higher authority," he said.

"Who? God?" She snorted hopelessly.

"Not that high, *signora*. I'm going to Rome to plead Celestina's case to Pope Innocent."

She grabbed his arm. "Hold on while I gather some things."

"Why?" In was unimaginable to him that she'd make such a request.

"Because I'm going with you."

Rinaldo's mouth slacked. She was indifferent to God but a pope she couldn't wait to see? Though there was no fire in the oven, he broke into a sweat. It was not possible for her to go with him for as many reasons as he had fingers, but mostly he needed to be fleet of foot. Nello and the damn Dominican wanted Celestina in the worst way. Time was everything.

"But *signora*, the road to Rome is perilous," he said.

"But you'll never get into the Vatican without my necklace." She said it like it made perfect sense.

He slapped his hands to his forehead, watching as she scurried down the Via Scalia to her apartment. He looked to the south. He could leave, but to be rude to someone's grandmother was wrong. He began to pace, pausing to pick up a black mourning ribbon in the corner. He smelled it. Almond.

I'm coming, Celestina.

The bakery door banged open. He slipped the ribbon inside his pocket. Simona clawed three bottles of red wine.

He raised an eyebrow. "I see you're ready for the Vatican."

She plopped an overfilled mesh bag on the counter. There was fruited bread, chunks of cheese, and a piece of jewelry she'd surely stolen from the tomb of Cleopatra. When she held up the red necklace, the glint from the sun bouncing off the rubies nearly blinded him.

"That thing must be worth as much as half the de' Medici Palace," he said.

She wiggled her eyebrows.

"But the forests and mountains on the way to Rome are full of robbers," said Rinaldo.

She dropped it back in her mesh bag. "It's worth the risk. The ruby necklace is the one and only thing that will surely get us an audience with the Pope."

"But what does he have to do with a necklace?"

"You'll see," she said, grabbing her wine and bag.

Rinaldo followed her out the door, freezing at the sight of

an old horse with broom-handle tips for hips. It was hitched to a dilapidated wood cart.

"Well, take the reins and let's go see the damned Pope," said Simona.

He blanched before it all. His plan was going downhill fast.

)(

The old horse Castagno grazed on dry grass while Rinaldo pounded a nail to fix the cart's wheel. Three days of hard travel in a wood-wheeled cart on old roads had broken his patience.

"This is all your fault," Rinaldo mumbled under his breath about Simona. "I could have walked backward to Rome faster than navigating this old cart and horse. And all the while Celestina is withering in that hell hole."

Simona slapped a mosquito. "My granddaughter is strong, and she comes from good stock," she said, pointing her thumb at her chest. "Me."

The hammer slipped and slammed Rinaldo in the knuckle. "Earlier you were crying about her," he said, sucking on his wound.

"I know, I know. But once we're in Rome, you'll see. You'll kiss my feet."

Rinaldo spit. "You can kiss my—"

Simona shoved a hunk of bread in his mouth.

Rinaldo chewed and rubbed his neck. If his numbers were right, he and Simona were to arrive at the Vatican that afternoon.

He must convince the Holy Father that Celestina was no more a witch than Simona was the devil.

"I'm going foraging for lunch," said Simona, taking off up and over a hill.

Past the small hill, he heard her burp. Then an empty wine bottle came flying over the slope. Simona *was* a demon. He felt sick.

He studied the pockmarked path that led to Rome. Simona's plan, to use her ruby necklace to tease Pope Innocent into an audience, gave him a shiver of panic.

Not that she wasn't pretty enough to succeed; Celestina's grandmother was striking, more so when considering her age. But everyone knew that all popes denied themselves desires of the flesh to remain holy.

He glanced north. The sun was warm on the side of his cheek. He missed Settignano, but they'd come too far to turn back now. His feet tingled. *Do not run away, SanGiorgio.* Instead, he chugged up the small incline to check for Simona.

She was a few feet away. "Look at these," she said, holding up two eggs three times bigger than that of a chicken. "It's as if someone was hiding them from us. But I found them and now they're ours."

"Are you sure we should be taking those?" The eggs looked too good to be true.

"You're too young to worry all the time, Herculino. Mother bird's probably dead so the eggs will die anyway," she said, breaking and whipping them up in a clay bowl.

She added the berries and a torn basil leaf that she'd gathered, and then drizzled a line of her sweet raisin wine. She poured Rinaldo a cup. The yellowy *zabaione* was thick and rich and sweetened his mood as it filled his stomach.

Simona handed him a chunk of her bread spread with olive oil and honey, and he devoured that too. After the delicious feast, he yawned.

"We can sleep after Celestina's safe," she said. "Even though I hate that son-of-a-bitch Pope"—Rinaldo cringed at her profanity—"he's the only one who can help my granddaughter."

"*Signora*, you cannot go into a meeting with a pope with that cheekiness," said Rinaldo.

She pushed more *zabaione* at him.

"No more," he said.

She glanced around, "But we can't let it go to waste."

Castagno whinnied, long and low, a warning. Something smelled worse than a scrap heap. A heartbeat later, Rinaldo discovered the source of the stink.

The brown bear was as tall as a one-story building. It towered on its hind legs over Simona. Its black nose twitched. Clearly, it had come calling for *zabaione*.

Rinaldo rose slowly. He tried to keep his voice even. "*Signora*, don't turn around. For once in your life do as I say. Leave the *zabaione* and get to the cart."

She frowned at his words and turned around. And then screeched. The bear answered with a roar that shook the branches of the pine trees.

Rinaldo tossed her over his shoulder and ran to the cart. He threw her in, jumped in, and slapped the reins against the horse's haunches. "Castagno, *andiamo*! Let's go."

The cart lunged forward. He glanced back. The bear was devouring their food.

Simona tried to grab the reins from Rinaldo. "The path is bad and the horse is going too fast. We're going to break another wheel. Slow the horse until we get on a road built by Rome," she said.

"Quit telling me what to do." He wrestled back the reins.

They hit a ditch. Rinaldo flew forward, toppling over the back end of Castagno, onto the ground. The cart's front wheel had cracked in half.

"*Merda*," said Rinaldo, spitting out sand.

"Who's the stubborn one now?" Simona pursed her lips.

Rinaldo swiped red grime from his tunic. *Red*. He froze at the realization. "Do you have the red necklace?"

Simona excavated it from the top of her blouse. "Safe between my apples," she said.

He sighed in relief and then unhitched Castagno and helped Simona onto the horse's back. They started again, Rinaldo on foot and leading Castagno.

Buy now the sun was on fire and Castagno's mouth started to spot with foam. Rinaldo led the ancient horse and *Signora* to a narrow stream where they drank their fill. Afterward Rinaldo was still feeling nervous about the heat and the old ones and led them to cool off under the shade of a craggy apple tree while he went off by himself, hopeful that a few moments of solitude would strengthen him to get them all safely through the rest of the journey, for the sake of Celestina.

It wasn't long, less than one-quarter of an hour before he began to head back to Simona and Castagno.

"*Hooonk*."

Rinaldo spun around.

The heavy wings fluttered, slapping his face. A monstrous black goose with a blood-red beak and diamond collar flicked its black dagger tongue.

"*Hooonk*."

A man holding its leash emerged from the brush.

"How do you do, I'm *Signor* Nucitelli and my feathered friend here is Ottavia. You and nonna over there ate her eggs, and she isn't happy about it." Nucitelli had a wild singsong voice, a purple brocade coat, and Simona's rubies around his neck.

"How did you get that necklace?" Rinaldo sounded as

furious as he was.

"I plucked them from the old goose," said Nucitelli. "Payback."

Rinaldo shot a look at Simona in the distance. She was on the ground, bound and gagged. His stomach roiled seeing her that way. He felt murderous toward the pair of blond foreigners who loomed over her.

Rinaldo's gaze flashed back at the necklace. "Give it back."

He lunged for Nucitelli's neck, but the older man was fast and kicked a bootful of dirt in Rinaldo's face.

Rinaldo stumbled back in a hacking fit. Nucitelli kicked more dirt at him.

"Untie *Signora*, or you will be sorry," Rinaldo coughed.

The heavier blond brute kicked dirt in Simona's face. She curled up defensively. It crushed Rinaldo's heart to see her in distress.

"*Hooonk*."

Rinaldo grabbed the bird by the throat. "Hurt *Signora* again," his voice cracked, "and I will break the neck of Ottavia."

A challenging gleam flickered in Nucitelli's eye. "Do it."

Rinaldo angled away. It was clear no one believed he was able to hurt the bird and so he was left sounding like a fool. Nucitelli laughed smugly. The blond brutes brought Castagno over and in one leaping swirl Nucitelli mounted the horse.

The old horse grunted under the man's weight. The blonds jumped on poor Castagno, too.

Rinaldo stood horrified, still holding a screeching Ottavia, as Nucitelli kicked old Castagno in the ribs. "Go ahead and cook and eat Ottavia, for all I care," said Nucitelli. "I have a hen house full of Ottavias back in Pisa."

One hard kick later and Castagno was in full gallop, the three men bouncing on his back, getting farther and farther away.

Rinaldo unhanded Ottavia and she fluttered off into the brush. He ran to Simona, skidding on his knees over to her, untying the scrap of cloth binding her mouth. "Hurry, Herculino," were her first words.

He yanked the knot binding her wrists. "I'm going as fast as I can."

He helped her to her feet. "Let's get going before they get away," she said.

"Get away?" Though old, Castagno was still a *mille* times faster than Simona. "We're never getting back your necklace," he said.

"You just wait and see."

"I can't believe I let all that happen." His voice cracked. "I'm so stupid."

She stroked his cheek in a motherly way. "That is true, Herculino."

He clenched his jaw.

"But you are far braver," she added.

"Not really. The whole time I wanted to run away."

"But you didn't."

He gave her a weak smile. "But how can we have an audience with the Holy Father without the necklace?"

"I still have the most important thing," she said.

He wiped his nose with his sleeve. "What's that?"

She brushed the dust from her shoulder. "My womanly *carisma*."

He looked toward Rome, just in the distance. It felt far away as Transylvania.

On the outskirts of Rome, Rinaldo threw up his hands. The

wall that guarded the Vatican and surrounding vicinity looked impenetrable.

"I didn't know there'd be a wall, and whenever there's a wall, there are guards. And I hate guards," he said.

Simona raised a finger. "*Aspetta*. Be patient."

He hung back, watching as she swayed up to a watchman. The guard's hair matched his gray Swiss Guard uniform. Simona pulled a flask from inside her blouse. Rinaldo did not like what he was seeing.

The watchman drained a long swig. Rinaldo picked at his fingernails, hoping he wasn't going to have to fight. Raisin wine turned people ugly.

His fear turned to alarm when the watchman cocked his head for Simona to follow him in what Rinaldo saw as the wrong direction. He cleared his throat, loudly. She beckoned him to join them.

"Why are we walking away from the church?" Rinaldo talked hard in her ear. "Is he taking us to the Vatican prison?"

"Of course not," she said.

"But we're going away from St. Peter's. I was thinking we could talk to the Holy Father tomorrow after he said Mass."

Simona waved her hand at him. "Don't be silly, Rinaldo. He only says Mass in the Basilica on special occasions. We'd never get to him that way, anyway. Thousands attend Mass here each day. That's what Claudio says."

"Claudio?"

"Our guide."

Rinaldo eyed the Swiss Guard's formidable sword. "You mean the watchman, who can slice us in half at any moment?"

"*Sì*, the watchman." She winked at Claudio, who returned a lustful smile. "Our new friend here has a room for us on the high ground overlooking the church. Claudio says there's always a nice breeze at the Villa Belvedere."

Rinaldo stumbled on Simona's heels. "Villa Belvedere?"

"It's where the old man stays to keep cool in the warm months," said Simona.

"So, we'll be so close to him?" Rinaldo, for once, was beginning to feel hopeful that his plan could work.

"Claudio said yes," said Simona.

Rinaldo pulled at Simona's elbow. "How did you get Claudio to tell you this special news?"

"How many times do I have to say it, Herculino? It's my womanly *carisma*."

He fell back, praying that Simona was able to tamp down her womanly *carisma* long enough to keep them from getting thrown out of Rome before they had the chance to petition for Celestina's life.

18

Celestina stood before the window. The rain came at her sideways.

"I wish I would die of Typhoid Fever," she said into the torrent.

"*Ma Mie...*" Geneve's voice was weak. "Do not wish to die."

Celestina twisted the water from her hair and then sidled next to Geneve, as always in shackles. "But we might as well be dead. This isn't living."

Geneve batted open her eyes. "You know I never was able to finish telling you about my dream as we were so rudely interrupted by torture. May I speak of it now? It was about your Rinaldo."

"You may always speak about Rinaldo," said Celestina, pulling at the wet sack that passed for her dress.

"I see a little smile. That is good. And St. Catherine agrees," said Geneve. "After all, it was she who gave me my dream. She brought me to a quarry where the marble is as white as a baby's teeth. It's in the Tuscan mountains. Perhaps you've heard of the place called Settignano?"

Celestina's ears perked up. "Of course, I know it. It's

Rinaldo's little *borgo* in the hills," she said. "How do you know things that are impossible for you to know?"

"It's not important how I know, but that you listen," said Geneve.

"Lip buttoned," said Celestina, making the gesture.

"In my dream, Rinaldo hammers rock," said Geneve.

Celestina shivered, watching the onslaught of rain through the window. She was able to picture Rinaldo swinging his mallet, muscles rippling, which was an image to behold. "Go on," she said.

Geneve took a breath that seemed to rattle her bones. "And, so, he chips and sculpts the stone. And then I see that he has carved a great fire from the marble."

Celestina leaned in. "Spectacular waves of fire in rock? I've never looked upon such a sculpture. Tell me more."

"*D'accord.*" Geneve's head dropped. "All right, but let me rest for a moment."

Celestina clasped her hands under her chin, willing Geneve strength.

Geneve licked her cracked lips. "I am ready now," she said.

Celestina pressed her fingers in a steeple.

"Rinaldo's feet are in the fire but still he lifts you in his hands, unwavering and far above the flames to keep you protected. All in one, he sacrifices himself to keep you safe, while at the same time offering his thanks to God for the opportunity to do so," said Geneve.

Celestina's gaze darted to the corner. Rinaldo's packet remained untouched, but soon the puddle on the floor from the rain would catch up to it. After he escaped with Zola, she'd lost the wherewithal to open it. It had never felt like the right time.

But all at once she was unable to contain her curiosity.

She scurried for it, unraveling the leather tie with the white marble crucifix affixed.

She slipped the cord over her neck and fingered the hanging cross. It was cool and smooth. How she'd missed wearing Rinaldo's betrothal gift.

Hands trembling, she unfolded the paper. When she saw the image on the page, she was astonished and immediately regarded Geneve, who smiled knowingly. It was exactly as Geneve's dream described.

"But...but...how could you know?" asked Celestina. "You've been shackled the whole time with no opportunity to peek inside the packet."

"Stop looking at me," Geneve said thinly, resting her head against the wall. "And pay heed to his picture."

Celestina studied the way he sketched her hair, which flowed in waves and curled into delicate spiraling peaks. She reddened at the way he draped a flowing gown over her body. One shoulder remained covered, while the other was presented bare, exposing a hint of her swelling breast.

But it was how he depicted himself that truly enflamed her cheeks. How strong he looked, holding her high in his arms, as though delivering her onto the heavens. His determined jaw, strapping shoulders, and *scalpellino* square chest showed his indomitable spirit.

The muscles in his arms were long and rippled as a bull's. Smiling, she thought that was a secret message to her, of happier days and the pet name she'd once bestowed upon him. Torino, her little bull.

Tights, covering his rock-hard bottom, rested low on his slender waist. If Geneve were not present, Celestina would have kissed the paper.

After dissecting every detail, she now was able to view

the picture as a whole. Rinaldo had drawn himself standing in a grand fire. Inside the flames floated images of her grandmother's bakery, the Vines, and the two of them—she and Rinaldo—entwined in the desire that burned between them.

She bit back tears, so proud of the remarkable way he'd conquered movement and meaning on the page. And then she saw something she was unable to believe she'd missed. In scrolling script, he named his masterpiece, "Celestina's Burnings."

And to think she had wanted to die.

She steadied against the wall. "You are right, Geneve."

"About what, *Ma Mie*?" Geneve asked.

Celestina sighed. "I have been such a fool."

One corner of Geneve's lips rose in a smile. "And so now one question remains: What will you do to remedy it?"

She hunkered down, thinking about Geneve's question, trying to find an answer in her mind, when the torch light down the corridor caught Celestina's attention.

With haste, she refolded Rinaldo's sketch and hid it in the hay so it would stay dry. Nello must not see her with the drawing or he'd steal it. His key jiggled in the door lock. He'd brought Fra with him.

"Monsignor has asked to see the Frenchwoman," said Fra.

Celestina leaped to shield Geneve. Nello elbowed her out of the way.

"But I didn't escape. How dare you?" shouted Celestina.

"The Frenchwoman makes her own trouble." Fra nodded at Nello. "Take her for the *strappado*."

Nello carted her in his arms down the corridor. "*Nooo!*" Celestina roared fire, but Fra's icy exterior remained unmelted.

"Speaking of escape," he said. "I've put out the call to the

Reform. The *scalpellino* is to be executed on sight."

She moved about, breathing hard, unable to stay in one place and staring at the floor wishing for a rabbit hole to fall through to get away from one of the two most monstrous men in all of Florence and beyond.

Her grandmother was right about everything.

"Tell me," asked Celestina. She was overcome with the need to know how the game ended, a game more impossible than chess, a game where the women never win. "What does Monsignor want of me?"

"For your grandmother to suffer," said Fra.

Celestina's heart tripped at Fra's flippant reply. "And how does he do that, make her suffer?"

"Your temptress ways provided Monsignor with the means. Don't you see, Fraulein?"

Other than seeing that he and Monsignor possessed demonic minds, she saw nothing. "I...cannot follow..."

"Your grandmother hurts because you are in prison. You hurt because the Frenchwoman suffers. It's a circle of pain," he said.

The twisted way they thought made her head spin. "And what does Monsignor want of Geneve?"

"Same thing you've wanted, Fraulein. To save Florence from witches, especially one as powerful as the Frenchwoman," Fra said.

Celestina staggered back. The words coming out of Fra's mouth were true, painful and horribly familiar. But that was the old Celestina. She had put behind her so many of her backward thoughts, but also the best part of her—her memories of Papa—was fading away as well. Somehow, she had to get rid of the bad and keep the good.

"And you, Fra, what do you want of me? Or have you

already won while I'm losing everything?"

"I want to keep you safe, Fraulein."

Her mouth fell open. Did he never stop with that absurd explanation?

"Caging a woman to keep her safe? But who am I to be kept away from?" Her voice shook.

"The natural and supernatural. In other words, evil."

"But this place is choking me with evil and danger. And I'm not safe, so you're losing now, too."

He scratched his chin. "I never lose. But now I see that you need more to allow you to know how much I care about you." His words and tone were new. There was more than a hint that he wanted to make her happy. "I will pray for a solution that will bring you more comfort," he said.

He stepped back outside the cell, mindfully shutting the door. The lock clicked, and so did an idea.

By the time Fra was half way down the corridor, she'd come up with a scheme that tipped the game in her favor. Under Fra's thumb, she was destined to die in Bargello. There was no end in sight to her imprisonment, and it was only a matter of time before she succumbed to hunger, thirst, or torture gone deadly wrong.

To die without professing her love to Rinaldo was unthinkable.

But her plan gave her sorry life new meaning. It would bring comfort to Rinaldo and Simona, all by using Fra's desire for her against him.

19

Celestina slept restlessly between prayers, asking St. Catherine to keep Geneve safe. It had been more than a day, plus another half since her friend had been taken to the torture room. Celestina could only hope her friend had famously escaped.

A nearly silent shuffle outside her bars gave her a start.

Celestina's gaze swept the dark cell. "Geneve?"

A deep cough knifed the quiet. Her palms started to sweat. He'd come.

"Show yourself," said Celestina.

He stepped in a beam of moonlight streaming through her window. Flipping back his hood, he said, "I thought you'd be asking about the other, Fraulein. Lombardi's daughter."

"She's nothing to me."

"We bear something in common, then. The agreement that the blonde is not worth the wages it costs for a man to go searching for her. But I thought perhaps you'd be mooning for the one who escaped with her."

"Of course not," she said. It pleased her that earlier she'd sized up Fra Brucker correctly. An eager desire was coming off him.

His hand gripped an iron bar, knuckles gleaming white. "So, you *didn't* pray I was your quarry grunt, returning for you?"

She slipped Rinaldo's necklace over her head to keep it out of Fra's sight, stroking the Christ figure with her thumb. "I denied him once on your orders. Why on earth would I expect him to return?"

"To escape, and to take the Frenchwoman with you this time."

"If I loved him as you seem to believe, would I care about what happened to the Frenchwoman? It would be too much risk and she is not much to me, either." Celestina shrugged. Her ability to lie had much improved in prison.

"*Ahhh*, I see, Fraulein. So, you denied the grunt because, why? You love me or fear me?"

Though the question suggested a trick, Fra's attention had veered from Rinaldo, which was her intent. "I fear no man," she said in her best impression of Geneve.

"Aren't you afraid of God?" He scratched at the iron bar with his fingernail.

"Who says God's a man?" She pressed Rinaldo's cross to her heart.

"Come closer, Fraulein."

She hesitated before standing. Rinaldo was the only man who'd ever touched her. In her heart, that's how she'd wished it to stay, but Fra was the only chance she had to see Torino once more. Taking a deep breath, she advanced.

Threading his hands between the bars he grasped her shoulders. His touch was as pleasant as the barb of a hornet, but she denied her urge to twist away.

St. Catherine, be with me.

The success of Celestina's idea hinged on Fra's unbridled desire for her. And, for the Tribunal of Faith to see that Monsignor was worse, not better, since returning from Siena. She prayed that this time, after witnessing Monsignor's deranged actions and words, they'd send him away forever for his unjust *vendette* against Simona, Geneve, and the women in the Passage of Witches.

She caught Fra looking at Rinaldo's cross between her fingers. "Is that a weapon?" Before she was able to answer he slapped it out of her hand. It hit the floor and rattled, echoing her nerves.

She held her breath, praying he didn't recognize it from when he ordered Magnaccio to cut it from her neck.

When Fra pulled her roughly to him, she squeezed hold of the greasy bars and braced to keep back. It was clear Fra had bigger, more personal, things than Rinaldo's cross on his mind.

"Fra...what are you doing?" She tried to hold onto her fragile control.

"Something...for which I'm going to burn in hell," he said and drew her in forcefully. The stink of barley wine on his breath nearly made her wretch.

The moon behind them fell dark, and so did his face, but that appeared to give no pause to his turbulence.

His hand found her breast and smothered it. Her nipple hardened under his grinding palm and she ached to crawl out of her skin. When he squeezed, she gritted her teeth. Her back stiffened in response to his heinous touch.

And then he let go. Her breast, once so feverish under his hand, cooled. Fearing he might leave before she was able to set in place the pieces of her plan, she served him hard words.

"What kind of godly person are you?" The question came

out like a thunderbolt of indignation.

With the clouds having passed by the moon and the new light, she was able to witness him thrash about. God almighty, she thought, *her* words torched *his* ears. For her, that was a first, and a good step forward.

"I assumed...the iron bars between us...would hold me back but I succumbed to my worst demons," he said in a broken whisper.

Through the bars she struck him on the shoulder, over and over, feeling within her a vengeful surge of excitement. Like a stoic, he didn't flinch.

"So, you make me endure your...groping...as my penance?" She stopped hitting him to catch her breath.

"But you did nothing." His voice was taut. "What could I possibly absolve you of?"

"The *strappado*," she said. "You took my punishment."

"I took the torture for you willingly. Monsignor can strip me of everything I've fought for. But for you, I will face any wrath, with no thought of payment or penance."

The crack in his voice was real. At that moment it was clear that she held power over his heart. It was time to enact her idea of a trial and to convince Fra to lure Rinaldo to the proceedings so her Torino may know of her love for him. Also, Celestina's case had to be big enough to put Monsignor once again front and center before the Tribunal of Faith.

Fra cupped her chin with his hand. She feared her disgust radiated outward, which would ruin everything. But he seemed not to notice her disdain. For once she was grateful for his conceit; it seemed he was unable to imagine that he was repulsive.

He coerced his tongue past her lips. She hated the way it felt, like a worm wriggling in the dirt, and tasting nothing like berries and lime, how Zola described Rinaldo's sweet kisses.

While his tongue poked inside her mouth, she pulled up near memories of her and Rinaldo at the Vines. As long as she was able to retain Rinaldo's face in her mind, she was able to erase Fra's.

She only forced herself to look at him when she sensed he was fumbling about with the fasteners on his cape. That's when her jaw, like his *cappa*, hit the floor. She'd only seen stone sculptures of nudes—never before the front of a fully naked man. And certainly not with his manhood on guard and with its own hooded *cappa*.

The key clicked in the lock and he was inside her cell.

Like a drunken swordsman, he stabbed her in the stomach, missing her slit. When a violent spray ejected from it, dousing her with warm foam, she lunged back.

His sticky vinegar soiled her lower parts, dripping down her legs. She mopped up what she could with her filthy gunnysack dress but it was all over her.

"*Verzeihung.* Sorry. I didn't mean for that to…I'm stupid… so stupid at this." He floundered about as he redressed.

She held a steady glare, praying his apology was true to his heart because she needed him raw and exposed if her trick was going to work.

"Why won't you leave me alone?" Celestina stepped back. "You know nothing of love. The thing you once said to me applies to you now. You prostrate yourself. Before me, before Monsignor, before God—"

"But…I'm going to get you out of here," he said.

She threw back her shoulders. "How?"

"I…I don't know yet," he said. "But I realize things now, things that I didn't understand before. I thought I could keep you safe inside the prison, the way the monks at the abbey kept me. But now I know that trapping a person is no way to have them, or keep them."

It enraged her at how careless Fra was, dangling her freedom before her and then snatching it back.

From here forward she must strike the correct tone—that of a hurt lover who he owes—for him to buy her idea.

"If you care about me, then do this," she said.

"Anything."

"Get me a trial before the Tribunal of Faith."

"If it's what you want, but why do you want it?" he asked, clearly puzzled.

"Since I am the only person alive that Simona loves, I believe Monsignor would like nothing more than for me to turn against my grandmother. If you bring my grandmother to the trial, I will accuse her of being a witch. It won't kill her outright, but will instead cause her to die a *mille* small deaths, for the rest of her natural life."

Fra regarded her with somber curiosity. "Until this moment, I'd assumed such an admission from you was impossible."

She flipped her hand, acting like she'd intended forever to turn in Simona. "But that's what I thought Monsignor wanted—to torture Simona in a slow death. It's my job as a soldier in the holy army of the Reform to find witches, is it not?"

"Yes. It's good. You've learned well. That's a good thing," he said eagerly. "But are you sure? The woman is your grandmother, after all. I suppose that must mean something to you."

"In my ignorance, what I once considered Simona's idiosyncrasies, I've now learned were signs that she is a witch. If anyone asks ever again, I will deny that we are related. I want no association with a demon such as Simona," said Celestina, shrugging as though she was finished loving Simona.

God, she prayed she was convincing.

Fra looked ready to jump out of his clogs. "Yes, Fraulein," he said, pounding his fist in his palm. "Exactly right. Yes."

She sighed inwardly, pleased that he'd bought her little performance. And now, with Fra's eyes gleaming in surprised delight, she decided to spring the details of her plan.

"Well, then answer me," she asked. "As vice supreme knight of the Reform, do you have the power to call forth the Tribunal?"

"It is within my jurisdiction. Absolutely."

Relief escaped her lips. "Then there is one condition." She folded her arms.

He reached out and then pulled back. It was clear he was worried that any single action he undertook had the potential to displease her.

"Tell me, Celestina." It was the first time he'd used her given name.

"The trial must take place in the middle of the Piazza del Signoria."

He looked doubtful. "A public trial?"

"I know that you are not a Florentine, but I've often seen trials in the piazza. Large spectacles, open to all. I want you to force everyone to attend. Ring Montanina three times if you must," she said. "The stonecutter from Settignano must be there, and for that to happen he must be given immunity against his charges of attempting to help me escape. I assume that is within your power as well."

"Of course, it is. But why him?" He sounded jealous.

"The stonecutter likes my grandmother," she said. "He must leave my trial heartbroken knowing that I accused her of being a witch. *Signor* Lombardi's story that she used magic to raise her parakeet from the dead will be my evidence."

Fra scratched his chin. "I see...and so...?"

"That way I can be done with the *scalpellino*, but rest knowing that though his affection for me was foolhardy, it should not cost him his life. We don't need that guilt, do we?"

"It is true, I don't need more guilt," said Fra sheepishly.

"Also, Monsignor will rest knowing that my grandmother will suffer every breath of her life. Victory for you, me, and Monsignor, all the way around."

A circle of victory.

She held her breath, willing that her words were good enough to convince Fra.

"Before I go along with this, I have one condition," he said.

"What is that?" She awaited his answer, toes curled.

"Upon your confession at trial, I will demand that Monsignor free you from this snake pit and then we can...you and I...after you're free...we can?"

She exhaled, and then remembered to act pleased. "I agree to that."

"Before this moment, I have never wanted to be second best, not in my faith or the Reform, but there's something about you, Celestina, that makes me want to follow you, and you alone, to wherever you lead me," he said.

She gave a slow nod, as though she understood and agreed while trying not to shudder in revulsion at the glassiness in his eyes.

"Until the trial, then," he said.

She cinched her gunnysack to her chest. "And see to it that I get a new dress," she said. She wanted to look nice for Rinaldo.

"I'll order up one to match the color of your hair," he said, and she forced another smile.

Moments after Fra left, at the exact moment that night turned to day, Celestina swept up Rinaldo's necklace and slipped it on her neck.

Her shoulders shook as she sobbed soundlessly. Fear of failure caused turmoil in her soul. There were too many ways for her plan to fail—and fail miserably.

"Are you all right, Celestina?" She startled at Anastasia's voice.

Celestina gave a sullen nod.

Anastasia handed her a rag through the bars. She pointed at Celestina's thighs. "That's the way it happened to me with Padre Ernesto. He came to me in the dark, always pushing his *cazzo* in my slit. Finally, I could take no more and I cut off his rod and threw it to the pigs, who gobbled it up."

Celestina swiped at the sticky cream clinging to the inside of her legs. Her stomach curled at the terrible things that happened to Anastasia. "And that's why they deem you a witch?" Celestina asked.

"I'm here for murder, and they say my pigs were demons," said Anastasia.

"Our jailers are the demons," said Celestina.

Anastasia gave her a pained stare. "Did he hurt you, Celestina, the way Padre Ernesto hurt me?"

Celestina assured her, "He did not enter me."

"But he gave you a shot." It was Giovanna. She pointed at the stiff mess of Fra's *acido* drying on the rag.

"His vinegar washed over me, that's all," said Celestina.

"That doesn't mean you're safe from getting his baby," said Giovanna.

"Impossible," said Celestina. "He did not enter me."

"Remember Uranus and Venus?" asked Giovanna.

Celestina's hand flew to cover her *patata*, considering the Greek myth. After the Titan Cronus cut off the god Uranus's *cazzo* and cast it into the sea, Uranus's daughter Venus leaped from the waters.

"That's an old story, not the truth. That doesn't happen to ordinary people," said Celestina.

"Remember when we thought Geneve sprung from the moon?" asked Giovanna. "She's so perfect I still sometimes believe that's where she was born."

The inside of Celestina's mouth turned to dust. It was clear that once in a while babies just happened.

"Celestina has always been stupid." It was Juliana.

Celestina stared at her incredulously. She hadn't expected such viciousness from the girl. "Why are you calling me a bad name?" asked Celestina.

"How can you turn in your own grandmother to those monsters?" Juliana banked her fists to her hips.

"*Aha*, that." As heartbroken as she was that Juliana could think so low of her, Celestina was pleased that her idea had meat to it, enough so that Juliana believed she could do something so awful. Celestina whispered, "It's a trick."

Juliana's face softened. "So, you're not giving up *Signora* Simona?"

"Never, but Fra must think so."

"*Aha*, now I see." Juliana smiled wide.

They slammed shut their mouths at the clamor down the corridor. Nello was dragging Geneve. He was followed by Capo.

Celestina's heart dropped.

"Get back, or you're next," Nello bellowed at them all.

Giovanna, Anastasia, Juliana, Celestina, and all the women up and down the Passage of Witches were reaching between the bars for Geneve.

Capo banged his club against the cages, but the prisoners didn't retreat. Celestina was heartened. Geneve's special goodness was unmistakable to all, well beyond the cell they shared.

As Geneve neared, Celestina saw that her friend was only a hint more alive than a rag doll and in far worse shape than before: one eye was swollen shut, a shoulder was slumped with the bone protruding sideways, and her feet were blackened with bruises.

Capo dug at the lock with his long key and Nello threw Geneve inside. Celestina caught her in her arms. The Frenchwoman was a sack of bones. Celestina was unable to hold on as Nello tore Geneve from her arms and then clamped the frail woman's wrists in wall chains.

Behind Nello's back, Capo handed Celestina a chunk of cheese. He pointed at Geneve. He turned before Celestina could nod in thanks.

Celestina stared at Geneve with horror suffocating her heart.

How could Celestina ever dare to think that she was able to beat Fra and Monsignor? Her plan now seemed unfathomable.

20

Rinaldo awakened to the echo of a Gregorian chant filling his small room.

Monastery priests rise as early as quarrymen, he thought, rubbing his neck. But they slept on beds of nails, it seemed.

Kneeling on the ceramic tile floor, he prayed that Celestina stayed safe in her cold prison cell, wishing they could trade places.

As he dressed, he wondered how Simona was faring. He'd last seen her wobbling on raisin wine and seducing Claudio, the Swiss Guard who'd procured a room for her next door at the convent. Rinaldo shook his head. Poor nuns.

But his real problem was the missing necklace. He'd been counting on it to secure a meeting with Pope Innocent. In Simona's mind, those jewels were their best opportunity. She'd been so sure of it that Rinaldo had never thought past the rubies.

The priestly song filled the monastery corridor. He opened a thick wood door and stepped outside onto soft, dewy grass. A colony of green and yellow monk parrots squawked in a nearby cedar tree, shading him from the Roman sun, which glowed like gold.

From his vantage point he was able to view the Basilica of St. Peter within the walls of the Vatican. His *scalpellino* eyes went straight to the crumbling brickwork at the back of the basilica. He shook his head at the disrepair. What a shame. He and his brothers could build special scaffolding and have the cathedral mortared and shored up in no more than seven days.

He surveyed the hill from the Pantheon to the pastures surrounding Castel Sant'Angelo, his gaze settling on the Pope's simple white cottage, not a rock's throw from where he stood. He stilled in awe and savored his proximity to the most important man on Earth. Somehow, he must meet the Holy Father.

Rinaldo then scanned the courtyard in front of the villa, curious about the downgrade of the hill that had been terraced for gardens. Pacing back and forth, he studied the new construction.

All at once the idea of creating frescos inside churches and palaces made his stomach flip like he'd eaten a rotten eggplant. He'd never be the next Ghirlandaio—or Alessandro DiCapria, for that matter.

It was the open canvas of the land before him that called to him now. Here he'd be able to mix his *scalpellino* skills and his artistic eye to create movement in living things. He pictured gardens of stone and metal sculptures among topiary and blossoming trees. How he wished to work here.

His mind raced, imagining the Holy Father strolling in the gardens and then stopping to rest on a marble bench, which Rinaldo had carved with his own hands. He smiled, envisioning families in the courtyard for festivals, weddings, and outdoor Mass.

A group of laborers assembling outside the Pope's villa caught Rinaldo's eye. Bearing hammers and chisels, they laughed and pushed each other, and a wave of homesickness hit Rinaldo like a sack of rocks. These men were the image of his brothers and cousins.

He rubbed his chest to slow his quickening heart and then edged up to a young man about his age who had set himself apart from the rest, making him the easiest to approach.

"Hello friend, I'm called Rinaldo SanGiorgio. How do I go about seeing the Holy Father?"

The young man smirked. "You? The Pope?"

"Never mind." Rinaldo reddened.

Rinaldo started to turn away, but to his surprise, the *ragazzo* called him back. "Pollauiolo is meeting with him now. And we're stuck here waiting for Master's orders. I hate this shitty garden."

Rinaldo shuffled back, aghast at the ungrateful way the *ragazzo* spoke of the Holy Father's garden. It was the opportunity of a lifetime, but the moody *ragazzo* was in such bad humor he was unable to understand his good fortune.

"When Master returns, point him out, *per favore*. I want to ask him if he can deliver a message to the pontiff."

The *ragazzo* spit on the grass. "Polly is a son of a bitch."

This rotten *ragazzo* was giving Rinaldo a bad taste in his mouth. "Why do you speak so ill of your Master?" he asked.

"He drives us like slaves," said the *ragazzo*. "I want to paint frescos inside the church, like a real artist. My father makes me do this grunt work to straighten me out from my big ideas."

Rinaldo softened, seeing his old self in the bad-tempered *ragazzo*. "*Aha*, I thought that once, but no longer. I would give anything to work here, in the fresh air among these men, creating sculpture from stone and flora," said Rinaldo.

The Roman sized up Rinaldo. "We look enough alike. I'm called Marsillo, and you can be me."

Perhaps it was common in Rome to switch names, but Rinaldo did not understand the purpose. "But what's my benefit of being you and not me?"

Marsillo handed Rinaldo his mallet. "I have this job, and you want it. I quit. It's yours, SanGiorgio." He saluted sloppily and disappeared through the trees.

Rinaldo stared after him while the other men hooted and clapped. One slapped Rinaldo's behind as if he were a hero. Rinaldo was unsure what took place exactly, but it seemed the others did not like Marsillo. Rinaldo, personally, liked the idea of being accepted by these men.

In the middle of it all another man, of forty years or thereabouts, walked down the path, leaving the Holy Father's cottage. By the way the laborers reacted to him, falling quiet and turning toward him with respect, Rinaldo figured he was Master.

A couple of workers who carried themselves like capos separated from the rest of the group to speak with Master in private. His dark, bushy brows jumped at their news, which Rinaldo assumed had to do with Marsillo's leaving. Master's gaze found Rinaldo. Rinaldo flushed and tucked his arms to his sides, wishing he was able to disappear. He had no idea how Master would take the idea of a switch.

As he neared, Rinaldo saw the unkempt thatch on Master's head and dirt-smeared smock. He was no fancy Leonardo da Vinci. Rinaldo immediately warmed up to Master Pollauiolo.

Master extended his calloused hand. "I'm called Antonio, one of the del Pollauiolo brothers. As surrogate of the Holy

Father, I lead these men in God's work, to create a garden worthy of the Almighty." They shook heartily. "You look of good heart, of strong stature, and of better nature than Marsillo. What's your name, son?"

Rinaldo's mind flashed back to when Master da Vinci asked him the same question. Back then his response was windy and weak. But he'd grown confident because Celestina alone had made him feel strong and proud. And that's the way he said his name this time.

"So, I hear you want to join us," said Master Pollauiolo.

Rinaldo's head spun. Master possessed the hands of a laborer but spoke as smooth as a priest, and was humble and smart, all at the same time. If only Rinaldo knew how to speak as well, he'd be able to explain that he was in Rome to plead for the Holy Father's intercession to free Celestina.

With all that flying around his head, he was only able to stammer, "*Ho...ho...ho...*"

"*I-I-I* what? Did you swallow a cat, SanGiorgio? The Pope hates cats, you know, thinks they carry the plague," said Pollauiolo. "But don't get ahead of yourself. You don't have the job yet. Holy Father has the final say over who works in his gardens."

Rinaldo sputtered, "*Na...Na...Naturalmente...*"

A capo handed Rinaldo a scroll, charcoal pencil, and thumbnail-sized pot of sepia powder. Rinaldo rubbed the red dust between his fingers.

"Take those supplies and create a sketch that the Holy Father might like, one that could be turned into a sculpture for his garden," said Pollauiolo.

Rinaldo's heart jumped. "The Pope will judge my sketch?"

Pollauiolo chuckled. "*Si*, SanGiorgio. Now create a worthy drawing, one he falls in love with. And do it fast. I am to meet with him again within one-quarter of an hour."

Rinaldo clutched the scroll to his chest. He must use the opportunity to send a direct message to the Holy Father. But he had no ideas.

Do not run, SanGiorgio.

"Are you ill, SanGiorgio?" asked Pollauiolo.

Rinaldo cleared his throat. "No, Master."

"Then draw!"

Rinaldo unrolled the scroll and stared at the creamy paper. He shook out his hands as if that helped him think. His mind was blank as the eyes of a barnyard turkey. Master had said Rinaldo needed to create a drawing that the pontiff would fall in love with. Fall in love with...

Desperation drove him to bend a knee and bow his head in prayer in front of Pollauiolo and the men. He felt a flush creep across his cheeks, but presenting Pollauiolo with a blank page would be more embarrassing.

Jesus, help me be smart for Celestina's sake.

All at once his hand burned with fever and like a fiery arrow, an image of the perfect sketch shot through his mind.

It might not be exactly right for a pope's garden, and it was a risk, but deep inside it felt right—though why Rinaldo was unsure. Perhaps some secret idea of Simona's leeched out of her heart and into his.

With great glee and no reservations, he filled the page and at the end, he used his baby finger to dab the sepia dust around the throat of his figure. In the bottom corner, he wrote the single name of his subject.

He snapped the paper at Pollauiolo, who studied it intently, and then looked up at Rinaldo as if he had suddenly turned more interesting.

"I will have your answer soon," said Pollauiolo, careful

not to show one way or the other how he felt about the picture. Pollauiolo then rolled up the scroll and legged it up the path to the show the Holy Father.

As the others set out to work the gardens, Rinaldo twisted the cherub charm at his neck. He was almost happy for the distracting smack at the back of his head.

"I've been looking all over the—"

Simona's gaze floated over Rinaldo's shoulder. He twisted around to discover that she was looking not at Pollauiolo, who strode down the path from the cottage, but at a round figure that made Rinaldo's soul tingle.

The portly religious wore a white skullcap that covered wisps of golden-red hair. The heavy and sizeable gold cross around his neck shimmered in the sun. His clerical habit was whiter than the clouds in the sky. Everything about him glowed.

In doing what felt natural, Rinaldo dropped to his knees and folded his hands prayerfully. Sparkling, ruby-encrusted slippers appeared before Rinaldo. He snuck a sideways peek at Simona, standing with her hip cocked and sizing up the rotund religious.

The first words from her mouth were, "If it isn't Cibo, or should I say, *Innocent*?"

Rinaldo cringed and Pollauiolo stumbled backward. Her disrespectful tone could get them thrown out. To Rinaldo's amazement, the pontiff chortled.

"Young man," his voice was deep and resonant, "are you the artist who created the drawing of my Simona and her necklace? The necklace that I gave her long ago?"

Rinaldo jerked. Had Pope Innocent called Celestina's grandmother "my Simona?" It was clear she had not exaggerated the role the necklace could play in their success.

Rinaldo swallowed once, to tame his voice. "*Si*, Your Holiness."

"You drew my Simona with her necklace, but when I look upon my old friend, I see it is missing at her throat. Tell me, do you know what happened?" asked the Holy Father.

Rinaldo grimaced. "*Signor* Nucitelli and his goose Ottavia, along with some blonds from the north, stole it from us on our journey to see you, Your Holiness."

"I see," the Holy Father said thoughtfully. "Rise, please, young man."

Rinaldo leaped straight up. He stared at the young grass peeking up from the dark dirt beneath his feet.

"You may look at me," said His Holiness.

It was Pollauiolo who spoke next. "This young man with the talented hand is Rinaldo SanGiorgio." He faced Rinaldo. "I believe you will fit into our brotherhood, SanGiorgio. His Holiness and I invite you to join me and my men to build this garden."

Rinaldo rubbed the middle of his forehead. "I do not wish to disrespect you, Master, for my dream is to work with you and these men. But the first reason for my visit to Rome is to ask His Holiness to pardon *Signora* Simona's granddaughter from prison. Celestina DiCapria has been accused of being a witch, but she is an angel."

The Holy Father glanced at Simona. She nodded in solemn affirmation.

"Excuse *Signora* Simona and me for a few moments," said the Holy Father. His tone was grave.

Master grabbed Rinaldo by the sleeve and pulled him back. The strain of addressing the Holy Father had made him dizzy. Rinaldo gladly followed on Pollauiolo's heels down the incline toward the other men. He couldn't get far enough away in order to calm down.

Soon Innocent called over Master. They spoke in hushed tones, with Simona standing on the sidelines. After a few moments, Master returned and slapped Rinaldo on the back. "Pay is one gold florin a month, plus living arrangements."

"But I cannot stay," said Rinaldo.

"The Holy Father gave his permission for you to go back home and save your girl and return to us when you can, which I hope is soon. It's going to be hard being down a man."

He and Master shook and then Pollauiolo joined the others to do God's earthly work.

Rinaldo rubbed his fluttery stomach and paced around an old oak so he wouldn't take off running. He snuck a peek at the Holy Father and Simona. They appeared to be arguing with great passion. It made him jumpy and he was unable to stand looking at them any longer.

It seemed like forever, but some half an hour later, he saw Simona stepping spritely down the hill, coming toward him. He glanced past her shoulder and the earth dropped under his feet. The Holy Father was no longer present.

Rinaldo swiped the air. "You ruined everything with that rude mouth of yours, didn't you?"

"Go around to the stables and pick out a horse," she said, ignoring his question. "There is no time to waste. We're going back to Florence."

Seething, he planted his feet. "I knew you'd get us kicked out of Rome."

"Oh, Herculino, you have so much to learn. We did not get kicked out. Quite the opposite: he's coming with us."

Rinaldo looked around. "Who's coming with us?"

"Cibo."

Rinaldo jerked his head back. "His Holiness?"

"Call him that if you want, but when I knew him, he was anything but holy. He's accompanying us to Florence by special papal cavalcade. Before three days' time, Celestina will be free."

She started for the convent to collect her things but paused to catch her breath. "Cibo has already sent scouts ahead to investigate her condition and account back to us while we travel. We should know what is going on with our girl soon. I only pray to God we're not too late," she said.

"Where are these men? I will ride with them."

"That's what I fought with Cibo about until he explained that these men are spies. Cibo feared that if Baldasare got wind of you riding with them, it would put our girl in the gravest of danger."

Pollauiolo's men all swung to look as Rinaldo flew past them for the stables. He swore he'd be back with them one day, with Celestina as his bride.

Or die trying.

21

Celestina dragged her chains across the Piazza della Signoria, past the burning stake. Metal scraped the cobblestones. None of it mattered. Today she would face Rinaldo and tell him, and all of Florence, that she loved him.

"If we're late, Monsignor will see that I'm whipped." The strain in Capo's voice was real. It surprised her. Everyone, it appeared, was at the mercy of Monsignor.

She readjusted her "new" dress. Another gunnysack, albeit less faded. But it was too big. She hiked her shoulders to keep it from slipping.

"What are you talking about?" she asked Capo, glancing around the piazza. "We're already here. Everyone else is late for my trial."

Where is Rinaldo?

"You don't know anything," said Capo. "Your trial takes place on the other side of the piazza. Now move." He tapped the end of his club against her *culo*.

The memory of Fra's hard *cazzo* against her stomach shot through her, and hot with that thought, she spit in Capo's face.

He stared at her incredulously with her spittle hanging

from his lips.

She swallowed heavily. Her foul reaction stunned even her. Vengeance had been delivered against the wrong man. She braced for Capo's fist.

But he simply licked his lips and said, "You taste like figs."

It had to be a trick. He was going to club her in the knee when she least suspected it.

"Just beat me and get it over with," she said, hunching into her shoulders, awaiting his blow.

He leaned in. "Fig me again," he said and opened his mouth.

"Just get me to my trial," she sighed, but in her heart, she was grateful that it was Capo, and not Nello, escorting her.

"*Va bene*, all right, Baker Girl." He pointed at Palazzo della Signoria. "It's that building."

She dug her feet into the cobblestones. "But why do you direct me *inside* city hall? Fra Brucker promised a public trial."

"Monsignor was very clear," said Capo. "Your trial is way up inside the *torre*."

Her gaze climbed the outside of the Arnolfo Tower to the big clock, it's one arm on nine. "But Fra promised an *outdoor* trial," she said.

"Public trials are for nobles, courtiers, and clergy who bring in herds of lawyers and enough people to fill the Coliseum. You and I are little more than *contadini*. Peasants like us only get small, indoor trials," Capo said.

Betrayal squeezed her heart. Fra had acted all-powerful, but he was a nothing. She faced the heavens and stared into the sun. How could she be so blind to believe that she could beat him?

Now the only person she was able to think about was

Rinaldo. There was still a chance that part of her plan would work. "But my people might not be able to find me inside the tower," she said.

"My people?" mocked Capo. "You mean that outlaw SanGiorgio?"

She stamped her foot. "I'm waiting right here for Rinaldo."

Capo's answer was to throw her over his shoulder. She kicked the air and pounded her fists against his back.

"Your fists are as troublesome as mosquito bites," he laughed and moments later lowered her at the foot of a steep staircase that led up to the Arnolfo Tower.

Her heavy chains clanged against the tile as she stumbled up the first step. Wide-eyed, she gazed up the endless stairs. She set her jaw and tried again. Rinaldo was possibly up there, waiting.

"I know you can't wait to see your *amichetto*." Capo scooped her in his arms. "I can't believe I'm doing this for someone else's sweetheart."

Perhaps the strain of prison had softened her brain but bouncing up the stairs in Capo's hold wasn't awful. God willing, she'd be leaving in Rinaldo's.

Two hundred steps later, Capo set her down at the top. If she'd had any doubts where her trial was going to take place, they vanished. Inside the courtroom keys tinkled, chairs scraped the tile, and deep-voiced chatter echoed.

Capo nudged her through the arched doorway. Her nose was assaulted by the stench of perspiring old men in stained black robes. They looked her up and down as if she were naked. She tried straightening her dress. A kind tap from behind reassured her that Capo was watching her back. She glimpsed from mustache, to beard, to shaved face. No Rinaldo.

A man about Simona's age, or thereabouts, bustled

over. He wore a floppy black *berretto*. "Good morning. I'm Magistrate Falso, your *avvocato*."

But this Falso fellow did not feel like her anything. She mumbled, "What does that mean?"

"I'm on your side for the trial," said Falso.

Before she was able to ask if Rinaldo had been informed of her trial and whether her grandmother was able to be present, Falso fell back to straighten a row of chairs.

Capo sighed. "Falso is bought and paid for by Monsignor. Everyone knows it, but no one does anything about it. *Coniglio!*"

Her heart twitched nervously. What good was a lawyer who was a big chicken? Without Rinaldo there yet, Capo was the only one on her side.

She checked for Rinaldo once again. Scribes holding feather pens scribbled in books, turnkeys fussed with the many instruments hanging from their belts, and assorted priests whispered among themselves. A white-bearded healer in an orange robe rummaged through his leather bag.

In the far back stood a man with shoulders of an ox who bore a red tunic with a single black stripe on the sleeve.

"Torturer," said Capo, answering her unspoken question. "And he's nothing like the goats running the torture room in Bargello. That man is *il diavolo*. The devil, I tell you."

She sunk into Capo, her gaze traveling up a rope that was slung over a hook screwed into the ceiling. Another *strappado*. Her mouth turned dry as straw.

Capo guided her to a small stool in the front of the courtroom, helping with the weight of her chains as she stepped up. Her vantage point was good. She was able to see the door. Now she'd not miss Rinaldo's entrance.

Silence fell over the courtroom. A triumvirate of Roman

Catholic bishops bearing gold shepherd staffs emerged from behind a black curtain. They wore identical dour faces, purple clothes, and skullcaps. Pectoral crosses hanging from green silk cords graced their necks. They took seats behind a polished table that was as ornate as the trio of bishops themselves.

Capo bowed his head. From the side of his mouth, he whispered, "The Tribunal of the Faith. Your judges."

Je me attens a mon juge, c'est le roy du ciel et de la terre, she mouthed silently.

She checked the doorway for Rinaldo, and her heart shrunk. Capo elbowed her in the rib. "Look up front. Pay attention to what I'm going to tell you."

She gave a sickly nod.

Capo pointed at the bishop closest to her. "Corso is *gonfaloniere*." The top third of the bishop's face was all silver-and-black eyebrow. On his right was the banner of Pope Innocent VIII, red silk and embroidered with gold keys. On his left was St. Peter's banner, gold silk and stitched with red keys.

"The *gonfaloniere* is the mallet. He makes sure the trial follows the rules of the church. And so that you know, Corso is all business and strict—and I'm saying strict *for even a bishop*—but he also hates Monsignor and the Reform," said Capo.

Celestina raised her eyebrows. "That will surely count in my favor."

"Who can tell?" Capo shrugged. "He always looks like he's just swallowed sour milk."

She glanced at the marble crucifix hanging from her neck. "I'm only here to see Rinaldo anyway."

Capo twisted his lips.

"Why such a funny look?" she asked.

"I don't see anyone from the public here," he said.

"Rinaldo might be lost, but he will find me." She glanced at the doorway.

Capo cleared his throat. "Let me finish telling you about the Tribunal." He pointed at the middle bishop. "The fat-bellied one is Pagolo, the *esecutore*. He presides over the trial. Next, to him, the one with the curly hair is Iacopo. He's *capitano*. That son of a bitch has a heart of lead."

She was unable to hide the hope in her voice. "Do Pagolo and Iacopo hate Monsignor too?"

Capo twisted so his back was to the Tribunal. "It's the opposite. Pagolo and Iacopo favor the Reform. Don't say anything stupid for them to use against you."

"But only a year ago they sent away Monsignor, and he's worse now, surely they'll see that," she said, envisioning the truth rising to the surface at trial.

"Everything's changed," said Capo. "Since last year the Reform has taken a strong hold of the Tribunal. They're mostly political now."

She teetered on the stool. Capo caught her elbow. "Keep steady, Baker Girl," he said.

"Court is ready to begin." Corso banged his fancy slipper on the table. At least the bishop against Monsignor seemed to be running the trial.

"You have to get two of those three bishops on your side, and nothing's guaranteed. *Buona fortuna*, Baker Girl. Good luck," said Capo.

"Capo?"

He swung around.

"*Grazie*," she said, adding, "If my plan works, I may never see you again. So, before you leave, I must know something."

"Ask fast."

"Why are you so nice to me?"

A cloud passed his green eyes. "You remind me of someone who *I...I...*"

"Tell me."

He rubbed his hand on his chest, over his heart. "My wife. Oliva was beautiful in the way you are. And smart. I always see her in your face, and that makes me be nice to you."

She had no idea Capo was a young widower, and she ached for his loss. "*Amico mio*, my friend, I'm so sorry," she said.

"*Grazie*. Olivia died with the birth of our baby, a boy we named Tonio. That's my real name, Antonio."

"My mother died giving birth to me, too," said Celestina. At that moment she missed the mother she never knew the way Capo must always yearn for his Olivia and Tonio.

"Perhaps that's also why I favor you," he said. "Somewhere inside my soul, I must believe that you're like Tonio."

"*Sono grato del tuo aiuto*," she said, "I'm grateful to you forever, but if you will, please do one more thing. Find Rinaldo for me."

He gave a strong nod and then slipped out the door past Monsignor, who was making his entrance. His *magna cappa* shimmered blue in the light streaming from a small window. Fra trailed Monsignor. His gaze cut straight to her.

"Where's Rinaldo?" She mouthed the words at him.

He flinched.

As he took a seat in the gallery, she stared at him with such venom that her vision clouded.

Corso clapped three times, giving Fra reason to look away from her. *Codardo*, she seethed. Coward.

Corso started, "Monsignor Baldasare, who is also a judge in the Catholic Church, will prosecute the case against *Signorina* DiCapria."

Celestina gasped. Monsignor was the prosecutor?

"*Bon giorno, Signorina* DiCapria," said Monsignor.

She shook her head. *No. No. No.* Never had she expected to go against Monsignor, one on one.

"Begin, *per favore*," said Corso.

Monsignor tapped his fingers on his stomach. "My first question for *Signorina* DiCapria is this: Explain how Simona the Baker raised her pet bird from the dead."

Celestina rose on her toes, peering over Monsignor's head. "Where's Rinaldo?" Sweat beaded her upper lip.

Monsignor waved his hand across the span of bishops. "These are important men, with important things to do today. Now answer, *signorina*, or else."

It took everything in her power to hold back from crying. "But I was promised Rinaldo would be here." She aimed her words at Fra. "I am not saying anything until I see Rinaldo SanGiorgio."

"The *scalpellino* does not know about the trial," said Fra from the gallery.

She glowered at him, breathless with rage.

"But it's not what the Fraulein might think," Fra added.

Monsignor's deep voice cut through the courtroom. "*Basta*. Enough explanations."

Fra retreated deep in his seat. She held her glare on him— the good little altar boy who always obeyed Monsignor.

"*Signorina*, you must now testify. Tell us about your grandmother and her bird," said Monsignor.

Celestina sucked in her cheeks. Without Rinaldo, she was no longer playing.

"Answer, or we will dig up Simona from whatever rock she's been hiding under and make her tell us the story," said Monsignor.

"What do you mean hiding?" asked Celestina. "She's at the bakery, as she is every day of her life, *si*?"

"No," answered Monsignor. Falso concurred with the bad news.

Celestina jerked. "Where is she then?"

"No one can find her," said Monsignor.

A drop of sweat rolled into her left eye. It burned and blurred that half of the room. "But she never leaves the bakery, except to sleep." Celestina blinked to focus. "How long have you been looking for her?"

"Days," said Monsignor.

Celestina's mind flipped upside down. It groped for an answer. Perhaps witches stole Simona's soul. But Geneve said that never happened. Wherever Simona was, Celestina feared her grandmother was in mortal danger.

She turned to Fra. "You act like you know everything. Now prove it. Where is Simona?"

"She's missing, like the *scalpellino*," said Fra, throwing up his hands.

Celestina flew off the stool for the door. She had to find her grandmother and Rinaldo.

A large watchman trapped her by the waist and swung her over his shoulder, chains and all.

"*Va' all'inferno*," she screamed, kicking. "Go to hell, all of you. I need to find Simona and Rinaldo."

The watchman banked her on the stool and then cuffed her ear for good measure. Stars swirled inside her head. She was unsure if it was Montanina ringing or her ears.

"Stay put, or you'll get worse next time," said the guard.

Monsignor quieted the courtroom. "We will find the grandmother in due time. The question remains, *Signorina* DiCapria, did Simona raise a canary from the dead using Love

Magic?"

Celestina turned humbly toward the Tribunal. She must say the words in the right way to show the Tribunal how devious Monsignor was in calling her grandmother a witch. She had to save Simona's reputation, and life, wherever her grandmother was at the moment.

"My grandmother had two identical yellow canaries," she started. "They fought until she separated them; one stayed at the bakery and the other in our apartment."

"We do not have all day," said Monsignor.

"There is a small hole between the wall of our bakery and *Signor* Lombardi's *farmacia*. Simona's bakery bird liked to sing, but *Signor* Lombardi hates all things beautiful.

"He complained, 'That bird's song gives me a headache.' And then, one day the bird was dead, by poison. And everyone knows *Signor* Lombardi is an expert in potions—"

Monsignor interrupted, "You'd think we were in the audience for Dante's Divine Comedy. Quicken your story, *signorina*. Soon it will be time for lunch."

"It was clear *Signor* Lombardi killed Simona's bird, so my grandmother played a trick," said Celestina. "She lured the *signore* into the bakery with a loaf of his favorite prune-filled bread. After he filled his stomach, she told him to watch as she rubbed her dead bird's tummy. Secretly, she had switched it with the live bird from our apartment, which she had hidden in her sleeve.

"When it seemed as if the bird had resurrected from the dead, *Signor* Lombardi began to cry like a baby. He was so frightened. My grandmother told him if he hurt the bird again, he'd be cursed. That's when he told everyone who listened that Simona was a sorceress. The good part was he never touched one of her singing birds again, and that's all she wanted."

"Your grandmother must be a saint," said Monsignor in his most sardonic way.

Celestina implored the Tribunal. "Monsignor is no different than *Signor* Lombardi. You sent Monsignor away once after he instigated my papa's murder. And now he wants to ruin my life to spite my grandmother, because she picked another, long ago. Please send him away before, one by one, he kills all the women in the Passage of Witches."

She slumped, having said everything she intended, and it exhausted her to the bone. She could barely stand.

Monsignor clapped slowly. "Nice story."

"It's the truth." Her voice was weak. "I swear on Papa's soul."

"The soul that is locked in purgatory? The same place where your grandfather will wither when he dies," said Monsignor.

Her hands, and then her feet, and finally her whole body convulsed. To speak of her Papa, and also of her no-named grandfather, was more than she was able to bear.

"Tell me my grandfather's name, or shut up about him," she screamed at Monsignor. "And go and die for talking about my Papa."

Monsignor stepped forward and drew back his hand. *Whack*. The pain from his slap sizzled up her cheek, and her eyesight blackened for a short spell. But she was proud of herself. Though she nearly fainted she had the presence of mind to react as little as humanly possible. Like Geneve, Celestina would never again give Monsignor the satisfaction of knowing he'd hurt her.

At the same time, the courtroom erupted.

Fra pushed past the others, his eyes trained on her the whole time. Watchmen threw their hands upon him, reining him back.

Bishop Corso looked satisfied, suggesting he was pleased that she'd made noise at Monsignor's expense. But Bishop Pagolo glowered at Celestina menacingly while Bishop Iacopo leaned over, cupping his mouth, to whisper to Pagolo.

Monsignor's voice cut through the pandemonium, "*Silenzio.*"

Watchmen threw Fra Brucker back into his chair. The rest in the gallery settled down.

Monsignor's big ears burned red. Repercussion was coming.

She turned quickly to Falso. As her supposed advocate, he'd done nothing for her, but if he found a way to grant her this one wish, she'd gladly call it even. "May I go now? I must find my grandmother and Rinaldo."

"Go where?" Monsignor interrupted while Falso buttoned his lip. "You're not leaving," said Monsignor.

She boldly met his gaze. His self-satisfied face mocked her.

"You have not tricked a single man in this courtroom into believing that your grandmother had two birds," Monsignor said.

"I have told you the truth." The strength in her voice surprised her. "And now it is your turn to do the same. Who is my grandfather?"

Monsignor's lip curled. "You are in no position to bargain, *signorina.* You have three heartbeats, to tell the truth about your grandmother, or we will make you talk. One, two—"

"There is no more to tell."

"Three."

The whoosh of rope ripping against the ceiling hook cut through the stunned silence. In the corner, the torturer prepared the *strappado*.

"Hang me as payment," shouted Fra Brucker as he struggled against guards. A watchman covered the friar's mouth.

"Capo," Corso called, looking around. "Where's that guard?" Capo came running into the courtroom, pausing for a moment to give Celestina a thumb down. She struggled to breathe. It felt like she was getting choked. He'd not found Rinaldo.

Corso ordered Capo to unlock Celestina's ankle chains and to take her to the corner. "Don't fight the rope, it won't hurt as much," whispered Capo.

The torturer bound her wrists in thin twine. His touch was dry as a snake and she wished to jump out of her skin. He threaded the thick *strappado* through the twine and then wrapped the other end of the rope around his hand. He drew it down, which raised Celestina off the floor. She hung by her wrists behind her back, swaying above the courtroom.

Though there was great stretch in her shoulders, a week and a half inside Bargello had made her lose weight. It would have been far worse if she were heavier.

Monsignor tipped back his head, examining as she dangled in the air. "You have also been accused of hearing the voices of saints. Is that true?"

Fra Brucker broke free of the watchman gagging his mouth. "They're trying to catch you in a trick, Celestina. Do not speak."

She pressed her lips together.

Monsignor now posed as the true torturer. "Add weight," he said.

The torturer's lumpy young assistant tied a boulder around her ankle. The extra weight set her shoulders on fire.

"Drop her," said Monsignor.

The rope jerked. The bounce was hard. Her shoulders seared.

"Have you ever had intercourse with Satan?" asked Monsignor.

"What?" She was unable to keep silent at so outlandish a charge. "Of course not. I have never...with no one," she said, suffocating tears filling her throat.

"Torturer, lower her," said Monsignor.

The rope whirred against the hook and she collapsed in a heap. Her right shoulder blazed in agony.

The torturer untied the big rope and then the twine from her wrists. Her bloodied hands flopped to her side like dead fish.

The healer with the beard and orange robe stepped forward and knelt before her, examining each shoulder. Without warning, he shoved her right shoulder into place. Her scream could have curdled wine into vinegar.

Corso banged his slipper. Celestina's panting was the only sound in the courtroom.

"Since we cannot get a straight answer from *Signorina* DiCapria, she must be given a virginity test. Healer, take her," Monsignor said. The damned Falso said nothing in her defense.

Fra Brucker fought to break free of the watchmen. "Barbarians! In God's name, leave Celestina alone."

A beefy guard lifted her over his shoulder and dropped her onto a dirty cot behind a makeshift curtain in the back of the courtroom. Another guard was there. He was greasy-faced. She refused to look at either as she contemplated this virginity test, of which she'd never heard.

Perhaps the healer stood on the other side of the curtain

and asked if she'd sinned, like a priest in a confessional. She'd swear her modesty was intact. Fra had not entered her, after all.

With the back of his hand, the healer edged the curtain open. Her heart fell. Would he ask her questions face to face? It was embarrassing, but she'd endured far worse.

At the behest of the healer, the watchmen pinned her shoulders to the cot. She fought, trying to scratch out their eyes, but it was two against one. They each took hold of a knee and spread her.

"Do you two idiots know what you're doing? I don't need to be held down to answer a question," she said, squirming.

The watchmen grinned salaciously at each other.

Celestina shouted at the healer. "I swear on St. Catherine's soul that I am a virgin."

The guards snickered. The healer patted her knee. "It's not a talking test, *signorina*. Relax and it won't hurt."

"How can I relax like this?" Her voice cracked. "And relax for what?"

The watchmen bore down hard on her legs. Mortified that her dress had bunched around her hips, leaving her *patata* out in the wide open, she wriggled but was unable to move it so it at least covered her private area.

A thick, cold, and sticky substance was smeared around her bottom. "What are you doing?" she demanded of the healer.

He stuffed a balled-up sock into her mouth. She gagged violently as he shoved his hand inside her bottom half. Her heart nearly exploded. Flesh ripped. The sock silenced her choking screams.

"Almost finished," he said. Something slipped out. Horrified, she was unsure if it was his hand, or her own *merda* sliding out of her bottom. He removed the sock, and she coughed long strings of saliva. The watchmen released her.

She pressed her hands to her heart, breathing wildly, hoping to God that it was over. The healer's face was stone and gave her no comfort. When the watchmen stood her up, allowing her to straighten her dress before re-entering the courtroom, she dared to believe they were done.

She was shaking so hard that it was hard to balance back on the stool in the front of the courtroom. She looked only at the floor, refusing to see any of them. The only thing keeping her from going crazy was the satisfaction of knowing for certain she passed the test.

"And what is the result of the virginity test?" asked Corso.

Celestina licked her lips. She couldn't wait to look up to see their disappointment when it was declared that she was a virgin.

The healer cleared his throat and raised his hand. "No blood," he said. "*Signorina* DiCapria is not a virgin."

"Liar," she cried.

"Quiet," demanded Corso.

The healer continued, "But there is more."

She grimaced. What more? She was either a virgin or she wasn't. And she most certainly *was* a virgin.

"There is swelling deep inside *Signorina* DiCapria. The prisoner is with child."

Her hand flew to her stomach. How could she be with child? No archangel had appeared to her, speaking of an immaculate conception.

The courtroom turned deafening as the healer, Monsignor, and Falso consulted with the bishops at the Tribunal's table. Fra stood alone, pulling at his clerical collar.

Corso waved his hands over his head. The courtroom

hushed and Monsignor stepped forward.

"Since those accused of heresy are not allowed visitors, and intercourse is not allowed in Bargello, the court is left to conclude that *Signorina* DiCapria is carrying the child of the devil, who chose to visit her in the dark of the night," he said.

Celestina weaved back and forth on the stool. The accusation was ugly nonsense. "I never even slept with Rinaldo, let alone the devil," she cried.

Her mind raced as to the whereabouts of Rinaldo and Simona as the Tribunal conferred. How she wished to see their faces. Finally, Bishop Iacopo stood. "It is the decision of this Tribunal that..."

She sobered in a heartbeat. She checked for Bishop Corso, the one who despised Monsignor. He was her only hope to stop this farce and tell the truth. When he avoided looking at her, she turned to ice. It was clear that Monsignor had gotten to Corso, and that the *gonfaloniere* was now corrupted.

"*Signorina* Celestina DiCapria will be beheaded in the courtyard of Bargello at midday tomorrow," said Iacopo. "Afterward, the body will then be taken to the Piazza della Signoria to burn at the stake."

"God sees everything." It was Fra, voice booming. "He sees you bishops. He sees you, Monsignor. He knows you have sentenced Celestina to death to hurt her grandmother, for only God knows what reason. This ruling is a travesty!"

The courtroom erupted in shouts, fists, and flying shoes.

An invisible drape of blackness fell over her as Montanina cried. Once for a beheading. Twice for a burning.

Capo swept her off the stool, clamped her in chains, and guided her through the door. She peered down the long flight of stairs, and then fixed her stare at her stomach. If there were truly a baby inside, how could she feel so empty?

"I am a virgin, Capo," she said. "I swear on my grandmother's soul."

Capo glared in the direction of the healer. "That healer is one son of a bitch, Baker Girl. He'd lie for two *scudi* to line his orange pocket."

Falso called after Capo. The young watchman twisted back to confer, releasing his hold on her.

It was then that Geneve's voice snaked through her ears, "*Ma Mie*, you must escape."

The pages of her memory flipped back to Rinaldo's face, begging her to flee from Bargello with him.

And now she had another chance; a chance to escape it all.

Leaning forward, she teetered at the edge of the staircase. Lifting her leg out straight as far as it would go in the chains, she drifted headfirst.

"Celestina!" Fra Brucker's voice startled her and she caught herself.

She spun to scream at him for stopping her. But when she saw what he'd done, she simply stared.

There he was, flat on the floor, prostrate, like her on the first day they met when the Reform was righteous and new.

He lifted his face. "I know I am not Rinaldo, but I have loved you too, though badly. I will be there for you tomorrow. You will not die alone, Celestina. Until then, don't do anything to taint your soul."

His eyes were a mix of red tears and gray guilt, a murky violet. At that moment, she saw him as he might have been if his mind had not been twisted by the likes of men like Monsignor.

She took one last, longing look down the staircase before Capo grabbed her by the elbow and pulled her firmly back.

, hundreds of them, resounded against the proper Roman road and then halted in the span of a single heartbeat. It was twilight. Rinaldo looked in awe at the Swiss Guard, courtiers, grooms, cooks, and every stripe of religious. They moved through *Italia* like a perfect army.

It was still a bit less than a day's ride to Florence. With affection he tugged the ear of Fumo, the handsome gray *stallone* he was lent to ride. They still had a few roads left to travel together.

After making camp, Rinaldo perched on a log, eating his veal and rosemary stew, waiting for papal scouts to deliver word of Florence. He'd had no news of Celestina or Simona since leaving Rome, although earlier he'd seen Simona being escorted by an elderly bishop into the papal red and gold carriage. Rinaldo figured she was doing better than her granddaughter.

A streak of torchlight ripped through camp. "Remount," cried a young cardinal on horseback. "We ride through the night."

Rinaldo dropped his bowl. The cardinal's tone was full of alarm. "But why?" he asked.

The cardinal on horseback swung around. "*Signorina* DiCapria is due to lose her head at noon. His Holiness has ordered us to ride double time. The Holy Father and the rest of the caravan will follow at our heels."

Rinaldo shot to his feet. "Celestina is to be beheaded?"

"Yes, in the courtyard of Bargello," said the cardinal.

"But we might not reach her in time." Rinaldo jumped on Fumo. Within a few heartbeats, the stallion was in full gallop.

The young cardinal caught up to Rinaldo, flashing a scroll. "This is the stay bearing Innocent's seal. We can stop the execution," he said.

"If we can get there on time." Rinaldo urged on Fumo.

"Her fate is in God's hands," said the religious.

And the demons who bear the names Brucker and Baldasare, thought Rinaldo.

23

Celestina crouched in the corner of her cell, clawing at her hair. In her mind, she was ripping out Monsignor's tongue.

"Stop hurting yourself, *Ma Mie*." Geneve's sharp tone cut through the miscarried thoughts swirling in Celestina's head.

"Hurt? Pulling my mop doesn't hurt," Celestina growled. "My shoulder hurts. No wonder the church loves the *strappado*. It's charitable. The torture that keeps giving."

"At least they haven't stolen your humor," said Geneve.

Celestina felt the creep of small feet across her back. She glanced at her shoulder and spotted a rat. Swatting it, she sent it sailing across the cell. It hit the wall with a thud.

She retreated back to the corner, watching in horror as the creature seized and then stiffened. Every decision she made hurt something. She wanted to harm Monsignor and ended up killing an innocent animal. With only hours left to live, her life was going in the wrong direction.

The rush of blood pounded in her ear. Rinaldo's crucifix rose and fell on her chest with each breath. So few, precious heartbeats left.

An image flashed behind her eyes of Rinaldo walking the streets of Florence lost in a daze. Next, she pictured Simona with her head in the hearth wall oven.

St. Catherine, give me a sign that they are safe if you're even bothering to listen anymore.

Never before had she ended a prayer with such contempt.

"Ha. Why do I bother? God has turned deaf to my prayers," she said, making sure Geneve heard. "Why should he listen to the pleas of a witch?"

"Do not say such things," said Geneve.

"*Perche no?*" Celestina challenged. "Why not? It's true. I slept with Satan, they say."

Raising her shackled hands, Geneve reached out. "Come here, *Ma Mie*."

Celestina's chin dropped to her chest. Unable to hold Geneve's undying faith against her, she sidled up to her friend. "Never give up on God," said Geneve.

"But God has given up on me, and you, and Juliana, and Anastasia, and Giovanna. But I, at least, have given Him a reason. I've lied, dishonored, and committed adultery—with a religious."

Celestina shook her head at her own words. What the men said about her sounded false in her ears.

Geneve stroked her cheek. "*Ma Mie*, the love of God is in you, and all around you. But if you pull your hair and thrash at helpless animals, you will never be quiet enough to feel Him."

"There's no hope," said Celestina.

"There's always hope," countered Geneve. "God doesn't make mistakes."

"Tell that to the poor rat." Celestina glanced at where she'd last seen it. It wasn't there. She looked questioningly at Geneve. "I thought I killed it."

Geneve returned a satisfied look. She nodded at the far corner. Celestina watched the rat lick its paws, grooming after its near-death ordeal.

"See what I mean," said Geneve.

Celestina slipped Rinaldo's marble crucifix off her neck and over Geneve's head. It lay dominant on her friend's sunken chest, but it suited Geneve, with her oversized faith. "Take care of this after I'm gone," said Celestina.

"You will wear it again one day soon," Geneve said.

"Where I'm going," Celestina stared down the empty corridor, "No one is allowed a crucifix."

Bong.

Celestina's stomach lurched. This time it was Montanina calling for her head. She caught a glimpse of Capo down the corridor, nearing the cell.

She lunged away from Geneve's embrace and crawled around the cell searching for a weapon—a nail or a shard of wood—for which to impale her heart before she was dragged to the courtyard for her beheading. Anything not to face that ax; anything not to have her head sit atop a stick.

Celestina threw up her hands. The cell was scattered with straw, centuries of tears, and the echo of Geneve's advice. Yet there was nothing to end her life, like the soulless, hopeless witch she was.

Capo's key clicked in the lock. He gently opened the cell door. His face was drawn in sadness. "It's time, Baker Girl. *Il boia* waits."

"The executioner can go to hell." Celestina slammed her back against the wall. "Go away, Capo." With the ferocity of a cornered dog, she kicked at him.

He caught her by the foot. "Don't make this harder, Baker Girl." He swiped his eye with the back of his sleeve.

Celestina toppled, excited at the opportunity that her skull might crack against the stone floor and she'd bleed to death like Papa in the piazza outside Santa Maria Novella. At least she'd die with Geneve present and not at the hand of the executioner.

But a soft hand cushioned her head before it could hit the floor. Celestina snapped at the girl in the cell next door. "Damn it, Juliana, why did you save me?"

"Because you are going to save me," Juliana said. "I dreamed it. And Anastasia and Giovanna—you're going to rescue them, too."

Capo now had Celestina's hands behind her back. He fumbled with the knot because of her thrashing. He finally got her to straighten up.

She looked flatly at Juliana. "I'm sorry to tell you, but you're not Geneve and your dreams mean nothing."

Juliana stretched her arms for Celestina, but Capo ordered her back.

"I will see you soon, Celestina," said Juliana.

"No, you won't." Celestina turned away. "You're going to heaven."

Anastasia and Giovanna held hands between the bars, tears streaming down their cheeks.

"Let's go, Baker Girl. They're all waiting," said Capo, leading her out of the cell.

Geneve called her name. Celestina dug in her heels. Capo sighed impatiently but let up. "I remembered one last thing to tell you, *Ma Mie.*"

Black spots splotched before Celestina's eyes. She was going to faint.

Geneve rattled her chains. "Give me full your attention, Celestina."

Celestina nodded limply.

"If there is even the tiniest chance, by all and any means you must escape," said Geneve.

Celestina bit back a cry. "For me, the Father in heaven doesn't work that way."

Geneve answered, "But God is made up of three parts: Father, Son, and Holy Ghost."

Celestina cried, "I told you I've given up hope on God and Jesus."

Geneve's voice strained. "I understand *Ma Mie*. But until your last breath, you must never doubt the power of the Holy Ghost."

"Please, Baker Girl, we have to go," said Capo. The lock clicked behind her for the last time.

In spite of what Geneve said, Celestina was going to die with regret. Rinaldo would never know the depth of her love for him.

So much for the ever-great Holy Ghost.

Celestina stared down the stone staircase that led to Bargello's courtyard.

Her bound hands shook behind her. Though she was unable to see the *animali*—that's what Simona called the fiends who camped at every execution—she heard them whistle for her head.

Il boia, the towering executioner, looked at her through a pair of holes in his black hood.

Montanina bonged twice. She balked. Two for a burning. Was Montanina already calling for her to burn at the stake? But she still had her head.

Glumly, she gazed in the direction of the Piazza della

Signoria. Was some other poor soul getting burned? What if they died at the exact same time? Was it possible their souls could get mixed up?

"God doesn't make mistakes." Geneve's words made her quake. There was no escaping hell—not for Celestina.

Montanina's echo passed. In the courtyard below, whistles for her head grew louder. She tried to block out their cries by picturing Rinaldo's brown eyes, silky hair, and neck so strong it would break the executioner's ax.

Il boia unexpectedly yanked an eyeless sack over her head. She tried to buck out, but then he cinched it tight around her neck. It was nearly impossible for her to breathe.

She thrashed about, in a state of utter alarm. Had she inhaled her last good breath without knowing it? There was no end to their torture.

He strong-armed her down the stairs with her feet barely touching the steps. The *animali* cried, "*Strega!* Witch!" The executioner dragged her across the courtyard.

And then he lurched to a stop, and she wrenched to a halt with him. The vicious barks of the *animali* fell silent. Like the quiet before a tornado, the air stilled. Birds hushed. The executioner's hand fell from her arm.

She turned her head this way and that, but it was useless. She was unable to learn anything with the hood blinding her.

St. Catherine, what should I do?

"Escape." It was Geneve's voice in Celestina's head.

Celestina jolted to action. She scampered back ten steps and then paused, neck buried in shoulders, wondering why the executioner's swift fist hadn't crushed her head like a mallet.

But it was St. Catherine who answered with a flaming kick to Celestina's soul. With a big grunt, she doubled over.

St. Catherine's message was loud and clear. Celestina needed to keep moving.

She slithered back, holding her breath. How was it possible that *il boia* did not notice that the convict was fleeing? She knew better than to stop to think about it. She wanted no more of St. Catherine's answers.

She quickened her pace, feeling along the way with her bare feet, stopping only when the back of her heel scraped a stone bulwark. She tapped her toe around, surmising she'd made it all the way to the wall surrounding the courtyard. Now she must guess where the gate was located in order to escape the prison grounds.

But she had no sense of what direction she was facing. Somehow, she had to doff the hood so she was able to see. And then she'd make an all-out dash for the gate.

Dropping to her knees, she picked at the knot binding her hands. Capo had done a bad job tying, and it surrendered easier than she expected.

As she grabbed the hood to pull it off, a pair of rock-hard hands clamped her shoulders.

She shrieked and then slumped, aborting her attempt to lift the hood. At least with her face covered, the *animali* were unable to see her cry in failure. She'd been so foolish to hope. Hope didn't exist for her. Who did she think she was—Geneve?

She blinked into the blackness of her hood...why was *il boia* now tenderly massaging her shoulders? A rush of cool air swept over her head. Who was lifting her hood?

She recoiled from the blinding sunlight. Slowly she focused, starting to see pieces of her new existence. Brown eyes flecked with gray, dark hair the color of balsamic, and pink lips shaped like the mountain in the Florentine sun.

And then the whole picture emerged. She saw the most

handsome face in all the heavens. It was the face she dreamed of, the face she wished for her children.

All at once her immediate past came rushing back. Her hand flew to her neck. She checked for a seam but there was no line; an expert had reattached it.

Apparently, beheading did not hurt.

Also, dying was not terrible.

Somehow, she'd made it to heaven, and it was perfect.

)(

The bloodstained grass beneath her was a surprise, as was the stench of unwashed bodies. Celestina hadn't expected heaven to look like the courtyard at Bargello. Or smell like the *animali*.

The Almighty also appeared different than she expected. Wide-shouldered and rangy, He was the twin of Rinaldo SanGiorgio.

Her entire spirit tingled. "God?" she asked.

"Not likely." His chuckle was rich as cream.

"Wait, am I dead?"

He cradled her face in his rough hands. "You are alive."

She took a few pokes at his rock-hard arm. Her breathing quickened. "Are you the real Rinaldo?"

"Don't you mean Torino, your little bull?" he asked and swept her into his arms.

She floated there. How she yearned to savor the moment, but sands of the hourglass fell fast. Any time now *il boia* would notice his prisoner was missing. She started, "Rinaldo...before I die—"

He tapped his finger on her lip. "*Shhh.*"

She glimpsed the executioner. Inexplicably, his broad back was turned away from her, though he was only a short distance away. She ran a shaking finger over Rinaldo's smooth brow.

"Geneve was being threatened and that's why I was unable to escape with you. And one more thing, before they take my head, I have three words to say: I love you."

"You are not going to die," said Rinaldo.

She cleared her throat and shot a glance at *il boia*.

"Have faith," he said. After setting her down he grabbed her hand. When he started in *il boia's* direction, she tried to break away from him.

She bared her teeth at him. "I trusted you," she screamed and beat against his chest.

"Stop fighting," he said, weathering the blows.

And then as if to prove his point he purposely dragged her past *il boia*. The executioner, as well as the *animali*, stood silent, awestruck in something beyond where she was able to see.

She lifted on her toes but only recognized Monsignor, who wore an expression as stony as a statue of Caligula. Sheer fright swept through her. Whatever this was that she was getting away with, Monsignor would put a stop to it.

As they passed him, incredulously, he didn't seem to see her.

But Fra Brucker did. They shared glimpses. Without breaking stride, Rinaldo knocked Fra's shoulder. It was a hard hit and delivered on purpose. The impact rocked through Rinaldo and shook her.

Oddly, Fra took the blow without defense. Rinaldo plowed on.

A moment later the air filled with a joyful voice. "Granddaughter!"

Celestina broke from Rinaldo. Lingering thoughts of Fra

all but disappeared as she pushed through a clump of *animali* for Simona.

"I never thought I'd see you again," said Celestina. The first thing she noticed was that in her absence Simona had turned into a bird. She was careful not to hug her grandmother too hard. It seemed her ribs might crack.

"There is someone I want you to meet." Her grandmother nodded at a man standing in a grandiose beam of sunlight, a one-of-a-kind picture in white and red.

A bright gold pectoral cross, with a richness and heft, the sort of which Celestina had never seen, hung from a silk cord around his neck. Behind him was a platoon of religious soldiers.

Celestina openly stared.

"Remember before, when you asked about God," said Rinaldo. "*Ecco.* Simona and I have delivered your salvation. May I present the Servant of the Servants of God."

Celestina's breathing slowed and the courtyard closed in around her.

The image of a flame, barely bigger than a wisp, flickered over Pope Innocent's head. Her mind went to Geneve. It would be just like her friend to petition the Holy Ghost to introduce Celestina to him.

"Holy Father?" Celestina asked, in awe.

"Yes, granddaughter."

It was Simona.

Celestina blinked and the flame was no more. She faced her grandmother questioningly before her gaze drifted back to the Holy Father.

The way he smiled reminded Celestina of Papa. Also, the Holy Father shared the exact coloring of Cri. Celestina scratched her head and whispered at Simona, "Pope Innocent looks like Cristoforo Colombo and Papa?"

Simona visibly stiffened. Celestina's heart skipped a beat at the sight of Monsignor, now beside her grandmother. His mouth twisted more than usual.

Bracing, she asked Simona, "Is the Pope's real name Cibo?"

Simona traced the grass with the tip of her slipper. "Yes, granddaughter, Giovanni Battista Cibo."

Celestina reeled back as if she'd been punched in the chest. "Are you...*sure*?"

Simona sighed. "Even I cannot lie before a pope."

Celestina stammered, "What...are you doing here with him? What are *we* doing here?"

Simona cleared her throat. "Cibo and I have something to tell you."

)(

In the center of the prison courtyard, in front of the *animali*, and all the angels and saints, Simona admitted, "We share *una nipote*."

Celestina's gaze bounced between Simona and Innocent. "A granddaughter?"

The Holy Father beamed.

Gold and silver swirled inside Celestina's head. "Simona, you must end your game and explain."

Simona looked her straight on. No dramatics, no wine, no screaming. Finally, it seemed, Simona was ready to talk.

"I was fifteen years old. Cibo and Baldasare were students," said Simona. "It was my job to bring them their daily bread. Cibo was no more than a boy, with no commitment to the church—"

"And I loved her."

The foundation under Celestina rocked at the deep tremor of Innocent's voice. Had she heard correctly? Pope Innocent loved Simona, as a woman?

"And I love you," he said with conviction directly to Celestina. "As God loves you, wholly and without judgment. From this day forward, you are formally my niece."

Celestina grabbed Rinaldo's arm. "But...I thought...I might be your granddaughter?"

"You are." Simona's tone was sharp as a pick. "Niece and nephew are what he calls all his forbidden progeny."

Rinaldo gasped, "*Tutti*?"

Celestina echoed, "All?"

Simona grunted. "God knows how many."

One of the cardinals, a tall and elegant man in a rouge habit and *biretta*, broke from the others.

"I am Cardinal Lorenz." The timing of his interruption was perfect, as if he was much practiced. "And now it is time for papal business."

He faced a quartet of Swiss Guard. "Open the door beneath the stone staircase," said the cardinal. The ancient panel was unlocked and four more guards emerged, escorting three shackled prisoners.

Upon seeing them, Celestina's first urge was to flee. Her second was to fall over in shock. Rinaldo seemed to read her mind and encircled her safely in his arms.

Bishops Corso, Pagolo, and Iacopo—the entire Tribunal of Faith—were dressed in sacks and bound in chains. The *animali* returned to their awful ways and yelped and barked laughter. She almost joined them.

"Holy Father, have mercy." Iacopo bowed before Innocent, and then in front of Celestina. It felt odd to be on the receiving end of a bishop's groveling. "We were not told that *Signora*

DiCapria was your granddaughter."

Simona shouted in Pagolo's face. "Hang them all from the *strappado* until their arms rip off."

"*Ferendae Sententiae*," said Pope Innocent. "Sentence has already passed: The daily *strappado* and life in bondage."

As they were hauled up the stairs, the clamor of their chains diminished. Still, Pope Innocent glowered after them.

Celestina straightened her back, growing taller. She was grateful Fra had stopped her from falling down the stairs. Bearing witness to true justice was satisfying.

All at once the courtyard was in an uproar again. *Gli animali* shoved forward, pushing their way off the premises.

Ahi, Celestina thought and smirked. They know better than to let Innocent turn his powerful eye on them.

With the courtyard nearly cleared, Cardinal Lorenz beckoned Monsignor and Fra. Pope Innocent held out his ring for Monsignor to kiss. Monsignor deliberately turned away. Innocent flicked his finger against his nose, a signal to rid him of the stench of Monsignor's disrespect.

Fra, however, bowed and kissed St. Peter's Ring of the Fisherman, sitting large and heavy on Innocent's finger.

Innocent turned to Monsignor, saying, "I prayed the beauty of the mountains and the splendid Cathedral in Siena might have calmed the hell fire that has always burned inside you. I was wrong."

Monsignor peered down his nose at Innocent. "Call it what you want, but I am unwavering in my mission. Funny how it used to be your mission, too," said Monsignor.

Innocent pressed his fist to his mouth contemplatively. "The rest of the boys in our circle put away their dream of a new religion," he said. "They became adults and placed their faith in the Roman Catholic Church. But not you, it seems. You still believe in civic glory, the destruction of secular art and culture, and Christian renewal. And it will be your undoing."

Monsignor smirked. "*Ahi*, Cibo, you've always been too pragmatic. Not enough of a dreamer. Don't you see, my movement will not *die*." He paused to let his words sink in. "Lorenzo de' Medici is gone, and the de' Medici are nothing if not feckless without '*il Magnifico*.' As we speak, my popular republic is taking root."

"You are mad," said Innocent.

"But I have the youth on my side," said Monsignor. "Long after you and I are gone, my purifying campaign will be the law of the land. Long live the Reform."

Celestina saw Innocent wobble. Cardinal Lorenz extended his elbow for Il Papa to steady himself, but the Holy Father waved off the offer.

Celestina feared that Monsignor was winning the fight.

But then her grandfather seemed to get another wind. "I don't know whether you truly believe in the Reform, or if you are using it as a way to get back at me for winning the love of a girl, one we both loved."

Celestina sought out her grandmother. Simona's gaze was pinned on Monsignor.

"Is that what you tell yourself, Cibo? That the Reform was started because Simona spurned my love? Tell that to the thousandfold who follow me as their leader," Monsignor said.

A pained look crossed the Holy Father's face. "Your jealousy and ambition have turned you into an agent of the underworld, Baldasare."

"So says a vain pope who calls himself Innocent," Monsignor spat.

"*Bene*." Innocent fingered his gold crucifix. "Very well, Baldasare. You've had your say. Now it is time for business."

"Monsignor Guilio Baldasare," said Cardinal Lorenz. "You are sentenced to death for damning Lorenzo de' Medici on his deathbed, an act that has brought him grave illness, of which he has nonetheless survived."

Celestina recoiled with such force she almost knocked over Rinaldo. Monsignor's head turned red and fat as if it was going to explode.

"He's not dead? Well, you have no proof of anything then," said Monsignor, his voice coming from his throat like a wild wave.

"Every conspiracy has a witness, Baldasare. There is no question as to your guilt," said Innocent. "You are banned from receiving the sacrament of communion and sentenced to death."

"I demand a trial," raged Monsignor.

"A public trial?" Innocent raised an eyebrow. "Like the one promised my niece?"

As guards descended on him, Monsignor accused Fra. "It was the Austrian. He made the promise to her."

"I know," said Innocent. He turned his back on Monsignor. "*Hai finito*. You are done."

Monsignor's eyes cut for the gate. A wall of Swiss Guard circled him, thwarting any chance for escape. Capo joined them. Celestina noticed their professionalism seemed to rub off on him.

"I order the Swiss Guard to escort Monsignor Baldasare to the prison tower at Piazza della Signoria, where he will be tortured until he makes a full confession, upon which time he will be put to death by burning. May God have mercy on your soul, Baldasare," said Innocent.

Capo shoved a dirty sock in Monsignor's mouth, which silenced his protest. But Monsignor, bucking like a crazed donkey, broke halfway free of the Swiss Guard, and finding Fra, grabbed the younger man's arm.

Fra shrunk away. Celestina would always remember Monsignor's look at that moment, like he'd been slapped in the face.

Next, Innocent regarded Fra Brucker. "Now I will deal with you."

Fra bowed before the Pope. "And what is my punishment, Your Holiness?"

"Your letter to me was instrumental in Baldasare's arrest. I have considered that in my decision."

Fra raised his head. "That is true, Your Holiness. But I am guilty of other things. Serious sins."

"I will hear your private confessional," Innocent said.

The muscle in Fra's jaw twitched. "Thank you, Holy Father, but I want my confession to be heard by all. I believe it is my right to make amends to those I've pained."

Celestina's hand flew to her lips. *Mio Dio.* She could not allow him to talk out loud about the way he touched her. Had he considered the consequences? It could ruin everything with Rinaldo.

"What is it that you want to confess?" asked Innocent.

Fra knelt before him.

"Wait," said Celestina. When she spoke up unexpectedly, Rinaldo blinked like she'd thrown salt in his eyes.

She faced Pope Innocent. "I know this man, and I do not need him to make amends to my face. What I'd like, as one of his victims, is to deliver Fra's punishment...please...Uncle?"

Fra Brucker, as usual, caught up in his own desires, began, "Bless me, Holy Father, for I have sinned—"

Innocent held up his hand. "*Basta.*"

The friar clamped his jaw. Celestina pressed her hand to

her stomach in relief.

A faint smile crossed Innocent's lips. "All right, niece. What do you believe Friar Brucker's punishment should be?"

"I ask for a merciful punishment."

"Why?" Rinaldo's voice was like a whip.

"Rinaldo, please—"

"Never mind 'please.' Fra and his Reform Boys have destroyed half the art in the heart of Florence. Why should he be given mercy?" Rinaldo's cheeks reddened.

Her heart ripped in half. Rinaldo was right, but it was only part of the story. She must make him understand. "I've witnessed Fra grow and become better."

Rinaldo glowered at Fra. "The Dominican was no child when he joined the unholy trinity of Monsignor and *Signor* Lombardi," said Rinaldo.

She stammered, "*Questo e vero*...that's true, but—"

"*Ma che cosa?* But what?" Rinaldo threw up his hands. "He's the monster who jailed you, who kept you away from the love of your grandmother. Away from *me*."

Rinaldo's *scalpellino* muscles twitched for a fight. If he ever learned Fra had been but one heartbeat away from stealing every mite of her modesty, he might crush the young friar to dust. And then Rinaldo would end up swinging under the hanging tree.

Celestina faced Innocent. "Fra is no saint, and he must pay a price for his actions. But on his behalf, I beg for leniency."

"Why do you protect him?" Rinaldo demanded.

An image of herself, teetering at the top of the stairs at Palazzo della Signoria, flashed before her. She remembered the sharp urgency in Fra's voice, pulling her back.

"Fra Brucker saved my life once. Now I ask my uncle to spare his."

She reached for Rinaldo's hand. His jaw was set so tight she thought it might crack. But then his chest rose and fell in a deep breath. Gently, he took her hand.

"Trust me," she said.

Rinaldo gave her hand a gentle squeeze, quieting her trembling.

Innocent rocked on his heels. "It is true I cannot deny my nieces and nephews. It is my worst weakness, so I have reconsidered my punishment."

He looked down upon the friar. "Thane Brucker, I excommunicate you from the Roman Catholic Church. You are barred from receiving the Eucharist and from using your religious title," said Innocent. "Anything you have in your possession will be confiscated by the Vatican."

The ex-friar's body visibly pulsed. A Vatican priest handed him a set of tights and tunic. She looked aside when he stripped his clogs, habit, and *cappa*—she never wanted to see him naked again.

With a simple change of clothing, he'd gone from fierce blue and black to bland beige. Even his eyes paled.

He looked at the Holy Father. "I suppose you will be needing back Shadrach."

"Of course," said Innocent. "The *stallone* shall be delivered to a master that cares for him."

"It is right and just," said the ex-friar, head bowed. "The way I treated him...I'm ashamed."

Innocent gave a stern nod. "Now go, Thane Brucker, and use this time to repent and reform, with the intention of one day returning to the body of Christ."

And then Pope Innocent VIII turned his back on the man Celestina would now think of as Brucker.

The ex-friar flashed a glance at Celestina, but she refused

to meet his gaze, for Rinaldo's sake. The last she saw of Brucker was his back as he slipped past the prison gate.

Holy Father raised a crooked finger at Cardinal Lorenz. "And see to it that this *Signor* Lombardi is punished."

"Unbelievable," Simona sighed. "It takes a visit from a pope to clip that son of a bitch."

The Holy Father raised a second, and then a third, finger. "And I almost forgot. Take care of that healer and whoremaster as well. They must be made to atone for their sins against my niece."

Celestina nodded gratefully, catching the Holy Father studying her with admiration.

"You are free," he said. "Go and make a good life with Rinaldo SanGiorgio. And, perhaps, visit your uncle once in a while."

She cleared her throat. "Uncle, I beg of you one last thing."

"Yes, niece?"

She licked her lips with cautious hope. "Four good women have been wrongly imprisoned. Juliana, Anastasia, Giovanna, and Geneve Romee. I seek their pardon."

"My mercy is for you alone," he said plainly.

She flinched at the disinterest in his tone, and then glanced at the second story of the prison, remembering Juliana's words: "You are going to save me."

Celestina pushed up her raggedy sleeves and showed him her bruised wrists. "If you deny my friends their just freedom, then put me back in chains."

"Be still," cried Simona.

Celestina ignored her grandmother, but Rinaldo proved more difficult. He edged in front of Celestina, pleading, "Holy Father, don't listen to her. She is starved and knows not what she says."

Celestina elbowed Rinaldo out of the way. "He does not speak for me and neither does Simona. I refuse to live free while good women wither."

Cardinal Lorenz clapped his hands. "Silence," he demanded. She did as she was told—they all did—but her insides boiled.

Rinaldo clutched her hand, and the throb of his frightened pulse told her that he was scared. "Don't do this," he whispered. "I will break in and free them all for you."

"No, Torino. You're the best man in the world, but they cannot live like escaped convicts. They must be truly free."

Innocent cleared his throat. "I see that my niece has the passion of a lioness. Of course, she does. Chivalry runs in the blood of all Cibos."

Rinaldo's strong grip tightened. She too felt a sliver of hope.

"But we are also much too indulgent of our young," Innocent said.

Simona stumbled in place and Rinaldo slammed his fist against his eye. Celestina presented her hands, palms face up. "Chain me. I surrender," she said.

"Put your hands down this instant, niece." Innocent's tone was overpowering. It took every drop of her resolve to hold her hands in place.

He shook his head disappointedly and then faced Capo. "See that the women my niece speaks of are pardoned."

Capo pounded his chest with a snap. "Yes, Holy Father." Simona's head fell back and Rinaldo leaped straight up like a frisky mountain goat.

Innocent turned to Celestina. "Now, will you please put down your hands?" He rubbed his brow as though he had a headache. "I cannot stand to see my niece standing with her arms raised in rebellion like some radical."

She fought back a victorious smile. "Yes, Holy Father." She made a show of dropping her hands. "I owe you a favor, so please, allow me to repay you. What would you like?"

He studied her. "Answer one question."

"I will do so thoughtfully."

"Tell me one thing about my nephew, Alessandro. What did you like best about your father?"

She was unable to contain her smile. "Papa's art," she said without hesitation. "Oh, Holy Father, you should see the paintings and statues of his *putti*."

For the first time, she saw Innocent's grayish-white teeth. "Very good," he smiled. "I will see to it that one of his pieces is added to the Vatican collection."

Excitement washed over Celestina. She bounced on her toes. "Yes, yes, thank you, Holy Father. Now everyone will remember Papa—"

And then she froze. Defeat pulsed in her throat.

"But what's wrong, Celestina?" asked Innocent.

She stared at her feet. "The Reform smashed many, perhaps by now all, of his statues." She flushed with shame to have been associated with such heathens. "His frescos are on the walls of churches, and unless we pick up the whole building and bring it to Rome, there is nothing to display."

Rinaldo cleared his throat. "If I may..."

She regarded him quizzically as he slipped over his head the golden necklace bearing Papa's winged angel.

He dangled it before Innocent.

"If it's all right with Celestina, please put this gold *putto* charm in the Vatican museum," said Rinaldo. "After my *Celissima*, it is the best thing her papa created."

Celestina nodded with great vigor.

"It will be done," said Innocent, securing the charm in his hand.

"There's one more thing, Holy Father," said Rinaldo.

"Yes, my child?" said Innocent.

Rinaldo pulled from his pocket a black hair ribbon. Celestina was startled to see it. She'd thrown it in the corner on the day that Montanina rang three times.

Rinaldo presented it to Pope Innocent. "Here is a memento of your niece, the ribbon she wore in her hair." Rinaldo inhaled its aroma. "It smells like her bakery, of almonds. I thought you might like it to remember her by."

Innocent took it and held it against his heart. He appeared as touched as Celestina by Rinaldo's thoughtfulness. "I'd like a private moment with you, *Signor* SanGiorgio," said the Holy Father.

Rinaldo approached shyly. The religious laid his thick hand on Rinaldo's shoulder. They spoke together softly while Simona massaged Celestina's shoulder as if she was kneading dough. How she'd missed her grandmother's touch.

Rinaldo swaggered back.

"What did he say?" Celestina whispered.

Rinaldo beamed. "He gave me Shadrach."

"You will look handsome together," said Celestina.

His smile was tight like he was keeping a secret.

She asked, "What else?"

"You'll know soon enough."

She regarded him with excited curiosity until Innocent beckoned Cardinal Lorenz.

"There is one more thing," said the Holy Father. "According to our young friend *Signor* SanGiorgio, there is a guard called Nello who watches the women and is sinfully consumed with lascivious thoughts. Have him transferred to a men's corridor, for all time."

At that moment her love for Torino grew tenfold.

"Simona?" It was Innocent. Her grandmother cocked an eyebrow. "May we drop you off?" he asked.

"I'll take a ride to the bakery in the gold carriage." Simona wiped invisible dust from her shoulder. "Give my neighbors something to gossip about—for at least a *mille* years."

"I was hoping you'd say that. It has been too long since I've seen the old place."

The Holy Father's gaze lingered on Simona's face and Celestina stared after them as they left arm in arm, past the iron gate.

){

Rinaldo withdrew the ermine cuff he'd salvaged from Celestina's dress, burning on the stake outside Bargello that day, and rubbed it against her cheek.

"How are you so perfect?" she said.

"It's my manly *carisma*," he said.

"*Mio Dio*, Simona has rubbed off on you," she clasped her chest in laughter.

"There are some people I want you to meet." Celestina clutched Rinaldo's hand.

They dashed up the stone staircase, down the musty halls of Bargello, and through the Passage of Witches. She couldn't wait to deliver the good news to those who believed in her when she didn't believe in herself.

Juliana squealed at the sight of her. Celestina reached through the bars and hugged the girl like they were long-lost sisters. "Capo will begin arranging for your freedom," said Celestina. "Anastasia and Giovanna, you too."

"I never gave up faith," said Juliana. Anastasia and

Giovanna stood stunned.

"I foretold it," said Juliana, chin out and chest high.

Juliana would never know how close Celestina came to failing. "Seems you do have a bit of Geneve in you." Celestina's gaze ricocheted around her former cell. "Where is Geneve?"

Juliana stared at her feet. Giovanna and Anastasia glanced at one another nervously.

Celestina's voice shook. "Tell me, Juliana."

"Two rings for a burning," she said.

"Geneve..." Celestina's voice trailed off.

"After Capo came for you, Nello took away Geneve," said Juliana.

Beneath Celestina's feet, the floor opened into a bottomless pit.

24

Celestina dropped to her knees at the foot of the burning stake in the Piazza della Signoria. If the stones and ash of Geneve's remains weren't digging into her skin, telling her it was real, she'd have thought this was all a nightmare.

"They burned my friend," Celestina said. Inside, where her soul once was, there was a black hole.

Rinaldo fingered through the ash and exhumed his white crucifix. Its leather strap was wrapped around a folded-up sheet of paper. He opened it to discover his drawing, "Celestina's Burnings."

Celestina stared at it in disbelief. "I gave Geneve the cross when I thought I was going to lose my head. I couldn't bear the thought of it being swept away in blood," she said.

Rinaldo sniffed the drawing. "The paper doesn't smell like smoke," he said.

"It's been hidden in the hay in my cell since I opened it. Geneve must have rewrapped the picture and brought it with her to her burning," said Celestina.

"Look," said Rinaldo. "The marble cross remains unblemished and its leather strap wholly intact. The drawing did not burn. I am not so sure your Geneve burned either," he said.

Celestina held up her hand for him to stop. "I know you are trying to protect my feelings, but I am no longer a child in need of stories."

"Can you please be quiet, even for one moment, so I can speak?"

"Go on," she sighed.

He raised his crucifix and drawing. "If these were anywhere near your Geneve at the time of her burning, wouldn't they be burned up, too?"

She rubbed her pockmarked kneecap. "I suppose so."

Rinaldo scooped a handful of ash. "And wouldn't this dust at least be warm?" And then he wrapped his hands around the burning stake. "And wouldn't the temperature of this be high instead of low?"

She clutched her stomach. "It would," she said, daring to agree.

Rinaldo leaped up and she allowed him to pull her along. "There was no burning today, *Celissima*. I think your Geneve escaped."

Celestina blinked at an image that appeared above the burning stake.

"I see a flame," she said.

Over the ashes danced the wisp of fire. She stared at it, but it yielded no faces of Monsignor terrorizing or Papa bleeding. This flame was pure hope.

She pointed and asked, "Do you see it, Rinaldo?"

He looked there, and then at her like she bore two heads. "I think prison has made your eyes funny," he said. "There's no fire before us."

The flame surged and the black hole inside her filled with

a golden glow. Wherever Geneve was, she was setting the world on fire.

Celestina raised her gaze to the heavens.

Thank you, Holy Ghost.

)(

Rinaldo led her over the Ponte Vecchio, the old bridge, past butcher stalls, deep and dark like catacombs. The bloody smell of raw meat hung heavy in the air over the River Arno.

When a flea-bitten dog licked blood off the ground under a hanging pig's head, she retched.

"Look at the river," said Rinaldo. He stroked her hair as she rubbed her nose on his shoulder, attempting to stifle the stink.

Rinaldo's musk was different than she remembered. He had the air of new places and foods. He smelled like Rome.

"Let the water's pretty color calm you," he said.

The unusual hue the sun cast on the Arno was a luscious shade of violet. And Rinaldo was right, the color did soothe her. Until that moment, color was practically a distant memory. In Bargello, most everything was black, gray, and blood red.

As they walked past the Pitti Palace and through the Roman Arch, Celestina's ears danced at the rising and falling calls of laughing doves—*croo-doo-doo-doo-doo*—that followed them all the way deep into the Vines.

She rubbed her hand over the stone mushroom cap where she'd once sat and posed as Rinaldo's muse. It seemed a century ago. He held up his finger. "*Aspetta*," he said. "I'll be right back."

"Be fast. I don't want to live another heartbeat without you," she called after him.

Rinaldo returned with a mound of purple grapes. Sliding

beside her on the rock, he dangled the bunch over her mouth. She snatched one in her teeth. Sweet juice burst inside her hungry mouth.

He held the last grape to her lips, leaned in, and nibbled. He then stopped where their lips touched. The scent of grapes on his breath intoxicated her. She pressed harder against his mouth.

When he pulled away, she went cold as death.

She raked her fingers through her hair, what was left of it after hunger made it loose on her scalp, and stared openly at the clumps. She scratched her hip. The bone stuck out like that of a starving mule.

"Is it that you no longer find me desirable, is that why you stopped our kiss?" A cynical inner voice knifed at her thoughts.

Without pause, he punched himself in the side. "Ouch," he moaned.

She blinked at him, aghast. "Why'd you hit yourself, you stupid sausage?"

He rubbed his injured ribcage. "To show you I would endure anything for you," he said. "And your beauty."

"That may change when you hear what happened in prison," she said.

"I don't need to know anything." His voice had a hard edge.

"But I need to say it," she said. "I have endured much, which did not hurt me as much as make me stronger. But there are things you must know."

Rinaldo's eyes flashed savagely. "What did he do to you? I will kill him," he said, brandishing his fist.

Celestina set her jaw. What Fra had done, she could never speak of. Not one detail. Rinaldo must not avenge her honor. If caught, he would be hanged.

"I cannot, I will not ever speak of it. But at the trial, there were accusations made public that you must know of, so they may never be used to divide us," she said.

He took a purposeful breath. "I will honor your wish and listen to what you choose to reveal," he said. But his vengeful tone betrayed him.

She took a deep breath. "The healer told the Tribunal some things about me, and they were bad."

He cupped her face in his hands. "What were his lies?"

She swallowed hard. "That I wasn't a virgin, but that's not exactly true." She glanced away, not wanting to see his reaction.

"The Tribunal's decree means nothing to me," he said.

The pulse in her neck twitched. "But there's more, and it's much worse." Carrying the devil's baby was an accusation so damning that it was practically unthinkable, and here she was, having to explain.

"I cannot hear another word from their lying mouths. Nothing they say can ever come between us. I care only about you," he said. "Now allow me to erase their ugly voices in your head."

His protest was sincere, and she was certainly more than willing to never speak of it aloud. But she feared she'd never be able to forget. "I wish you could, but their voices scream in my head."

With a stroke of his thumb, he erased her tear. "Then my love will speak louder."

"And then you'll break my ears." She caught herself in a giggle.

"Then I'll just have to kiss them back together."

Passion radiated from her soul. "Kiss me now, Torino, and do it the way I imagined in prison."

Rinaldo swept his warm lips across hers. Her back arched and she was newly awakened. From behind closed lids, she saw the sunlight shimmering between the leaves. No more gray prison ceiling.

Beneath the droopy limbs of the ancient willow, she doffed her dress. Spreading her arms, she let the clean aroma of pine wash over her.

Once she'd planned to make love to spite her grandmother and Simona's long-ago burnings. Now she knew that was childish. Being in love wasn't always warm and soft as a soothing flame. Sometimes it nipped and bled from the sharp, icy edges. It was the difference between Rinaldo and Brucker.

Rinaldo stepped out of his stockings, and she glimpsed his growing manhood. They had nothing to fear with only the animals to see them. Glorious privacy. It was a gift. That's what she believed Geneve would say.

He led her to a patch of new grass and lowered her gently. Contessa de' Medici's mattress could not have been softer. Her fingers played with the light hair dusting his chest while his warm tongue glided between her breasts. Her heart nearly leaped from her chest in ecstasy. His fingers skimmed past her waist. He cupped his hands around the back of her hips and slid inside her.

Warm wetness shot through her legs. She squeezed to keep his warm stream from flowing out. At last, she and Rinaldo were one, bound together forever.

A family.

25

Out of respect for his *Celissima*, for they were not yet married despite their most perfect coupling, Rinaldo turned his back to slip on his tunic. He plucked a long blade of grass from under the olive tree and tied it in a circle.

Celestina was already wearing her miserable prison sack.

Kneeling on the grass, he presented his makeshift ring. "Will you please get a new dress and marry me, Celestina DiCapria?"

A cloud of concern passed her eyes. In her mind, she was somewhere else. *That damned ex-Dominican; she's thinking about him.*

"Perhaps you didn't hear me," Rinaldo repeated, trying to remain calm. "May we wed?"

"I should go see Simona." She stared at the tree.

He understood immediately. Rinaldo slipped the grass ring inside his slipper. He should have asked permission. "Let's go ask your grandmother," he said, jumping to his feet.

"But I don't know whether to kill Simona or kiss her." Her voice trailed off. She seemed not to have heard a word he said.

"If she hadn't kept Pope Innocent a secret, I may have

known my grandfather...excuse me...my uncle...for years," said Celestina.

"Secrets are poison, it is true," Rinaldo said, trying to suffocate thoughts about the ex-religious and what he may have done to her back at Bargello.

"Simona...and Monsignor...argued about a man named Cibo. I never knew that was the Holy Father's given name." She was becoming fitful.

He pushed back the wet lock of her hair sticking to her flushed cheek. His heart hurt for her and for what she must now go through. The hard part—knowing the truth of her family's secretive past—was just beginning for her.

"Celestina...*Celissima*. Listen to me."

She blinked. "Yes, Rinaldo?"

He looked to the heavens to find the right words. "Try to see it this way," he started. "If there were no Cibo, there'd be no Celestina. Without Celestina, Rinaldo would still be in love with a painting of Venus hanging in the de' Medici Palace. Now, how pitiful is that?"

"You're crazy." When she smiled his heavy heart lightened.

"Crazy for you." He stroked her cheek. "So, can we start over?"

She smoothed his hair and he eased her back, pushed aside her dress, and pulled down his hose. In long, fluid strokes, the way he polished stone, he massaged his way inside her. Her body melted, free of strain.

After he peaked, he rolled off her. Hands resting on chest, he breathed with deep satisfaction.

She poked him in the ribs.

"Why do you stab me, my love?" he asked.

"I'm waiting," she said.

"For what?"

She cleared her throat, waving her left hand before his face.

"*Ahhh*, yes." He knelt on one knee and dug around his slipper for the ring of grass. "Celestina, *bella*, will you be my bride?"

She straightened. "*Si*, Rinaldo."

He slipped the ring over her finger. "I will make your family proud."

With gentle lips, she kissed her ring. "And if the boycott hasn't closed the bakery, I will support us by baking *biscotti* while you find a master to study fresco."

"But Celestina, *bella*, you have missed so much. I've been promised a sculpting apprenticeship in a grand garden," he said.

The long, dark lashes shadowing her cheeks swept up. "Tell me," she said, bouncing on her knees. "No, don't tell me. Let me guess. Ghirlandaio? No, not him, he's too mean. Master da Vinci? No, he's too famous. I know. Giotto. No, no, no. I think he's dead."

Rinaldo fell back laughing.

Celestina threw up her arms. "I give up."

"Master Antonio del Pollaiuolo." He said the name proudly.

She jumped to her feet, pulling him with her. "I've never heard of this Pollaiuolo. Papa never talked about him, but he must be a great sculptor to get you to change your dream from painting fresco to carving stone. Is he new in Florence? It seems there's so much I've missed. I can't wait to see and hear and taste everything. Take me to his studio. I want to sneak a peek at him."

"All right. All right. But you'll have to wait a bit. He's in Rome."

She stepped back. "Rome?"

He needed to tell her everything so she'd get excited again. "I'm going to sculpt marble statues for the gardens at the Villa Belvedere, your grandfather's summer cottage on the high ground overlooking St. Peter's. Wait until you feel the breeze on that hill, *Celissima*. On hot days you can come and watch me work and cool off."

Her head jerked back. "Your work is at St. Peter's Cathedral?"

"*Si*," he said. Why she seemed upset he didn't know. Perhaps it was too much news. "That's where Master Pollaiuolo works. It is perhaps why your papa never mentioned him."

"I see. Of course," she said.

Rinaldo cocked his head. "Is there something wrong, *Celissima*?"

She stepped back. "You have already accepted this apprenticeship?"

He nodded with vigor. "*Si*. And Master Pollaiuolo is paying *me* to learn. It is the same way Ghirlandaio pays Michelangelo to work in his studio. Master Pollaiuolo says I'm a natural."

She glanced back in the direction of Florence. "You seem so happy."

The way she said it sounded like that was a bad thing. "But I am," he said with caution. "So why do you look so sad?"

"I'm *not*," she said, raising her voice.

But he felt her resistance. "You are willing to move to Rome, aren't you?" he asked.

"Of course," she said. "If that's what you want."

His shoulders fell. How could she not be thrilled at his chance to rise from quarryman to a floristic sculptor in a single lifetime? "You will love Rome, I promise. Rome is the center of the world."

"I know, I know." Her chin dropped to her chest. "It's just everything has been moving so fast since I left Bargello. And what about Simona? Who will she worry about without us around?"

"Your grandmother can come with us," he said gleefully.

She looked at him flatly. "Have you ever met Simona?"

Masterful persuasion was not his gift, it seemed. "But as wife and husband we must begin our own life in our own way," he said.

"Of course. I know that." She said it like she was alone with her thoughts.

He scowled at the gray squirrel hanging on the side of the willow chirping at him. "But sculpting is what you said I should do, and you were right. Everyone was right. "

"You will be a fine sculptor." There was a bit of rebuff in her tone.

He feared she was finding him unhumble, so he quickly changed his approach. "I'm no Donatello, that is true. But my whole life I've chipped stone. And I love the flowers and trees." He swept his hand across the flora in the Vines. "We will have more than enough money to live in a nice apartment in Rome."

She tapped her finger against her chin. "I see you have thought all this out."

He paced back and forth. "Of course. That is what a husband does. Makes plans for the future."

"And you have done that," she said. "Now give me a moment to breathe."

He pressed his hand to his stomach. He had more to tell her but waited for a few heartbeats. "I hope you feel better because I have another surprise," he said.

She grabbed hold of a willow branch. "What now?" Her

tone was skeptical, but what he was going to say next would fix that.

"I asked the Holy Father to marry us," said Rinaldo.

"At St. Peter's Cathedral in Rome?" He hadn't expected her to react with such dread.

"*Sì*. Wait until you see it, Celestina. It's said that the art there is a *mille* times better than at the de' Medici's."

She put up her hands. "Can we slow down and consider some other ideas?" she asked.

He clutched his chest. Her words were a blow. "But it's the best idea. It's the Pope, for God's sake."

"Stop pushing," she said.

And then the unthinkable crossed his mind. With the utmost trepidation in his voice, he asked, "Does slowing down and thinking of another idea mean that you don't want to marry me?"

Her head dropped back as though she was looking to the heavens for an answer.

He took in a trembly breath.

"Of course I want to, and with St. Catherine at my side," she said and held his cold-as-ice hands in hers.

He exhaled. "Then what is the problem?"

"I don't want to be the first Catholic in the history of the world to be married by her grandfather half a country away at his church. It feels wholly unnatural to me. *Capisci?*"

A lump in his throat the size of a boulder choked him. He'd been so stupid.

Jesus, please help me make this right.

Like a bolt of lightning, an idea struck him. He was so happy he nearly jumped out of his slippers. "*Celissima*, I know the perfect place."

She slapped her hands to her cheeks. "Oh God, where

now?"

He glanced at Settignano in the distance. "There's this little tabernacle I know of, outside and underneath the grand oak tree."

Her eyebrow kicked up. "I'm listening."

26

Settignano, Six Weeks Later

Celestina's wedding veil caught on the peeling chestnut bench. She pinched the ragged edge of a large sliver of wood and withdrew it from the veil, flicking the shard past Shadrach's white rump.

She rocked back and forth in the gentle sway of the horse cart with a feeling of foreboding tickling the inside of her stomach. Rinaldo hadn't yet seen her, and their *anellamento* ceremony had already hit a snag.

Also, she still had no idea whether or not Simona had prepared a dowry.

She took a glimpse of her grandmother, looking over her shoulder down the Via Desiderio. Behind them stood the rolling Settignano mountainside, with fields of purple grapes baking in the bright morning sun. There was little else to observe, which made Simona's interest in the world behind them seem all that stranger.

As Celestina smoothed the skirt of her silver-embroidered *cioppa*, the cart hit a hole in the road. A sudden bout of dizziness overcame her and she clutched the edge of the bench.

She checked on the poppy garland crowning her head, relieved the flowers were safely in place. She'd been strangely pale the past few days, and she loved the way the reddish-orange flowers cast a blush upon her cheeks. More poppies were bunched and bundled for a bright bouquet.

Celestina snuggled against her grandmother, vying for Simona's attention. Soon it would no longer be just the two of them. But Simona was still fixated on the road behind them.

But Celestina couldn't be too angry, not when her grandmother had gone above all expectation in pulling together Celestina's wedding ensemble. It was truly *magnifico*—fit for a de' Medici—but it had cost too much. She'd paid twelve *lire* for *gorgia di piccione*, silk that mimicked the color and texture of a dove's downy chest.

Normally the cost would not sink Simona, but the Reform's boycott of the bakery had taken its toll. There was no money for flour or rent. Simona would never admit it, but the bakery was close to nailing shut its door.

This led Celestina to believe there was no money for a dowry either, but as usual, Simona was closed lipped.

Celestina once again turned to check for a *forziere* in the bed of the cart, thinking in the excitement she may have missed it. But there was no special wedding chest for Simona to present to Rinaldo's family unless she planned to bestow upon them a bale of hay.

A brown-haired boy of about twelve years, holding Shadrach's reins, called back. "Not much farther to Cappella del Vannella."

They were getting close, and soon she'd be exposed. Celestina fanned herself with her hand. If there was no dowry, the SanGiorgios could stop the ceremony.

Celestina stared painfully at Simona's back. "What are you looking for?"

"Don't worry about it," said Simona.

Celestina's frustration unfurled. "This dress cost too much and we ran out of money before you could buy a *forziere*." Celestina threw up her hands. "Now we have nothing to bring the SanGiorgios. Am I correct?"

Simona waved her hand dismissively. "Everything's taken care of. I hope."

The worry made Celestina want to throw up. Her hand flew to her mouth. What had she been thinking? Her father was a journeyman artist. Her grandmother was in debt. And she herself was a prison bird. Of course, there was no dowry.

The cart rocked to a halt at the outdoor chapel where she and Simona were greeted by a smiling band of men with broad chests and women slim as willow branches. Celestina felt the blood drain from her face. The SanGiorgios were bound to ask about her dowry.

A lean man with leathery skin and a bushy mustache twisted his cap in his hands. "I'm Jacopo, Rinaldo's papa."

He pointed to a woman with brown eyes that sparkled like quartz in the mountain sun. She smiled like Rinaldo. "This is Maria, his mamma." Now Celestina understood the source of Rinaldo's warmth.

Celestina turned to introduce her grandmother, but Simona's neck was like a turtle's, stretched and looking far down the road. Interrupting her might cause a scene. It was best to wait.

"I'm called Benedetto, Rinaldo's oldest brother." He was the tallest and offered his hand as she stepped off the cart.

"Luca," said the stockiest, taking her other hand. He bore the same eyebrows as Rinaldo, arched and strong. He pointed to a pair of pretty brunette wives and fidgety children. Her heart melted seeing them. Rinaldo's nieces and nephews looked like a cadre of little Torinos.

Finally, she saw Giacobbe and felt more at ease.

"Welcome to the SanGiorgio family, Celestina. I pray every night that you and my wife can be friends again," he said.

Celestina looked straight at Zola's thickened middle. They had gotten married while Celestina was still in Bargello, over concern of Zola's growing condition.

Celestina's tenuous composure was at its limit. She couldn't bear to think about whose baby Zola was carrying— Giacobbe's or Rinaldo's?

Besides that, Zola shot her a look of satisfaction that stabbed Celestina's heart like a Roman gladius. Zola had everything and she knew it, and Celestina didn't even have a dowry.

"Do not go near my granddaughter." Her grandmother had apparently taken a reprise from studying the Via Desiderio and witnessed Zola's smug look.

Zola scrambled back. "But Simona, Celestina and I are going to be sisters now. One day our children will play as cousins."

The SanGiorgios nodded tensely. Simona, however, didn't heed the strain in the air—or, more likely, didn't care.

"After what you did to Celestina? You call that being a sister?" asked Simona.

Celestina was bolstered by Simona's loyalty, even while an unusual taste filled her mouth. Bitter metal. Perhaps her insides jostled from the envy over Zola's pregnancy, but Celestina felt as if she might throw up. She took in a deep breath of mountain air.

"No more of the past," said Celestina, hoping a different subject would snuff the bubbling volcano inside of her.

Simona raised one finger. "I never forget."

An awkward silence hung in the air until Giacobbe skidded far around Simona to get to Celestina. "*Grazie*, sister," he embraced her awkwardly. "Thank you for not digging up the old bones."

"Time for *anellamento*," said Jacopo, quickly taking Celestina by the elbow and seizing the moment of peace.

His arm was as strong as the root of a thousand-year-old olive tree, and there was no way she was able to stop the proceedings while she awaited word of a dowry.

They stood before a long cobblestone aisle, where at the end of it a large wooden crucifix hung in silhouette from the stone-peaked cupola.

A silver-haired woman with a proud air stood beside the cross. "That's my sister, Pia. Sings hymns like an angel," said Jacopo.

Pia burst forth with a chorus of "*Monstra te esse matre*." The *Ave Maris Stella* had never brought tears to Celestina until that moment. She fought her urge to cry but the words "show that you are a mother" had stirred her.

"I know. You miss your mamma on your wedding day," said Jacopo. He drew a linen cloth from his pocket and wiped her face.

"That must be the problem," she said and rubbed her stomach.

Jacopo pointed to a friar standing beneath the cupola. She leaned in for a good look. He had a fringe of hair that matched his fraying missal. "My youngest brother, Fra Pepe," said Jacopo.

"Everyone here is related to you," she said, while her gaze

hunted for Simona.

Fra Pepe waved them forward. Arm in arm, to the lilt of Pia's voice, she and Jacopo proceeded. Celestina pressed her bouquet into her stomach. A dark cloud blanketed her and she felt like she was suffocating in a cover-up of irreparable proportions.

In these few short moments, she'd grown to love Jacopo and Maria and couldn't bear the look of disappointment on their faces when they learned she came with no dowry.

She was on the verge of blacking out. "I am unable to continue," she said finally, digging in her feet. "I have something important to confess—"

But Jacopo was not looking at her. His heart was in his eyes as he stared admiringly at the altar.

She followed his gaze, and when she saw Rinaldo, dressed in a *farsetto* of brown velvet and a vest trimmed in *vai*, the fur of the gray squirrel, there was no fight left in her. Jacopo started again for the altar, supporting her all the way.

He paused under the cupola, patted her hand, and slipped away to stand with Maria. And then there was only Rinaldo. His gray-brown eyes caught hers, and never once through the entirety of their vows did their gaze drift apart.

Fra Pepe asked for the ring and Rinaldo dug inside his vest pocket. She sucked in her breath when she saw it. Made of white marble, it was spiraled in gold.

She stammered, "Did you...make it?"

He cast down his eyes. "With my own hands."

When he slipped it on her finger, her stomach tightened. His gift to her was the moon and stars, and she had nothing to give in return.

"Go ahead, nephew," Fra Pepe said. "Kiss your bride."

She tried to withdraw, to stop the charade. With no

dowry, their marriage was illegitimate. They must not seal their future with a kiss, or they would both be living a lie. But Rinaldo simply leaned in farther and brushed his lips against hers.

She stiffened to break his hold. He seemed unaware of the fire and ice dueling inside her and pressed harder, dissolving her resolve to dust. She kissed him back as though it was to be their last.

Fra Pepe cleared his throat in an unsubtle manner, and she and Rinaldo tried to separate. It was only when Fra Pepe barked an intentional cough that they managed to pull away. Deep laughter rumbled among Rinaldo's brothers.

"Time has come for the bride to present her dowry," announced Fra Pepe.

A whimper escaped her lips. The hour of reckoning was upon her. "Simona?" she called thickly.

Rinaldo's brothers, most likely sensing her distress, left in search of her grandmother.

She stood frozen as Rinaldo rubbed her back. She wished his hands had the power to make her disappear.

Then Shadrach, who'd become the most pleasant fellow since Rinaldo had taken over his care, whinnied like his tail was on fire. The clamor of horse hooves in the distance cracked the air.

The SanGiorgios fell silent, looking fixedly at an ornate gold carriage drawn by a quartet of black stallions. It charged down the road threateningly, the driver whipping the horses much too aggressively for so modest a road. It skidded to a halt at the end of the cobblestone aisle before them.

The SanGiorgio men tensed. Rinaldo had said often that the Settignese mistrusted outsiders. It was clear they'd never seen a patrol such as this in Settignano, and they were on guard.

Ten watchmen, gray coats flaring, jumped from the cart. Each bore a red patch embroidered with white keys on their chest pockets. The driver, who'd driven the horses like his brains were scrambled, wore a *barbuta*. The T-shaped helmet was adorned with a gray-blue feather.

"Swiss Guard," said Rinaldo, staring at them hard. "I know them to be good men, yet still they are soldiers. And the driver, he looks different. I don't know what to make of him."

She'd never seen anything like it either. The driver, for one, seemed more foe than friend.

Rinaldo turned to her. "For the love of God, stay with Mamma. They could be imposters and this could be a dirty trick. I don't want to lose you again, like at the sabbat."

At first, she bristled, but then forewent the urge to argue. Last time he tried to protect her he ended up hanging from a tree. She watched the back of his broad shoulders as he approached them.

Each guard held a weapon. Half bore pointed pikes and the other five had broadswords. Her misgivings increased by the heartbeat. If there was a fight, Rinaldo could fall injured or dead.

Meanwhile, she felt the carriage driver staring at her. Though the mask partially obscured his features, there was a familiarity about him. And then she saw it. His eyes were the color of the feather in his helmet. Recognition stabbed at her like a spike to the stomach.

It can't be him.

But she'd never met another living soul with eyes that color of gray-blue.

Her gaze darted to Rinaldo. If he identified the driver, there would surely be a battle between them—to the death.

It was then that a Roman guard, speaking as though he were the leader, took command.

"Which of you is Celestina DiCapria?" he asked.

She stepped back. Surely, she'd done nothing to warrant such attention. She was struck with another bout of dizziness.

"Who wants to know?" Rinaldo stepped forward. He was acting like the Swiss Guard would do her harm, even though her grandfather was pope. It was as if Rinaldo sensed a troublemaker among one or more of these men. She'd learned to trust his misgivings about certain people and was now wary herself.

Jacopo pushed up his sleeves. Rinaldo's suspicion seemed to be rubbing off on everyone. "Say the word, son, and we'll throw these Roman clowns out on their ears," said Jacopo. It was then that the side door of the carriage flung open.

And out stepped Simona.

Relief rippled through Celestina. Simona was safe. Jacopo threw a murderous look at the Romans and then asked Simona, "Did these dirty dogs hurt you, *signora*?"

Simona raised her hands. "I've been expecting them, Jacopo."

Warily, Jacopo backed off, but he continued to glare at the Romans.

"We come bearing wedding gifts, a dowry if you will, compliments of Pope Innocent VIII," said the leader.

Celestina looked on incredulously. Four other guards hauled out an ornate chest made of poplar and gilded in gold that, judging by the puffiness of their cheeks and the redness of their faces, must have weighed the same as a small elephant.

It had to be a dream. She was most certainly dreaming. And in that dream Rinaldo was pressing his palms to his cheeks, staring at the *forziere*. The other SanGiorgios were present in her dream as well: Jacopo with his mouth hanging, Maria openly weeping in joy, and Giacobbe smiling widely. But Zola, whose face was pinched in jealousy, made Celestina realize that this was no dream. Zola's reaction was much too real.

"Celestina's uncle left instructions for the newlywed couple to open the gifts in front of their guests," said the lead guard.

Simona broke out in a wide smile and waved for Celestina and Rinaldo to start. "Let's see what your uncle, who's really your *grandfather*, gave you," said her grandmother.

Celestina felt the stare of the carriage driver bearing down on her. She flashed a glance. Elbow on knee, he was taking her in.

She covered her face behind her bouquet, watching Rinaldo lift the lid. But the presence of the driver was distracting her. He needed to leave.

The glint of gold from inside the chest nearly blinded them. The flash gave Celestina an idea. Her grandfather's dowry had given her new confidence, and with an air of authority, she faced the lead watchman.

"My husband and I can manage the rest." Celestina threw back her shoulders and glared at the driver. "The niece of Pope Innocent VIII dismisses you. Return to Rome."

The driver in the metal mask cocked his head. She could imagine his smirk.

The lead guard bowed quickly. "As you wish. I will inform your uncle his gifts were properly delivered."

The steely-eyed driver snapped the reins and his team of horses lurched forward and around in a circle. Guards jumped aboard the fast-moving carriage and a cloud of road dust followed the company down the Via Desiderio.

Celestina braced her hand on Rinaldo's shoulder and watched until the carriage was out of sight.

While all was well at the moment, she worried about what would happen when Rinaldo and she arrived in Rome for Rinaldo's apprenticeship in the Vatican gardens. It would be nearly impossible for Rinaldo not to run into Brucker, whether the former friar was cloaked or uncloaked in the T-shaped helmet. The thought made her stomach twist.

Rinaldo steadied her. "*Celissima*, you are pale. Perhaps you need to sit down. We can open the chest later."

But she would no longer allow Brucker to taint the moment. Not for Rinaldo, who was so excited, or for Simona, who had pulled off the impossible.

"Don't talk nonsense. Start," said Celestina.

She caught Simona's eye and mouthed, "*Grazie.*"

Simona wore an expression that said, "What were you worried about?"

From the trunk, Rinaldo lifted a roll of canvas. He unreeled it and then broke into a smile.

"What's in there, brother?" Benedetto leaned forward.

"A walnut-handled hammer," said Rinaldo. From the way he bounced it in his hand, it looked weighty.

Then Rinaldo counted the remaining contents. "Eight chisels for carving marble and alabaster, and they are even finer that those belonging to Master Pollaiuolo. I can do great work with such tools."

Celestina was overjoyed for Rinaldo.

He dug around inside the chest and whistled appreciatively. "There's something for Simona."

"I don't want anything of Cibo's," she said.

"You're going to want this, trust me."

Rinaldo raised the grand ruby necklace. The cut of the

gems caught the sun and the SanGiorgios gasped. Rinaldo clasped it at Simona's neck. "Il Papa got it back from *Signor* Nucitelli, it seems."

Simona fingered it at her neck. "Cibo's gouty and old, but he's still a *tipo tosto*."

Celestina shook her head, pleased with this grandfather of hers. Who knew the Pope was a tough *ragazzo*?

"Help me with this." Rinaldo motioned for Cobbe. Together they hauled out a thick silver box at least a foot high. Rinaldo unclasped the lid, revealing a bounty of Greek, Roman, and papal coins.

With shaking hands, Rinaldo exhumed a note hidden in the treasure and handed it to Celestina. She ran her fingers over the embedded papal seal and read the letter aloud. "'To be divided three ways: among Celestina and Rinaldo SanGiorgio, Jacopo and Maria SanGiorgio, and Simona.' And it's signed by my grandfather...my uncle...whoever."

Maria gasped. Jacopo swayed as if he'd drank too much *grappa*. Luca caught him before he hit the ground and guided him by the elbow to sit on the stone bench.

"Now that's what I call a dowry." Simona rubbed her hands together. "The bakery is back in business."

"But there are more gifts." Rinaldo waved over Fra Pepe. "Books."

Rinaldo set a Bible in Fra Pepe's open hands. He held on to another, its twin. The set was encrusted in a rubies, sapphires, and emeralds.

Fra Pepe flipped the heavy gold cover. His eyes turned to circles the size of communion wafers. "God in heaven, nephew. Holy Father has given you The Urbino Bibles, volumes one and two."

Simona nearly careened over. "*Madre mia.*" Cobbe

steadied her.

Fra Pepe stroked the cover. "Davide and Dominico Ghirlandaio helped illustrate these holy books."

Celestina spoke softly. "Fra Pepe? *Zio?*" But the Bibles had his full attention. "Uncle," she said louder.

He could barely look up from the words on the page. "*Si?* Yes, Celestina?"

"If Rinaldo agrees, we would like you to have the Urbinos," she said.

Fra Pepe sputtered, "*Mai*, no. I couldn't possibly. They're too much—"

Rinaldo slapped him on the back. "Enjoy them, uncle."

"Have you two gone crazy?" cried Simona. "The Urbino Bibles are worth more than half of *Firenze*."

"More than half of *Italia*," swooned Fra Pepe.

In high soprano, and at the perfect time, Pia warbled, "*Gloria!*"

"Pepe, these books will allow you to fulfill your dream to build your own church. People will come from all over Europe to see the Urbinos," said Jacopo.

Fra Pepe nodded, speechless.

Rinaldo clasped Celestina's hand. "Time to go." They planned to spend the night in Florence before heading to Rome. She was overcome with fatigue, and couldn't wait to lie down to catch her breath.

"But there is still one gift," said Simona, lifting from the chest a black-and-white chess set made of the finest marble. There was a letter attached, sealed in wax with the initial "C."

Celestina read the note aloud: "*Buona fortuna. Zio Cri.*"

She stared at the words. How funny. Uncle Cri? Colombo? She looked questioningly at Simona.

Her grandmother's face soured as if she had swallowed a

Sardinian bat. "I know what you're going to ask, so I will just say it. The man is your uncle."

Celestina folded her arms deliberately. She was too tired to play around. "Quit teasing."

Simona looked her dead on. "I am telling the truth. Cristoforo Colombo is your father's half-brother. He is the son of Anna Colonna and Cibo."

Celestina stuttered, "Cri...was the boy...who Monsignor stole from Anna?"

"Yes. Cibo ran around like a wild boar in his younger days," said Simona.

Celestina shuffled back a step. "Our hair *is* the same color. All these years...that's what you and Monsignor fought about?"

"Some of it."

"Did Cri always know?"

"I think he always felt a special connection to us after Anna brought him to the bakery that one time. He seemed compelled to return, anyway. But I don't believe he knew his relationship to Alessandro and you," said Simona, "until now."

"So, you've told him?" asked Celestina.

"Cibo did. I won't be alive forever, and Cibo doesn't look so good. We wanted you to know that you had blood-family in this world, even if it is that *bastardo* Cristoforo."

Celestina looked around. She was far more than pleased. She had everything she ever wanted before her. To put the final seal on it she turned to Rinaldo. "Kiss me now, Torino."

He attacked her lips, and she returned the favor. The SanGiorgio *ragazzi* whistled and clapped. She pulled away from Rinaldo for a heartbeat to breathe and caught the sight of Zola kicking the box of priceless coins.

A nearby church chimed twice; its elegant sound was

nothing like the bellow of Montanina, so this was not the call for a witch burning. Instead, the delicate hum floated in the air, each ring representing a seed implanting on either side of Celestina's heart.

If Geneve were there she'd tell Celestina that was a sign. And now Celestina realized that the stirrings inside her were different than mere stomach sickness. It was part of something bigger.

"Tingle. Tingle for a baby," Celestina whispered lovingly to her stomach.

And then she doubled over in agony. A duel started within her belly. Her hands flew to her middle to quell the madness, but the moment she touched her stomach, her hands burned.

After withdrawing them, they cooled immediately. What had happened was reminiscent of the time she'd handled Geneve's dress inside Bargello, a time of great foretelling.

She looked upon her hands and stumbled back in horror. "Torino?" They shook as she showed him. "What is happening to my hands?"

Taking hold of each, he examined them every which way and then shrugged. How could he not see what had manifested?

The left was cast in gray-blue, and the right was tanned in brown with flecks of gray. Her hands were the colors of two sets of eyes that had become more familiar to her than her own.

She began to breathe violently.

"Is everything all right, my love?" Rinaldo asked with utter concern. "*Calma*," he said softly, as if speaking louder may cause her to shatter.

"Calm down?" she cried, swatting away his hand as he tried to soothe her. She then clutched her sides to keep the seams of her white dress from unraveling.

Now, Montanina, in the distance, called for a head. Celestina lurched as if she'd been sandbagged from behind. Then came another bong from the big, black bell. She swiped the sweat from her brow. The heat of two tiny flames burned deep inside her.

Her hands had prophesied twins, and that they'd each possess a set of eyes much different from one another.

But the babies have to be Rinaldo's.

After all, there'd been no penetration with Brucker back at Bargello. But what about Giovanna's tale of Venus, springing to life from the sea? That was not normal. Neither was one hand glowing brown-gray, while the other radiated gray-blue.

She stared at the sky and stroked her neck to soothe the burning toward the back of her throat. At that moment the heavens transformed from soft pastel to a hard hue of bluish-silver. Brucker's color was doubling down on her.

Dreadful thoughts about her babies' fatherhood began to gestate.

Celestina dropped to her knees, and then stretched flat on her stomach. She needed to settle her mind, but instead, her thoughts flared. Inside her head, she was back on the Via Scalia on the day she'd met Brucker when he was still Fra.

She'd fallen to the position of surrender then, too. And she was also confused. Why did he make her repeat the last four words of the Lord's Prayer? Aside from the obvious, she'd been unable to wrap her mind around the depths of the phrase, "deliver us from evil."

But, now, it was clear what Fra meant.

She didn't need to wear a black dress and hang on a stake to get burned by him.

Author's note:

The Renaissance was not all art and enlightenment. From the 15th to the 17th centuries, witch-hunting was a major sport in much of Europe. Tens of thousands of people, almost all women, were put on trial, tortured, and burned at the stake.

Fanning the flames of witch mania was the *Malleus Maleficarum*, the infamous witch-hunting manual that circulated throughout Europe. Written by Heinrich Kramer and Jacob Sprenger, and first published in Germany in 1487, it is one of the deadliest pieces of literature in the history of the world.

Its message, which was to identify, interrogate, and convict witches, spread throughout Europe rapidly due to the innovation of the Guttenberg printing press in the middle of the 15th century. It also succeeded in no small part because of the obsessive fear, ignorance, and hatred of women that existed among some monks. That book alone helped send some 2,800 "witches" to their deaths.

The papal bull, which appears at the beginning of the book, was written by Pope Innocent VIII. The bull, a formal proclamation, sealed with a leaden *bulla*, gives no indication of the Vatican taking a dogmatic position with regard to witchcraft, according to Italian Journalist Ruggero Marino in his book, *Christopher Columbus, The Last Templar*.

Marino hypothesizes that the fundamental idea of the bull was to maintain that the Catholic Church had always recognized the possibility of a demonic influence among humanity. According to Marino, Innocent's fight against witchcraft served to protect the natural world and defend life from death and fertility from sterility.

Marino also suggests that Pope Innocent VIII was the father of Christopher Columbus, who I refer to in the novel as Cristoforo Colombo, his name in Italian.

Marino believes Columbus studied ancient texts and maps from the Vatican Library, access to which was granted by Pope Innocent. Marino hypothesizes that Columbus merely stumbled onto the New World when in fact he was looking for a New Jerusalem; a new religion, combining the spiritual wisdom of the three faiths: Christianity, Judaism, and Islam. Innocent, who had a Jewish father and Muslim grandmother, was the perfect individual to further Columbus's journey, according to Marino.

Besides Columbus, Innocent fathered two other known children before he entered the clergy: a son, Franceschetto Cybo; and a daughter, Teodorina Cybo. I took the liberty of creating another son, Alessandro DiCapria.

Along with witch-hunting, bonfires were common in Florence throughout the 15th century. The charismatic Dominican Friar Girolamo Savonarola led the most famous— the Bonfire of the Vanities—in 1497. His followers rampaged Florence, burning thousands of objects: cosmetics, books, art, and the like. The fictional Reform Boys are based on the *Piagnoni*, Savonarola's devotees.

The Reform is an interpretation of the *Frateschi*, the

political party of Savonarola, known for his prophecies of civic glory, destruction of secular art and culture, and call for a Christian renewal—and of declaring Florence the New Jerusalem. The character of Monsignor is loosely based on Savonarola.

With the exception of the famous artists mentioned in the novel, all other characters are part of my fiction family.

The following books and academic paper proved invaluable in my research for *Celestina's Burnings*:

The Agony and The Ecstasy by Irving Stone; *Christopher Columbus: The Last Templar* by Ruggero Marino; *Daily Life in Renaissance Italy* by Elizabeth S. Cohen and Thomas V. Cohen; *Under the Devil's Spell* by Matteo Duni; *Joan— The Mysterious Life of the Heretic Who Became a Saint* by Donald Spoto; *A Short History of Florence* by Franco Cardini; *Dressing Renaissance Florence: Families, Fortunes & Fine Clothing* by Carole Collier Frick; and *Columbus's Religiosity and the Millennium* by Luciano G. Rusich.

Acknowledgment

I'd like to thank:

The Literary Wanderlust team, foremost Publisher Susan Brooks, first for favoring my tweet on #PitMad, and then for taking a chance on me. I am forever grateful.

Also, my editor, the fabulous Sharon Salonen, who let me get away with nothing, for which I'm deeply appreciative.

Mentor and Poet Kathleen Ripley Leo; Linda Gors Fletcher, editor extraordinaire; and, Susan Glover, whose support was immeasurable. You're all so smart and generous. Prosettes forever!

The men of Pub Prose: Perry Zimmerman, Don Beyer, Jerry Birdsall, Peter Huntley, and the late Allan Feldt.

Two great writing coaches: Author Rayne Hall and Story Master Michael Hague. Also, Novelist Louise Knott Ahern, Capital City Writers; and, Judge Christine Fichtner Stahurski, Wisconsin Romance Writer's Fab Five Contest. And, one great photographer, Jim Liska.

These wonderful people for decades of friendship, reads, and laughs: John Cusumano, Mike and Mary Lynn Harrison, Holly Shreve Gilbert, Kathy Paige, Pat Smith, Sue Reid Casey,

Debbie Meagher, Kris Turnwald, Longacre Bunco Babes, and Botsford lunch buds.

And especially, Kathy Ciolfi, Marie Coombs, Paula Pasche, Beth Valkevich, and Judy Wilczewski – best-friend medals all around.

All the Schiavi's, Basirico's, Pedersens, and Cavelliers, especially Rita Pedersen, Michael and Diana Schiavi, Joe and Kelly Schiavi, Carri Lee, and Carol Pedersen-Teevens. Also, Angela and Luciano Rusich, whose knowledge of history and Italian culture proved as priceless as their friendships.

My family: Beth Pedersen Schuler and Chase Schuler; Nick and Gemma Pedersen: and Christina and Ruh Fardin. Also, the bellissimi grandchildren Sofia and Chip.

My husband/soulmate, Brian Pedersen: "Grazie mille."

And, finally, St. Padre Pio, who said, "Pray, hope, and don't worry."

About the Author

Annemarie Schiavi Pedersen's stories are a rare chance for readers to visit the Italian Renaissance, a time of artistic enlightenment and medieval darkness. Those passions create a dangerous mix for her sensual and sometimes scandalous characters.

She studied journalism and history at The University of Michigan and is an award-winning author, journalist, and editor. She proudly shares a blood line with Petrarch, the Renaissance poet whose lyrical prose about smiles and eyes inspired Leonardo da Vinci's Mona Lisa.

Annemarie and her husband Brian live in Metro Detroit. Between working on her stories and texting all day with the rest of her family—her three kids, their spouses, and the bellissimi grandchildren—she's constantly writing.

Follow Annemarie Schiavi Pedersen on:

facebook@annemarieschiavipedersenauthor

twitter@schiavipedersen

Instagram@schiavipedersen

Renaissance Romantics...Because History has Hotties, too...blog at annemarieschiavipedersen.wordpress.com

CPSIA information can be obtained
at www.ICGtesting.com
Printed in the USA
LVHW090230130120
643416LV00001B/161/P